BEYOND THE STORM

Book II
Beyond Those Hills Series

BEYOND THE STORM

Vernal Lind

© 2007 by Vernal Lind. All rights reserved.

Pleasant Word (a division of WinePress Publishing, PO Box 428, Enumclaw, WA 98022) functions only as book publisher. As such, the ultimate design, content, editorial accuracy, and views expressed or implied in this work are those of the author.

No part of this publication may be reproduced, stored in a retrieval system or transmitted in any way by any means—electronic, mechanical, photocopy, recording or otherwise—without the prior permission of the copyright holder, except as provided by USA copyright law.

Unless otherwise noted, all Scriptures are taken from the King James Version of the Bible.

Scripture references marked NASB are taken from the New American Standard Bible, © 1960, 1963, 1968, 1971, 1972, 1973, 1975, 1977 by The Lockman Foundation. Used by permission.

ISBN 13: 978-1-4141-0843-8
ISBN 10: 1-4141-0843-5
Library of Congress Catalog Card Number: 2006907959

TABLE OF CONTENTS

Prologue	7
Chapter 1	9
Chapter 2	15
Chapter 3	27
Chapter 4	35
Chapter 5	45
Chapter 6	55
Chapter 7	63
Chapter 8	73
Chapter 9	83
Chapter 10	95
Chapter 11	107
Chapter 12	119
Chapter 13	127
Chapter 14	137
Chapter 15	149
Chapter 16	157
Chapter 17	165

Chapter 18	173
Chapter 19	183
Chapter 20	191
Chapter 21	203
Chapter 22	213
Chapter 23	219
Chapter 24	227
Chapter 25	235
Chapter 26	245
Chapter 27	251
Chapter 28	259
Chapter 29	267
Chapter 30	273
Chapter 31	283
Chapter 32	293
Chapter 33	301
Chapter 34	311
Chapter 35	321
Epilogue	331

Prologue

August 1940

Storms often marked turning points in Matthew Anderson's life. Now he stood on the front porch of his farm home, watching ink-black clouds and sharp lightning bolts orchestrated by claps of thunder. A storm of worry began to twist his spirit every bit as turbulently as the churning clouds twisted in the sky. A hard rain pelted the dry ground and Matthew's dark premonition took hold. Something was about to go wrong.

Life had been going well. Matthew loved his wife, his five children, and the rest of his family more than life itself. Intertwined with his love of family were his love of the land and his love of God.

Though he had been trying not to worry, anything that hurt his family caused the darkness and worry to take over. It was a weakness within him.

"Lord, help!" he said, "Are you telling me something? Or is this just part of my stupid weakness?"

The words of an old hymn entered his mind. His worry began to fade as he sang the words in his rich tenor voice.

Jesus, Lover of my soul,
Let me to Thy bosom fly,

Beyond the Storm

While the nearer waters roll,
While the tempest still is high!
Hide me, O my Savior hide,
Till the storm of life is past;
Safe into the haven guide:
O receive my soul at last!

Calm settled over Matthew once again. The storms of life would come and go just as the lightning and thunder had come and gone. Rain began to fall gently, nourishing the earth.

Chapter 1

September 1940

Matthew Anderson glanced at his brother. P.J. had a record of causing trouble and his remark signaled he was at it again. But would his brother dare change the course of events after today's welcoming celebration? Family and friends and community people had gathered to welcome Matthew's niece Corrine and her husband Warren to the family farm.

Matthew stood by his favorite oak tree in the yard of this farm where he'd grown up—the farm that should have been his. He wanted to spend a few moments alone before more family members and friends arrived.

Today was one of those golden September Sundays. The brilliant yellow of the poplar and ash trees with red maples in the distance and dark red sumac nearby accented the beauty of autumn. Matthew sometimes wondered if heaven could be more beautiful than the hills and valleys and lakes of Minnesota. He loved this land where he'd grown up.

Matthew looked across the lawn toward the big house, where Ma and Ellen and his sisters were arranging tables and chairs. There would soon be many more family members and friends visiting and milling around. His sons were there. He took great pride in his children. James and Johnie, looking more like men than boys, were with their cousin Jake over by the barn. His baby son, seventeen-month-old Michael had been placed in the care of his daughters, Margaret and Carol. His daughters, with their cousins Beth and Irene, were trying to help the women.

"The farm is mine!" P.J.'s voice echoed in Matthew's mind as if the words spoken had been said yesterday rather than three years ago. There had been an understanding between Matthew and Pa from the time Matthew had been a youth that one day he would own the farm. Matthew had worked his whole life to make the farm a good and productive one. His life's sweat was in this land, and it was where he expected to spend the rest of his life. When P.J. had spoken those words, Matthew's world had crumbled.

After P.J. claimed the home farm, Matthew and Ellen had bought their own place. The stress and resentment of his brother had destroyed Matthew's health and brought him close to death. But Matthew survived the deadly ulcer attack that would have killed most men. The following spring they moved to this richer and better farm. He was much better off on the new farm. In the years that followed he walked the path of forgiveness and experienced new life.

Pa had died eight months ago and Matthew thought of Ma being alone in the little house. Then Corrine and Warren had moved into the big house close by and they checked on Ma frequently. It seemed almost too good to be true. Then P.J. had dropped a bomb. His son wanted the farm. If P.J. carried through with what he'd said, everything would change.

Matthew's eyes went to the front porch where his tall, dark, and menacing brother stood. P.J. was approaching fifty. His dark hair was graying slightly. He held his six-foot frame well. People seemed to notice his handsome and striking features.

Matthew had never felt he measured up to his brother. He was shorter than P.J. by two inches and his sandy brown hair had strands of gray and was thinning now. At forty, Matthew was strong but he remained thin. His physique did not have the rugged strength of some farmers.

Matthew's thoughts were interrupted as more people arrived. The hayfield was filling up with cars, just as it had three years ago. That had been the day of Ma and Pa's golden wedding anniversary. That day would be etched in his memory forever. Yes, it was that wonderful day of family closeness that was suddenly destroyed when P.J. revealed the terrible truth—that the farm actually belonged to him.

Matthew left his post by the tree and went to mingle with people. Soon he was talking with family and friends and neighbors. Then, he

Chapter One

caught sight of Warren, walking by himself toward the garden. He hurried toward his niece's husband. "Warren, is something wrong?"

"No, Matthew, nothing's wrong. I can't believe how right everything is."

Matthew could see the younger man was overcome with emotion. "It's just a neighborhood and family gathering. Only you're the excuse. We wanted to welcome you and Corrine and the girls."

"I can't believe how good people have been. When I lost my farm in Wisconsin, I thought life was over. I didn't know how I could face the future."

"We're your family. We care." As Matthew said the words, he realized Warren was becoming as much a friend as a relative.

"I've always liked this big house and the farm. It seems to invite people to come. I'm fortunate to be able to rent it. It's almost too good to be true. This is the community where I'd like to grow old."

Matthew hoped P.J. wouldn't betray Warren too. "You're family. We want you here."

"I don't know when I've been as terrified as I was the day the bank foreclosed on my farm in Wisconsin. Corrine was ill; there were the three girls to think about; and I didn't know where to go or what to do."

"I'm glad you came here."

Ellen's voice interrupted. "Matthew. Warren. We're going to have a short program."

Matthew and Warren joined the crowd. Warren and Corrine's piano had been carried out on the front porch. Ellen sat on the piano bench. Martha, his oldest sister, stood on the front steps. The crowd quieted and a gentle breeze rustled the leaves on the trees.

"Welcome," began Martha. "I'm happy all of you could be here today. This is the day to welcome home my youngest daughter and her husband. Welcome home, Corrine, Warren, girls. We're delighted to have you in our community. It's great to have three of my granddaughters close by."

The audience applauded.

Matthew noticed his sister's graying hair and the lines on her face—gentle lines. She had grown older. Her life had not been easy: hard times on their farm in Wisconsin, health problems, and her husband's death. But she had the inner beauty that belongs only to the kindest of people.

Martha continued. "This is another celebration as well. Corrine and Warren are celebrating their tenth wedding anniversary. This couple has weathered some storms and difficulties, but now they are safely settled in our community. Let us sing our best wishes to them."

Without further introduction, Ellen played the introduction to the birthday-anniversary song. "Happy anniversary to you...." The crowd sang lustily and without announcement added a second verse asking God to bless the couple.

"Celebration and thanksgiving go together," Martha said. "We must acknowledge the Lord in all our ways. I'm calling on Pastor Strand to lead us in prayer and say a few words."

The crowd settled down. Some people found chairs while others stood or sat on the ground. The front yard became an outdoor auditorium.

Matthew thought of the many times Pastor Strand had been part of family gatherings: baptisms, funerals, weddings, anniversaries, and countless other events. As the pastor opened in prayer, Matthew breathed his own prayer of thanksgiving and added a prayer of concern. "Please don't let P.J. cause any trouble for Corrine and Warren. Keep them safe in this place."

"How good and pleasant it is when brothers live together in unity!" Strand went on to read the rest of the psalm, but Matthew's thoughts stayed on the first words.

After the pastor finished the psalm, he began to reflect on the words. "We are brothers here, and that includes sisters as well. As we welcome you to this community and congregation of believers, we become your brothers and sisters. Already we have come to love and care for you. You have quickly become part of our lives."

The Pastor's talk continued. When he finished, Martha ushered her three granddaughters to the piano. As Ellen played, the girls sang the familiar words to "Jesus Loves Me." The three children had captured the simple beauty and truth of this song. Matthew felt great pride as four of his five children sang a traditional family song. His sister's three children joined them.

> *Children of the Heavenly Father,*
> *Safely in His bosom gather.*
> *Nestling bird nor star in heaven,*
> *Such a refuge n'eer was given.*

The song always revived old memories in Matthew and re-affirmed his faith. Ever since Pa had died, it seemed more important than ever

Chapter One

before to claim his heavenly Father as his own. In his many hours alone at work in the fields, Matthew enjoyed the company of this Father.

Matthew's eyes turned to his wife as she played the piano. Ellen remained beautiful and petite even after seventeen years of marriage. The program was informal and short. The group sang several songs, including the song about the tie that binds. Matthew felt the truth of the words, "the fellowship of kindred minds is like to that above." This was indeed the good life—a foretaste of heaven above.

As the program ended, his second sister, Victoria, took charge. Her roles as teacher and principal seemed to spill over into all other situations. She was definitely in charge. The women brought out the afternoon lunch: hot dishes, sandwiches, Jell-O, cakes, desserts, along with coffee for the adults and nectar and lemonade for the children. Pastor Strand started the Table Prayer and quickly people lined up for their lunch—in reality, a feast. The talk and laughter and community and family togetherness filled the hour that followed. Then, almost as if a signal had been given, people left. Most of the guests were farmers and needed to get home for chores. Milking as well as other farm tasks were waiting.

Matthew saw P.J. walking toward his car. His brother's earlier comment clouded Matthew's mind like a summer storm or perhaps like the threat of world war. He had to make sure P.J. wouldn't cause trouble.

"P.J., wait."

"Sorry, Matthew, I'm in a hurry. I have to make another trip to the city."

"It'll just take a minute." Matthew hurried over to his brother.

P.J. spoke abruptly. "Be quick about it."

"What did you mean about Larry settling here? Corrine and Warren have moved in, and they depend on this place for a living."

"Oh, don't worry so much." P.J. opened the car door.

"I thought you made a change in your life. You said you'd make things right for the family. And letting Corrine and Warren live here is best for the family."

"We'll work things out. Making things right for the family also means that I'll look after Larry and help him. He's my son. He's more important than a niece."

"But your son knows nothing about farming. He has no interest."

P.J.'s dark features looked more menacing than ever. "He will learn."

"But Warren's settled here. He's planning to rent for another year and then buy some of the land."

P.J. seemed to sneer. "That's his problem." With those words, P.J. slammed the car door and drove down the road toward his lakeside home.

"Warren's become like a brother," said Matthew aloud to himself. "I can't let P.J. destroy his life the way he almost destroyed mine."

Chapter 2

The following weekend Mother Earth displayed the gold of autumn. Some of these autumn days seemed to be etched in vivid color, leaving something never to be forgotten. P.J. had left on a business trip, and Matthew hoped his brother's plans would not work out. The beauty of autumn and harvest work caused those concerns to fade from his mind.

The days of harvest meant satisfaction for Matthew. His efforts of spring and summer were now rewarded. And family comradery added to this satisfaction.

"Dad, let me take over. You need a break." Ever since Matthew's brush with death, his sons had tried to make his life easier. Now James took the fork from Matthew and began pitching bundles of wheat onto the threshing machine. The well-dried bundles went through the threshing rig quickly and easily, generously yielding high-quality wheat. This was a good harvest.

Matthew slid down the stack to the ground and walked away from the dust that surrounded the area. He was proud of his children. Sixteen-year-old James, a huskier taller version of his petite mother, was winning honors as a junior in high school. This son would go far. Even though he was the dreamer, James showed concern and consideration for others.

As he surveyed the situation, Matthew noticed Johnie and James competing as to who could throw in the most bundles. He was ready to shout a warning, but just then his brother-in-law Ed shouted, "Hey there, boys. Slow down! You'll jam the machine." Ed always carefully checked the machine while his son Jake took charge of leveling off the wheat in the truck. It amazed Matthew that the boys thought of threshing as play rather than work.

Matthew hated to admit he had a favorite child, but he did. Fifteen-year-old Johnie was that favorite. Johnie, now almost six feet tall, was taller and huskier than both his father and James. Johnie loved the farm and the land much the way Matthew did. And Johnie had a mechanical ability that Matthew did not have. Matthew loved horses and had never become very handy with tractors and these new machines.

Matthew relaxed, enjoying the sight of a good harvest brought in. Then, without warning, a cloud darkened his thoughts. The sharp words of his brother penetrated his thinking. "The farm is mine. I've got the control. It's mine to do with as I wish."

He tried to put away thoughts of P.J.'s control and manipulation. After all, P.J. had said a few months ago that he would make things right for the family.

Matthew wondered why these dark thoughts had come to mind at this time. Perhaps they came to remind him how good God had been—-how God had led him to a new and richer farm than the old home place.

Out of the corner of his eye, he saw his two daughters waving to him and motioning. Margaret, a thirteen-year-old freshman in high school, looked more and more like a young woman than a girl. Carol, a year younger, still remained a little girl.

The girls ran toward him. "It's dinner time!" they shouted. "We have company."

Matthew knew his cousin Pete was coming today, but who was the company the girls were excited about? He waved back, indicating the threshing crew would soon be on their way.

Within minutes the tractor and threshing machine were shut down. James, Johnie, and Jake ran ahead. Matthew wished he had half their energy. He and Ed walked briskly behind them.

Out of the corner of his eye, Matthew thought he saw a brown uniform, reminding him that the United States would likely be drawn into war. He dreaded the thought that his sons might fight in the war.

From inside the house came excited talk. The men and boys quickly washed themselves in the basins of water outside on the porch. As he

Chapter Two

and Ed entered the kitchen, the talk quieted and attention focused on a young man.

"Mr. Anderson," said the young man. "Could you use another hand on the threshing crew?"

Matthew smiled broadly. "I hardly recognized you, Joe. That uniform changes you."

The two men shook hands. Then Matthew opened his arms and Joe Nelson hugged him as a son would hug his father. It had only been in recent times that Matthew had been able to show this kind of affection. This blond nineteen-year-old had changed from that hired boy of a year ago to a well-proportioned handsome young man.

Joe stepped back and looked at those around him. "I'm home." His voice had a catch in it. "I've missed you."

Matthew found himself at a loss for words. He envied Ellen and others who always seemed able to say just the right thing.

"We're happy you're here," said Ellen. "Why don't you sit down? Dinner's getting cold."

Later, Matthew would remember this time as one of those perfect days, a day he wished would never end. Lively conversation followed with Joe at the center of attention. He saw that James and Johnie and Jake looked up to Joe with admiration. Perhaps they were thinking of joining the army as Joe had done.

When the conversation lagged, it was Margaret, who asked a question causing Matthew to wonder if she looked to Joe as someone other than a big brother.

"How long do you have vacation?" she asked. "I hope you'll stay here all the time."

James laughed. "It's not vacation. It's leave."

Ellen interjected her comment. "You're welcome here as long as you like, but I think you'll want to see your mom and dad."

Joe looked down, avoiding the gaze of those around him. "Mom and Dad are always so busy, and I don't like the city."

"Stay here the whole time!" added Carol.

"Thanks." The next words did not come easy. "I'll be shipped out in just a few weeks—probably the South Pacific."

"I think I'll go sign up!" exclaimed Johnie.

"Me too," added Jake. "You know where the excitement is."

"You're not going until you've finished high school," Matthew objected. His boys probably thought of the South Pacific tour of duty as one grand adventure. He knew better. "War is likely to happen." Matthew drew a deep breath. "War is serious business."

The conversation quieted as the group concentrated on eating. Then finishing, Ed spoke up. "We have work to do. We need to get through threshing today. The weather can change quickly. We have plenty of help now, so we should make it."

Something in those next hours was painted permanently in Matthew's memory. He couldn't put his finger on what it was. September weather in Minnesota could be just about ideal, not too hot and not too cold. The sun shone and the sky displayed its clearest and most vivid blue. The yellows and reds seemed even brighter than they had a few days ago.

Joe's presence encouraged the boys to work even harder. Matthew stood back, observing the fruits of his labor and enjoying the way the boys had fun doing their work. Ed drove the truckload of wheat to the elevator in town and returned with a large check, indicating the high quality and quantity of the wheat. Farm life, usually so hard and back-breaking, rarely moved this smoothly. "I have been blest," Matthew said aloud. "Every good and perfect gift comes from above."

Farm life has its rituals. The threshing, finished by late afternoon, meant the evening chores of milking cows still needed to be done. With Joe and the boys eager to get the work finished, Matthew felt he was in the way. He stood back and let them do most of the work.

Supper followed after Matthew and Joe and the boys washed themselves behind the house in tubs. Running water and bathtubs had not yet found their way into this rural area.

Saturday night traditions included allowing James and Johnie to take the Model A into town. Tonight Joe went with them. First they'd drive up and down the streets; then later they'd walk around meeting friends and pursuing some of the girls they knew from their classes. On occasion a new girl would arrive on the scene and the boys would compete for her attention. These rituals had not changed since Matthew's day, except for the fact that cars had replaced horses and buggies.

Matthew drove the rest of the family to town in the trusted '35 Chevy. Though unhappy that they were not permitted to go with the boys, the girls got out of the car and walked around, meeting their friends. Ellen took care of grocery shopping for the week and Matthew visited with friends and paid bills.

Saturday night rituals ended before ten. After all, Sunday was the day for worship and was also a special time for family and friends. Cousin Pete

Chapter Two

was visiting at Ma's with his wife Alice, and Matthew looked forward to seeing them on Sunday. In some ways Pete seemed more like a brother than a cousin. After all, many summers during his growing up years he had lived with the Andersons.

Oak Ridge Church was full that Sunday with the regular attendees plus a number of visitors. As the organist finished the prelude, Matthew looked around to check on the boys. James and Johnie sat in the back row with their cousin Jake. Matthew wasn't quite in favor of that, but he'd keep an eye on them. Beside him sat Ellen and the two girls; and Michael sat contentedly in his lap. Joe, looking so dignified in his uniform, sat beside Matthew.

This morning his sisters Victoria and Martha had decided to attend their home church here at Oak Ridge. They sat across the aisle and farther up front near Corrine and Warren and their three girls. Ma sat next to Martha, but seemed very much alone without Pa. Just behind him in their usual place sat his sister Mary and her husband Ed and their two girls. As the organist began playing the opening hymn, two couples were ushered to the front in the last remaining spot. Sure enough, P.J. and his wife Rita had decided to come, and they were followed by Pete and Alice. That meant all the Andersons were present on this special Sunday morning.

Surrounded by his family along with his church family, Matthew felt a sense of security.

After church at noon, the family met at the home place for dinner. They gathered near Ma's little house where the picnic table was filled with platters of fried chicken, hot dishes, and much more delectable food. Because the family was growing, these gatherings were becoming more difficult to arrange. But today four generations spent time together.

Matthew hoped to have some time with Cousin Pete. As they finished the last of their apple pie, Pete suggested they walk over to the barn and talk. Pete must have something on his mind.

"How is your mother doing alone at the little house?" Pete asked.

Matthew glanced at the big house, where he and Ellen had lived for fourteen years. "Well, Corrine and Warren are renting the land and the house, of course. They've been good to Ma. They look after her to see that everything's OK."

"It's great they're here to look after Aunt Elizabeth. I'm glad for that."

Matthew agreed. "I don't think Ma could be alone here without them. P.J.'s gone so much that we can't depend on him."

"What P.J. did wasn't right." Pete had avoided this subject for three years, but now he said, "I don't know why he wants to own the farm."

Matthew felt words were unnecessary. The two men walked in silence.

"Do you miss this home place?" Pete stopped and looked back toward the big house. "I miss seeing you and Ellen and the kids in that house."

"Well, Pete, I missed the place for awhile, but I've come to love my new farm and my—or rather, our home. This new farm belongs to me and not to the family or someone else."

"I'm glad things have worked out for you." The silence that followed told Matthew that Pete had something else he wanted to say.

"Matthew, sometimes I envy you and the kind of life you have. Ellen's a wonderful person, and you have five great kids. I feel I'm missing something."

"Yes, God has been good to me. But you have Alice."

Pete picked up a rock and threw it against the large oak tree. "Being married to Alice hasn't been exactly easy."

The words surprised Matthew though he had always seen Pete's wife as a rather persnickety lady.

Pete continued. "Yes, we've been married twenty-five years, but I don't know how well I can survive another twenty-five the way your folks did. I can never do things right. And she's getting harder to live with all the time."

"I'm sorry. But she's always pleasant, and she's a pretty lady. Ellen thinks she has such good taste in clothes."

"I can't disagree with that. But there's more to life."

Matthew waited for his cousin to go on.

"Going to church this morning reminded me of some important things I'd forgotten. God and all those good things seem so far away in the city. I work crazy hours in the iron mine. I get good pay, but there's not much else."

Matthew wanted to say the right words but feared something wrong would come out. "God is everywhere. We have to take time for Him."

"God seems closer here in the country." Pete turned away, deliberately it seemed. "Our lives are empty. I wish we had children. They are a blessing."

Chapter Two

"That's right. But our children all regard you like an uncle. I know that's not quite the same as having your own children, but they always love seeing you."

Pete paused and then went on. "I've been doing something I shouldn't do—at least your mother would be shocked. When I get off work at eleven or twelve, I stop at a bar. There's such good comradeship. No one's critical. Everyone accepts me."

Matthew tried to hold back, but the words came out. "You know that's not right. Going to those places never solves the problem."

"Underneath I know that. But it's unpleasant to go home to Alice. And the comradeship in the bar along with a few drinks helps me get on with life."

Matthew feared what this was doing to Pete. "I'm sorry. I said too much."

"No, you're right. How did you get so smart?"

Matthew laughed. "I never considered myself the smart one. I didn't even finish eighth grade. I have Ellen. She's the smart one."

"I think I know what I have to do."

Something within seemed to guide Matthew. "After my brush with death, I realized how empty and weak I was. I discovered the only way I could survive and go on living was to come to the Lord with all my burdens. Something happened then and there. I can't tell exactly when, but I came away a changed person."

Pete didn't hesitate. "You've found what I need and want."

At that moment he heard the voices of Margaret and Carol along with their cousin. "Dad, company is coming."

Matthew knew immediately that some of the neighborhood friends were dropping by so they could visit with Pete and Alice.

The brotherly talk ended. In minutes, Matthew and Pete were in the midst of a crowd of people. Neighbors, friends, and more family milled around, visiting with Pete and Alice. Everything blended together to make one of those perfect days, but even the most pleasant of days comes to an end. Such was the case. After another lunch, actually another feast, the neighbors and friends left. Pete and Alice had to leave to return to work on the Iron Range. Matthew and Pete had no chance to finish their talk together.

As Pete got into his car, he called out. "I'll be back in November for hunting. We'll talk then."

Matthew wondered if the talk would ever take place.

Beyond the Storm

Monday evening, Matthew figured he should check on his mother. He knew Ma would experience a letdown after the big weekend. And he wondered if she knew anything about P.J.'s plans.

Mother and son shared a few moments of quiet talk. Ma looked to him more than ever for support and company. Matthew knew, better than anyone else, how much she missed Pa.

As Matthew stood on the porch ready to leave, P.J. drove up in his black Cadillac. "I didn't think you'd be back so soon."

Ma looked happy to see her son.

P.J. hurried up the steps, hugged his mother, and gave her a kiss on the cheek. "I've got to hurry back to the house. I have some work that needs to be done."

"Why must you hurry, son. Can't you come in and visit?"

"Sorry, Mother," came P.J.'s abrupt reply. He walked back to his car.

"Wait, P.J. I need to talk to you." Matthew managed to keep his brother from opening the car door. He turned to Ma. "P.J. and I have business."

"OK," said P.J. reluctantly.

Matthew motioned for him to follow. They walked toward the barn, out of the hearing range of Ma.

"P.J., last spring you made promises to make things right. I thought you'd turned over a new leaf. You can't mess things up now for Corrine and Warren. That would leave Ma completely alone."

P. J. was quiet, not answering Matthew. Since P.J. had faced the truth about his shady business, things had been different. Mafia-type characters had not been around. After such a change, how could P.J. suddenly turn around and hurt his family?

As they walked, Matthew sensed something was wrong. P.J.'s comments were evasive. What was he holding back? Had his big brother run into some new difficulties with his former associates? He knew that breaking with the criminal element could be difficult, even impossible.

As the two men walked away from the barn toward the big house where Corrine and Warren now lived, Matthew felt a twinge of sadness. He looked at the house and remembered his youth spent there and also the fourteen years of living there with Ellen and his children. Now the place that had been home looked strangely unfamiliar.

Chapter Two

"That place has many happy memories," Matthew said. Then he added, "Corrine and Warren have been good to Ma. They look after her. You need to let them stay here."

P.J. looked away.

"Is something wrong?"

P.J. hesitated. "Well, I might as well tell you. Larry's in deep trouble. I need to get him away from the city. This is the only way."

Matthew gasped. "But why? Larry isn't interested in farming. He's hardly ever been on a farm."

"He's always liked the farm. He's wanted to be here."

"But that's not fair to Warren. They were all set to rent the land and possibly buy. They've put money into the land, and they expect a fair return. There isn't room for Larry here."

"I was hoping you'd understand." P.J., usually so confident and sure of himself, fidgeted in an awkward way.

Matthew began to list more objections. "But will Larry help take care of Ma the way Corrine and Warren have? Corrine checks every day."

"I'll be nearby, too. We'll see that everything's all right."

Matthew didn't believe his brother. "P.J., you're gone much of the time. I thought you resolved to make things right. I thought you were signing the land back to Ma as rightful owner—and that the benefits would go to all her children, not just you."

"I'm in a bind. And Larry needs a means of support."

Matthew felt the old anger returning. "I think there's something more. The draft is being re-instated, and Larry is a prime candidate. I bet that's the reason."

P.J.'s face reddened. "War is something terrible. I don't want my son killed on some battlefield."

Immediately, words came to Matthew. He clenched his fists. "Yes, but we owe something to our country. When I turned eighteen, I registered. I was ready to serve if necessary. I don't want my sons in danger either, but if necessary, they will serve their country. It's an obligation. We can't ignore our duty."

P.J. backed away. "I'm surprised you feel so strongly about this. You were always the peace-loving brother."

Matthew could have said more, but he held back his words. "History repeats itself. You did a similar thing to avoid being drafted in the Great War. You knew Pa would not approve of what you were doing. And

Pa would not approve of treating Warren and Corrine this way. You're disgracing your family."

"I'll see that Ma's taken care of. That's all that's important."

Matthew thought of something else. "Have you told her?"

P.J. said nothing.

"That's just your style."

"Perhaps," began P.J., "I can do something about Corrine and Warren. I'll see. I'll think about it."

Fortunately for P.J. the door of the little house opened and Ma came out. "Ellen just called. She was worried when you didn't come home."

Matthew turned to his mother. "I'll be on my way." Then to P.J., he whispered loudly, "Don't you dare force Corrine and Warren to leave." Matthew held up his fist.

"I'll think about it," P.J. answered.

Life returned to a normal routine after the events of the weekend and Monday. Matthew hoped P.J. would not carry out his plans. Martha left because a daughter needed her. Victoria returned to her teaching. Matthew saw less and less of Mary and Ed. They were occupied with farm work and their three children. His own four children were back in school, busy and involved. At home, seventeen-month-old Michael livened up the household.

During the days that followed, Matthew enjoyed Joe's companionship. Like old times, they did the morning chores together. Joe loved plowing the fields, and that meant Matthew had time for other tasks around the farm.

One afternoon while Matthew, Ellen, and Joe were drinking their afternoon coffee, Joe made an announcement. "I'd like to go to the cemetery and pay my respects to Grandma and Grandpa."

Matthew sensed the young man's sadness, but it was Ellen who spoke. "You miss your grandparents, don't you?"

There was a catch in Joe's voice. "I feel alone in the world—as if I have no family. My parents have their own lives in the city. I don't really have anyone."

Ellen walked over and placed her hands on Joe's shoulder. "You have us. We're your family. We love you."

Chapter Two

"I don't know if I could face being in the service if I didn't have you to come back to. I've been thinking about Grandpa and Grandma. I'd like to say goodbye to them."

"Joe," said Matthew, "would you like me to go with you to the cemetery? I haven't stopped there for awhile."

"I'd like that."

Matthew and Joe drove to the cemetery. Matthew thought of Joe's grandparents and their kind ways. John and Johanna Nelson had been like second parents to him when he bought their farm. As Pastor Strand had said, "Those people were the salt of the earth. They were what godly Christian people should be."

Matthew stopped the car at the cemetery entrance. As a child he had loved to play with other boys in this place. As he and Joe walked down the main path, it seemed to Matthew that he was returning to a bygone era. Ma and Pa were young, and dozens of people of an earlier generation were present. He wished they were actually present so they could talk. There were questions he wanted to ask.

They soon stood before the tombstones of John and Johanna Nelson. Joe knelt, not saying a word. In that moment, Matthew realized how fortunate he was to have Ellen and the children as well as other family.

Joe turned to Matthew. "I miss them. They raised me. Why didn't I appreciate them when they were alive? There's so much I'd like to talk to them about." He rose and turned away from the new gravestones. "Do people ever appreciate those they love while they're living?"

The question surprised Matthew. "Now that I think about it; most people don't appreciate their loved ones until it's too late. I miss Pa; I wish I could talk to him about what to plant and about how I should do certain things. Most of all, I just wish I had him around."

"Mr. Anderson," Joe began slowly, "I don't care to say this, but I'm scared of what's coming when I'm shipped out. There are some rough guys around who do things I'd never dream of doing. And I don't know if I could kill somebody—even in battle."

Matthew realized the words could have easily been his own twenty years ago. "I guess you do what the government says your job is. You're fighting for our country, to keep us safe."

The two walked on. A bond of understanding existed that would not be broken even with a separation of thousands of miles.

Matthew and Joe found themselves at the Anderson family plot.

"You miss your pa, don't you?" Joe stooped down and picked away a blade of grass. "I thought your pa was a great guy, very much like you."

The compliment surprised Matthew. "I've never felt I could live up to Pa's strength. Those old immigrants had a strength that my generation doesn't have."

Joe did not hesitate. "You have that strength."

The two stood in silence.

Matthew turned aside. "Do I have that strength?" he whispered aloud. "I need it."

A cowbell nearby sounded, reminding Matthew there were chores to be done.

Chapter 3

Matthew drove at high speed down the country road the six miles to the home place. Warren had called and desperately needed help with a calf being born. Matthew knew how important every minute could be.

He hurried to the barn where he had worked so many years. Warren greeted him. The cow mooed loudly, apparently in great pain.

Matthew went to work, massaging and petting the cow. He spoke gently, "Come, now, Bessie, you'll be all right. You have some work to do." He gave a gentle poke. The cow stood up.

Matthew continued to massage and felt movement within. The calf's front legs appeared.

"OK, let's pull."

In a moment the calf was pulled into the world. Matthew set the calf close to its mother.

"Matthew, you seem to know exactly what to do. I thought Bessie was in big trouble. You saved the day."

"These things come with time—experience."

The men proceeded to clean up the afterbirth.

Warren looked away. "Your dad used to say you had a special touch that animals responded to."

Matthew thought a moment. "Maybe that's because I think cattle have personalities just like people. And animals are good company when people aren't around."

Warren's face told Matthew there was something else troubling him. "Is something wrong?"

"I'm not sure. I need to talk business with P.J., but he's hard to pin down. It almost seems he's avoiding me." Warren paused and then went on. "I've had rough going. I had nothing when I came here. Corrine's mother helped out in the beginning and other people extended credit. Now with the crops in, I need to settle what debts I can. And then I owe P.J. rent."

Harsh memories of the past entered Matthew's mind. "I hate to speak badly of my brother, but he's hard to deal with. He can be generous one minute. The next minute, he's a tyrant."

Matthew watched the cow lick the newborn calf. He saw that Warren also shared the special joy that comes with a new life.

At the same time, Warren's dark eyes showed an even darker worry. "I need to ask another favor. I was wondering if you'd go with me to talk with P.J. I need all the moral support I can get."

Matthew nodded agreement.

Warren looked at his clothes. "I guess I better clean up before we go."

"No," said Matthew. "This is a farm and we're talking farm business. We'll go just as we are."

The two men were about to leave the barn when a door opened. There stood P.J., very much out of place in his tailored suit.

"Hello, Matthew. Warren. Warren, I want to see you."

"And I want to talk business with you."

P.J. brushed the request aside. "I'm getting some more beef cattle shipped in. They'll be here in a day or so."

Warren looked surprised and puzzled. "But that's not part of the agreement. I'm a dairy farmer."

P.J. went on with explanations about the advantage of raising beef cattle. Warren and Matthew tried to interrupt, but P.J. continued with seemingly inconsequential information.

Warren's face reddened. "P.J., stop, we need to talk."

"I'm in a hurry. I have to get to the cities on business."

Matthew interrupted. "You always have that excuse. Warren has some business matters you need to settle right now."

Chapter Three

Matthew moved over to block the door.

Warren began his explanation. "I've had some money problems. I guess you know that. I have bills to pay. What I'm trying to say is that I can pay only part of the rent."

P.J. smiled, looking almost too happy. "Well, I'll give you a good deal for the coming year."

"But I'm not ready for beef cattle. We don't have the proper fences in place. And I'm just getting my dairy herd established. I don't think I can handle beef as well."

Matthew began to suspect there was more behind P.J.'s plan. His maneuverings were never that simple.

"Well, if you want to rent another year, you're going to have to make room for my beef cattle, or rather Larry's beef cattle. Otherwise, you know what you can do."

"But what's Larry going to do here on this farm?"

P.J. looked away. "We'll work that out. He's going to come home here to farm. He can share this farm. He'll live here too."

Warren objected. "There's not room for both of us."

"It's a big house, and there's plenty of land. You'll have to make room."

"But you've agreed to rent to me with the option to buy. And I've fixed up the barn and the sheds. I have the right to stay and be in charge of this farm." Warren's face turned an even deeper red. Matthew knew Warren had a temper. Warren grasped the pitchfork tightly.

P.J. started to leave. Then he turned. "Well, I guess it will be simple enough for Larry to move in and take over the beef cattle. Then you can just get out."

Matthew felt his own anger rising within. History was repeating itself. P.J.'s resolution last spring to change his ways meant nothing.

"OK, I'll work with your beef cattle. But that means you pay me well."

P.J. turned to Warren and Matthew. "I'll pay you well. You've got a big house here. It's comfortable. Larry and his wife will live with you. And you can train Larry so that he can farm."

Matthew gasped.

Warren stumbled over his words. "You expect me and my wife and girls to be crowded into our house with your son and his wife! Larry is a misbehaving spoiled brat that no one should have to live with."

Warren stepped forward and P.J. moved away.

"You forget the painting and work I've done here. You promised I could rent with the option to buy within two years. Or don't your promises mean anything?"

Surprised by Warren's anger, P.J. spoke the next words carefully. "I believe, Warren, I said that there would be a possibility of your buying the farm. But you aren't even able to pay the rent."

"But my work and painting should count for part of the rent."

"The rent's due right now. Your painting wasn't in the agreement. You did that on your own. And there's nothing to stop me from kicking you off this land if you don't pay."

Matthew trembled in rage. He knew how Warren felt. That intense anger and helplessness had almost destroyed him.

"But," began Warren again, "I painted the house and barn, repaired the barn and outbuildings because I thought I could buy the place. That work in itself is worth the rent. And you say you can kick me out if I don't do what you ask me to."

P.J. straightened himself and moved toward the door. Matthew stepped out of the way. "Yes, you must remember that I own this place. It's mine to do with as I wish. And if I want Larry to have the place, that's the way it will be."

Before Matthew realized what was happening, Warren picked up the pitchfork and moved directly toward P.J. "You miserable cur." The words of profanity that Warren yelled were totally uncharacteristic of him.

P.J., in his desire to leave, stumbled over the threshold of the entrance.

Warren raised the pitchfork. "You're too rotten to live. You deserve to die!" He held the fork above P.J., ready to stab him.

"Don't do it! He's not worth it!" shouted Matthew.

P.J. cringed. Then he struggled to his feet. He stood, wiping the barn dirt from his suit, and began to back away.

Matthew spoke the words Ellen had once said. "P.J., remember you must answer to a higher authority. You will stand before Almighty God and you will have to account for what you have done."

P.J. walked to his car and got in. As he began to drive away, he yelled out the window, "You can get out!"

Chapter Three

An hour later, Matthew sat at the kitchen table with Warren and Corrine. As he glanced around his old home, he noticed the small amount of furniture that was in the house. Warren and Corrine were poor. How could anyone be as heartless as P.J.?

Coffee and a few cookies or a piece of cake usually calmed people in any kind of crisis. It did not help now. Matthew put aside a half cookie. Warren held his cup, not even drinking the coffee. Corrine's eyes were filled with tears.

"I don't know how much good it will do, but we need to rally the rest of the family and confront P.J.," Matthew spoke with assurance. "Martha should be back in a few days. And Victoria will not be afraid to speak up. P.J. will have to listen."

"Mom has already helped us so much," said Corrine. "I hate to ask for any more help. She's always helping one of us girls. And she isn't young either."

Warren set down his cup and began to speak, his voice choked with tears. "I'm such a failure. I lost your mother's farm in Wisconsin. The bank took everything."

"That wasn't your fault," comforted Corrine.

"Don't blame yourself," said Matthew. "Thousands of farmers lost their land. Pa and I were fortunate."

"It's like a curse!" Warren pounded his fist on the table. "Greedy people out to get the honest guy who has little."

Inwardly, Matthew agreed.

"We'll figure something out." Corrine wiped her tears and went to stand behind her husband, placing her hands gently on his shoulder. "The girls and I are with you every step of the way."

"Yes," agreed Matthew. "And so are the rest of the Andersons minus P.J. And so is the community."

"Thanks." Warren looked up for the first time.

"Let's not say anything to your grandmother yet. It's tough enough for her getting used to living alone without Pa," Matthew said.

Corrine smiled. "We have each other and our girls."

Two days later, Matthew and Ellen stood at the front door of P.J.'s grand lake home, a house in the grand tradition of the most elegant homes in Minneapolis or Chicago. Ellen rang the doorbell, then Matthew knocked loudly.

After what seemed far too long, Rita answered the door. Without saying hello she announced, "P.J. is very busy. I'll tell him you called."

Ellen marched in. "We have important business to discuss."

Rita replied curtly. "It can wait."

Matthew followed Ellen as she went right in and down the hall to the library office. Rita protested.

Ellen knocked on the door, and then walked in. "Hello P.J. We have business—matters that can't wait."

Rita pushed herself forward. "I tried to tell these people you were busy. They don't realize how much work you do."

To Matthew's surprise, P.J. greeted them in a cordial way. "You know, Matthew and Ellen, I did want to talk with you."

Rita looked rebuffed. "Well, then, I'll leave you to talk business."

P.J. turned to his wife. "Why don't you make some coffee? And aren't there some muffins left from breakfast?"

"I'll see."

Matthew wasn't sure how to respond to P.J.'s charm. P.J. had a way of being a tyrant one minute and changing into a charming host the next.

"I've been meaning to get over and spend some time with Mother, but I've been busy. How is she doing?"

"She's doing well," said Ellen. "Corrine always checks on her. Those three little girls are a blessing."

P.J. went on to talk about Cousin Peter and to ask about the kids. Rita brought in coffee and muffins for them to enjoy. Rita, though reserved, became the proper hostess.

After other talk, Ellen interrupted. "We have to get down to business. It's about Warren and Corrine. It's important that they stay right where they are."

"I agree, but I have Larry to think about." P.J. smiled, exuding self-confidence at the same time.

Matthew felt a need to remind P.J. of his promises. "Remember, last spring, how you promised to make things right. You would let this land and home benefit the whole family. And who benefits most from Corrine and Warren being here? It is the whole family, not just you."

"But Matthew, I have to be concerned about my own son just the way you would be concerned about your children."

Chapter Three

Rita interrupted. "And, remember, Warren was responsible for losing Martha's farm."

Matthew felt the heat of old anger stirring within.

P.J. turned to his wife. "Don't bring that up, please."

Ellen, always the quick thinker, spoke up. "That was the result of the dry years and the Depression. It was not Warren's fault."

"Remember," said Matthew, "that Warren might very well move out if you don't treat him right. There are other farms and houses for rent."

P.J. seemed to relent. "I hope Corrine and Warren will stay. They're a great help to Mother."

"And why don't you have Larry live in your house?" questioned Ellen.

Rita didn't waste a moment. "We have friends and business associates who will be visiting us. These are important people. In fact, tonight all the bedrooms are filled. We wouldn't have room."

"What about the cabins?" asked Ellen.

"They are only summer cabins."

"Who exactly are these people?" Ellen questioned.

P.J. avoided looking at Matthew and Ellen. "These are new business associates. They're not the ones who were here before. And friends, of course."

"You're saying these are honest people, not questionable characters." Ellen had a way of being direct.

"They're good and honest." P.J.'s protests didn't quite have the ring of truth.

P. J. tried to change the direction of the conversation. Matthew and Ellen got up to leave.

P.J. walked with Matthew and Ellen to their car. "We'll work things out. Everything will be all right for Corrine and Warren. Don't worry."

As Matthew and Ellen drove down the lane to the home place, Ellen asked the question that Matthew was forming in his mind. "Do you think we can trust P.J.?"

"P.J. says whatever he thinks people want to hear. He destroys people's lives, but we can't let him."

Matthew stopped the car by Ma's house. Ellen appeared to be deep in thought. Finally, she spoke.

"There are powers and principalities at work here. I'm afraid there's something terribly evil at work with Paul John Anderson."

Matthew added, "How could Ma have such a son as P.J.?"

At that moment Elizabeth Anderson appeared on the steps of her little house. She had begun to show her more than seventy years. But there was a kind, serene gentleness that showed in her face.

"I was hoping you would stop by. I just wanted to be with my children."

And, even though he was a forty-year-old man with five children and a wife, Matthew needed his mother.

Chapter 4

The ideal weather of September changed without Matthew realizing it. The moderate dry temperatures became hot and humid. He needed no weather forecaster to tell him that a storm was likely.

"Matthew," Ellen called to him as he and Joe got out of the car. "Your mother phoned. I don't know what the problem is, but I think you'd better go over."

Matthew quickly got back into the car and drove to the home place.

As he drove up the driveway, he noticed something different. There were no cattle around the barn, and everything seemed strangely empty and quiet. The big house was all closed up. Why would all the windows be closed with these hot temperatures?

Elizabeth Anderson met her son as he got out of the car. "Matthew, I'm glad you're here. I don't know what I'm going to do."

"What's wrong? Where are Corrine and Warren?" Matthew stopped abruptly and looked down the road that led to P.J.'s house. "And what about P.J.? Isn't he around?"

Ma clenched her fists. "I don't know what that son of mine did, but he'll soon put me out of my own house and home."

Matthew knew what this was about. "You mean Corrine and Warren have left."

"Why did Corrine and Warren keep this problem from me? And you knew about it too."

"Yes, but I thought we could get P.J. to change his mind. And we didn't want to worry you."

"I'm not some weak wilting violet. I've learned to face tough situations."

"I'm sorry, Ma." Matthew wanted to stoop down and kiss his mother, but he restrained himself. "Where did Corrine and Warren go?"

Ma began to relate the situation. "Corrine came over early this morning and said goodbye. They had everything from the house loaded up. The cattle truck came and picked up the cattle. They were out so fast I didn't know what was happening."

Matthew repeated himself. "But where did they go?"

"They said they could move into some old house on the Robertson property down the road. And Glenn said they could rent some acreage there."

Matthew remembered that Glenn was ready to rent out some of his land because his boys were planning to go into the army. "Did you talk with P.J.? What did he have to say?"

"First, he said he was busy. Then he came over. We talked, and I'm afraid I wasn't very nice. He left and said he had business in the Cities. He said Larry was going to live in the big house."

Matthew tried to comfort his mother as best he could. Keen disappointment replaced his belief that P.J. would try to change his ways and make things right. His brother had once more become the jerk he had been most of his life. On the other hand, Matthew couldn't help wondering why Warren had moved without even coming for help.

In the usual tradition, Ma made coffee, and mother and son had coffee and cookies. Ma calmed down, but her face still remained flushed from anger.

"Maybe it's best you come live with us. I know it will be OK with Ellen," Matthew suggested.

"I never wanted to be a burden to my children. I've always wanted to be independent. I'm used to looking after people, not being looked after."

"There comes a time," said Matthew.

"I'm three score years and ten, plus two. That's a full life. It will soon be my time."

Chapter Four

"No, Ma," protested Matthew. "You're strong and healthy. You can have many years ahead of you. Grandma lived to be well over eighty."

"I was so comfortable here with Corrine and Warren in the big house. They were there and they helped me. Now, I feel so alone. And the great grandkids were just wonderful. I loved having them here."

Matthew reached for his mother's hand. "We're only a phone call away. We're nearby whenever you need us. And Mary and Ed are close as well."

The shadows deepened and Ma switched on the light. Matthew looked west and noticed the dark clouds. The house was heavy with heat. He hated to leave Ma, but it was time for him to go home. Ma tried to reassure him that she would be fine.

As he drove away from the home place, he had an uneasy feeling about the events of the day as well as the weather. He took a last look at the big house and realized how empty it must be with no one living there. A house like that was meant to be filled with people and life.

"I miss my old home," he said, just as thunder rumbled in the distance.

That evening, Elizabeth Anderson sat alone at her kitchen table. She turned off the lights so she could look outside and watch the progress of the storm. A few rain drops fell, and that seemed to end the storm.

In her mind she saw her oldest son. She never knew exactly what business P.J. had, but she knew he dealt with shady characters. He was not honest. Matthew had told her how P.J. had been ready to take his own life. He had drifted far from the values she had taught him. She thought of Scripture and the way she tried to bring up her son. "Train up a child in the way he ought to go, and when he is old, he will not depart from it." This son had departed from the way. Would or could he return when he became old?

Elizabeth rose and stood by the front door. The big house looked lonely and empty. She remembered the excitement when she and John and all the children moved into the big new house. That had been a great event in their lives. Then, shortly after Matthew married Ellen, they had built this "little house." It had been home to Elizabeth for more than fifteen years now.

Only last night, she had looked out to see the comforting lights of the big house. She knew that Corrine and Warren were there. If she needed help, they would be over in a minute. But P.J. had changed all that. What had P.J. been thinking? Warren had worked hard to make the farm a better one. Why would P.J. decide that Larry should move here and farm? Larry was no farmer.

Elizabeth walked into the bedroom, feeling keenly the emptiness of her life now that John was gone. She put on her nightgown and lay down to sleep, but sleep evaded her. Only a sheet covered her and yet she was wet with perspiration. Finally she dozed off. Disturbing objects and people moved through her dreams. She stirred in her sleep as she became aware of lightning reflecting from the mirror of her dresser. Thunder rumbled in the distance. September thunder storms could be violent.

A deeper sleep finally came. Her husband walked into her dreams. "Be careful!" he kept saying. "Be careful." Elizabeth had the feeling that something dreadful lurked nearby.

Suddenly, light was everywhere, and at that same moment thunder filled the bedroom as if everything were about to explode. She sat up, completely awake. The lightning must have struck nearby. She moved quickly to look at the barn and then at the big house. There was no evidence that either had been struck.

Outside the rain poured for a few minutes and then stopped. She opened the windows and door. Cool autumn air poured into the house. The storm was over.

As she returned to her bed, she wished as she had many times before, that John were here. It was always such a comfort, knowing he was next to her.

She was exhausted, but sleep evaded her. If only Corrine and Warren were nearby, she would feel safe. She tried to stop thinking. She followed her old routine of counting eggs rather than sheep. Sleep finally came, but P.J., dark and menacing, filled her dreams. She had spent more nights worrying about him than all the rest of her children put together. He was the most talented and brilliant. He could have been a movie actor or a governor or a president if he'd put his mind to it. But somehow, this son could not be trusted. Instinctively, she knew that from the earliest years, but she didn't want to believe what she knew in her heart.

In her dream Elizabeth found herself in P.J.'s extravagant house. She sensed something dark and evil as she walked through the rooms. She couldn't believe P.J. could afford such a mansion. Half awake, she

Chapter Four

remembered P.J.'s greatest deception: first getting John to sign the farm over to him, and then neglecting to sign the farm back as he had agreed. That deception was causing no end of trouble.

As the nightmare continued, she found herself running beside P.J. They approached a cliff with a thousand foot drop below. P.J. was on the ledge and about to go over. Suddenly a bright light blazed. She screamed as the light obscured everything and P.J. began to fall.

Her own scream wakened her. As Elizabeth's mind cleared, she became aware of a flickering light. It seemed at first the light was part of her nightmare, but then she realized the light was real. It can't be morning yet, she thought. Out of habit, she reached over to touch John. As she started to say something, she remembered that he was gone.

She jumped out of bed, feeling all the aches of her seventy-two years. She moved fast, opening the front door. She smelled heavy smoke. She ran down the steps and to her horror she saw the big house enveloped in flames.

A barrel of emotions filled her mind. It seemed the fire would destroy everything. "Lord, what do I do now?" she prayed.

"I'll call Mary and Ed!" she said aloud. "They're closest." She cranked out the three long rings on the wall phone, hoping she wouldn't wake up everyone on the party line. She wasn't sure of the time, but it had to be the middle of the night.

Elizabeth's hands shook as she waited for an answer.

"Hello," Mary sounded frightened.

"It's your mother here. The big house is on fire."

"How bad?" Mary's voice became shrill.

"It looks bad. What should I do?"

"Ed and I will be right there."

Ed's voice sounded in the background. "Call the operator. She'll call the fire department. Call Matthew!"

"Yes." Elizabeth's heart beat madly. She could barely talk. She had heard of people having heart attacks at such times.

"Are you all right, Ma?"

Elizabeth found her strength returning. "I'll be all right. Come fast. I'll call the fire department."

Elizabeth rang the long ring for the operator, probably waking the woman from a deep sleep. She waited impatiently.

Finally the operator's voice asked for the number.

"Help! This is Elizabeth Anderson. John Anderson farm. The big house is on fire! Call the fire department! And hurry!"

She heard the operator ring for the fire chief who would set off the fire alarm that would probably awaken half of Lake View. Then, a long ring for the local line signaled to seven other families that there was an emergency.

Elizabeth collected her thoughts, quickly putting on a dress and stockings. She could not stop trembling but felt a sense of relief as Mary and Ed drove up.

She looked at the house she had loved and taken care of. The flames were everywhere. Light reflected in the second floor windows. She knew it was too late to save the house.

"Ma, are you all right?" Mary was at her side. "Did you make the calls?"

"I haven't called Matthew yet."

"I'll do that, now," said Mary. "It looks as if the fire may cut off electricity. You'd better get out the lamps."

Elizabeth looked away from the dreadfulness of the fire. Mary rang for the operator who answered immediately this time. The operator rang for Matthew.

"Matthew, it's the big house. It's burning."

At that moment the transformer blew, and the lights went out.

Matthew was not surprised. His instincts had told him something would happen.

He hurried back upstairs to awaken Ellen and tell her of the fire. The children were all sleeping.

"We need to get there fast," said Matthew. "Will the children be OK?"

"They'll be fine," said Ellen.

Ellen and Matthew dressed quickly and in minutes were in the car. As he turned onto the highway, Matthew saw the fire, though still several miles away. The fire was like an avenging demon. He drove hard, taking the curves as fast as he dared.

Ellen cautioned him. "I don't think there's anything we can do about the house."

Chapter Four

Memories flooded Matthew's mind. "I can't believe what I'm seeing." He remembered the nightmares he'd had that night. It was almost as if those nightmares were warnings of what he now saw. Ever since that thunder crash, he'd had a premonition that something was going to happen.

The driveway was already crowded with cars. Matthew decided to park on the road, and he and Ellen hurried toward the crowd and Ma's house. The fire trucks from town had arrived, and volunteer firemen were surveying the situation.

"Let's hose down the little house," yelled someone from the fire department. "There's nothing to do about the big house. Let's not take any chances with the other buildings."

Matthew and Ellen stood back with the many neighbors who had gathered.

His good friend and old neighbor, Glenn Robertson, hurried up to him. "There wasn't anything we could do. It was too late. We got a few things out: an old desk and that oak table you left."

Matthew, overcome with shock and memories, could say nothing.

"We're just stunned." Ellen placed her hand gently on Matthew's arm. "How did it start?" she asked.

"Lightning, we think," answered Glenn.

Matthew remembered Pa's words and repeated them. "And when it's lightning, it seems to have an extra power. It's as if there are little fingers that reach out."

Matthew looked up and saw the flames angrily destroying the attic. He remembered those rainy days of childhood when he had played up there.

In the crowd a few feet away, Matthew caught sight of his mother. Mary stood beside her. He wished he could shield Ma from this terrible happening. "Ma, are you all right?"

"This is too much." Ma kept looking up as the fire raged on. "It's as if my whole past is burning up."

One of the firefighters yelled to the crowd. "Get back! The chimney's about to collapse. It'll send flames and debris this way!"

The fire had a personality all its own. Flames everywhere reached out with fingers of destruction. The heat intensified as glass shattered and fire leapt through several windows. The firefighters tried to move the crowd farther away from the building.

Matthew became mesmerized by the leaping flames. Suddenly there was a deafening roar as the chimney came down. At the same time, the beams of the second floor collapsed. Noise and confusion followed as people moved away from the danger. There was nothing to do.

Matthew shivered even as he felt the heat of the fire. His eyes smarted from the smoke and intensity of the fire. The house that contained so many memories of his childhood as well as those of his first fourteen years of marriage was no more.

Ma's voice was shaky as she spoke. "We worked so hard to build the house. And my mother's emigrant trunk was in the attic."

Matthew wanted to say comforting words, but words would not come. Ellen gave her mother-in-law a hug.

"But those are only things," Ma said. "We haven't lost anyone. We're all alive."

Matthew couldn't hear the words as the noise of the crowd remained intense.

Matthew saw the firefighters checking the barn and other outbuildings. "Thank God, the wind's blowing the other way."

Ma reached her hand to Ellen. "Do you think we should make coffee for these people? They did everything they could. They even moved the woodpile and the old stuff from the shed."

"Come with me," said Mary. "Ellen and I will take care of coffee. Maybe we can make some sandwiches."

Another flurry of activity followed. "The straw pile's on fire," some one yelled.

In moments, men were pumping water and running toward the straw pile and the barn. The firemen hosed down the roof and sides of the barn.

Matthew rushed to help, but soon felt his help was unnecessary. The small fire was quickly put out.

Elizabeth Anderson stood on the porch. Various neighbors tried to comfort her. She was a woman who did not easily give way to tears, but now she sobbed, "Oh, why did this happen? I don't understand. I don't understand."

As quickly as the tears had come, Elizabeth dried them.

The hour that followed was a time of activity and some confusion. Mary and Ellen brought out cups of coffee and quickly made sandwiches. The firefighters and some of the others welcomed the refreshments.

Chapter Four

Some of the firefighters watched so that sparks would not fly away and ignite elsewhere. Ed, who had worked with the firefighters, came to the house. "It should be safe; the fire's out." Then he added, "It won't be long until it's time for chores."

People began to leave, neighbors as well as men from the fire department. The last firefighter gave some advice. Soon only Matthew and Ellen and Mary and Ed remained. They sat at the kitchen table in tired silence.

"I don't know what to do." Ma looked sad and alone. "I'm numb. I miss your pa more than ever. He'd know what to do."

Matthew did not hesitate. "Ma, you're coming with us. You shouldn't be alone here."

Ellen agreed.

Elizabeth Anderson looked away. "Oh, Matthew, no. I can't be a burden to you and your family."

"Ma, there's no question about it."

Mary added, "Yes, Mother, that's what you should do."

Ellen rose and walked into the bedroom. "You come in and we'll pick out a few things. You can come back later and pack more.

Ma quietly followed. "I'll stay a day or two."

She had a look of emptiness and sadness that would haunt Matthew for days to come. Mary and Ed left, and Matthew listened to the words of the two women as they rummaged about in the bedroom.

Slowly and meditatively, Matthew walked outside and watched the sun peek into a new day. He stood before the ruins of the big house. Smoke smells filled the air. The fire had wiped out a part of his life.

Ellen's words interrupted his thoughts. "Matthew, we're ready."

"Ma, it's hard to believe," Matthew said as he picked up the old suitcase.

Her usual strength gone, Ma looked frail and old. "Half a lifetime of memories wiped out. But life goes on."

The sun brightened the world, and golden leaves of autumn glistened in the morning sun, but Matthew found it difficult to see the beauty and look beyond this storm.

Chapter 5

October 1940

Something about a bus and a bus station fascinated Matthew. A bus symbolized travel that went beyond the familiar hills where he'd always lived. He had dreamed of going far away, but opportunity had never come his way. Or at least he had never taken that opportunity.

Matthew and Ellen had brought Joe to the River Falls Bus Depot. This departure was different from others they had experienced. This one marked an uncertain future for the young man they had come to know and love.

Joe stood tall and straight. "Goodbye Mrs. Anderson." He gave Ellen a hug. "I'll miss you."

"Please call me Ellen."

Joe choked back tears. "I can't do that. You deserve respect. You're like a mother to me."

Matthew extended his hand. "And call me Matthew." Then he opened his arms and Joe hugged him. He felt Joe trembling—-overwhelmed with emotion and no doubt fearful of what he would soon face.

Joe stepped back, his deep blue eyes glistening with tears. "Could I call you Dad and Mom? You're more than just my boss and his wife. I need a family to come back to."

"We'd be honored," said Ellen. "In many ways, you seem like another son. But we can never replace your own parents."

Overcome with emotion Matthew began, "We'll miss you."

"Dad." Joe spoke the word with pride as he extended his hand. "A handshake seals the bargain."

Matthew, more than almost any other time, wanted to say something profound. Only one word escaped his lips. "Son."

"Joseph Nelson, we love you. We will pray for you every day," Ellen said as she hugged him.

"Thanks, Mom."

A harsh voice interrupted. "Last call. The bus is leaving. Last call."

Joe grabbed his duffel bag. "It's time. I'll miss you." He hurried into the bus, not looking back.

Matthew and Ellen saw through the bus window where Joe sat. He held up his hand and waved.

Other parents and friends pushed past Matthew and Ellen to shout their last goodbyes. The noise of people and the grinding of the bus gears punctuated the farewell.

Matthew and Ellen stood on the sidewalk as others left. They watched the bus as it disappeared. Then, slowly, they returned to their car.

As Matthew and Ellen left the city of River Falls, Matthew remembered the new problems that lay before them. "We need to stop and check on Ma."

The charred remains of the big house reminded Matthew of the fire that had destroyed the place a few weeks ago. The acrid smell of charred wood remained. The foundation and basement with some partially burned boards and some unrecognizable objects were all that remained of the house.

Elizabeth Anderson had insisted on returning to her own little house. Neither Matthew nor her other children could convince her differently.

They walked briskly up the steps to the little house. Ellen knocked on the door and stepped in. "Mother Anderson," she called.

The two called out several times. There was no answer. It was totally uncharacteristic of Elizabeth Anderson to be out of the kitchen or the

Chapter Five

living room. She was always working on something. Matthew's heart beat fast, fear crept in. Had something happened to Ma?

Matthew hurried to the other door and looked out to see if his mother had gone outside. Ellen checked the kitchen stove. It was cold. No pot filled with hot coffee for anyone who might stop. And the sink was filled with dirty dishes that hadn't been washed for several days.

"This isn't like Ma," said Matthew. "Something's got to be wrong."

A frail sounding voice came from the bedroom. "Is that you Matthew? I guess I didn't hear you."

Elizabeth Anderson stepped into the living room, still wearing her nightgown.

"Mother Anderson, are you sick?" Ellen hurried to her mother-in-law's side.

"I don't know what's wrong with me." She wiped her eyes. "I'm tired. I can't seem to get anything done. If I do something, it doesn't turn out right."

"Ma, you've been crying."

Ma brushed aside the remark. "Let me get dressed. I'll make coffee."

"I'll get fire started in the stove. This time of year the kitchen stove keeps the house comfortable." Matthew saw that he needed to make a trip to the woodpile. He motioned Ellen to go out with him.

Ellen seemed to know what her husband was thinking. "Your mother shouldn't be alone. She needs to come with us."

Matthew picked up several sticks of dry wood. "I think you're right. Let's not waste any time."

When his mother came out of the bedroom, fully dressed, she looked at the cold stove. "I thought you were going to start the stove for me."

Matthew laid down the sticks of wood. "We changed our minds. Ma, we don't think you should be here alone. You're coming with us."

Ellen added, "Why don't you bring a few clothes along with your nightgown. Stay with Matthew and me. We'll come back later and get everything you want."

"Please, no," pleaded the old woman. "I can stay here myself. P.J.'s nearby."

The mention of P.J. reminded Matthew that he needed to confront his brother once more.

Before anyone could respond further, a sharp knock at the door interrupted the next words.

The door opened. Ed stood there, obviously upset and shaken. "I saw you were here. I'm afraid I have some bad news."

Ma didn't hesitate to speak. "It's Mary, isn't it? I've been so worried about her. That terrible cough."

Matthew, too, had been afraid something was wrong.

"I took her to the doctor this morning," began Ed. "We'd been doctoring before, and we went into River Falls for X-rays. I'm afraid the X-rays proved what we were afraid of. She has TB."

"Oh, Ed," said Ellen, "I'm so sorry."

"The doctor said we have to move fast. So I'm taking her to the TB sanitarium. We don't know how long she'll have to be there."

Ma turned and walked away. "I've lost one child already. Another one stole the land from me. I can't lose a third child. That's too much for an old woman to bear."

Ellen moved close to her mother-in-law, putting an arm around her shoulder. "There are things that can be done. Many people overcome TB."

"I always thought I'd have this little house to live in. And then Corrine and Warren were so good to me. Before that I had the two of you." She looked up at Matthew.

"You still have us," said Ed forcefully. "That jerk of a son of yours can't take this house. That is clear."

"But, don't worry about me," said Ma. "We have Mary to think about."

The four talked of Mary and the impact this would make on the children. Ed added, "I think I've already found a hired girl. Beth is in high school and can't handle school work and all the house work."

Matthew's mind traveled back to childhood days when he and Mary would play together. It was hard to think of this thirty-nine-year old woman as the same little sister who had played with him.

"I've got to get back to work. I have more work than ever." Ed left as abruptly as he had arrived.

"How much more do I need to face?" questioned Ma. "I can't take any more."

Matthew took charge. "Ma, you're coming with us. Ellen will clean up the spare bedroom. We can make that place real comfortable."

"I'll help you pack a few things," Ellen offered.

"I think I need to see P.J." Matthew shifted uneasily.

Chapter Five

"You go ahead," said Ellen. "I'll help with packing and putting things away."

Matthew drove the half-mile to his brother's ostentatious mansion. He dreaded the meeting, but maybe he could help improve the situation. He kept recalling his brother's resolution to make things right.

As luck would have it, Matthew found P.J. outside, polishing his Cadillac. One of the few things the brothers had in common was the desire to keep their cars looking good.

They greeted one another. There was a coolness that had developed recently.

"What brings you here, brother?" P.J. put aside the towel he had used in polishing his Cadillac.

"I think we have some problems," began Matthew.

P.J. quickly responded. "Oh, Rita and I will look in on Mother. You don't have a thing to worry about."

Matthew felt himself stiffen. Silently, he prayed that God would calm him and give the right words. "You made a promise last spring. Remember that day in the cemetery? You were going to see that this farm was run for the benefit of the family. You promised."

P.J.'s face reddened. "Did I say all that? I think I was upset."

All at once, Matthew's words came easily as if his tongue had been loosened. "What you did years back may have been legal. But what you did was wrong and immoral. You were to sign the land back to Ma and Pa. This land should now belong to Ma. Actually, it should be mine."

P.J. started to say something but then stopped.

"And now Corrine and Warren need a farm. They should be back on *this* farm."

"But remember, Larry is a nephew, a grandson. Doesn't he have as much right as Corrine and Warren?"

"Larry knows nothing about farming. And where's he going to stay? There is no big house any longer. If Corrine and Warren had stayed, they would have been there to stop the fire."

"I offered Corrine and Warren chances to stay. It was a big house, and Larry and Joan could have lived there also."

"Why should Warren and Corrine have stayed? Your terms weren't fair."

An interruption came in the form of a large dark car driving up. Matthew thought he recognized the man who got out. The man, at least six feet four inches tall, had the body of a prize fighter with broad shoulders and beefy arms. He crossed his arms and ambled toward Matthew and P.J.

"Good afternoon," the man said.

Matthew and P.J. greeted him.

"I have a message for you, Paul John Anderson." Even without a verbal threat, the voice announced danger.

Matthew felt himself becoming tense. He had thought the Mafia element was out of the picture. P.J. had guaranteed that.

"I'm listening," answered P.J., meekly.

"You stay clear of the area east of here. That's our area. If you try any business there, you'll find out what we do." The man flexed his muscles. "Bad things happen to people who double-cross the boss. Is that clear?"

P.J. looked puzzled.

"Remember what happened to Jack Barlow. Did I make myself clear or must I do more?"

P.J. stepped back. "I understand."

"I noticed you had a little fire a ways down the road. It's not only lightning that starts fires." He turned to go. "You have a mighty nice house here, Paul John Anderson. Things can happen, you know."

The man didn't wait for an answer. He got in his car and drove away.

Matthew watched the car disappear. "I thought you were done with those goons. You know how the community feels about these characters."

"I swear, Matthew, I'm not associated with the crime syndicate."

"I don't believe you. Your word means nothing."

P.J. backed away. "I need to go. I have work to do."

Matthew followed. "We're not done yet. There's other action we can take."

"Please, wait." P.J. very rarely pleaded; he usually bullied and controlled.

"What will happen with Larry? Where can he live? With you and Rita, I suppose."

P.J. began moving toward the house. "He'll stay here at first, but we'll be building. Maybe we can even start this fall. We have business associates who will be with us in our house. We're working to make some cabins ready for winter."

"I have more to say." Matthew grabbed P.J.'s arm.

Chapter Five

P.J. pulled away from him. "Don't try to tell me what to do."

Matthew found his courage returning. "It's about time you listened to what I'm going to say. You have much to answer for. You have God to answer to."

"Come on," P.J. mocked. "So you've got religion. That's fine for Mother and Ellen. It's a woman's thing. But be a man like me."

"Brother, I'll be man enough to stand up to you. God only knows that some people have been afraid to. We all know about your drinking and carousing. You managed to get Cousin Peter to go back to his drinking. And you've been to the doctor with heart problems. Strong drink does things to a person's judgment."

P.J. looked down. "How do you know all this?"

"Ma figured it out. She saw Dr. Baker come out. And Dr. Baker talked with Ellen."

"He had no business doing that."

"Now, let's come back to your promises. You were ready to take your life. You knew Pa would have been disappointed in you. In fact, he might not have had that heart attack if it hadn't been for you. And you know that."

The last words stunned P.J. He said nothing.

"You know you've done wrong. You have to change. And now Ma is beside herself. You know she needs people and help. For now, she's coming home with Ellen and me. But you have some responsibility."

"What wrong with Ma?"

"If you had treated Corrine and Warren better, they would have been there when she needed help. You forced them out. Now it should be your duty to check on Ma."

P.J. repeated his question.

"Ma's feeling terrible right now. She's alone. Winter is coming. You are having serious problems. And just now, Mary has to go to the sanitarium. She has TB."

"Oh, no!"

"Rather than helping this family, you're destroying everything around you. You can't hurt any more people."

"I'll do what I can to help Mary."

"The best thing you can do is make things right on this farm. If I had been here, owning and running the farm, these problems would not have taken place. Now, the best thing you can do is to get someone to run the farm the way Corrine and Warren did, or else get them back."

"I don't know where Corrine and Warren are."

"They're just a few miles from here."

Rita's sharp voice called from the front porch. "Paul John, there's an important telephone call for you. They're in a hurry."

"I've got to go. I'll see what I can do." P.J. hurried into the house.

Matthew stood for a moment, watching his brother. He muttered to himself, "P.J.'s a total jerk. He won't do a thing."

As Matthew walked into Ma's little house, Ellen met him. "Your mother is not well. We need to get her to the doctor, but she doesn't want to go."

"That's Ma for you." Then he added, "I don't think my talk with P.J. did any good."

"That figures." Ellen pointed toward the bedroom door. "She's lying down again. She's decided she should stay here."

Matthew knew he had to be firm. It seemed at this point that he had become the parent who needed to look after his mother.

Matthew said a silent prayer, asking God for strength and wisdom. He sat down on the bed. "Ma, we need to look after you. It's my turn now. Come with us. At least for tonight."

"I don't want to be a burden to my children," she said weakly.

"We'll worry about you if you stay here alone." Matthew went on to give more reasons why she should leave her home.

A few minutes later, Matthew drove down the driveway. Ellen sat in the backseat. Ma sat in front beside him. As Matthew reached the end of the driveway, Ma began to sob uncontrollably. Matthew stopped the car.

Through the tears, Ma began to talk. "I don't know how I can go on. What purpose in life can I have? Why doesn't God take me home?"

"You have a purpose here, Mother Anderson." Ellen's voice had a firmness and authority. "You have five grandchildren at our place as well as other grandchildren and great-grandchildren. They all love you. You have a special connection with them."

Matthew looked back at the home place and realized the changes of these past years. He remembered his mother's wise thoughts.

Chapter Five

"Ma, life is never easy. Change is a part of life. You've said that. The Lord will guide us into and through these changes. Living life means meeting these changes and adjusting to them."

Ma dried her tears. "I'm sorry. I guess I was feeling sorry for myself. I'm alive, and God has a purpose for me here."

"That's right," said Matthew. "Each one of us has a purpose. And God gives us the strength we need."

Chapter 6

"Matthew," announced Elizabeth Anderson a week later. "I need a ride home. I'm feeling better now. I want to sleep in my own bed."

Elizabeth saw the glance between Matthew and Ellen. She hated the idea that people felt they had to look after her.

"Ma, do you think you're ready to be alone? It gets lonely. And there's no one close by."

"I'll manage." Then she added, "Besides I'll have company tomorrow night. Your cousin Peter's coming and he'll be staying with me. And Alice, too."

Once again, Elizabeth saw Matthew look to his wife for help. Matthew had a good wife—one with a lot of common sense. She'd understand a woman's point of view.

Ellen did seem to understand. "Matthew, why don't you take your mother back to her house after chores?"

Matthew nodded. That settled the matter.

Elizabeth spent the next two days baking and planning. She had Matthew take her to town where she bought ample supplies of groceries.

Ellen sent a good supply of milk and butter and some other staples. The cellar would keep the milk and meat cold. Elizabeth had no intention of getting one of those newfangled refrigerators. Such things were an extravagance. Sometimes she wondered about the need for electricity.

The evening shadows deepened. Elizabeth sat in her chair beside the window, tired from hours of work. Half awake and half asleep, she found her private world invaded by dark thoughts. She saw Corrine and Warren and the three girls now living in that decrepit old house that should have been torn down. Glenn Robertson had been kind enough to let them move there. But would that place even provide decent warmth during the winter?

Her thoughts turned to P.J., who had caused so much difficulty. She thought back to her own life. During those years when P.J. was young, she was a harried mother. In fact for some time after Lucille's birth, she had not been well. Martha and Victoria adjusted well, but P.J. had been rebellious from his earliest years.

Had she done something wrong with P.J.? Somewhere during those years she had experienced a spiritual renewal. She had dedicated herself to the Lord. The girls responded well, but P.J. had been different. At times, he would do everything she expected, but then he would change to an entirely different person. He was charming from his earliest days. A born salesman, he could talk others into almost anything.

She wondered if she had done the right thing by sending him to Prairie Center to stay with a cousin during his high school years. That cousin did not share any of her values—and certainly not her faith. P.J. had stayed away four years. Elizabeth had suspected he might be living a double life, the dutiful son in front of her, the prodigal whenever he was out of her sight. By nature she was trusting and wanted to believe the best of everyone, especially her children.

Her thoughts turned to her other children. Martha was the perfect daughter, the ideal mother, always ready to help. Why did Martha have to be away so frequently? It was good that she was now living in Lake View; at least she lived close by.

Victoria was completely different. She was now both principal and teacher in the local high school. Tall for a woman, she had dark hair and dark striking features—in many ways like P.J. She immediately commanded respect of everyone, especially her students. She always enforced her rigid moral code.

Chapter Six

She still missed her third daughter, Lucille, in so many ways kind like Martha. Lucille had exhibited weakness and tiredness from childhood. She had a weak heart. Why did this precious girl, filled only with kindness and goodness, have to die young? Life wasn't fair. Elizabeth had experienced some of her deepest darkness at that time.

Then there were Matthew and Mary. Matthew, always the quiet one, who felt he didn't quite measure up. Had she done something to make him feel that way? Of all her children, he was probably the most sensitive and caring. Matthew deserved to have the farm that P.J. had stolen. No one else could have forgiven P.J. the way Matthew had.

And Mary, her youngest. Elizabeth was tired by the time Mary was born. She hadn't been ready for another child, and didn't really want one. Perhaps Mary sensed that. She was undeniably her father's favorite. John Anderson was older when she arrived. He took more time to have her sit in his lap and tell her stories.

Now would Mary, so strong most of the time, be able to face her illness? Would she gain strength and recover and come home? It didn't seem fair that an old lady should see her children suffer this way.

"Dear Lord," she whispered. "I need your strength. Otherwise I can't go on. I can't face this world alone."

In that moment an almost audible voice came to her. *You are not alone. Lo, I am with you always even unto the end of the world.*

A peace settled over Elizabeth—-a peace she did not understand.

She spoke aloud. "Lord, I have You. And You have given me my family. I have Matthew and Ellen and the kids. And Mary will recover. I pray that she will. I know that You will heal her. And I have Martha and Victoria. They are both strong women of faith. They are here for me."

The phone interrupted. She rose and answered.

"Hello, Grandma, it's Corrine."

"How wonderful to hear from you."

"Grandma, I'll be over next week. I'm sorry we had to leave so suddenly. Warren and I felt we couldn't go on living there under those circumstances."

"I miss you." Elizabeth sighed. "I do understand."

"And I'm sorry the house burned. I can't believe that grand house is no longer standing."

Tears stopped Elizabeth from saying anything.

"I've not been feeling so well. Otherwise I'd have been over sooner. I can't even begin to describe how awful this experience was. Warren can't take any more setbacks. And neither can I."

"I wish we could have done something."

Elizabeth felt uncomfortable. She knew there were listening ears on the party line. Neighborliness sometimes turned into nosiness. Anyhow, the whole neighborhood probably knew what P.J. had done.

Elizabeth felt less alone after her talk with Corrine.

Darkness had settled when Peter arrived. Elizabeth heard the car, saw the lights, and hurried to the door. She had already cooked a fresh pot of coffee.

"Welcome home," she said as he entered.

"Aunt Elizabeth, it is good to be here." He took her in his arms. "It's been too long since I've visited you."

"Where's Alice?"

Peter began to make excuses for his busy wife.

When he stopped talking, set his suitcase down, and sat, Elizabeth poured a cup of coffee and simply said, "Peter, you're not fooling me. Something's wrong."

As Elizabeth put out sandwiches and cookies and cake, Peter began to talk. "It's a long story. I know it's my fault."

"Then, can't you try to make it right?"

"Well, it's this way: Alice's family has always been more important than I am. I've played second fiddle to them all our married life. That's how it started."

Elizabeth began to quote, "When a man leaves his father and mother, he must cleave unto his wife. That's God's command. And a wife must leave parents and cleave to her husband."

Peter continued to pour out his heart to his aunt. "I confess now that I've been going the wrong way. It's been too easy to stop at the bars for companionship. Alice was either gone or wouldn't talk to me."

"Drink is never the answer."

Peter looked down. "I know that. I've made a resolution to stop drinking. I've been going back to church, and I haven't had a drink in two weeks."

"You're on the right track. The Lord will help you work out the problem."

Chapter Six

"I guess that's why I came. I haven't been here much for several years—except for the trip last month. I want to spend time with you and the rest of the family."

Aunt and nephew visited for several more hours. Finally, Elizabeth announced, "I think you'd better get to bed. You're going to be up hunting early in the morning."

"I guess so. But visiting you is far more important than any hunting." He kissed his aunt on the cheek and said goodnight.

A few minutes later, Elizabeth sat on her bed and bowed her had. She whispered aloud, "Peter's on the right track. I planted those seeds of faith long ago when he lived with us. I must pray for him and Alice."

And that is what she did. In minutes she slipped into a deep and restful sleep. Even at seventy-two, life was good.

After chores the next morning, Matthew returned to the home place. He never enjoyed hunting, but he went for the companionship and for the pleasant walks through the woods. He found Peter and his mother seated, drinking coffee, and visiting.

It was Peter who invited him to sit down. Soon the three were visiting about old times and childhood shenanigans.

Finally Matthew looked at his watch, noting the late morning hour. "I thought you came to go duck hunting."

Peter laughed. "I'm afraid that was just an excuse. But I'm eager to get outside."

"Give me half an hour, and I'll give you noon dinner," interrupted Ma.

Matthew stood up. "Remember, both of you are invited to supper at our place tonight."

Ma stood up and opened the trap door to the cellar. "In just a few minutes I can warm up some pork. I'll fry a few potatoes and open some canned corn. And we'll be set."

Matthew and Peter agreed. "Let's get our hunting gear ready. Then we'll eat."

The two men got their gear ready, then ate their noon meal, and soon were on their way to the east end for hunting. The sunny, warm October day meant that the ducks would hardly be flying over. The two cousins spent their time walking and talking and enjoying the warmth of autumn. They spent more time in the woods than by the sloughs and lake.

Late in the afternoon, they approached P.J.'s mansion. Peter expressed his surprise at what he saw.

Even now Matthew felt pain about his loss of the family farm. "P.J. got control, and this is what he did."

"What about all those cabins?"

"That just happened this summer. P.J. and Rita rent them or let their guests stay there. It's mostly for some of those rich guys from the city."

"I notice there's a bit of traffic by Aunt Elizabeth's house. How does she feel about that? And about P.J. taking over?"

Matthew looked away. "She knows what P.J. did was wrong and unfair. I think she still blames herself and Pa for not being more careful."

"P.J. has a way with people. He looks honest. But I wouldn't want to buy a used car from him."

Matthew took out his pocket watch. "Pete, I'm afraid it's time for chores. I told the boys I'd be back in time to help."

The two men walked away from the woods and slough to the road. A voice called out. Matthew turned to see P.J.

"How about coming over for a drink?" P.J. called out.

"No thanks," Pete replied. "I'm laying off all liquor. It only gets me into trouble."

"Come now, Cousin, you can take a little drink. Any strong man can take a drink."

Matthew felt anger rising within him. "You heard the man. He said 'No.' Liquor never helped anyone."

"Come now, Matthew, just because you've gotten weak, doesn't mean Pete can't have a few drinks."

Pete walked over to P.J. and shook his hand. "Thanks for the offer, but no thanks."

"You can at least come over and see my house and the cabins and visit a bit."

Pete consented. Matthew reminded him of the supper invitation and walked back to Ma's little house and his car. He had more than a few misgivings. P.J. had a way of talking people into almost anything.

Chapter Six

"They're finally here," yelled an impatient Johnie to his mother and sisters. "We can eat."

Ellen and the girls moved into action, making the gravy, mashing the potatoes, and getting the meal on the table.

In his mind, Matthew knew what had happened. He walked out to welcome his cousin and mother. Peter looked unsteady. No doubt he had given in to P.J.'s offer.

As Ma walked ahead through the kitchen door, Matthew whispered to Pete. "You gave in to P.J. You've been drinking."

"The temptation was too strong. Now I feel awful. I disappointed Aunt Elizabeth."

"I'm getting you some coffee right away. And watch what you say."

Peter Anderson was one of those people who became friendlier and funnier when he had a few drinks. He quickly became the life of the party. He regaled James and Johnie and Margaret and Carol with his stories of the characters he worked with. He made working in the mines seem like the most exciting job in the world.

In her usual outspoken manner Carol blurted out, "Cousin Peter, you sure smell funny."

Peter did a quick comeback. "I guess I put on too much cologne. Some of that French stuff."

Johnie muttered, "You drank that cologne." Peter did not hear the comment.

Matthew looked at Ellen and then at his mother. Ellen gave him that knowing look. Ma looked away, embarrassed by what was happening.

As Ellen began to serve dessert, Peter excused himself. Matthew knew his cousin needed to use the outhouse. And he had to move quickly. Johnie laughed under his breath. The others smiled. An intoxicated relative was a new experience.

When Peter returned he announced, "I guess I'm tired. That outdoor air and duck hunting is more exercise than I'm used to."

The family members began to eat their pie. Suddenly Peter's head came forward. Ma looked alarmed. Matthew immediately recognized what was wrong. Peter was asleep.

"It's nothing," whispered Ellen. "He's had a little too much."

The rest of the family ate quietly. Ellen and the girls cleared the table.

Matthew went over to Peter and nudged him. Peter wakened with a start.

"What's wrong? Where am I?"

"You fell asleep. Give me your keys."

"Why?" Peter objected.

"You know why. I'll drive Ma home. And, Johnie, would you drive Peter's car and take him back to Ma's?"

Peter stumbled out of his chair. "I'm sorry. I guess I didn't think."

Ma followed her son, disappointment written all over her face.

CHAPTER 7

Elizabeth Anderson listened to the last of the organ music from Dr. Christian. She always loved hearing the words of the announcer, "Dr. Christian, the only show on radio where the audience writes the script. Stories right from the heart of America, woven around the beloved American character, the family doctor."

Her thoughts moved away from the radio play. P.J. was turning out to be a first-rate scoundrel. He had coaxed Peter to have a few drinks, and that resulted in drunkenness and embarrassment. She thought of the suspicious characters in P.J.'s life. Why was this happening? She hadn't brought up her son to live this way.

The five-minute newscast came on. War with Germany was almost a reality. In all probability the young men in her family would be drawn into this fight. The death of her nephew in the Great War left an indelible impression in her collection of memories.

Without warning, the newscast cut off and blackness filled the room. The electricity had gone out. A loud pounding on the door startled her. Waiting until her eyes became accustomed to the dark, she stood close to the door, but didn't open it.

A desperate voice called out. "I need to find P. J. Anderson fast. It's a matter of life and death."

Elizabeth wondered if it could really be a matter of life and death. "Who are you? Why is this important?"

Beyond the Storm

The door opened. A large man barged in. Elizabeth backed away, trembling uncontrollably. The man must have realized her fear and promptly apologized. "I need to see Mr. Anderson immediately. It's a big business deal and if I don't see him right away, he'll miss a great opportunity."

Elizabeth tried to stay calm, reassuring herself that this was just business and there was no danger involved. "Just go down to the gate near the barn. You'll see where to drive. And please close the gate."

"Thanks ever so much. I'm sorry if I frightened you."

The man hurried toward his car. Elizabeth stood by the open door and watched as lights from another car appeared. A man got out of that car. She heard him speak to the big man.

"Is this the way to P.J. Anderson's?"

The large man's gruff voice questioned, "Who are you?"

She didn't hear the name or the answer. But she heard the next words. "Anderson said this would be a good hideout. The law won't be looking in a faraway cabin."

The cars drove away, but those last words haunted her. Was her son associating with criminals and even hiding them? How could she have raised such a prodigal?

Elizabeth slept little that night. When she did doze off, it was only to awaken and to relive the horrors of the fire. Before dawn she got out of bed and found that the electricity had come back on.

She stoked the fire in the kitchen stove, put on the coffee, and began cooking her oatmeal. As she did these chores, she began to feel a dreadful, sharp pain in her stomach. By the time her oatmeal was ready, she found she had no appetite. Chills went through her body, both chills of fear and some other kind of chills. She knew she had to do something. But she waited. Matthew would be doing chores and so would her son-in-law. Ed was closer, but he had so many added responsibilities with Mary away in the sanitarium.

She doubled over in pain, but waited. It seemed to take forever for the seven o'clock hour to come. Now Matthew would be done with milking and the early chores.

Once Elizabeth called Matthew, she knew she was in good hands. Within the hour, he had her in the car and they were on their way to see Dr. Baker.

Chapter Seven

Baker poked and probed and finally said, "Mrs. Anderson, I think I know the problem. You've had a gallbladder attack. You've had some upsetting times and that seems to make everything worse."

"It was awful," Elizabeth said. "For awhile I thought I was dying."

"That's no surprise. With all you've been through these last months, it's no wonder you're not feeling well." Baker helped her off the examination table. "I'll give you some Milk of Magnesia, and you can buy some more in the drugstore. You'll have to watch your diet. I'll write out a list of foods you should avoid."

"Thanks. I guess the good Lord still wants me to live."

Baker smiled. "You have many good years ahead of you."

As they approached Matthew, the doctor spoke loudly and emphatically to Matthew. "Your mother needs some looking after. She should not be alone. Do you suppose Martha could come and stay with her?"

Elizabeth quickly objected. "Martha has her own life. And when she gets called away to help her daughters, she should be free to go. I can manage. I don't want to impose on my children."

Matthew, usually so gentle and quiet, spoke with authority. "Ma, you're coming home with me. You'll stay with Ellen and me and the kids."

Elizabeth was ready to object, but she thought back to the dark night and the fire and the loud knocking on the door. "I hate to put you out."

"Ma, you looked after me when I was little. It's time for me to look after you."

Ellen looked down on her mother-in-law, who lay on the bed in the guestroom. "You need to rest."

"I'm sorry to be so much bother. Last night those men scared me half to death."

"I think we need to do something about that. Now you rest."

Ellen saw the deep, furrowed lines in Elizabeth Anderson's face. Her mother-in-law had experienced what no mother should have to go through.

"There's nothing anyone can do. P.J. has control. No one can stop him."

Beyond the Storm

"We'll see about that." Ellen closed the door and stood in the hallway thinking about Matthew and the five children and the new situation they now faced.

Ellen wasn't sure what she should do. She knew it would be hard for Matthew to stand up to his brother one more time. She began to consider a new plan of action.

That evening as supper ended, she called Matthew aside. "I think I need to try to do something about P.J. I know how hard this is for you. I'd like to have Johnie take me over. I'll talk with him."

"But he's my brother. I should take care of it."

"My dear husband," Ellen pleaded, "you are the kindest man in the world. You've stood up to your brother, but it hurts you terribly. I'd like to try facing him alone."

Matthew hesitated. "When I think of how he hurt Pa, I become angry. And now that I see how frightened Ma is, I'd like to give him a good beating. I'm afraid I'd get out of control."

"That's why I'd like to try going alone. I have a plan."

"Let me go with. You can talk."

"Matthew, not this time. Please let me do this alone. Your mother could use your attention tonight."

Matthew reluctantly agreed. Ellen then asked Johnie to drive her to P.J.'s home.

Ellen often wished she could drive, but she had grown up in an era when most women did not drive. She might be well-read and well educated in most areas of life, but not driving was one way where she was not a modern woman.

As they drove the six miles, she found herself looking at her son in the driver's seat. With thick blond hair, bright blue eyes, a six-foot frame and attractive features, he had become a handsome young man. While James might be the son "after her own heart," Johnie was the dependable one for moving into action.

Ellen turned to Johnie and started to ask a question about school, but then noticed something. "What's happened to your eye? Don't turn away."

"Oh, nothing," he grunted.

"Turn this way."

"Mother, I'm driving. I can't."

Ellen leaned over. "You've got a lump and a black eye. Tell me what happened."

Chapter Seven

"Just a little scuffle. That's all."

"There's more to it, and I want to know what it is."

Johnie hesitated. "It's Jake. We had a little disagreement."

Ellen began to realize there was more behind this. "I've observed that Jake has become something of a bully now that your Aunt Mary's away."

Johnie repeated, "It's nothing."

Ellen cleared her throat, telling her son she meant business.

"OK, Mother. It was this way. Jake was making fun of someone."

"But you're bigger and stronger than he."

"It wasn't really between Jake and me. I couldn't take it any longer. He called James a sissy and weak because he plays the piano and likes music and writes stories. I decided I had to do something."

Ellen waited for him to go on. Though she didn't believe in fighting as a means to solving problems, she had to admire Johnie for standing up for his brother.

"I'm not smart like James, and I wish he liked more of the outdoor things. But he's a brilliant student, smarter than I'll ever be. I might tease him, but no one has the right to make fun of him the way Jake did."

"I don't believe in fighting, but you were right to stand up for James."

"Sometimes I get really angry at Jake and other bullies like him. I want to fight when someone takes advantage of him."

Mother and son drove on down the driveway of the home place. To Ellen's surprise, a car stood outside Elizabeth Anderson's house. "Johnie, stop at Grandma's house." She got out of the car and walked up the porch steps. Johnie followed close behind.

Ellen knocked on the door. She heard voices.

The door opened. "Hello, Aunt Ellen. Hello Johnie."

Ellen looked aghast. "Larry, what are you doing here?" Before her stood this younger version of P.J. Anderson. Larry had the dark handsome features of his father and some of the same charm.

"Dad thought I should stay here now that Grandma's at your place. That way, I'll be near the cattle and the other chores."

"But, Larry, you don't have the right just to take over someone else's house. This is still your grandmother's home. You should not be here."

"Dad and Mom say it's OK. Besides, with all their guests and visitors, their house is a bit crowded."

"You have no right."

Larry showed some of his father's bullheadedness. "Dad does have the deed to the property. He has control."

Ellen bit her tongue.

Larry, quick to note the hesitation, suggested, "Why don't you come in and meet my wife."

Ellen stepped into the kitchen with Johnie right behind her.

"This is Joan."

The young woman couldn't have been more than twenty. Though little more than five feet tall, Joan had a presence that captured attention. Her hair was as light as Larry's was dark. Her other features exhibited gentleness and sweetness. Ellen immediately liked the young woman.

After the introductions, Ellen announced, "We need to be on our way. We have business with your father."

"He's at the house, but he's awfully busy," Larry reminded. "Mom and Dad have company from the cities."

"This is important!" Ellen's voice had that no-nonsense tone.

Johnie led the way to the door and Ellen followed.

As Johnie drove down the lane to P.J.'s house, Ellen noted a number of cars parked outside as well as cars parked by several of the cabins. A talk with P.J. was not going to be easy.

Ellen led the way to the front door. She was glad Johnie was beside her. He might be only fifteen, but he was bigger and stronger than many mature men.

Ellen rang the doorbell.

Rita appeared, dressed in a tight dress, tailored, no doubt, by one of the stores in Chicago. "We're busy. Couldn't you come back some other time?"

Ellen stood erect, her five feet two inches commanding respect. "No. What I have to say demands immediate attention. I can get the authorities and then P.J. will have to pay attention."

"All right, if you must. I'll get him. We have guests. And it's our dinner time."

Ellen wasn't used to the ways of the city. For farmers dinner was always at noon. Only big-city people talked about having dinner after seven o'clock at night.

P.J. appeared. "You wanted to see me."

"I think you may wish to discuss this in private—unless you want everyone to hear."

Chapter Seven

P.J. motioned for them to follow into the kitchen. A hired girl stood at the kitchen counter, cutting the pies. P.J. went to her and whispered, "Take the pie and plates into the dining room and serve it there. Then you can go to your room for awhile."

The girl obeyed. She seemed to be afraid of her own shadow.

"Why don't you sit down?" invited P.J.

"No, P.J., I'd rather stand." Ellen paused. "First, I'm going to remind you of a few things. You vowed to make things right with your family. Your treatment of Corrine and Warren was despicable. The whole neighborhood is upset."

"Warren chose to move. I can't help that."

Ellen breathed deeply, trying to control her anger. "Oh, yes, you could. You had given them the right to rent the house, and you had said they could buy."

"They misunderstood me."

Ellen noticed Johnie clenching his fists.

"But I didn't come to talk about Corrine and Warren; I came to talk about your mother," continued Ellen. "Your so-called friends or guests frightened her half to death. That was unconscionable. That must stop."

"I'm sorry. But she's safe at your place now."

"Yes, for now." Ellen moved toward to her brother-in-law. "But that little house is hers. And she plans to return. Larry has no permission—no right to be there."

P.J. hesitated. "Well, Mother isn't there. Why can't he stay there, close to the other farm buildings where he has cattle?"

Ellen felt a tightness deep within. "Larry has no business in your mother's house. Even the way you manipulated the farm ownership, Elizabeth Anderson has lifetime rights to her house. That is absolute. We don't need a lawyer to prove that. And Sheriff Walker may do other checking."

P.J. cleared his throat, obviously uncomfortable.

"Your mother is planning to move back home when she is well and strong enough. But one more thing: you keep those business partners or friends of yours from coming and going at all hours of the night. Other neighbors have complained."

"I'll see what I can do."

Ellen looked up at P.J. without flinching. "You better. If you don't make that change immediately, we'll contact Sheriff Walker. And I'm not sure you want the sheriff investigating."

P.J. looked away, visibly shaken.

Ellen hadn't noticed her son's anger rising. Johnie stepped closer to his uncle. "Uncle P.J., how can you treat people this way? You're a bully, the way you push people around. Bullies ought to be horse-whipped."

"Oh, come off it, kid." P.J. looked annoyed at his nephew. "You don't understand all that's going on today. Wait till you're a little older to get involved with adult matters."

"I'm old enough to know right and wrong. And if you're a part of this family, you know something about right and wrong too. You cheated my dad out of the farm. You forced Corrine and Warren off the farm when you promised they could rent or even buy. And now you take over my grandma's house without her permission."

P.J. straightened himself. "I have ownership of the land. There is nothing you can do about that, you whippersnapper."

Johnie pushed himself forward directly in front of his uncle. "If you weren't my uncle and an old man, I'd give you what you deserve. You're the worst low-life I've ever seen."

For a moment Ellen thought Johnie was going to give P.J. a black eye. Actually, her brother-in-law deserved whatever came to him.

P.J. backed away. "I'll see what I can do."

"You keep saying that, but I think you're a liar," shouted Johnie. "You deserve to be punished."

Rita opened the kitchen door. "What's all this noise about? We can hear you in the dining room." She walked over to P.J. "You need to come back to your guests."

Johnie was not finished. "You need to tell those guests they don't belong here. People around here are honest and good."

P.J.'s face reddened in anger. "Be careful what you say about my friends."

"Or what?" challenged Johnie. "They'll get rid of me the way someone got rid of Harlow!"

P.J. moved toward the kitchen door. "Young man, you can't say these things. There's a thing called 'libel'."

Ellen moved toward P.J. "We'll be going now. But your friends and your actions will come under close scrutiny. The sheriff will be involved.

Chapter Seven

There's no doubt about that. We'll give him a call tonight. He's already suspicious."

"No, please don't." P.J.'s tone changed. "I'll take care of things. I'll talk to my friends. I guarantee things will change."

"And," Ellen added before she went out the door, "I suspect if we get the right lawyer, we'll get the farm back."

Chapter 8

November 1940

As Matthew and Johnie finished milking, Matthew could see that Johnie had something on his mind. "OK, Johnie, go. It's too warm for good duck hunting, but go ahead and try. I'll finish the chores."

"Thanks, Dad." Johnie ran faster than any track star to pick up his gun and headed to the east sloughs.

Matthew smiled. He was proud of fifteen-year-old Johnie. He dreamed of this son working with him and taking over the farm. Johnie truly loved the outdoors and the land around him.

Matthew let out the cows and cleaned the barn. As he finished his tasks, he thought of the approaching winter. These unseasonably warm temperatures made winter seem distant. Something in his head, though, told him that it was time to haul wood for the cold winter days. The warmth of late autumn could quickly change to sub-zero cold and snow.

He still felt uneasy about Ma. She had consented to stay with them for the present. "When I feel a little stronger," she said, "I'll go back home." Ma shouldn't be in the little house alone. She needs some looking after.

Beyond the Storm

He looked to the hills. That's where his help came from. Sometimes the help was spiritual and sometimes he might sense a task he should do. He thought out loud, "We need to haul wood today. But I think I'll go out and hunt with Johnie for a little while first."

A distant explosion of gunfire startled Johnie as he walked along a small pond. The gunfire reminded him of what was happening in Europe and England and Norway. War frightened him. But as he basked in the warmth of the day, the war and violence seemed far away. Right now, he hoped Dad would come and join him even though Dad didn't care for guns and hunting.

Johnie loved the land—this land. He dreamed that this place would be his someday. He often came down here to the ponds to think, and now it seemed there was more to think about. School was such a drag; he wished he could have the freedom of the outdoors.

He looked and listened for sounds of ducks. The leaves crackled beneath his feet almost as if they were talking. The trees were bare of leaves except for the red oaks, which kept their leaves until spring. This unusual weather made November seem like a damp spring day. Though war seemed distant, Johnie couldn't help thinking about its horrors. The bombings in England with hundreds killed. The resistance in Norway. Other countries falling to the Nazis.

It was hard to understand this thing called war. Why would someone want to destroy the peace and beauty of a country? Fighting was foreign to these beautiful hills of Minnesota, and like his father, Johnie kept looking to the hills, thinking ahead to approaching winter and after that the beautiful green of spring and new life. He loved to watch these changes of nature and life. Monday would be Armistice Day and that meant a day away from school. He could hunt and enjoy the outdoors all day.

Johnie began looking ahead. Two years from now, he would graduate from high school—that is if he stayed in school that long. Would the war be over, or would he be in the army? Somehow he felt it was his duty to keep this country safe from the Nazis or anyone else wanting to destroy freedom. Like Joe, he wanted to fight for freedom. Joe was somewhere in the South Pacific, but Johnie figured when he went, he'd be fighting the Germans.

Chapter Eight

In his dreams Johnie knew after it was all over he would return to these hills. Perhaps he could come back a decorated war hero and take over this farm. These farms would provide food for a hungry world. What a great opportunity! What lay here and what lay beyond those hills held great promise.

"I don't think there'll be much luck with ducks today." Dad's voice startled Johnie.

"It's just good to be out here. I hate being stuck indoors. This is the life for me."

"You were deep in thought."

Johnie laid down his rifle and sat on a wet log. "I was thinking about war. We'll be in the war soon."

"I'm afraid so," said Matthew. Johnie could see his father sizing him up.

Father and son sat for several moments in silence with a special kind of communication taking place. Matthew added, "But if you farm, you could be exempt."

"I don't want that!" Johnie's emotion ran deep. "The Nazis stand for something terrible. It's my duty to defend our freedom. I'm not a draft dodger like Uncle P.J."

Matthew looked surprised. "I didn't realize you knew so much about your uncle."

"Yes, I know Uncle P.J.'s a real jerk. And he hasn't changed a bit."

Matthew nodded. "I guess you're right."

"Oh, I know more than you think, Dad. If war comes, I want to go. It's my duty."

"I admire you for that. But I'll miss you. I dread the thought that you will have to go."

"You never had to go, Dad, did you?"

"I turned eighteen and registered. I would have gone, but then on November 11 the war ended."

"How did you feel about war, Dad?"

"I hated it. I think killing is awful." As his father spoke, his eyes seemed to pierce through his son. "But I felt it was my duty to go. Especially since P.J. stayed out."

"But Cousin Pete went, didn't he?"

"Yes, he did." Matthew gazed into the distance. "And I think he has some problems left from that war. War hurts people in many ways, not just physically, but mentally as well."

"He drinks a lot, doesn't he?"

Matthew took off his cap and ran his fingers through his thinning hair. "I'm afraid he does. Drinking was never a part of our family life, but I'm afraid both P.J. and Pete drink much more than they should."

"People sometimes do really stupid things, don't they? Especially drinking."

"I've come to agree with your mother on that. Drinking can control a person. I made the decision a long time ago not to drink at all."

Johnie forgot about duck hunting as they talked of war and family and other concerns. He asked his father about many things until suddenly he changed the subject.

"How could P.J. take control of our old farm the way he did?"

Matthew hesitated for he liked to think before he said something. "There's not much to say. He did it by getting your grandpa and grandma to sign papers. They didn't know what they were signing. Anyhow, they didn't know how their actions would affect the family in the future."

"How could he get by with that?" Johnie tightened his fist in anger. "He took a farm that should have been ours."

Johnie could see the sadness in his father's eyes. He waited.

His father looked away and then spoke. "I had a hard time with it. You know how sick I was, but I had to forgive. I could do that only with God's help. And now I'm better off. This is a better land. The soil is much richer. Our family is better off."

"It still wasn't fair." Johnie felt ready to fight for his father against this injustice.

"Often, life isn't fair. I've learned that lesson many times. We can let the unfairness destroy us, or we can go on."

"Then, the bad guy wins, doesn't he?"

"No, the bad guy will lose out in the end."

"I wonder about that."

In the next moment Johnie wished he were little and could let his father shield him. He knew it was hard for his dad to talk about these personal matters.

Matthew seemed to be searching for words. "When P.J. took the farm, I had to let go. I had to let God take control. Only the Lord could free me from that anger against my brother."

"I'm afraid I don't understand."

Chapter Eight

"Son, we're alike in many ways. We both love this land. And I know that if you come to the Lord and ask for understanding, He will take care of you."

The moments that followed were more reverent than any church service.

Then Johnie broke the reverie. "But P.J. keeps pulling dirty tricks. You just can't trust him."

"Forgiveness is not a one-time shot," began Matthew. "God commands us to forgive and to keep forgiving—to forgive a brother seventy times seven if need be. I'm not always good at this forgiveness. I have to keep asking God for help."

"Then, everything isn't suddenly OK." Johnie wasn't sure whether he meant the words as statement or question.

Matthew smiled and placed his hand on his son's shoulder. "Life is a continuing process. The minute I think I have everything under control, I find a new problem. Then I have to turn to God again and again and again."

"In other words, you never have all the answers."

"That's life." Matthew stood up and looked to the hills in the distance. "Life is like traveling through these hills and valleys. There's always just one more ahead." He paused. "Each hill may bring a problem. We may overcome one, and then there's a new one."

"That makes sense."

"And the Lord leads us through the valleys and up the hills. Even though we forget, He still is there."

Suddenly, their talk was interrupted by activity. The ducks flew up at the other end of the pond. Johnie and his father raised their rifles. Their shots rang out clear to the hills and valleys that warm November day. They soon found they had shot enough ducks for a generous family meal.

Johnie put on his waders and collected the ducks they had shot.

"It's time to get back home for dinner," announced Matthew.

"I'd like to stay." Johnie didn't want to leave the peacefulness of the woods and ponds and lakes even for his mother's dinner.

"Remember, we have work to do. It's November and we need to haul wood. We have only a few loads home. We need more. You know how fast winter can come."

Even though he would have chosen to stay and hunt, Johnie returned home with his father. That afternoon, Matthew, James, and Johnie hauled many large loads of wood. After the tenth load was unloaded next to the house, Matthew announced, "Now we are ready for winter. Without wood, we would be in a bad way if a storm came."

Sunday morning, November 10, the atmosphere was different. The barometer was falling, and the cattle were restless. There was a driving rain. On Saturday the ducks and wildlife had been almost absent, but today large flocks of ducks headed south. It seemed the wildlife had received some signal of danger, and they were intent on escaping.

That Sunday morning, Johnie struggled with himself. When he saw the ducks flying, he wanted to hunt. But there was one thing taken for granted on Sunday morning in this house: church attendance.

"Dad," said Johnie as he and James finished the morning chores, "I'd really like to hunt this morning. This is good hunting weather."

Matthew appeared to be thinking before he answered. "You take the Model A to church. Leave as soon as the service is over. You'll still have time to hunt."

"I'd really like to go right away." Johnie thought a moment and then added, "I guess worship is something I should do first. Maybe God will bless me with more ducks then."

"What about working on Sunday?" questioned his brother.

"We can use the meat. We need to eat." Johnie never hesitated to answer or try to outsmart his brother.

Within an hour the family had dressed in their Sunday best for church. Johnie and James went ahead in the Model A. Matthew, Ellen, the girls, Grandma, and little Michael went in the '35 Chevy.

Johnie felt different during the short drive to church. As the heavy rain came down and then diminished to drizzle, he observed the way the rain cleaned everything. He felt a kind of cleansing within him. If this had been a week ago, he would have objected to Dad's insistence on church; now he accepted his father's way.

That morning the sanctuary was more crowded than usual. Perhaps the concern about war had something to do with that. When Pastor Strand began speaking, Johnie was surprised that the pastor's words expressed exactly what he had been thinking.

Monday would be Armistice Day, 1940. Pastor Strand began speaking. "If the Son makes you free, you shall be free indeed."

Chapter Eight

Johnie's thinking moved ahead. He had felt something of this new freedom. He had begun to realize that God was at work in people's lives. His mind moved from the sermon to other places, and he became only vaguely aware of people seated around him. He thought of the draft recently instituted. And there was all the dreadful bombing and killing in Europe. If he were in London, he might have to flee to a bomb shelter at a moment's notice.

Pastor Strand's words broke into his awareness. "We must be vigilant. 'Eternal vigilance is the price of freedom.' We must always be on guard. We must remember our freedom comes from God alone. We must commit ourselves to Him. When we commit ourselves to Him—when we give ourselves to Him—we have new freedom and new hope. If we stray from this, we become slaves to one kind of sin or another.

"Freedom is found in Christ alone. Now, what may this mean to us here on this day before Armistice Day 1940? What does this mean to the United States, one of the few countries to celebrate this day free from war?"

Johnie hadn't thought of how free this country was. Most places were not so fortunate. What about the draft? Would he be drafted or would he want to volunteer to go? He knew he must help preserve this country and its freedom. A kind of patriotic pride swelled within him. "This is a great and good country. It is worth defending." He whispered these words to himself.

Johnie returned once more to the reality of the present. The pastor continued. "We must look first to God, the true author of liberty. 'Our Father's God, to thee, Author of liberty, of thee we sing.' The song says it well. Again, I say: we look to God, our true author of liberty. Let us come to Him in thanksgiving. But as followers, we must be willing to stand for liberty—to stand for freedom in our corner of the world—perhaps in any corner of the world."

One thing about Johnie's mind, it was always on the move. He didn't care much for school, but that didn't mean he wasn't a thinker. He must fight for freedom. He must defend the weaker brother. He must even fight in a war if necessary.

The service ended. Johnie left the sanctuary, almost running to the Model A. In a short time he was in hunting clothes, walking to the swampy area in the east end. Faithful Rover followed him, ready to go after the ducks.

He couldn't help thinking of his cousin Jake, a serious troublemaker. He would not let Jake call James a sissy or weak. Johnie figured he had done the right thing when Jake went home with a black eye and bruises. Bullies had to be put in their place.

It wasn't long before his thoughts were interrupted by the arrival of the largest flock of ducks he had ever seen. He loaded and re-loaded several times. Within minutes he was sure he had his limit. Rover and he might have a problem finding all the birds he had shot.

Johnie returned home in the afternoon with his bounty. He was starving. Fortunately, Mother kept the pork roast warm for him. With some help from Mom and Dad, Johnie cleaned the ducks. He looked forward to the Monday meal of duck.

As the family sat down to supper, the phone rang.

His mother answered. It was obvious something was wrong.

"What's wrong?" questioned Matthew.

Ellen spoke quickly. "It's P.J. He's had a heart attack, and it's serious."

"Where is he?" Matthew asked.

"He's in the River Falls Hospital. I think we should go." Ellen stopped a moment and then whispered to her husband, "He's done some bad things, but he is your brother."

Grandma's puzzled expression said she hadn't heard everything. Ellen repeated, "P.J.'s had a heart attack."

"Oh no, it can't be." Grandma turned pale. "Not my son."

"We'll go. And, Ma, you come with us, of course. He wants to see you." Matthew turned to Johnie. "The weather is changing. We need to get a fire going in the furnace."

"We'll take care of that," said Johnie.

"Come down in the basement with me." Matthew quickly left his food. "We need to check the dampers and be sure we have dry wood. We need to get some more of the wood inside."

Johnie knew his father trusted him with these matters. Dad often said how well he could take over. When they returned to the kitchen, Johnie could see how pale his grandmother was.

"P.J. is not old…and he's strong," said Ellen. "He'll be OK."

"I'm praying for him," said Grandma. "But he hasn't taken care of himself. I'm afraid this is serious."

As his parents and grandmother got into the car, Johnie noticed a few snowflakes coming down. Obviously the weather was changing.

Chapter Eight

Later that evening, James and Johnie stoked the furnace. Outside the winds gained momentum. The hours slipped by, and Mom and Dad and Grandma did not return. Margaret took care of Michael. He was more fussy than usual, but he finally settled down, and the girls went to bed.

James and Johnie turned out the lights in their room. Johnie felt a strange emptiness without Mom and Dad nearby. He remembered the blizzard when Michael was born and Dad had to stay in River Falls for several days.

"Do you think God really answers prayer?" asked Johnie. "It's hard to believe He has time for everyone."

"I guess He does," replied James. "I pray a lot when things get bad. And they usually get better."

The house rattled as the wind blew hard against the windows. The wind gained momentum. More snow fell. No one knew it, but the storm of the century was on the way.

Chapter 9

Matthew paced the floor in the small waiting room. Would this night never end? P.J. was hovering between life and death. Could his brother survive this severe heart attack? A storm of emotions moved through Matthew's mind.

Ma sat with bowed head while Ellen placed her arm gently around her troubled mother-in-law. Rita paced the floor, smoking one cigarette after another.

"Why did my husband have to have his heart attack here in this hick town?" sputtered Rita. "Why couldn't he have been close to the big city doctors? They could do something."

Matthew wanted to respond, but a reply wouldn't help. He knew Ellen and his mother were quietly praying. The outcome was in God's hands.

Shortly after ten, Dr. Baker entered the waiting room. "P.J. seems better now. He wants to see you."

Rita interrupted quickly. "Perhaps I should go in alone. We don't want to tire him."

"You go first," said the doctor, "but he asked to see his brother and mother. Especially, he wants to see you, Mrs. Anderson."

Rita put out her cigarette and hurried to her husband's room.

"How is he, really?" asked Ma. "I want to know. I'm afraid it's not good."

"I don't know what to tell you about his condition. The heart can be terribly unpredictable." Dr. Baker motioned for them to sit down.

"He very much wants to see you," repeated the doctor and he took the old woman's hand. "You have to be prepared for the worst. I just want you to know, Mrs. Anderson. You must take care of yourself. We don't want you here as a patient."

Ma smiled through her tears. "I'll be OK. I'm not some weak houseplant."

Matthew realized once again that his mother had a deep strength that became more evident in moments of crisis. They waited a few minutes, and then Matthew took his mother's arm. "Let's go in now." He could feel her trembling.

As they entered P.J.'s room, Rita stood close to her husband. Matthew drew back, startled, when he saw P.J.'s ashen face. His dark piercing blue eyes had lost their brightness. His hair looked even grayer than Matthew remembered.

P.J. spoke with a forced brightness. "I'm feeling better. I'll be up in no time."

"We'll see," warned his wife.

"You need rest," said his mother. "You've been working too hard. God meant for people to have a day of rest."

"Mother, I'll be fine. Don't worry. And don't even worry about that house of yours. We'll check so that everything will be all right. And come next spring we'll build a new house, and Larry and his wife will be close by. That will be a good time for you to move back."

"I don't think I need to wait until spring."

"Oh, you wait until spring," P.J. continued, "Larry will be close by to look in on you."

Ma hesitated. "Perhaps."

An awkward silence followed. Finally P.J. spoke. "And how are all my nieces and nephews?" This personal interest came as a surprise.

Ellen filled in details about the nieces and nephews. It seemed to Matthew that P.J. was trying too hard to show an interest.

Matthew wondered about P.J.'s urgent request. "You wanted to talk with me. What is it you wanted to talk about?"

P.J. looked away. "Oh, that can wait. I'll be better in a few days. Then we can talk."

Chapter Nine

Dr. Baker returned. "I'm going to give you something to relax you, P.J. You need the rest. You'll fall asleep quickly when you take this medication."

"I'm going to stay here beside my husband." Rita sat in the one straight-backed chair in the room and began to light another cigarette.

"No cigarettes," said the doctor.

"Sorry," Rita managed to say.

Baker added, "You might as well lie down in the other bed and get some rest. P.J. will soon be sleeping."

Ma kissed her son gently on the cheek. "God be with you, my son. I'll be praying for you."

"Thanks, Mother."

When Matthew stepped out of the hospital, he knew instantly that the weather was changing. It was colder than when they'd gone in a few hours earlier. "This weather is strange. I feel something in my bones," Matthew shivered.

"This reminds me of the way it was before another storm," Ma began. "Back in 1888, there was a storm that everyone still talks about. Many children died in that terrible blizzard, especially in North Dakota."

The drive home was tough going because of sleet and snow. By the time Matthew and his passengers finally arrived home it was late. A strong wind had developed. Inside, the house was warm and snug. There were no sounds from the children, so the three exhausted adults dropped into their beds.

A different world greeted them in the morning. Everything was white, and the wind swept the snow into drifts. It was Armistice Day, a holiday for some people, but not for farmers. Chores still had to be done and the harsh wind and snow made them much harder. After chores, Matthew entered the kitchen and knew instantly that something was wrong.

"Dr. Baker called."

"It's not good, is it?" Matthew feared what Ellen would say.

"P.J. has taken a turn for the worse. It seems he has pneumonia. Nothing seems to quiet him. He wants to see you."

"I should go," said Matthew. "I don't understand why he didn't talk last night."

"I told him we'd try to get to the hospital." Ellen proceeded to get Matthew's breakfast on the table. "Dr. Baker said the roads are getting bad. We can't waste much time."

Matthew moved toward the bedroom to change clothes. "You better stay here with the kids."

Ellen raised her voice. "You're not going alone, and you're not going without breakfast."

Matthew sensed Ellen's concern about him. Ever since that close call with death, Ellen had watched him carefully. He quietly agreed and went to change clothes.

"Your mother isn't up yet. I think it's best if we don't wake her." Ellen put out the toast and finished frying the eggs.

Matthew had to force himself to swallow. He sat picking at his food when the boys bounded downstairs ready to eat. Then it was out to the car to put the chains on. The temperature was dropping rapidly so he poured antifreeze into the radiator to prevent it from freezing up somewhere between here and the hospital. He put two sacks of feed in the trunk to weigh down the car and give it more traction. That would help in heavy snow. He threw in an old blanket so that he would be ready for almost anything.

When Matthew went inside, the girls were eating breakfast. "We'll drive you to school, but if the weather gets worse, ask the teacher to send you home."

Johnie couldn't help teasing Carol. "You have school and we don't. Ha ha!"

Carol didn't waste any time answering. "We get out earlier in the spring than you do."

Margaret announced, "I'm going with Carol. I'm visiting my old school today. In a few years I'll be a teacher."

Matthew felt relieved that Ma was not up yet. There was no need for her to make another trip to River Falls. There must be something urgent for P.J. to insist that he come back again on such a stormy day.

Ellen gave directions for taking care of Michael even though the boys felt they knew exactly what to do. Their grandmother would take this opportunity to spoil her youngest grandson. Matthew gave directions to his sons about the chores that needed to be done. He expected to be back by milking time in the evening.

Matthew, with Ellen by his side, found the roads weren't as bad as he had expected. The six miles of township roads had some ice and drifts.

Chapter Nine

When he came to the state highway, the driving was easier except for the gales of wind and the snow coming at them. They passed Lake View, where he took off the chains, and then drove on toward River Falls.

Matthew concentrated on driving in the windy white vagueness of the storm. The conversation was limited to figuring out where he was on the road. He met few cars. Several times, he came dangerously close to the ditch.

They approached the hospital. The building took on a different meaning. It could be a place of hope, but it might well be a place of suffering and death.

"I'm afraid for Ma if something happens to P.J." Matthew said as he parked the car.

"It will be hard, almost a repeat of what happened to your father."

Matthew agreed. "P.J. has a lot to deal with. His conscience must be bothering him. I don't know how he can live with himself."

As they approached P.J.'s room, Matthew realized the truth of his last statement. Rita met them, her face showing signs of tiredness and strain. "I don't think you should see him now. He's very upset."

Matthew stopped abruptly. "But he asked for me. He wanted to see me."

Rita stood blocking the doorway. "He's rambling on in all kinds of ways. I don't think he knows what he's saying. The pneumonia and fever have affected him."

"We understand," said Ellen, "but Dr. Baker called and said we should come. Matthew is going in to see his brother." Her last words had a tone of authority.

Rita hesitated.

"It doesn't look good, does it?" Ellen reached out for Rita's hand.

Tears came to Rita's eyes. A woman, usually in control, was obviously not in charge now. "I'm afraid he's not going to make it. And I can't reach Larry or Noreen. Larry took off for the cities. I feel so alone."

"We're here for you." Even as Ellen spoke, it was clear she had never felt close to her sister-in-law.

"Thank you." Rita began to cry. Ellen put her arms around her and they awkwardly hugged each other. "I'm so afraid. I feel as if I'm losing everything."

"We're praying for P.J.," said Ellen.

"I wish I had your faith." Rita wiped the tears from her eyes. "Paul John and I have never had much time for religion and church."

"The Lord is available to all who call on Him." Ellen's words did not seem to comfort Rita. "He helps us through our problems."

"I've been too busy." Rita moved away from the doorway. "And now I may lose everything."

"We're going in," announced Ellen. "He asked to see Matthew, and we must honor that request." Matthew and Ellen walked into the sick room though Rita obviously did not want them to.

P.J.'s eyes were half open and he seemed awake. He didn't notice Matthew and kept on muttering something. "Dad, it's mine. You signed it over. It's all fair and square. I didn't want to hurt you." Then, his voice trailed off.

Ellen stood close to P.J. "Matthew is here to see you. You asked for him."

P.J. opened his eyes. "This pain is unbearable. I feel so cold. Don't they have enough fuel to heat this place?" He added some expletives as he repeated his complaints.

"It's not cold in here. It's you," said Rita.

"I need more blankets."

As P.J. spoke, Matthew noticed the ashen death-like gray of his face. P.J.'s handsome features now appeared grotesque and distorted—almost evil.

"I feel awful. I've done some bad things. If I ever get out of here, I want to make things right." P.J. kept thrashing about on the hospital bed, his talk becoming so jumbled that no one could understand.

"Paul John's out of his head. He doesn't know what he's saying," shouted Rita.

Matthew knew exactly what was tormenting his brother.

As P.J. became more determined to talk, Rita became more agitated. "He's getting worse. I think you should go. Your being here makes him worse."

"Stay! Please stay!" P.J. called out in all the voice he had. "You're my brother. I've done some terrible things. I want to make everything right." P.J. kept repeating the words. "I want to make everything right." His voice trailed off.

"He's upset, don't you see?" said Rita. "And he's getting worse."

P.J. shouted the next words. "I'm freezing. My legs feel prickly and cold. What's happening to me?"

Chapter Nine

P.J.'s eyes closed, and briefly he seemed to drift into a deep sleep. Then, he wakened and opened his eyes. He threw his blanket aside. "It's terribly hot. They turned up the heat way too high."

"Keep your blankets on." Rita tried to put the blankets back in place.

"They're after me. I can't get away. They're going to kill me. They'll destroy me!" P.J. thrashed about on his bed. P.J. stopped moving about and seemed to relax. "I gave up the business with those men. They won't come after me now."

For only a moment he relaxed. Then P.J. threw his blankets aside and began to yell in panic. "It's dark now—so terribly dark. Where am I? This place is awful. It's blacker than any black I've ever experienced."

Ellen turned to leave. "I think we better get the doctor."

Once more P.J. quieted. "The light...the light. It's so bright. It's blinding me. This heat is unbearable. Rita, is that you? Matthew, are you there? The light's so bright. Matthew... Rita. You're just shadows."

P.J. quieted down and seemed to drift off to sleep. Dr. Baker came. In whispered tones, Rita tried to explain what had happened.

Dr. Baker whispered, "He may be having another spell. There's not much we can do at this point." He placed his hand on P.J.'s forehead. "P.J., you need to be quiet and rest. Rest is the best thing for you. There's nothing you can do here now except relax and rest. Don't try to talk."

P.J. seemed to drift off to sleep. Then, he sat up. "It's hot, so very hot. Where am I?"

"It's OK, darling, you're here in the hospital."

Dr. Baker motioned to Matthew and Ellen.

Rita sat beside the bed, holding her husband's hand. Matthew and Ellen followed Dr. Baker as he left the room.

Dr. Baker spoke in an ominous tone. "These things can turn around. Hold on to that hope, but don't depend on it."

"It's out of our hands," said Ellen.

"Yes," agreed Dr. Baker. "Some matters are in God's hands. I learned that from the two of you."

When they came to the end of the hall, a nurse-receptionist greeted them. "I don't think you should try to get back to your farm. Many roads are blocked. You'll see what I mean when you go outside."

Beyond the Storm

A foreign and unfamiliar world greeted them outside the hospital. Matthew cleaned off the snow that covered his car. "I think we better try to make it home. I'll put on the chains. We can't leave Ma and the kids alone in this storm."

The snowplow had cleared some snow from the state highway, but high winds had blown it back and the road was covered with snow. The wind driving the snow also made visibility nearly impossible. Matthew was glad it was still daylight.

As he turned south of Lake View, he began to realize this was not going to be an easy trip home. The heavy clouds would bring darkness much earlier than usual. The car heater was not keeping up with the wind-driven cold and Matthew and Ellen soon found they were freezing. Matthew stopped several times to clean wet snow from the windshield.

The driving became more and more impossible. Matthew figured they had gone only two miles south on the township road when it seemed as if the light of day had been turned off early. They approached a wooded area. Everything was white. Without warning, the car jolted to a stop. Matthew stepped on the accelerator, but the car would not move. He stepped outside the car. He gazed ahead and saw a drift taller than he was.

Matthew returned to the car, shifting into reverse. With little warning the car tilted into the ditch and began sinking into the snow.

He opened the door and surveyed the situation. "I don't think we're going to get any further. We're stuck."

"What can we do?"

Matthew felt a growing fear. "We can't stay here. This storm is worse than I thought, and it's getting colder."

Ellen shivered. "I'm worried about the kids and your mother."

"All we can do is take care of ourselves here." Matthew began to give directions. "Get the blanket from the back seat. There's a schoolhouse a short way back. We'll find shelter there."

As they walked, the wind and snow felt like knives coming against them. The wind left them breathless. Ellen nestled close to Matthew. They turned their backs to the wind so that they could avoid the biting flakes. A terrible cold permeated Matthew's body and spirit.

He tried to wrap the blanket around Ellen. The temperature, which had been warm and spring-like yesterday, had now fallen. The driving wind made the temperature feel as if it were below zero.

For a brief moment the wind abated and Matthew could see something other than white. Finally, the school came into his line of vision.

Chapter Nine

It seemed to take hours to walk a short distance. Everything, including the school, seemed foreign and unnatural. The darkening shadows of evening added to the uncertainty.

Ellen leaned on him more and more as they walked. All at once, he felt her go limp. He knew she was cold and exhausted.

Matthew had heard of people freezing to death a few feet from safety. "We've got to make it," he said aloud. "For the sake of the kids and Ma, we can't give up."

Ellen stumbled forward. "I can't go on."

Matthew lifted her up. "Don't let yourself go. Stay awake."

Ellen, usually so strong and capable, responded weakly. "I'm so cold and tired. I just can't move."

Matthew stumbled and found himself facing another drift. "Ellen, try to walk. We're almost to the schoolhouse."

The two found strength to push themselves through the drifts. "Let's hope the school's not locked," said Ellen.

Matthew tried to open the door. The door was locked. With Ellen following, he went around to the north side in a space where the wind had blown away the snow. He checked the three basement windows. As he tried the third window, he let out a shout of joy. It was unlocked.

These rural schools could be found every few miles and often served as places of refuge. It was hard to think of the country without these centers for the community.

Matthew crawled through the opening first and then helped Ellen in. The dark basement seemed warm and safe—a relief from the piercing snow and wind. They stumbled around until Matthew found the furnace and a few pieces of wood. There was probably more wood out in the woodshed—at least he hoped so.

Ellen's energy and clear thinking seemed to have returned. She felt her way around in the darkness. "I have a feeling there should be kindling wood nearby." Her hands found the dry sticks. "The teacher had everything ready for morning." Ellen found a table. "Here are some matches. I guess my years of being a teacher come in handy."

"You're always the teacher," Matthew added, tenderly.

As his eyes grew accustomed to the dark, Matthew discovered more wood farther back in a corner. Within minutes, he had a warm fire going. The warmth of the furnace told him there had been school for part of the day. Most country schools did not close for the Armistice Day holiday.

The two found their way to the stairway and the entry room. Ellen spotted first one jacket and then another. "Let's put these on for extra warmth."

Ellen found two of the larger desks and pulled them near the register where the heat came up from the furnace. At least this area would be warm. Matthew felt the cold drafts from the windows. Outdoor temperatures were steadily dropping.

"I hope all our children are safe," said Ellen.

"I wonder about the animals—and the chores. And can the boys keep the furnace going?" Several times Matthew went down to the school basement to make certain the fire in the furnace would not go out.

Matthew and Ellen talked for a time and soon found themselves exhausted. They lay down on the hard floor near the register. Matthew felt Ellen's soft hair against his shoulder. With warmth coming through the register, Matthew fell asleep with Ellen in his arms. He felt the warmth of love as they slept, safe from the storm that could kill.

Outside the blizzard raged on.

P.J. struggled for breath. His mind replayed what he had said through the years. "Religion is for sissies—for women and children." "Religion keeps people in line." "I'm not at all sure there is a God." "It's stupid to follow these rules and regulations."

Then, echoes of sermons and Scripture played in his mind. "Work out your salvation with fear and trembling." He had not trembled before. Now he was frozen and shook with fear. "It is appointed unto men once to die and after that the judgment."

Was this the judgment he had heard of? The judgment he had felt would never come—or at least it would come far in the future. He was glad his mind had cleared so that he could write a letter to Matthew.

Suddenly he felt very hot. It seemed as if fire was consuming him.

His family passed before him. Dad, the patriarch of the family seemed very much alive. Dad beckoned to him. Then words came from his father's mouth. "You must change your ways. You promised to make things right."

A hard feeling came to P.J. He felt like one of those rocks in the field that could feel nothing. "I'd like to believe!" he yelled out.

Chapter Nine

Mother came before him. She was reading her Bible, as she did so often. "Do as your father says. He is a wise man."

P.J. wanted to move and do something. "I can't! I can't!" he yelled out.

Martha always did everything right. He resented her. This kindly matron pointed her finger at him, scolding.

Victoria. They were alike in so many ways. But Victoria had taken the respectable route, becoming a teacher and a principal. The whole community admired Victoria. He envied her position. And there she was saying, "I told you so. Your sins will find you out."

Somehow, Cousin Pete got into the picture. For years, he had been like a brother. Pete was shouting at him. "You dirty old man. You got me into the way of drinking and worse things. Thank God, I got away from you."

Each person disappeared as another came forward.

Lucille. Oh, how he had loved this little sister. And why did she have to die? Lucille seemed to be pleading. "Big brother, don't go on this way. You're making big mistakes. Please come back to your family."

He wanted to talk with Lucille and take her in his arms and comfort her. But in a split second she was gone.

Then there was Matthew as a little boy. He had loved this little brother who looked up to him. But Matthew was entirely different both in appearance and in outlook. While P.J. had striking dark features, Matthew was blond. While P.J. was forceful and aggressive, Matthew was kind and gentle.

He saw himself playing with Matthew. But there was a side that loved to lord it over this little brother. He saw himself teasing and tormenting Matthew.

Then Matthew became an adult. Now Matthew stood in P.J.'s mind with his five children and Ellen. He had always looked down on Matthew as weak, but Matthew seemed to have everything. A loyal, intelligent pretty wife. Five children who would be a credit to any man. Even now, he would like to prove to Matthew that he, Paul John, was in charge. But he loved this brother. Matthew's forgiveness and kindness had been evident many times.

Matthew was calling to him. "Please don't go on this way. You're hurting Ma and Pa. You're hurting many people."

Matthew disappeared in a flash. Then Mary came. In many ways Mary was like Victoria, strong and forceful. But he saw her now in a hospital bed. Would TB destroy her? He saw tears in her eyes. "Don't go on this way," she pleaded.

Finally his wife appeared. Rita, strong and in charge, scolded him. "Get up, Paul John, you've been sick long enough. You need to tend to business, or else we'll be in trouble."

Once again cold seemed to penetrate his whole body.

Then the cold was replaced by intense heat, more intense than the heat of the hottest summer day.

A voice seemed to call him. "Paul John Anderson. Paul John Anderson."

Was this the Angel of Death?

He saw the Oak Ridge Church of his childhood. There was the stained glass window with Christ holding the lamb. Christ seemed to beckon, and then He disappeared.

"I want to believe, but I can't."

P.J. let out a piercing shriek. He became vaguely aware of Rita and several nurses around his bed. A bright light pierced his awareness. Then, everything went black.

Chapter 10

Earlier that day as Johnie had watched his parents drive out the driveway, he said, "I guess we're in charge. It looks bad outside."

From the kitchen window Johnie saw only white. The barn was not visible most of the time. The snow seemed to increase in amount and ferocity.

Johnie, always the practical one, added, "We might as well get the morning chores done."

Elizabeth Anderson appeared in the doorway. "Good morning boys. I didn't realize it was this late." The kitchen clock showed 9:30.

"Mom and Dad went to River falls. P.J. wanted to see Dad." Johnie hesitated, not wanting to worry his grandmother.

His grandmother began to prepare herself some oatmeal. "I'm afraid P.J. may not make it. It doesn't seem fair to lose both P. J. and your grandfather in one year."

"Oh, Grandma! Uncle P.J. will be OK. He's a tough guy." James tried to comfort his grandmother.

"Family deaths often come in threes. I don't like the thought." Her oatmeal simmered.

At this point, a cry came from the living room where little Michael had been playing. "I'll take care of Michael." His grandmother pushed aside her oatmeal and moved into the next room. "You boys have plenty to do. It's a good thing you didn't have school today."

Beyond the Storm

"At this rate," said Johnie, "we won't have school tomorrow either." His voice displayed his animated anticipation.

The house creaked as a violent gust of wind blew against it. All at once there was the sound of a door blowing open. "It's the porch door." Johnie hurried out to close it.

Johnie returned and announced, "This is some winter storm."

The boys put on heavy coats and left the warmth of the house. The walk between house and barn took more time and effort than they had ever experienced. They let the cattle out for water. The cattle moved quickly to the water tank and just as quickly returned to the barn, huddling against the outside wall. The boys worked fast, cleaning the barns and dishing out feed for the cattle. The cows, uncomfortable and coated with ice and snow, eagerly returned to their stalls. This weather was too uncomfortable for either man or beast.

While James fed the chickens, Johnie went to the pig house and found the door had blown open. The pigs were huddled in the far corner. He usually didn't feel sympathy toward pigs, but even these creatures demanded sympathy in this storm. He poured their feed and quickly latched the door.

"Even the animals seem to know something's wrong," said James to his brother as they met outside the barn.

Johnie spoke loudly as the wind blew in their faces. "I think we'd better hitch up the horses. Margaret and Carol shouldn't be in school."

"I'm glad Margaret decided to visit Carol's school today. That means Carol isn't alone."

For once the boys agreed on what to do. They went into the house to tell their grandmother.

"I don't want you boys taking any chances." Elizabeth Anderson spoke with the sternest voice that Johnie had never heard. "I remember the blizzard of '88. It was terrible and many people froze to death."

To James and Johnie, taking the horses and the sleigh was an adventure, one that didn't happen often. The cold and snow of the blizzard stimulated them to action—certainly they didn't consider this short drive dangerous.

Chapter Ten

As James went out the kitchen door to the back porch, he heard his grandmother saying, "Be careful!"

James had heard about blizzards, but he had never experienced a dangerous one. To him, a blizzard meant a vacation day and the adventure of digging out. Johnie took charge, hitching up and driving the team. James, satisfied to go along for the ride, looked into the storm with its sharp knives of wet snow. The township road was quickly filling with snow. The horses held back at first, but then seemed to sense an urgency of this special mission.

High drifts were making the road impassible for cars, but the horses struggled through. Johnie directed them to leave the road and cut across fields to the school. They had to go many roundabout ways to avoid the snowdrifts that were growing higher by the minute.

It took more than forty-five minutes to drive the mile and a quarter to the school. When the boys arrived, they saw that other fathers and brothers had the same idea. Johnie tied up the horses and James entered the school.

"I'm glad you came," said a very young teacher, Miss Wilson. "I was afraid to let Margaret and Carol cross the hills and fields in this blizzard."

"We thought we better come get them." James couldn't help noticing how pretty this young teacher was. She seemed hardly older than he. "But you shouldn't be out in a blizzard either," he added.

"Oh, I'll be fine. I live with the Gustafsons, just a quarter-mile down the road."

The door opened again and snow swirled in. Johnie, caked with snow, entered and called out, "I think we should hurry. It's getting worse. The horses are cold and restless."

Margaret and Carol gathered some books and their lunch pails and put on their coats.

James motioned for the teacher to get her coat. "Miss Wilson, we'll take you home." Johnie quickly agreed.

The boys sat in the front of the sleigh while Miss Wilson and the two girls sat in back. When they let Miss Wilson off, Mr. Gustafson came out and warned them. "This is not an ordinary storm. People have frozen to death in storms like this. It's like the blizzard of '88."

"We'll be careful," Johnie called out. "Thank you, Mr. Gustafson."

The boys passed the school again and began the trip home. Snow and sleet came against them like avenging hurtful demons. James heard the warnings of Grandma and Mr. Gustafson echo in his mind. Even when everything seemed white and their direction unclear, the horses knew the way home. They left the pastures and fields and arrived at the road. Their earlier tracks had almost completely disappeared and new drifts swept in all the time.

Finally, after struggling through drifts almost to their bellies, the horses brought the four Andersons safely to the back porch. James helped the girls off the sleigh. Then the brothers unhitched the horses and put them in the barn.

"I wonder where Mom and Dad are." Johnie paused and then added, "Maybe we can call the hospital."

"I wonder if they're on the way home?" said James.

As the boys entered the kitchen, James smelled the delicious aroma of roast beef, accompanied by home-canned peas and potatoes and gravy. Grandma had prepared their usual solid farm dinner.

"I'm starved!" announced Johnie.

"I knew you would be. I'll have everything on the table in just a minute." Grandma cut the meat, Margaret mashed the potatoes, and soon everything was ready.

James turned on the radio. No sound came.

"The lights went out an hour ago," said Grandma. "This weather looks bad."

"Have you talked to Uncle Ed?" questioned James.

"I did shortly after you left. But now the phone lines are down."

Johnie started to pass the food, but Grandma stopped him. "We have much to be thankful for. Don't forget the table grace and the blessing."

The family members bowed their heads. Grandma's glance seemed to signal Johnie to pray. "Dear Lord," Johnie prayed, "thank you for bringing us out of the storm. Please bring Mom and Dad home safely. And also make Uncle P.J. well. And thank you for this food. Excuse this short prayer because we're in a hurry and terribly hungry."

The rest echoed "Amen." Elizabeth smiled at the closing words of her grandson. "I think God understands your hurry. He may even have smiled."

"Does God laugh?" Carol asked.

"I think He's pretty serious with all of the problems of the world," said James. "We have terrible wars going on."

The family ate hungrily. A grandmother and four brothers and sisters plus little Michael ate their meal with no spats or fighting between any of

Chapter Ten

the children. There was a warm family feeling along with a sense of relief that all were safe. Grandma fed little Michael. He ate hungrily.

The blizzard continued and even worsened. After they finished dinner, the girls washed dishes while the boys went out to get more wood for the kitchen stove, a source not only for cooking, but for heat as well. The warmth of house contrasted sharply with the intense cold and wind and snow of the outdoors.

"Let's get out the games!" suggested James. Within minutes the old games of Authors, Pit, Old Maid, and Uno were brought out. Soon there was happy laughter and some light-hearted arguing. Pit, which involved everyone yelling and bidding and trading cards all at once, brought a high level of friendly, fun noise.

Meanwhile, little Michael crawled between the kitchen and the dining room between his siblings and his grandmother. The children played these games on the dining room table while Grandma began her work on several batches of cookies. Soon the smells of delicious chocolate cookies and what Grandma called "Old Fashioned White Sugar Cookies" filled the air. The aromas called the children back to the kitchen to test the cookies, warm from the oven.

Dark came earlier because of the snow and heavy clouds. Though electricity had come to their home two years ago, the children already took the convenience for granted. With the electricity out, they brought up the kerosene lamps from the basement. The lamps cast a warm glow in the kitchen and dining room as the children played and Grandma did her work in the kitchen.

"The cookies are ready," announced Grandma. "Take these first; they got a little dark. You can get your own milk."

The children, with Michael following close behind, were soon at the kitchen table—that is, all except Carol.

"Where's Carol?" Grandma asked.

There were some puzzled looks.

Margaret smiled, knowingly. "I think she went to the outhouse."

"Some day, we'll have indoor bathrooms the way they do in town," said James. "Then we won't have to go out in the cold."

Grandma shrugged her shoulder in a way that said such things were unnecessary nonsense. "The costs are high. We need to be satisfied with what we have. Tonight, I think we need to the use the slop jars inside."

Grandma went out through the back porch, opened the outside door and called. "Carol. Carol. Where are you?"

The blizzard literally roared.

She closed the door quickly and entered the kitchen. Her face pale, she gave a command. "Boys, you better go out and look."

When the boys did not respond immediately, she spoke sharply. "This storm is more dangerous than you think. Go! Go at once!"

"Yes, Grandma." They were not used to Grandma's sharp tone. James followed Johnie, and they put on jackets and hurried out, stumbling on the porch steps. Immediately it became difficult to tell where they were. The cold wind took James' breath away as he followed, and Johnie ran ahead to the outhouse. A high drift blocked their way. All at once a form struggling in a snowdrift emerged.

"Help me! I lost my way. I don't know where I am."

Johnie scooped up his little sister. Carol threw her arms around her big brother's neck. James breathed a sigh of relief and moved ahead to the house.

"I was so scared," she cried. "I lost my way. I couldn't see anything." Her tears flowed as she buried herself in the comfort of Johnie. "I couldn't breathe or anything. The wind was so strong."

Johnie comforted her even as he stumbled and they both fell into the snow. James then gathered his little sister in his arms. Johnie laughed as he extricated himself from the snow. James carried his frightened sister into the warmth of the house.

Grandma rushed to take off Carol's outer clothes. "Thank God, you're all right. You aren't to go out again. Not any of you—except for chores. We'll use the slop jars inside. That's an order."

"Yes, Grandma," said Carol. And Margaret echoed the same words, both being only too happy to obey.

"Well," announced Johnie as he put his jacket back on, "it's time for evening chores."

Grandma straightened Johnie's jacket. "Now, you boys stay together when you're outside. I know people who died coming back from the barn. That blizzard of '88 killed my best friend. It can happen in minutes, if you're not careful."

James couldn't believe the situation could be that serious. "You know we're going to need the lantern again because the lights are out. And today, it's so cold and windy we'll have to carry water into the barn. We can't let the cattle go outside."

Chapter Ten

The two boys found the work went very slowly because of the storm. They cleaned the barns, carried water to the cattle and horses, and then fed all the livestock. The wind and snow slowed them whenever they were outside. They heeded their grandmother's warning about staying together. They walked together to gather eggs in the chicken house, a job that usually belonged to their mother and sisters. As they went down the hill to the pig house, they almost lost their way. All paths had been obliterated, and even the most familiar became unfamiliar.

Once they finished these tasks, James and Johnie milked the cows in record time. In fact, they raced to see who could milk the most cows the quickest. But would the trucker be able to come and pick up the cream? In times of storm, this was always a problem.

Two very cold boys returned to the house several hours later.

"I've never experienced anything like this," said James as the delicious smells of a warm supper greeted him. "I wonder where Mom and Dad are."

"Your dad has good common sense." Grandma placed the leftover pork roast on the kitchen table. "And he knows a blizzard like this is dangerous. He has respect for the weather."

Grandma seemed to be her old self. James could see she thrived on these new responsibilities. He sensed that people had a need to be useful. Someday he would write the stories of this family and through the stories, he would present the love and warmth of this family.

They all sat down to eat. Grandma began to pray, and certain unspoken fears lurking in the background of her mind crept out. "Keep Matthew and Ellen safe from this storm. And if it is Your will, make my son well. You know how much I want him back home, sound in mind and body." She paused before she finished the prayer. "Thank you, Lord, for safety and warmth and food."

After supper, some very tired people sat around the kitchen table. The gas lamp did not give the bright light of the electric lights. No electricity meant no radio entertainment. James had the feeling they were cut off from the rest of the world.

"Well," said Johnie, "there'll be no school tomorrow or the next day. And maybe the day after that."

"And that makes you happy, I suppose," responded James. "You've never been crazy about school."

"I never wanted to be a bookworm."

Carol giggled. "You don't have to worry."

Beyond the Storm

Johnie gave her a friendly pat. James found a smaller lamp and left for the boys' room so he could read. One by one, each family member made an exit. Johnie stoked the furnace and the lamps were put out early that evening.

The house creaked and cracked from the cold during that night. Five children and their grandmother felt safe within the walls.

Early the next morning, James sat up in bed when he heard his grandmother's voice.

"Wake up James. Wake up Johnie. I'm afraid the furnace may have gone out. It's getting terribly cold."

James jumped out of bed and Johnie stirred at the same moment. Grandma repeated her words.

In minutes the boys were in the basement. The fire was almost out. Grandma had saved the family from a catastrophe by waking them. James realized how fortunate it was that they had hauled many loads of wood on Saturday. Johnie stoked the coals and James carried over the driest wood. It would not take long before the furnace would once more provide warmth for the whole house.

The temperatures had dropped below zero. Just forty-eight hours before, the temperatures had been seventy degrees warmer. The boys did the morning chores as usual. The truck driver who picked up the milk and cream did not come. The roads were blocked, but the boys found the additional milk cans so they would not have to dump the milk or cream.

By noon on Tuesday, November 12, Grandma looked tired. She had worked hard yesterday. This noon meant canned chicken and other canned goods. It was Carol who spoke what everyone was thinking. "I sure miss Mom and Dad. I wonder where they are. I wish they'd come home."

"We all wish that," said Grandma.

There was a slight hum. Margaret hurried over and snapped on the light switch.

"Yippee!" shouted Johnie. James and the girls added their shouts of joy. "We can see again."

"And I can read," said James.

Johnie looked out the window at the expanse of white. "I think we'd better hitch up the snow plow and try to get the roads open."

Chapter Ten

"Let's turn on the radio." James moved into the living room and switched on the radio. "We can get the news and hear about the storm."

The timing was right: "12:30 News." The announcer's words came through in a sharp, crisp manner. "This Armistice Day storm has been the worst in history. It has taken its heaviest toll on hunters. So far eleven hunters have been reported dead. A girl from St. Cloud went outside yesterday afternoon. Later, when the family discovered her missing, they went in search of her. She was found frozen to death this morning just a short way from her home. Other tragedies include…"

Each member of the family looked at Carol.

"I could have been that girl." Carol looked up at her brothers. "But my brothers found me."

Grandma seemed never to tire of reminding them of the seriousness of these storms. "You can't have too much respect for any blizzard."

The reports of the dead and missing continued to come over the radio. James felt fear and uncertainty settle over him. He knew Grandma and the others shared that fear. Even little Michael seemed restless and afraid.

"Do you think something could have happened to Mom and Dad?" questioned Margaret.

"We've had bad storms before. Your grandpa and I have instilled in our children a respect for the weather. The weather can be a friend, but it can also be man's worst enemy. Your dad knows that."

James realized the gravity of the situation. Johnie and Margaret and Carol all looked at Grandma. Little Michael whimpered.

Grandma spoke with an assurance that calmed her grandchildren. "This might be a good time to pray."

"Will prayer help?" Johnie stood up to get his jacket. "I wonder.... Why don't you pray?" he suggested.

James turned off the radio, and each one sat down with bowed heads. Grandma's voice had a quiver which betrayed her concern. "Dear Heavenly Father, we thank You that You have kept us warm and safe. Many are not so fortunate. We pray now for your children, Matthew and Ellen. We pray for their safety wherever they are. Bring them home to their children who need them. We all need and love them. We also pray for Paul John. Be with him. May he sense Your presence. Bring him back to us. We commit these and all our other family to You and Your tender care. Keep us safe this day also, and show us what we need to do. In Jesus' name, Amen."

Moments of silence followed. James saw tears fill his grandmother's eyes.

"That was better than any preacher's prayer," said Johnie. "You could have been a preacher."

Grandma smiled. "My task on this earth was to be a wife and mother, and now a grandmother."

Finally the storm let up and four young people dressed to go outdoors. These four might normally have argued or fought, but today were very much at peace. Even little Michael wanted to go out and play in the snow. Grandma decided the weather was still too severe for a boy not yet two years old.

The older boys found the shovels and began digging paths to the barn and outbuildings. By this time, the snow had stopped coming down, but the wind still blew harshly. The girls joined the boys and played and shoveled snow for a while, then decided it would be more comfortable indoors. That left the boys to hitch the horses to the plow. Johnie guided the horses, and James worked the crudely-made contraption that served as a snowplow.

The boys were soon laughing and having fun opening the driveway and then plowing some of the drifts on the township road. The temperatures kept dropping, but the wind lessened in severity.

That evening as supper ended, the lights flickered. Once again, the electricity went off, and the lamps were brought out. The children groaned in disappointment. "No radio programs," said Margaret. "No Dr. Christian."

"I have an idea," began Grandma. "There's a poem called "Snowbound." That would be just the right poem to read. I read it as a child."

"I read that poem in school," said James.

When the dishes were done, James lit a gas lamp and placed it on the living room table, where the most people could benefit from the light.

"Grandma, you read to us—just the way you did when we were little," said Carol.

The others agreed. Michael crawled into Grandma's lap. The light flickered, and Grandma began to read:

Chapter Ten

The sun that brief December day
Rose cheerless over hills of gray,
And darkly circled, gave at noon
A sadder light than waning moon.
Slow tracing down the thickening sky
Its mute and ominous prophecy,
A portent seeming less than threat,
It sank from sight before it set.

The white-haired grandmother read on, telling of each of the family members and the warmth of family life as they told stories and played games as the storm raged on. There were some stops in the story. The wind outside blew, and they felt their house creak just as the house in the poem creaked.

Then she read of the excitement when the storm ended. The boys dug their way to the barn and did the chores. Finally, Grandma came to the part where the old doctor checked on everyone's health and safety. And then the village paper—a week old—arrived. She read the final words:

Wide swung again our ice-locked door,
And all the world was ours once more!

James knew that he and the others would carry this memory throughout their lives. Grandma and the story would live on for generations.

They sat quietly a few moments. Then Margaret said softly, "That was a beautiful story. I love the poem." The others agreed.

"I'm thankful for my family." Grandma took off her glasses. "That's what's important to me. I love you all; God bless you all."

Little Michael had moved to Margaret's lap and was sound asleep. The wind blew harshly and the house creaked. Johnie stoked the furnace for the night. James went out and checked the cattle. The house was warm and safe. They could sleep now, secure from the cold and danger of the terrible blizzard.

The Armistice Day Blizzard of 1940 would soon end.

CHAPTER 11

Matthew slept fitfully that night of November 11. Lying on a hard floor next to a heat register was not comfortable, but at least there was some warmth. Ellen seemed to sleep better, relaxing against his body. The wind continued to blow throughout the night.

Habit caused Matthew to waken around five. The unfamiliar place and darkness startled him. He shivered in the cold and realized the fire might have gone out. He tried to move quietly away from Ellen. He stumbled against a desk and then found his way to the basement. His eyes gradually became accustomed to the darkness.

He knelt, trying to find the driest wood. Once more, he found the kindling and some larger sticks of dry wood. He was thankful that someone had the foresight to bring wood into the basement. Fortunately, the fire had not gone out completely. Within minutes, the fire produced warmth.

When Matthew returned to Ellen, she had awakened. Though the heat was beginning to permeate the room, they both shivered as they felt cold drafts.

"I think we'd better get to that farmhouse. It's not far," said Matthew. "Some newcomers live there—a young couple."

"We'd better wait until daylight."

Matthew and Ellen huddled together. They were hungry and their stomachs growled.

Beyond the Storm

It seemed to take forever, but finally the grayness of another stormy day appeared. As Matthew looked out the windows, he saw the outline of the countryside. The landscape revealed only white and the drifts of the storm. It was a strange, unfamiliar world.

Matthew checked the lock on the door. These school doors were usually locked with a skeleton-type key that wouldn't permit an exit without a key or breaking down the door. "I think we're going to have to crawl out through that basement window again."

As he prepared to climb out, Matthew observed, "It seems like such a long time since we left home yesterday morning."

"Time has a way of slowing down when we face a crisis."

Matthew pulled the window open, and snow came sifting in. "I think I'm going to have to burrow through some snow before we get out of here."

Matthew pulled himself up and pushed through the snow. Then he came back and pulled Ellen up through the window. He carefully closed the window. They were now both outside in the subzero temperature. The high drifts nearby seemed to cover everything. Matthew strained his eyes to see the farmhouse, but blowing snow obscured the view.

"We have to get to safety," Matthew whispered to himself. "We have to get back home, for the sake of the kids."

Walking was even harder than it had been the evening before. "We need to get some place fast," said Ellen. "This cold is unbearable. I'm afraid my hands are freezing."

Matthew held Ellen close to him. "Shake your hands. Then put them inside your pockets."

The two struggled through the hard drifts. They moved past the car, now almost completely covered with snow. Matthew helped Ellen as they tried to move around drifts and in some places through drifts.

"I know the farm place is just over this hill," said Matthew. "We'll be safe there."

Finally, Matthew saw the welcome sign of smoke coming out of the farmhouse chimney. "We're almost there!"

They stumbled over drifts as they walked down the driveway. Matthew knocked on the door, but there was no answer. He tried the door and found it unlocked. "Ellen, you go inside and keep warm. They must be in the barn doing chores."

Chapter Eleven

Matthew struggled through the drifts to the barn. He opened the barn door and saw a young woman emptying a large pail of milk into the separator. The startled woman let out a gasp.

"Sorry to frighten you." Matthew walked over and took the heavy pail. He realized this woman was in the last month of her pregnancy. "You shouldn't be doing such heavy work. I'll help you."

"Thank you, sir. My husband has so much to do. I wanted to help."

"I'm Matthew. My wife and I got stuck nearby late yesterday afternoon. We stayed in the schoolhouse."

"I'm Carol." As she said her name, Matthew felt a warmth and protectiveness. He thought of his own daughter.

A young man opened the barn door and said a surprised, "Hello."

Matthew again introduced himself and explained his situation.

"I'm Mike. We're running a little late today. I was feeding the pigs."

Matthew turned to the young woman. "You go inside. My wife's in your house so she could get out of the cold. She may have frozen her hands. I'll help Mike take care of the rest of the chores."

Though Matthew had his "good" clothes on, he helped the young man clean the barn and feed cattle and do the rest of the morning chores. As they finished, Mike gave a welcome invitation. "I'm starved. Let's go in for breakfast."

Inside the small farm kitchen, the smell of eggs and bacon frying and homemade bread toasting on the top of the stove welcomed them. The fresh coffee smell topped off the pleasant aromas.

The two men took off their jackets, washed their hands, and sat down.

"I don't know when a meal ever smelled better. I'm starved," said Mike.

Matthew sat down and bowed his head as Ellen passed the plate of fried eggs and bacon. Realizing the young man's awkwardness, Matthew quietly asked a blessing.

"I haven't been doing so well," said the young woman to Matthew. "Your wife's a godsend. My baby's due any day, and I've been having some problems."

Matthew and Ellen soon found that the young couple was having other difficulties as well. Their car had broken down, and they barely had enough food in the house. And now with a baby due any day, all their problems seemed to crash down on them at once.

"I had hoped to have the baby right here with some help. But Ma hasn't been able to come because of the storm."

"You need to get to a doctor," said Ellen. "I think we had better drive you to Dr. Baker as soon as we can."

Ellen placed another plate of bacon and eggs on the table and then sat down. The men were hungrily eating, and Carol seemed to enjoy the eggs.

"We can't afford a doctor," said Mike. "I'd do anything if we could. But I'm afraid we'll end up losing the farm. And then where will we be?"

"You can work things out with Dr. Baker," said Matthew. "He's a good man. He's not after your money."

Ellen reached over to Carol and took her hand. "My dear, I had my first four children at home. But for my last baby I really needed a doctor's help. I went to the hospital. That's the right thing for you—especially since you've had some problems."

"I wish I could. But how?"

"We'll find a way." Matthew looked at the worried couple and then at his own wife. How fortunate he was!

The four finished eating breakfast and settled back for some more coffee and talk. Ellen made a suggestion. "Why don't we see if we can get our car going? Then, we'll take you in to Dr. Baker's. You'll be safe when the baby comes."

Carol didn't seem ready to agree to this plan, but her husband wanted her to go.

As Matthew helped with more chores, he heard the sounds of the county snowplow a mile away. Mike hitched the horses to his homemade contraption that served as a snow plow, and they made an opening to Matthew's car. Then Matthew shoveled the car from under all that snow. A half-mile away, the county road would be open. Matthew felt a sense of relief when his car started. Matthew and Mike returned to the farmhouse to find Carol looking happier after encouragement from Ellen.

After the noon meal, Matthew announced they would be leaving soon. The young woman looked increasingly uncomfortable. Ellen had finally

Chapter Eleven

been able to convince Carol to go with them to town and to the doctor. Matthew had no doubt that this woman needed a doctor's attention.

Mike went ahead to plow the road so Matthew could keep on driving. Matthew maneuvered slowly through a plowed or partially-plowed road to the county highway. The narrowly plowed road made driving to Lake View somewhat easier. Finally they came to town and parked in front of Dr. Baker's home and office. Matthew breathed a sigh of relief as they brought the young woman into the doctor's office. On the other hand, the doctor could tell him nothing about his brother's condition.

Matthew then checked the winter driving situation. Some county roads would be open, but most township roads were still blocked. The roads south and east of town were not open. Matthew drove toward Victoria's house but soon found the side streets impassable. He parked the car and Ellen and he walked the short distance to his sister's home. As they were about to knock, Victoria opened the door.

"We've been so worried about you," she said, without even saying hello. "We knew you went to see P.J., but we didn't know what happened."

"Have you heard from the kids?" asked Ellen. "We're wondering if everything's OK."

"The phones in the country aren't working," said Victoria. "The lines are always down when there's any kind of storm."

Soon they found themselves welcome in the warmth of Victoria's home.

"Well, sis, you're getting quite a vacation," said Matthew.

"Yes, there was no school today and no school tomorrow—and maybe not on Thursday. But we'll have to make up the days in the spring."

Ellen handed her coat to Victoria. "I think we need a place to stay tonight. The roads aren't open south and east of here."

"You are most welcome here." Victoria took their coats and put them away in the closet. "What about P.J.? How is he doing?"

Ellen related briefly his condition yesterday. "But I don't know how things are today. The telephone lines are down. Dr. Baker didn't know anything. He will return to the hospital later this morning."

"I've been trying to call the hospital. I'll try once more." Victoria went to the phone and rang for the operator and spoke to her. She turned to Matthew and Ellen. "The lines are still down to River Falls, but the main lines should soon be repaired."

Matthew and Ellen began to relate their experiences of the past day, at the same time indicating their concern for the children at home alone with their grandmother.

"You two look exhausted. I think you need rest before supper. Then, we can enjoy the evening."

Matthew began to pace nervously. "I don't know if I could rest. I keep on wondering about Ma and the kids."

Ellen added, "I keep telling myself that they know what to do. But I am very weary. I will take your suggestions and rest for a few minutes." Matthew soon joined her.

An hour later, Matthew and Ellen entered the kitchen, refreshed from their time of rest. Both were so weary that they had managed to nap despite their concerns. In minutes, the three were seated at the kitchen table. Matthew found himself hungrier than he'd been in a long time. Though Victoria's cooking didn't compare to that of the other women in the family, it tasted great tonight, and he greedily ate her meatloaf.

"I haven't been this hungry in a long time." Matthew ate the last forkful of his piece of meatloaf.

"Well, there are more potatoes and peas and meatloaf." Victoria pushed the food closer to her brother. "And I have apple pie."

"You know, Victoria, I think we're eating because we're nervous. And because we haven't had much to eat these last days."

Victoria turned to her brother. "You were a fussy eater when you were a kid." She placed another slice of meatloaf on Matthew's plate.

Matthew devoured one more piece and then turned to the apple pie Victoria set down in front of him.

She cut him a large piece. "Now for some coffee. That always hits the spot. And I made egg coffee.

"That *is* special."

As they began to eat their pie, Victoria turned to Ellen. "Tell me more about Paul John. It's serious, isn't it? Do you think he's going to make it?"

Ellen looked at Matthew and then began. "When we were getting ready to leave, P.J. was restless. Rita thought we shouldn't see him. He was talking crazy part of the time."

Chapter Eleven

"That doesn't sound good."

"He was trying to say something," continued Ellen, "but we couldn't clearly understand what he meant."

Matthew's eyes were wet with unshed tears as Ellen went on. "P.J. kept saying, 'I'm sorry. I want to make everything right. I want to make everything right.'"

"What do you think he meant?" asked Victoria.

Ellen looked at her husband. Matthew returned the glance and explained. "I guess you don't know everything. I think P.J. is letting Larry have Mother Anderson's house to live in. I'm not sure what else Larry's doing. But I'm afraid it's not good. He's planning to have Larry run the farm, and he'll take everything that comes in."

"What!" Victoria's voice became shrill. "The rent from that land is supposed to go to Mother. There was to be no question about that."

"Well, that's the way it is," said Ellen.

"I thought it was dreadfully unfair when the land was signed over to P.J. And it was wrong when he kept it without signing it back." Victoria pounded her fist on the table. "I can't believe he'd cheat his own mother. I can't believe he'd go that far!"

"Yes, he would." Matthew found the old anger returning. "He has it all. He has a claim to everything. But I think he's sorry now about what he's done."

"P.J. and I fought as kids." Victoria's dark eyes showed sparks of anger. "And for some reason I knew he was never quite honest. He lied and cheated whenever he could. I guess that hasn't changed."

Matthew nodded quiet agreement.

Ellen, in a casual way, went on to tell the rest of the story. "P.J. seemed to be in torment. He kept saying he was sorry."

"I hope that was true repentance. I've started to think more about the future. And about heaven." Victoria paused a moment. "I wonder if our circle will be unbroken. I want my brother to be with us."

Victoria began to clear the table and Ellen helped. The routine tasks moved their thoughts away from the more serious concerns.

"Save your cups. We'll have some fresh coffee, and we can visit in the living room."

And that is what they did. The three talked of earlier times—of old neighbors. Victoria and Matthew spoke of childish things done and the way life used to be. The past once more became alive.

All at once, Matthew changed the topic. "I wonder about that young woman. And I feel concerned about Mike alone out there in the country."

Matthew and Ellen filled in the details of that story for Victoria.

"You're too kind for your own good, brother. People take advantage of you."

"I was just being neighborly," said Matthew. "I could walk up to Dr. Baker's and find out how she's doing."

The sharp ringing of the phone interrupted. Victoria quickly answered. Her side of the conversation revealed nothing.

Just as Matthew was getting ready to leave, Victoria announced, "Matthew, you don't have to go. First, there's no news about P.J. The young woman had her boy, and guess what they named him?"

"I can guess," said Ellen.

"Matthew is the name," replied Victoria. "And the young woman's mother and brother are on the way to the farm. So, Matthew, don't worry."

"I'm relieved." Matthew yawned and realized once more his tiredness.

Victoria brought out the fresh coffee and filled their cups. "Dear brother, you're a saint. You deserve this honor."

Ellen gave Matthew one of those reassuring looks. "Think of the way everything worked out. We came at just the right time to take the young woman to the doctor in town. And now her brother and mother are at the farm to help. And their warm house kept us safe from the cold."

"There were many coincidences. Life is filled with them."

Matthew didn't usually disagree with his sister. "I don't think they were coincidences at all."

"What seemed like coincidence," said Ellen, "was God's providence. This was His way of looking after us."

"But what about the people who are lost and frozen?" questioned Victoria. "Where was God's providence then?"

Those words and questions led the three into deeper discussions. Finally, Ellen said, "There are some things about God we will never understand in this life. But above all, He is sovereign. He is in control."

Outside, the wind continued to blow and snow filled in streets and roads once again. Inside warmth permeated the small family. Matthew felt the love and goodness that helped give this life its meaning. He prayed silently for his brother and for the safety of his mother and children.

Chapter Eleven

"Do you realize what time it is?" Victoria held up her watch. "It's almost midnight. I'm glad there isn't school tomorrow."

"Matthew will probably wake up at five, no matter what. He doesn't need an alarm clock when it's time for chores."

"I will want to get home as soon as possible. I hope everything's OK with Ma and the kids. They have all the work and responsibilities."

"I hope they're OK." Victoria showed her gentler side during these moments.

"I think the boys can do the chores and handle almost anything." Even as Matthew said the words, he realized something might have gone wrong during the cold and blizzard.

As Matthew and Ellen lay in a comfortable bed, Matthew observed, "This is a far cry from where we slept last night."

Ellen laughed. "It was harder for you than for me. At least I had you for a pillow."

Within minutes, Matthew and Ellen were in a deep and restful sleep that was much needed after the hard day they had had.

It was an hour after his usual five o'clock rising time that Matthew finally stirred. He thought of the children, but his exhaustion caused sleep to return.

It was almost eight when the phone rang. It was different here in town with only one ring that was repeated. Victoria's voice told Matthew something was wrong, seriously wrong.

Ellen opened the bedroom door and Matthew heard Victoria's last words. "Yes, I'll let the rest know."

"What's wrong?" Matthew asked as he hurried downstairs. Ellen followed.

Victoria's face, which usually showed a reserved aloofness, showed turmoil and concern. "It was Rita at the hospital. I have some bad news. P.J...," she faltered, "...P.J. died just a short while ago."

Stunned silence followed the announcement.

"We were prepared," said Ellen, "after seeing how bad he was the other night. I feared it was just a matter of time."

"I can't believe it," repeated Victoria. "How will Mother take this?"

"She's prepared."

Beyond the Storm

Several moments of inaction followed. But death has a way of moving the living to action. Victoria called Ed and found those phone lines were working. Then she tried calling home, but those phone lines were still down.

Death is something unreal whenever or however it comes. Each person responds differently. Matthew kept remembering the last moments with his brother.

After a small breakfast, Matthew walked uptown to find out about the roads. Many roads were not yet open. The state highway to River Falls was open though there were some drifts. A few county roads were open, but township roads were still, for the most part, blocked. This storm had been named "the Storm of the Century" and it surely had been. Only the old-timers still alive from the 1880's could remember that other worse storm. Finally, a train came through town, linking Lake View with the rest of the world.

Several hours later, the mail train came through. There would probably be no mail service out in the country for another few days. Cream and milk trucks would be able to get through to a few places and that would be about all. Life was almost at a standstill.

By early afternoon, Matthew and Ellen decided to try to drive the ten miles to their farm. They drove east several miles on the state highway and then took the county road south. The township roads that took them home the last few miles had a one-way track. Ellen looked intently at the road as her husband drove. It would be all too easy to drive into the ditch or a snow bank.

The drive seemed to take forever. Matthew got out of the car several times to shovel away drifts. After what seemed hours, the car and truck tracks ended, and there were only horse and sleigh tracks.

"I don't think we can make it any further." Matthew looked at the Andstrom place. "Let's stop here. I can walk home. You wait with these neighbors until I get the horses and sleigh."

Ellen protested. "I can walk, too."

Walking was not necessary. Mr. Andstrom insisted on giving them a ride home in his sleigh. Within half an hour, Matthew and Ellen arrived home.

As they rode up the driveway, they could see the boys had been at work with the snow plow. As the horses stopped in front of the house, the back door opened. They were greeted with shouts of joy.

Chapter Eleven

For that one moment, Matthew forgot about tragedy and death. Their children were all around them, asking questions. The children spoke of their adventures of the two nights and days.

"We're thankful you're home." That's all the children could say as the excitement died down.

"Where's Ma?" asked Matthew.

"Grandma worked so hard," answered Margaret. "I think she's all tired out. She's fast asleep. She cooked. I've never seen her work so hard."

Matthew knew he and Ellen had some tasks before them. He felt a sense of relief that his mother was resting.

"What about Uncle P.J.?" questioned James.

Matthew found himself choking with deep feeling.

"Your uncle died this morning," said Ellen. "It didn't look good from the beginning."

The children didn't seem sure how to respond. Not long ago, their grandfather had died, and they had experienced their first loss of a close family member. They had been close to their uncle at times, but there had been serious questions about the way he treated people.

Even when death greets a family, the routines of life go on. Once more, it was time for the chores. The large amounts of snow everywhere made the work take longer. While they did the chores, first cleaning barns and feeding cattle and then milking the cows and taking care of the pigs and chickens, Matthew felt a gnawing dread. It was one thing to tell the children about P.J., but how would he tell his mother?

After a time of quietness, Johnie began asking the questions.

"I keep wondering how God answers prayers. The storm made lots of people pray. Yet, some people froze to death."

"You keep asking questions we can't answer." James's voice showed hints of annoyance.

Matthew let the boys go on with their discussion but finally interrupting. "Well, boys, some things we don't know. But I think God has been busy answering prayers."

"Good, Dad. You have an answer. More than my bookworm brother." Johnie seemed ready to listen.

Matthew scratched his head, trying to remember all that had happened. "Remember last Saturday when I insisted we haul wood so that we'd be ready for winter?"

"Yes," replied Johnie. "I wanted to hunt. I hated the idea of hauling wood."

Beyond the Storm

Matthew continued. "We always pray for God to bless and keep and guide us." The boys nodded. "Look at how He made sure we had wood during the storm. If we hadn't taken in the wood, you could have had serious problems."

"We worked hard, but we kept warm," said James.

Matthew checked the milk pails to see they had been rinsed. "And your mother and I could easily have frozen to death when we went into the ditch. But we were near a school. We broke in and built a fire and kept safe and warm for the night. God knew where we needed to be to stay safe."

"Wow!" Johnie exclaimed. "That was some adventure."

"And we met a young couple. Mike helped us get our car out of the snow bank. Their car wasn't working, so we helped get the woman to town to Dr. Baker. Then she had her baby in the hospital just in time."

Johnie began to fidget, probably from hunger. "God must have been working overtime during that storm."

"And remember," interrupted James, "Carol went outside to the toilet and wandered off the path. She could have frozen to death, but we found her in time."

"You didn't tell us about that." Matthew gave his sons a questioning look.

Johnie always had the answer. "We didn't have a chance."

The warm lights of the house welcomed Matthew and his sons. The work of the day was finished, and the family was together and safe. Matthew dreaded the task before him: he must tell his mother about P.J.

Chapter 12

Matthew thought about the task before him. He couldn't leave it to Ellen. He had to tell Ma about P.J. before more time passed. Ellen had supper ready when he and the boys came in from chores. He couldn't put off the job.

Matthew went slowly up to her room, knocked on the door and entered. He never felt comfortable in a lady's room—even his mother's. "Ma, are you still sleeping?"

His mother stirred and slowly sat up. "I must have fallen asleep. When did you get back?"

"A few hours ago. You were sleeping. You must be exhausted."

"I guess you've spoiled me. I'm not used to working so hard."

Matthew cleared his throat, uncertain how he should go on. "Ma, I have something to tell you." P.J.'s tormented moments flashed through his mind.

"It's P.J., isn't it?"

"Ma, P.J. died this morning. He didn't recover from the heart attack, and he had pneumonia. There was nothing the doctors could do."

Ma looked very composed for just having heard the news. "Somehow, I knew this was going to happen. When you were called back, I knew it was a sign. Why must I live on and my son die before his time?"

"It's hard to understand. I'm glad I saw him the last time. I had a chance honestly to forgive him for what he did. I wanted him to live, but I knew there wasn't much hope."

"Did he suffer?" she asked. "P.J. always hid his hurts. He could be in great pain, but he never showed it. He broke his arm once and tried to hide it from us."

"When we saw him Monday morning, he was violently ill—delirious. He didn't know what he was saying."

"I'm glad I wasn't there." She folded her hands as if to pray. "I said my goodbye on Sunday night. It's not right that a mother sees her children die. It was awful when Lucille died, but to lose two children is unbearable."

"Life isn't always fair," Matthew said, "but Ellen and I and the children are here for you. We'll take care of you."

"I'm thankful for that. Each child is special."

"You've been working too hard these last days." Matthew took his mother's hand. "And P.J.'s death on top of all this."

"It felt good to work and be in charge. I felt useful. It gave me a real purpose for living."

"God has a purpose for you here, Ma."

Mother and son sat for several moments in silence. The love he felt for her and the love she had for him gave Matthew renewed strength.

Finally, Matthew broke the silence. "Ma, it's time to eat." As always, life and routine beckoned them to move on.

For Matthew the following days moved in slow motion. He did the chores and all the other work in a deliberate way. The children were home from school one more day because many roads were not yet open. Thursday afternoon the neighbors banded together to open the township roads. Contact with the outside world came with the opening of roads and the restoration of telephone service. The neighbors did extra work and plowing so that people would be able to attend P.J.'s funeral.

These days became a special bonding time between Matthew and his sons. That bonding happened many times, but especially that Thursday night. After getting everything ready for the next day, the three stood below the opening to the hayloft.

James asked, "Will Uncle P.J. go to hell? I keep thinking of some of the good things he did for us kids. I think of all those presents he gave us."

"Boy!" added Johnie, "we never got so many presents as we did last Christmas. And they were expensive."

Chapter Twelve

Matthew thought of the gifts P.J. had given—especially the large gift of money one Christmas. "Yes, P.J. had a good side. In a way family was important to him, and he could be generous."

Johnie clenched his fists as he spoke. "But he was dishonest and stole from people. He stole the farm from you, Dad."

"Yes, he did. Though he took it legally, he was dishonest. We know he did other things that were wrong."

"But will he go to heaven or hell?" James was not about to put aside his question. "Will the good things balance out the bad?"

"I can't answer that question. Only God knows. We're all sinful, of course. I know he was dishonest, and he was involved with criminals." Matthew couldn't help thinking of P.J.'s last tormented moments and he also wondered.

James always had good questions. "But Jesus forgave the thief on the cross, didn't he?"

"I think your mother would have better answers than I." Matthew paused a moment. "The last time I saw P.J., he seemed genuinely sorry. He wanted to make things right. He seemed as if he might be trusting in the Lord."

"Then, God would forgive him." James spoke the statement and then seemed to make it a question.

"God forgives the worst of sinners. We all need forgiveness," Matthew said.

"I know I do," said Johnie. "Sometimes I really feel like doing some nasty things. If someone does something to me, I want to get even."

"I've learned an important lesson." Matthew thought back on his life. "I've learned that if I don't forgive, I'll be in trouble. My bitterness toward P.J. almost killed me. I had to forgive."

"But, you had the right to be angry," said James "You had the right to get even."

"Yes, it wasn't fair," continued Matthew. "But I hurt myself by hating my brother. I hurt myself more than I hurt him. I couldn't go on living that way. There's a verse in the Bible that says something about hating our brother whom we have seen, then how can we love God whom we haven't seen?"

"That's deep stuff," said Johnie.

"It's important." Matthew wished somehow that he could impart these truths to his sons.

"Boy, I'm hungry!" Johnie turned to go. "We better get in for supper."

Matthew wanted to put his arms around his sons and hug them. Instead he just said, "I'm proud of you boys."

Friday, the regular routine returned. Carol skied to school, and Johnie drove the old Model A to Lake View High School. Somehow that car always started and got through places where other cars could not go.

The whole state was digging out from the storm. The storm hit some areas worse than Lake View and the countryside around. The funeral for P.J. was delayed until Monday with the hope that Rita's sister and mother and some Chicago friends and associates would be able to come.

During the next days many thoughts filled Matthew's mind. He kept seeing P.J. during those last tormented moments. P.J. said again and again, "If only I can get out of here. I want to make things right."

Life seemed to move slowly. With all the snow, the farm work continued to be more of a challenge. Matthew couldn't help wondering about the life of a farmer. There were times when this farm life seemed terribly harsh.

And then he wondered about Larry. Could this young kid, raised in the city, become a farmer? Larry, who was often rude and arrogant, had some of his father's charm. And, like his father, he would have a hard time admitting any mistakes. And what could he do about Larry living in Ma's house?

Monday arrived. This would be the day of P.J.'s funeral. To Matthew there was a touch of unreality. Memories of past funerals blended together.

The Anderson family sat together in the mourners' section. Matthew and his sisters were present as well as most of the nieces and nephews. The good news was that Mary had been released from the TB sanitarium for several days. Martha returned from Wisconsin with her two daughters. They stayed with Victoria in town. Cousin Pete and Alice came from the north country and stayed several days with Matthew and Ellen. Corrine and Warren were conspicuously absent.

Less than a year ago, these same people had sat in this church as they mourned the death of John Anderson. They might never again be

Chapter Twelve

together as a family. Matthew looked at his mother, seated next to Rita. What a contrast of women. Ma was dressed in a plain black dress; Rita in a suit with everything coordinated in the latest fashion. Fortunately, her rouge and lipstick were more subdued today. In Larry he observed a nervous younger version of P.J. What would the future hold for him? And what about Noreen, a younger version of Rita?

It was hard to concentrate on what was happening at the funeral service. In some ways this funeral was like any other. But then the reality would hit that this funeral was very different. It was his brother's, his own flesh and blood. It was P.J., a part of his generation.

Matthew's rich tenor voice joined the rest of the congregation singing one of his favorite hymns, "Blest Be the Tie that Binds." The family was together, but in a real sense were they? Each family member seemed to be pursuing something different in life. For some there was a sense of community, but for others the pursuit was leading them far away.

Matthew could still hear P.J.'s voice. "I'm in charge and don't you forget it." These memories of words and actions were scars, but perhaps they could be part of the healing too.

Pastor Strand spoke of timing and the way the Lord works. At that same moment other words of P.J.'s echoed in Matthew's mind. "Don't be stupid. Don't bring God into this!" How could his brother face death with these questions and uncertainties in his mind? P.J. had ridiculed Matthew for saying he believed in God. "God is for stupid, simple people, not for someone who thinks."

The pastor read the obituary. It seemed cold and impersonal. A soloist sang a song that Matthew didn't know. It was probably something fancy that Rita had chosen. Rita possessed none of the Anderson's family traditions and values.

Pastor Strand began his sermon. Matthew could not concentrate on the words. He felt no peace; his mind was in turmoil. He thought he had forgiven P.J. But it was as if the wound were once again opened.

As Pastor Strand continued, Matthew recalled more words of P.J. "That religion stuff. That's no more than a child's fairy tale. Religion's only good for women and children."

Matthew had never been able to argue with P.J. because his big brother always had the upper hand. Not only was P.J. older, he was stronger, and he definitely had brains.

"Jesus Christ the same yesterday, today, and forever." Those words triggered other memories like the happy occasion of Ma and Pa's fiftieth wedding anniversary. It was true! Scripture had once more affirmed his faith! This was not some feeble fairy tale as P.J. had said. Christ was indeed the Son of God.

Matthew thought of his own brush with death. In those moments when he thought his time had come, he had an encounter with Christ that changed his life. He knew God was real and was inviting him to live. This Jesus was the same then and now and forever. A peace had settled over him then just as it did now. It was a peace that felt as if he was being transported to a quiet lake that had barely a ripple.

Soon, the family crowded together in the snow-covered cemetery. "Ashes to ashes. Dust to dust," read Pastor Strand. There was something final about this goodbye. It was like the end of a long story, one of those newspaper serials. After many chapters of "To be Continued," finally "The End" had come.

As they left the cemetery to return to the church, Matthew felt a tap on his shoulder. It was Doctor Baker.

"I have a letter from your brother. He wanted to make sure you got this. He was troubled during those last hours. He wrote the letter during a short time when his mind seemed clear. I promised I would get it into your hands."

Matthew accepted the letter and thanked him.

Dr. Baker continued. "I didn't know if I should tell you this." He stopped in the middle of his thought.

Matthew anticipated the doctor's next words.

"I've been like P.J. in some ways. I've been pretty much of a skeptic—not sure if God was really there. Or if He did exist, I thought He didn't have much time for you and me."

Matthew felt as if he were a minister hearing a confession.

"Your brother was in torment during the last moments of his life. He said something like, 'God, I've rejected You too long. It's too late for me.' I've never seen such despair."

"I'm not surprised." Matthew felt anew a great sadness for his brother.

"P.J.'s death helped to make a believer out of me. I doubted God; now I know He's out there. More than that, I doubted the devil and hell. Now I know that hell is very real."

"That's something I haven't doubted," said Matthew.

Dr. Baker left and Matthew followed family and friends into the church, where they visited and had lunch. He thought how strange it

Chapter Twelve

was that the best family fellowship came at these times of tragedy and sadness. Why couldn't people learn to appreciate one another every day? Why did it take tragedy to bring people together?

Matthew returned to the business of work and life. It was strange how quickly everyday routines of life continued. Victoria returned to her teaching duties on Tuesday. Martha and Jane and Rachel left for Wisconsin. Pete and Alice made the return trip up north. And Matthew and everyone else went back to their usual work.

The next morning, Matthew returned to the house after morning chores. He sat down at the kitchen table, pouring himself a cup of coffee. He heard Ellen and Ma in the basement doing their weekly clothes washing. Even little Michael was confined there. Matthew was alone. He wanted to read this letter without people around. He was unsure of what it contained, and he had no idea how he would respond.

He began reading. "Dear Matthew, my brother..." The greeting was more affectionate than Matthew had ever experienced from P.J. "I write this letter, knowing something may happen to me. I feel you deserve to know a few things."

Matthew looked, but found no date. P.J. must have started the letter earlier and then finished it in the hospital.

He continued reading. "First of all, you know I had connections with the crime syndicate. I was on the edge, so to speak—not really a part of it. That's why both the law and the syndicate were after me. Some people thought that I had headquarters in my house by the lake."

As he read, Matthew heard P.J. saying the words. "I deeply regret all the hurt and concern this caused you and Ellen and the rest of the family. I never wanted to hurt you. I cut my connections with the syndicate, but I couldn't do it completely. They always wanted something. They practically owned me. It's as if I had sold my soul to them—like selling one's soul to the devil.

"If I am permitted to stay around, I believe I can make some things right. I would like to get our beloved farm back into the hands of the family. I'm not sure I can. The syndicate people seem to have gotten their fingers into everything that is mine, or was my family's.

"As I write this, the leaves are gone, but I remember the beauty of autumn. For the first time, Matthew, I can see why you love this area. It's a little bit like the Garden of Eden. But the terrible reality is that I've lost touch with all those good things—the church and the Bible. I'd like to believe, but I can't. It's as if I've gone too far, as if I've crossed a line to a point of no return.

"I don't know if you can believe this after some of the ways I've treated you: but I love you, dear brother. In a way, I've been jealous. I thought you were the one that Mom and Dad really loved. They treated me special because I was a visitor, but you were the most like them. Your children were fully their grandchildren.

"Again, I don't know if you can believe me. I wanted you to stay on the farm, but I also wanted to control things. I felt I knew better ways to make money, and I probably did. But those ways turned out to be wrong.

"Matthew, you must promise to take care of Mother. I know you will do that.

"I don't know what Rita will do if something happens to me. I can't see her settling in the country. I'm afraid one of my business acquaintances may have claim to the house—our mansion by the lake. Larry, right now, is a frightened child. If you can find it in your heart to teach him some of the ropes of farming, I will be ever so grateful.

"Again, I want to say that I never intended for you to move away from the home place. I thought we could all live close together as a whole family. I had that dream, but I know I wanted to be in charge. And I know I had no right to control the lives of others.

"I hope (I wish I could say I pray) that these things may be worked out. If something happens to me, Rita has been directed to return the major portion of the farm to you if we can clear the title. Larry will get eighty acres and some money.

"I hope when you think of me, you will think kindly. I know that I have often not been the brother I should have been. Your brother. Paul John Anderson."

Matthew sat quietly. The letter made many things clear. But now P.J.'s life was over. He would share this letter with the Ellen. He hoped that Rita would agree and that there wouldn't be any legal problems with other claims.

The kitchen door opened. It was Michael. "Daddy!" he called out. And soon the little boy was in his arms.

"My son, my son." P.J. would be forever in the past. Michael was the present and the future. The darkness of the past lay behind.

"I love you, Daddy."

"I love you, son." Matthew hugged the boy and looked outside to see the brightness of the sun reflected on the snow.

Chapter 13

"Matthew, I'd like to visit with Corrine," announced Ma. "Do you think you'd have time to drive me over?"

Matthew thought a moment. "Yes, let me finish some chores. I'd thought of checking on Warren and Corrine myself."

"Don't you think you should call first?" questioned Ellen.

"Martha told me their telephone doesn't work." Sadness showed in Ma's eyes. "I hate the thought of Corrine and those three girls not even being able to call for help."

Ellen nodded to her husband. "I think you need to visit. And I think you need to pay Larry a visit too."

"Yes." Ma's whole demeanor showed grim determination. "If I'm not living in my house this winter, Corrine should be there. She and Warren and the children need a warm and safe place to live."

An hour later, Matthew and his mother knocked at the door of the old dilapidated farm house.

"This house isn't fit to live in." Ma knocked once more.

Matthew heard the cries of a young child. He opened the sagging door and called out.

Corrine appeared, holding little Susie. "Sorry, I didn't hear you. Susie's been fussy. She can't seem to settle down."

Three-year-old, golden-haired Susie cried out. "It's cold. I'm freezing."

Matthew could see tears in his niece's eyes. He reached over and snatched Susie into his arms. She cuddled close to him.

Ma repeated more emphatically, "This place isn't fit to live in."

"We're thankful at least to have some cattle and a roof over our heads." Corrine motioned for them to sit at the kitchen table. "It's probably warmer here than anywhere else. The kitchen stove gives good heat."

Matthew looked down at little Susie. "You know I used to hold your mother just this way when she was a little girl."

Susie clung to her uncle a bit longer, then wiggled free and went to play with her blocks.

Corrine moved toward the stove. "I'll get some fresh coffee going if we have some left. I think we're almost out."

"Matthew," said Ma, "we're going to see to it that Corrine has all the food supplies she needs."

"No, Grandma, we can't accept charity." She looked down at Matthew, seated at the table. "Warren's in the barn finishing chores. He should be in any minute."

"We take care of family when they have a run of hard times." Matthew thought of his own children and how they were warm and comfortable. He couldn't help noticing the cold draft coming from the kitchen windows.

Ma stood up. "Matthew, we're going to do something about this now. If I'm not living in my house, Corrine and Warren and the kids can live there. It's not big, but it's warm and comfortable."

At that moment the door opened. Warren must have heard Elizabeth Anderson's last words.

"No, thank you. I don't want to be anywhere near that lousy character. Larry Anderson isn't fit to be around anyone."

"But this house is cold and drafty. Ma's house would keep you and the children warm."

Warren raised his voice. "I want nothing to do with that farm or any of those people. After this year, things will be better."

Corrine brought out cups and began to pour coffee. "Come, sit down. Coffee always helps."

Warren took off his jacket. Both strain and anger showed in his face.

Chapter Thirteen

"It's been awhile since I've seen you, and we missed you in church these last Sundays." Ma bit her lip as if her comments may have been taken as a reprimand.

"My suit's all wore out. I haven't any presentable clothes."

Matthew sensed Warren's embarrassment. "It's not the clothes that matter. It's what's inside—within the heart."

Warren cleared his throat. "My heart's not that great. I can't stand Larry. And even though P.J.'s dead, I think I hate him." He turned to Ma and added, "I'm sorry. But he was a first-rate scoundrel."

Ma looked away sadly. "I know my son did some terrible things. I'm sorry." Tears came to her eyes.

Matthew remembered all too well his feelings toward P.J. "I understand what you're saying, Warren. I went through some terrible times too, but finally I had to forgive P.J."

"You're a nicer guy than I am. I'm not sure I can do that."

"The coffee's getting cold. I'm sorry I don't have any cookies or cake." Then, Corrine checked the cupboard. "Here are some soda crackers."

Matthew and Ma and Corrine and Warren began to drink their coffee. Little Susie returned to her uncle's lap.

Ma began to speak once more. "Warren, please for the sake of your children, think about moving over to my house. Especially during these colder winter months."

Warren looked away. "I don't think I can."

"Think about it at least."

Warren's anger came out in other ways throughout their visit. "People are greedy," he said. "And then banks are all too ready to foreclose."

Matthew tried to calm him. "Yes, that's right. But some people went too far into debt."

"The bank in Wisconsin had me over a barrel. I couldn't go on without the loan. And then with crop failures, things just got worse and worse."

"I wish we had known," said Matthew. "We would have tried to help."

Warren clenched his fist. "I'm not a charity case. I want to make it on my own—not with charity from the family or anyone else."

Ma reached out to touch his clenched fist. "Warren. Corrine. We love you. And you've been hurt so badly. We want to do what we can. We're family. Please don't look at our help as charity."

Warren looked away. "Corrine says I'm too proud. I guess I am."

"Let us help," pleaded Ma. "That's what family is for."

Matthew stood up. "Ma and I are going to confront Rita and Larry. The little house can be your home for the winter. It's only two miles from here. We could even move the milk cows to Pa's old barn. That would work."

Warren seemed touched by the offer. "I can't believe how good you are. My own brothers would never do this."

Matthew thought of his neighbors and the people who had helped him. "The Lord wants us to take care of family and neighbors. That's His plan."

Corrine walked over to her uncle and gave him a hug. "Uncle Matthew, I love you. You don't know how much your kindness means."

Warren extended his hand. "Thank you."

Matthew and his mother waited at Rita's front door for an answer to their knocks. Finally, a young hired girl opened the door.

"We came to see Rita," announced Ma.

The shy girl hesitated. "She's in the library, but she said she didn't want to be disturbed."

"This is P.J.'s brother and I'm his mother." Elizabeth Anderson stood up straight, thus commanding respect.

"Come in." She pointed down the hall. "I think you know where the library is."

His mother led the way, opening the library door without knocking. "Rita, good morning. We need to talk."

"Good morning, Mother Anderson." Rita, dressed in a black dress, nodded to Matthew. "I'm writing thank you notes for those memorials."

Seeing Rita reminded Matthew that P.J. had died only weeks ago. His brother's death carried a touch of unreality.

Rita moved toward her mother-in-law, embracing her awkwardly. Matthew saw tears in the eyes of both.

"I still can't believe he's gone," said Ma. "It doesn't seem possible."

Rita agreed. "Why don't I have Elsie put on some coffee. Then we can talk."

Chapter Thirteen

Such hospitality was uncharacteristic of Rita. On rare occasions, though, she could be the model hostess.

As Ma regained her composure, she declined the offer. "We've just had coffee. And we have some business, and then we have to get back home for our noon meal."

Matthew remained silent and let Ma go on.

Ma came right to the point. "The house Corrine and Warren are living in isn't fit for anyone. I want them to live in my house."

"But Larry and Joan are there."

Ma's voice became commanding. "They can move. They can live here with you, or in one of the cabins."

Rita's voice became crisp and formal. "But, Mother Anderson, I have business guests coming from time to time. P.J.'s business guests are now my guests. Of course, Larry's taking over part of the business."

Ma's voice rose in loudness and pitch. "Rita Anderson, that house is mine. Even though P.J. took the farm, the deed says I have rights to the house for life. And I'm still very much alive. I may be around for awhile."

Rita's eyes seemed to shoot sparks. "Yes, you may live there for life, but that document doesn't say Corrine and Warren can."

Ma's strength seemed suddenly to evaporate. She began to cry. "And you would take an old lady's house."

Rita backed away.

Matthew wanted to take his mother in his arms, but he had never felt comfortable showing that much affection. "Ma, we'll work things out. You have your room at our place."

Ma began to dry her tears.

"I don't know what to say." Rita looked visibly shaken. "You realize I've lost my husband. I can't take much more. I'm just trying to go on living."

For a moment Matthew felt sorry for his sister-in-law. "We all miss P.J. But we have to do what's fair. And P.J. might be concerned for Larry, but he'd also want to look out for the rest of the family."

Ma looked away and spoke slowly. "It's pretty hard to move in the winter. It's almost December."

Matthew thought a moment. "What about Ma? She could decide to move back into her own home. Then, Larry would have to be out."

Rita's composure seemed to disappear. All at once the woman wearing a carefully tailored black suit that accented a trim figure and a face heavy with rouge and lipstick seemed to turn into a weak, lonely, and frightened woman. Matthew saw a side of her he had never before seen.

"I don't know what to do. I'm at my wit's end."

Rita sat down at the desk. Matthew was at a loss for words. His mother said nothing.

"I'm sorry. I probably shouldn't say anything. Ever since Paul John died, I've seen a side of Larry that I don't like. He's angry. He's been on the verge of striking me—and Joan as well."

"We can't permit that." Matthew looked down at Rita. "We have to do something."

"Larry's been taking over Paul John's business. Oh, I've tried to entertain and keep some things going. But Larry's been gone more and more, and he's dealing with some men I wonder about. My husband had learned to be careful with those men. Larry hasn't been careful."

Matthew almost shouted. "Those guys are crooks. P.J. was breaking off connections with them. They are dangerous. Larry could get into serious trouble. He's supposed to be farming."

All this while Ma had said nothing. Then she spoke. "Matthew, it's time we had a talk with Larry."

Rita trembled. "I can't help you."

Elizabeth Anderson viewed the empty spot where the big house had been. It was part of the past. She no longer felt this place was home. Part of her life had been destroyed, but she was not about to give up.

Matthew walked beside her as they approached her little house. She felt an uneasiness, even anger, for it seemed Larry had stolen the place from her. She wanted to remember P.J. kindly, but his terrible deeds prevented that.

"Matthew," a voice called from the barn. "I'm finishing chores. Larry should be back any minute."

Elizabeth observed her grandson's wife hurrying toward them. She suspected this young woman might be pregnant. She shouldn't be working in the barn alone. Where was Larry anyway? He should be doing the hard work.

"I'm glad you stopped by," announced Joan.

Chapter Thirteen

At that moment a car drove up and Larry stepped out. "Hello, Uncle Matthew. Hello, Grandma."

Elizabeth wanted to reach out and embrace this grandson, but something held her back. She also desperately wanted her own house back.

The four people made awkward conversation as they entered the house.

Elizabeth looked around at the familiar rooms. For a moment she just wanted to come home. Then, she thought of the loneliness. No one would be nearby...the big house was gone... and Joan had made the place unfamiliar. It didn't feel as if it belonged to her at all. This was no longer home.

Joan invited them to sit down.

"We'll stay just a minute," said Matthew. "It's time for noon dinner and Ellen's expecting us."

Elizabeth looked down; then her eyes alighted on Joan. The dirty barn clothes of this petite young woman couldn't hide her beauty. Larry had a good wife. But then she noticed something that startled her.

"Joan, what happened? Your eye." Elizabeth felt an overwhelming concern for Joan.

"Oh, it's nothing," she replied. "Larry's been so busy. He's had to take care of his dad's business, so I've done much of the farm work. I ran into something in the barn."

Elizabeth wondered.

Matthew interrupted. "Larry should be doing that hard work."

"You can't hide it. I have a feeling you're in the family way, and you shouldn't do all that work," Elizabeth said.

Joan's hand covered her black eye. "I realized only a few days ago that I am expecting. I'm used to hard work. I grew up on a farm, and I love that life. In some ways, I'm happy that Larry wanted to move to the farm. I'm right at home."

"I can't keep her in the house," said Larry. "She loves being outside, working with the chickens or the cows."

Elizabeth's eyes clouded with sadness. "Be careful. I used to feel the same way. Two years after your father was born, I found myself expecting. I guess I wasn't ready for another baby. Well, I did all kinds of hard work, and I ended up losing the baby."

Matthew gave her a look of surprise. "I never knew."

"It's not something a woman talks about. It's in the past."

"I'm sorry, Grandma Anderson. I'll be careful."

Elizabeth found her anger subsiding. Moving back to her home did not seem like a good idea.

Matthew changed the subject. "Actually we came because your grandmother may want to move back here. This is her home."

Joan turned to her husband. "We shouldn't have moved in here, but you said it was all right."

Larry spoke sharply. "This was my father's property. It now belongs to my mother, and it's coming to me."

Elizabeth looked to Matthew. She knew his stomach would now be churning with anger.

Matthew slowly responded. "But your grandmother has lifetime rights to live here."

"Yes, but she moved to your place. She's not here."

Elizabeth saw history repeating itself. "I don't know what to say."

Joan moved closer to Larry. "We shouldn't be here. This isn't right."

Larry suddenly changed his tone. "I'm sorry Grandma. We thought you'd be staying with Uncle Matthew. We didn't think you'd mind if we stayed here, and it's not good for a house to be empty. Mother and I have all those business people to take care of. This just seemed the perfect place to be. We should be near the farm buildings and animals anyway."

Elizabeth avoided the gaze of both Larry and Joan. "I guess we'll have to let things remain as they are—for now. I'll stay with Matthew and Ellen."

"Oh, Grandma, you're the best."

Elizabeth stood up straight, her five feet commanding respect. "But I plan to move back next spring. You can count on that."

"We'll move out next spring," said Larry.

"It's time for us to go." Elizabeth marched toward the door. Matthew followed.

That evening as Elizabeth read her evening devotions, she prayed. "Lord, I know I didn't do right by P.J. I made mistakes, but show me how to treat my grandson. Please help that sweet little Joan. And whatever it takes, show Larry the error of his ways. I pray that he will place his trust in You."

She turned off her light early. Little Michael was fast asleep. Matthew and Ellen were saying goodnight to James and Johnie and Margaret and Carol. With this family she had a sense of safety and well being. The

Chapter Thirteen

Lord was building this house. She heard the prayers of the children. She knew their course was charted well.

Sleep evaded her. P.J. appeared in her mind. He stood before her, his dark handsome features seemed as alive as ever. "Lord," she whispered aloud, "I can't do anything about P.J. But I can pray for each of my grandchildren."

As she prayed for each grandchild, deep peace came over her. Except when she came to Larry.

Chapter 14

Ellen's mind was far from her recipe. She had found a yellowed piece of paper with her mother's recipe for pumpkin pie filling. There was something special about making that pie. But she wanted to make a phone call first.

She was alone in the kitchen. Matthew and Johnie had gone out to the barn to check on a young calf. James was at the piano, practicing some of the school choir music. Carol and Margaret were in their room, and little Michael was playing on the floor near his grandmother who was busy knitting.

Ellen knew that making this phone call was the right thing to do. She rang central and gave the number.

The phone rang a long ring, two short rings, and another long. She waited, wondering about the delay.

Rita answered with a quick hello, as if she were being taken away from something far more important.

"I wanted to call and wish you a happy Thanksgiving," began Ellen. "The family will be together at Thanksgiving dinner tomorrow. We'd like to invite you and Larry and Joan. We have plenty of food."

For a moment the other end of the line was silent. "After what's happened, you want Larry and me to be with you?"

"Rita, we're family. And it's a holiday time. We'd like to have you with us, even if we've had our differences."

Rita still hesitated. "I'm sorry, but I'm expecting company. Larry and Joan are coming also."

"I know this will be a sad time for you with P.J. gone. It's time to put aside our differences and get together as a family. Maybe you could stop by for lunch later in the afternoon?"

Rita answered abruptly. "I'm expecting guests. I expect to be quite busy."

"I'm sorry."

"I think being around Corrine and Warren would be awkward," Rita added.

Ellen had to admit Rita was right. She hadn't really thought about that. She had only hoped a holiday would bring out the best in everyone.

"It's family time. And we'll all be missing P.J."

Ellen heard noise in the background. Rita spoke curtly. "I have to be on my way. Goodbye." The receiver clicked.

Ellen put down the receiver. "Well, I tried."

At that moment a car drove up the driveway. This would have to be Victoria and Martha.

Within minutes both women had brought in their old suitcases for their two-night stay. They settled in the kitchen, doing their usual Thanksgiving preparations. Elizabeth spoke with her daughters and then retreated to her bedroom, saying she was tired.

Each woman seemed to have an assigned duty. Martha peeled potatoes, Victoria peeled and pared apples, and Ellen worked with the pumpkin. Thanksgiving dinner would be a masterpiece. But this time the matriarch of the family was not participating.

Ellen may have been in charge of kitchen preparations, but Victoria led with the conversation. It seemed she was in a reflective, sentimental mood that was not entirely characteristic of this stern teacher.

"I'd like to express some thoughts that I don't usually talk about. In fact, we often don't say thank you to those people who mean the most to us. And that reminds me that I should talk to Mother."

"Well, Victoria, we're getting a little older." Martha rinsed off the potatoes she had peeled. "And when we're older, we take time to look back on our lives."

"Ellen, I can't begin to express how much being here means to me. It seems as if my roots are with you and Matthew. And each year I am reminded of the passing scenes of life."

Chapter Fourteen

Martha added, "And this is the place I would always come back to as well."

Ellen also had realized something about family. "Since my sisters and family are a distance away, you have become important. You've become like sisters rather than in-laws."

Victoria and Martha added similar sentiments.

"Tonight, I'm missing Dad more than ever," said Victoria. "It's almost a year ago that he became so ill. Even though he was old, I always felt I could go to him. There was something rock-like and strong about him."

After others expressed how they missed John Anderson, Victoria spoke again. "I've begun to realize our time on earth is short. And it's important not to take each other for granted. I may seem to take my family for granted, but I shouldn't. We are only together for such a short time."

Ellen wondered what was coming next.

"I'm haunted by the memory of P.J. I can't understand all he did. I don't think any of us realized the direction he was going. He was good looking and charming, and he had brains. He seemed to care about us, but he kept looking after Number One."

Ellen wanted to say more but she spoke only a few words. "P.J. didn't realize how much he was hurting people."

"What he did to Matthew was almost unforgivable," said Victoria. "And I wonder if he really meant it about making things right."

Ellen noticed Martha's eyes becoming glassy. "I think you're forgetting about Martha."

"I'm sorry. I didn't think."

Martha cleared her throat.

Victoria added, "That's one of my problems. I sometimes say too much."

"No, sister, that's all right. I'm afraid I'm having a hard time too." Martha stopped her work and looked away.

Ellen and Victoria waited for her to go on.

"I stopped to see Corrine and Warren and the girls. I know it's not right to speak ill of the dead. But I can't believe what P.J. did when he treated Warren so harshly, demanding either the money or making them meet his tough conditions. How could my brother be so terrible?"

Ellen held her tongue and then spoke. "And I'm afraid Larry isn't any better."

"I saw what that house is like. It was good of Glenn Robertson to let Corrine and Warren live in the house, but it's in terrible shape. It's cold all the time."

Matthew appeared at the kitchen door. "I think it's time we get over to Corrine's and Warren's and do some fixing up. The boys and I—and perhaps Ed—will go. The house doesn't have to be that drafty."

Ellen looked up, surprised. "Where did you come from?"

"You women were so busy talking you didn't hear me."

"I'm afraid for those little girls," said Martha. "They're freezing all the time."

"We'll see what we can do."

By this time, Ellen had put the pies in the oven. The baking pies filled the room with the fragrance of pumpkin and apple.

"I think it's time for coffee," announced Ellen. "I made some gingersnap cookies earlier today. Let's have a sample."

The fragrance, along with Ellen's announcement, brought the four children to the kitchen. Soon both children and adults were drinking coffee and enjoying fresh cookies. Ellen loved the warmth of family as Thanksgiving Day approached. But Mother Anderson was not present in her usual place.

In the midst of their lively conversation came sounds from upstairs. It was a scream or a loud shout.

"It's Ma," shouted Matthew. "Something's wrong."

Ellen ran upstairs, followed by Matthew. Victoria and Martha sat, dumbfounded.

As Ellen and Matthew looked into the darkened room, Elizabeth Anderson sat at the edge of her bed, crying. "Oh no, it can't be. Lord, you can't let this happen. You can't. You can't." At those last words she was shouting.

"Ma, what's wrong?" Matthew moved close to his mother. By this time Victoria and Martha, along with the four children, were standing in the doorway.

"I had the most awful dream. It seemed as if it really happened."

"What was it?" several voices echoed.

"It's Mary. I dreamed she had died, and I stood in front of her casket. I saw the three children there with Ed. They were all crying. It seemed so real."

Chapter Fourteen

Martha moved into the room and sat beside her mother, placing her arm on her shoulder. "Mother, it was only a dream. And remember Mary is getting better. She was home just a short time ago."

"But she's in that sanitarium, and she's so far away."

Ellen had felt concerned about Mary, but felt no need to voice her concerns. "We need to leave this in the Lord's hands."

Ellen's words had a calming effect. Elizabeth Anderson lay back. "I'm just a little nervous. I'm terribly tired."

Martha tucked the blankets around her mother just the way Elizabeth Anderson had done for each of her own children.

"I'm so tired now. I think I can sleep." Elizabeth closed her eyes.

The family members quietly left.

"I could use one last sip of coffee before bed," said Victoria.

Within minutes the family was once more enjoying cookies and fellowship. Life was good.

Thanksgiving morning, Matthew decided to do the chores by himself. He wanted to let the boys sleep. And Ellen had much to take care of in the kitchen.

He thought of other Thanksgivings and the changes through the years. One year ago, P.J. had been very much a part of the family and all the events. And Matthew had taken Pa pretty much for granted.

Just as Matthew finished the chores, a pickup drove into the yard. It was Glenn Robertson.

"Mornin' Matthew. I thought I'd stop. There's something I think you ought to know, and it's hard to talk in church without all kinds of people hearing."

Matthew greeted his friend and wondered what news was that important.

"It's about Larry."

Matthew audibly groaned. "What's he done now?"

"Well, we don't exactly know, but I happened to hear something."

"Sounds serious."

Glenn stepped closer to his friend. "I stopped at the Lake View Inn last night."

Matthew looked surprised. "That's not exactly a place you normally go, is it? That's where the beer drinkers hang out."

"You know me better than that, Matthew. My cousin Frank was staying at the inn and insisted that I meet him there."

Matthew nodded.

"We were sitting in a booth and Larry was in the next booth. He was meeting with someone from the city. They were whispering, but I have good ears."

"What did you hear?"

"I couldn't really see the other fellow, but he had a large amount of money. It didn't feel right. The man kept saying 'You have to hide it in a safe place.' And Larry said he had exactly the right place."

Matthew scratched his head. "I thought P.J.'s change of heart had solved the problem. But now Larry is going down the same road."

"I thought you'd want to know."

Matthew thanked his friend and Glenn left.

The next hour was filled with delightful confusion as family and guests readied themselves for the Thanksgiving service. Ma was her old self.

Matthew loved the quiet in the church before the Thanksgiving service. The word "sanctuary" meant to him a place of refuge. It was also a place where he often made decisions, decisions that became turning points in his life.

Larry. What could he do to stop his nephew from following in P.J.'s footsteps? Matthew remembered the little boy he had played with. How could this gentle little boy turn into a duplicate of his father?

"Lord, what can I do?" he whispered. "Lord, what *should* I do?"

The organist began playing Thanksgiving hymns. Matthew tried to put thoughts of Larry aside. In a moment he observed James at the piano. James would be playing as part of a piano-organ duet. The familiar strains of "Come Ye Thankful People, Come" sounded through the old church. Beneath his breath Matthew whispered, "I'm so proud of you, son."

As the hymns and sermon took place, Matthew silently prayed. "Lord, You have blessed me beyond all comprehension. A great farm. A good

Chapter Fourteen

season of growing. A great family. I'm proud of these kids. My sisters. Friends. Thank You."

When the service ended, he looked around for Ed and his family. They were not present. He knew there were problems. He missed Mary. He prayed for her healing. And then there was Larry. And he wondered what Rita might try.

Matthew was always amazed at Ellen and the way she could organize a big family gathering. Of course, she had Victoria and Martha helping her, and they were equally good in their own ways. But this year more than ever, Ma stayed in the background.

At noon sharp, Ellen announced. "We'll get the food on the table whether Ed and the kids are here or not."

As if by clock work, Ellen placed the turkey platter at the head of the table. The meat was already cut and ready to serve. Victoria and Martha placed other foods nearby. The five Anderson children and Warren and Corrine's three girls scrambled to find their places.

Just as the family members found their seats, Ed, Beth, Jake, and Irene arrived.

"Dad never gets ready on time," said Beth.

Ed gave her an angry nudge.

"That's OK," said Ellen. "You're just in time. We'll pray and then we can eat."

Ellen pointed to chairs at the big dining room table and the added picnic table. People seated themselves. "Let's all pray the traditional table prayer today. We must be thankful for the Lord's bounty."

Slowly, members of the group joined in the simple prayer. "Come, Lord Jesus, be our guest. Let these gifts to us be blest. Amen."

Never before had Matthew thought how inclusive this little prayer was. He envisioned Jesus as one of the guests seated at the table.

While many thoughts passed through Matthew's mind, there was happy and busy conversation. Margaret fed Michael. She had become a real little mother. The children, James, Johnie, and Carol, interacted as usual with their cousins Beth, Jake, and Irene as well as Warren and Corrine's three girls.

Beyond the Storm

Matthew couldn't help feeling happy that Martha would be settling in Lake View. And Corrine and Warren and their three girls would now be a regular part of these family gatherings.

This family gathering was like a movie. Sometimes much seemed to be happening, but then there were the quiet moments. Matthew experienced a warm feeling as the family spent those moments together. How quickly the meal ended!

"Anyone for dessert now?" asked Ellen. "Or shall we wait with the apple and pumpkin pies until later?"

The chorus of voices seemed to say, "I'm full. Let's wait."

And so, with little ado, the children—except for little Michael, who protested with loud cries—all went outside to find adventures of one kind or another.

The women gathered in the kitchen. Matthew and Ed and Warren found a corner of the living room to talk.

Matthew knew it was hard for most men to express feelings. He had learned to let go of feelings and express them to Ellen or Glenn or to God during his time in prayer. Such expression meant a great relief and release.

Some days Ed would speak those deeper feelings, and this was such a day.

Ed looked away from the other two men as he spoke. "Sometimes, I don't know what I'm going to do without Mary around. She kept us together. I never realized how important she was."

Warren stretched out his legs. "I don't know what I'd do without Corrine."

"I guess we men are pretty dependent on our wives," Matthew added.

Ed began to ramble on. "The house just doesn't seem right without Mary. It's empty. It's as if something is missing. And the kids…sometimes I don't know what to do."

Matthew listened, realizing his brother-in-law needed to talk.

"Beth is withdrawn half the time. She's going out with some boy and I'm worried about that. And Jake is angry all the time. He works hard some times; then other times he deliberately disobeys me. He's nasty to poor Irene."

Matthew wanted to say something comforting. "But Mary will be back. She looked so good at P.J.'s funeral."

Chapter Fourteen

"P.J.'s death was hard on her." Ed stared out the window. "She's had a setback."

"I'm sorry to hear that. We missed you in church this morning." The minute he said the words, Matthew regretted them.

Ed grunted. "I didn't feel like going, and the kids didn't want to—except Irene. Anyhow, I don't understand how God could let a good person like Mary suffer with TB. It's not fair. And, frankly, God makes me angry for letting this happen."

Matthew was at a loss for words.

"God doesn't seem to care for Mary or for what happens."

Matthew remembered all too vividly his own brush with death. "Ed, I can guarantee you that God does care. It's not clear why some of these terrible things happen. When I had my brush with death, God became more real than ever. I've had tough times, but God has guided me."

"I'm afraid I'm not good like you," said Ed. "I don't have your faith."

"Neither do I," added Warren. "I've had a difficult time understanding these hard times. And I can't help feeling angry at P.J. and the way he got me to rent the land and then backed out."

Matthew wanted to give more of a defense of his faith, but words would not come. Warren and Ed went on and on about the rough times and all the unfairness. Both seemed angry at God for letting such things happen.

As the two angry men ran out of steam, Matthew spoke. "We live in a fallen and sinful world. That's why these things happen. God doesn't want terrible things to happen, but they do because men are greedy and sinful. However, God guides His children through the tough times. He wants us to help one another."

Ed's anger appeared to subside. "Things have worked out for you and Ellen. This Thanksgiving dinner has helped me get my mind off my problems."

"And it got Corrine and me and the girls out of a cold house," added Warren.

Matthew stretched and stood up. "Ed, you and I and the boys are going over to that house. I've got some pieces of lumber. We'll fix the entry and do some work around the windows. And we'll put some straw around the foundation to keep out the cold and draft."

Warren interrupted. "We can't expect you to do all that work."

This time Ed answered. "We're family. We will help."

Matthew smelled brewing coffee.

Victoria entered. "Why don't you get the kids in? It's time for dessert."

Matthew hurried outside and called the kids. At first there was no response.

Then he heard Margaret. "We're on our way. But some are still back on the pond."

The adults soon were seated at the table, eating pumpkin or apple pie. Conversation was quiet and restrained.

Victoria, so often a take-charge person, announced to Matthew, "I think we should go over and get Mother's sewing machine. She's going to do more sewing now that she's here."

"Yes," said Ma, "I've decided I need to make myself useful. I guess I'll stay here for the winter. Next spring, I'm going back to my house."

Matthew wasn't sure Ma would be strong enough to go back even in the spring.

Suddenly the door burst open. Jake shouted the words, "Dad, let's go home right away."

"What happened to you?" demanded Ed. "You have blood all over yourself."

"Nothing. Let's go."

"Oh, no we're not going. We haven't finished our pie. There's pie for you and the rest of the kids."

"I don't want any dumb pie." With those words Jake left, slamming the door.

Victoria sat up erect. "That boy needs to learn some manners."

Ed's face reddened. "He needs to blow off steam."

The door opened with Carol and Irene entering first; then Margaret and the younger three girls, and finally Johnie and Beth.

"What happened?" demanded Ed.

"Johnie and Jake got into a big fight," said little Connie, Corrine's oldest daughter. "And Johnie won."

Ellen gave Johnie a stern look. "You know how we feel about fighting. There are better ways to settle differences."

"Johnie was mean to my brother," said Irene.

Ed glared at Johnie. "What's the meaning of this? You're bigger and older than Jake. Why did you beat him up?"

Irene repeated her accusations.

"That's not true!" cried Margaret.

Chapter Fourteen

Johnie, red-faced and obviously angry, quietly left the room. An awkward silence followed.

"I think we better go home," announced Ed. "Come, Beth and Irene. We're going."

Ellen tried to encourage them to stay. "We need to get to the bottom of this and work out the problem."

"This isn't the first time." Ed found his jacket. He turned to Ellen. "Thank you for the dinner. It was a great meal." With those words, Ed and his daughters left the family gathering.

Surprised and puzzled looks showed on the faces of all who remained.

Just then Matthew noticed that James was missing.

"Where's James?" asked Ellen. "We need to find out what happened."

Margaret, half in tears, began to tell the story. "Jake's a real bully. He started saying nasty things about James. He made fun of him for playing the piano. He said he was some kind of sissy."

"We've got to find him!" Ellen exclaimed.

"James is all right," said Margaret. "He wants to be by himself."

"What happened when Jake bullied James?" demanded Victoria.

Johnie quietly entered and spoke. "He pushed James around and made fun of him. James wouldn't fight. I couldn't stand to see what Jake did. I warned Jake, and he tried pushing me around. I gave him a good punch."

"What happened to James?" questioned Matthew.

"He ran off." Johnie's fist showed blood. "His feelings were hurt. He couldn't take any more of Jake's bullying."

Victoria rose to the occasion. "It sounds to me as if Jake got what he deserved. I shouldn't say anything, but he's running with a bad crowd. And he's turned into a bully."

Ellen cut several pieces of pie and brought out more cups for coffee or lemonade. "We'll settle this later."

Later that evening with company gone, Matthew and Johnie finished chores and washed up. Matthew enjoyed the warmth of the living room, but wondered about James.

"I'm worried about James," said Ellen. "He's been gone for hours. I know James often goes off by himself, but this is a little too long."

Just as Matthew was about to respond, a door opened quietly. James entered.

"We've been worried about you." Ellen showed that mother's concern.

"I'm sorry, Dad. I missed chores. I'll get up tomorrow and Johnie can sleep."

Matthew could see that James's eyes were red. He knew that the words of his cousin had hurt him more than any physical pain.

Matthew wanted to say what was in his heart. The words came slowly and deliberately. "James, I'm proud of you. You have talent. You will go far." He turned to Johnie. "I'm proud of you, too. You were right to defend your brother."

Matthew felt Ellen's hand in his.

CHAPTER 15

December 1940

Ellen knocked gently on the spare bedroom door. The sounds of James at his typewriter continued though others were in bed. She had been concerned about her son ever since the Thanksgiving fight. He kept to himself and always seemed quiet and preoccupied.

The typing stopped. James opened the door.

"Mother, did I disturb you?"

Ellen moved into the room and closed the door. "No, James. I've just been concerned about you."

"Mother, I've had school work, and I've had this terrific idea for a story. It's a story about the Armistice Day storm. I'd like to send it to a magazine."

"James, this is about something else. Ever since that episode with Jake, you've been different. You haven't been talking. You avoid your brothers and sisters. And you and I haven't talked."

"Sorry, Mother."

"Something's bothering you." Ellen stopped, waiting for an answer.

James hesitated. "Jake's a bully. He's not a nice person. What he said hurt me."

"He shouldn't have said what he did, but Jake's hurting, too. With your Aunt Mary away at the sanitarium, he's feeling lost."

James clenched his fist. "He's still a jerk."

Ellen smiled, knowing her son was right.

"I guess I'm different." James paused. "I'm not like the other guys. I love this farm, but I don't like tractors or machinery. I'm not good at sports. I love learning and music and writing. I just don't fit in."

Ellen took her son's hand. "My dear, you are unique. You have a special purpose. When you were very sick as a baby, we didn't expect you to live. I prayed fervently that you would live."

"You never told me much about that."

"I begged God to let you live. I gave the outcome to the Lord. I committed you to God, asking that He would have you and use you. And I know that is happening."

Ellen saw tears in her son's eyes.

"James, you have musical talent. And you can write. You have academic abilities far beyond most people your age. God will use that."

"But I can't see myself as a minister."

"Son, that's your choice only if it's what you feel God leads you to. God can use music and writing and academic accomplishment."

"But, Mother, I feel I'd like to be strong like the other guys. Look at how strong Johnie is. He's bigger and stronger than I am. I'm supposed to be the big brother."

The door opened a crack.

"You're strong in other ways."

"But Mother, I wish I could really be like the other guys. I'd like to be the one to help Johnie, not this way around."

Johnie opened the door quietly and stepped in. "James, I don't think this family could take two of me. You're strong in a different way. I haven't said it, but I do look up to you as a big brother. I wish I had your brains. I could never do half of what you can do."

"And I wish I could handle machinery the way you do. And I'd like to be tough like you."

Ellen wanted to hold both boys in her arms the way she did when they were small. "I'm proud of both of you. You'll always be my boys, but you're young men. And you're both strong—in different ways."

Johnie continued what he had to say. "I know I've got a temper. I can't stand to see a bully have control. Jake isn't that strong, but he thinks he's tough. I'm happy that I put him in his place."

Chapter Fifteen

Ellen smiled. "I guess if I'd been a guy, I would feel the same way."

"Thanks." James covered the typewriter. "I'm fortunate to have a great family."

"And," said Ellen, "I think it's time for bed. Tomorrow's Saturday, and there's work to do."

Awkwardly, James stood and extended his hand to his brother. "I'm fortunate to have such a good brother. I need you, brother."

"And I need you." The firm handshake tightened into a small contest. "James, you're stronger than you think."

The brothers moved to their bedroom. Ellen went downstairs and returned to Matthew. She was surprised to find him still awake.

"You must have been having a serious talk. Is James OK?"

Ellen slowly got into bed beside her husband. "You know we have a couple of exceptional sons. James was deeply hurt by Jake's bullying, but he'll be all right. He has unique talents and purpose. I think he knows that."

"James will go far. He's not made for the farm."

"And Johnie," she added, "I can't get over how big a man he's become. Actually, I'm proud that Johnie defended his brother. They're so different from one another, but there's a strong bond between them."

"I'm proud of our sons." Matthew yawned and added, "We've got some great kids. Margaret's wonderful the way she cares for people, and for little Michael."

"Michael seems so much like Johnie, it almost scares me. He's quite a handful, and so was Johnie. Even now, as a mother, I guess I worry, even though I shouldn't."

"And there's Carol." Matthew smiled.

"I think of her, and I'm not so sure. The others are on the right track, but I'm not quite so sure about Carol."

"Carol will turn out all right." Matthew paused a moment. "Think of all the years we've been together, and of all that's happened."

Ellen calculated the years. "Next year, we'll be married eighteen years. Five children. They're growing up so fast. Think of the changes during our time together."

"All those changes scare me." Matthew moved closer to Ellen. "What will the next few years hold? War? I think of the Nazis bombing England's cities. How long can America stay out of this war? How can we let these things happen? I keep wondering about Joe. What will he have to go through?"

Beyond the Storm

"Dear Matthew, it's out of our hands, and we won't solve these problems tonight. We can just be happy our children and your mother are safe within these walls."

"God is good. He will guide us."

Ellen lay for an hour, thinking. Then she drifted into a deep sleep. She felt safe with Matthew beside her.

Johnie had never liked school. He hated being cooped up with books and a lot of people. On the other hand, he loved Saturdays when he could be alone outdoors.

"You can go. I'll finish letting in the cattle," said Matthew.

Johnie grabbed his skates hanging on a peg on the barn wall. Followed by Rover, he was off to the pond. He didn't need to skate; he just wanted to feel the freedom and enjoy the pure, clean, whiteness of a winter day in December. When Johnie knelt to put on his skates, Rover licked his face.

He thought of the girls from school who liked him. Most seemed to like him better than he liked them. But then there was Laura, so dark and petite. She didn't seem to give him the time of day. Yet he knew she liked him.

Dad had always said he could go out on a date when he had earned enough money to pay his own way. He was too young to date at fifteen. Dad was pretty old-fashioned about such things. And Laura's father probably thought she was too young for a boyfriend.

Johnie stood up on his skates and glided along, avoiding ice that was covered with snow. Rover ran along close by. A young man couldn't find a better companion than Rover. This was freedom. This was the good life. As he turned around to come back to his starting point, he saw a figure nearby. It was Dad. Johnie quickly unfastened his skates and walked to his father. "You don't have to quit," Dad said.

His father seemed to be in one of his reflective moods. "This white snow is clean and good. I just like to stop working and enjoy it. There's no place in the world more beautiful than this."

"We agree on that," said Johnie. "I don't think I want to be anywhere else."

Father and son seemed to communicate without words.

Chapter Fifteen

"Dad, I've been thinking. Even though the teachers think I don't pay attention, I've been hearing and thinking about Hitler and the Nazis."

"I dread the thought of another war like the Great War. This one will be far more deadly."

"Hitler's a bully. We can't let him get away with it. He's making Germany into a bully for the rest of the world. And there's Japan, too."

"So you've been reading and listening more than we thought." Matthew sighed deeply. "There are no easy answers."

"If America goes to war, I know I have to go. I can't take the easy way out."

"But, Son, you'll be in school or farming. Farmers are exempt. Farming is an essential occupation."

"I'd hate to leave, Dad, but I know I'd have to. I'll soon be old enough."

"Joe feels the way you do."

Father and son walked back toward the barnyard and the house, deep in conversation.

"We're having an early dinner," Ellen announced. "Ed called. He can help with some carpentry work over at Corrine's and Warren's. I'll take some soup over for supper."

"How about the girls?" asked Matthew.

"I'm leaving them here to take care of Michael."

Johnie looked with admiration at Uncle Ed as he unloaded lumber. He wished he would become that strong. And this uncle had a way of giving orders, though Johnie didn't always like his arbitrary ways.

"Jake and I'll get to work on repairing some of the molding around the windows." Ed looked at Matthew. "You and James and Johnie can haul straw to bank around the house. Warren, come with me and show me the places that need the most work."

"Most of those windows need repair," said Warren, "Corrine can show you what's needed most. The tractor isn't working right now. I better take care of getting the horses hitched to the hayrack."

Johnie couldn't help noticing the condition of the barn. The cattle could always survive, but this barn was badly in need of repair.

Warren pointed to the snow that was near the house. "We need to dig away some of the snow so that we can get the straw right up to the house. I should have done something before the snows came."

Matthew asked James to work on the shoveling. It took only a short time to load the hayrack with straw. Johnie kept wondering why Warren hadn't thought of this sooner. The job could have been done by one man before the snow fell.

The next hours went by quickly. Ed gave most of the orders. With his carpentry skills, he did most of the nailing and measuring, assisted by Jake. The others cleaned up, ran errands, and did the other tasks.

As the men and boys loaded the pickup with unused boards and scrap, Ellen opened the door and called out, "Soup's on. We'll have an early supper."

When Johnie smelled the chicken soup, he realized he was terribly hungry. Several answered, "We'll be right in."

Suddenly Ed's voice sounded above all the other talk and noise. "Boy, what did you say? I want no more of your big mouth!"

Johnie couldn't hear what Jake said in response.

"You come here." Ed grabbed the stick. His six-foot solid frame towered menacingly over his five-seven son. Jake came reluctantly to his father.

"Dad, I didn't mean anything. You always take it wrong."

Ed flushed red with anger and yelled even louder. "It's time for a session behind the woodshed."

Ed grabbed his son's arm and dragged him behind the woodshed. Soon the sounds of a stick repeatedly hitting a human body could be heard.

"Don't, Dad. It hurts!"

The words of profanity coming from Ed were words that Johnie had rarely heard. His dad and the people he knew didn't talk that way.

Johnie and the others stood motionless, stunned by what was happening. The whipping continued.

Matthew, normally so quiet and gentle, ran to the woodshed. "Ed, you've got to stop. The boy's had enough."

Ed swore. "It's not up to you to tell me how to handle my kid."

Jake came out, hiding his face. The tough kid was sobbing.

Chapter Fifteen

Ed pushed Jake toward the pickup. He opened the door. "Get in! I've had enough out of you."

Johnie stood silent, not quite believing what had happened. The others said nothing.

"We're going." With those words Ed got in the pickup and drove away.

Warren motioned for the others to go into the house. "I knew Ed had a temper, but I didn't realize how bad it is."

"He's having a rough time now that Mary's away. He's at a breaking point," said Matthew.

Johnie entered the small kitchen last, following Warren, his father, and James. He began to understand something about Jake.

Ellen dished up the soup, and Corrine poured coffee and put bread and crackers on the table. Johnie was ready to eat.

"We couldn't help hearing all the shouting out there," said Ellen. "What happened?"

Corrine arranged chairs so that her guests could sit. "I'm glad the girls ate first. I hope they didn't hear all that profanity. They're upstairs playing with their dolls. It's the first time they've felt warm enough to be away from the stoves. Ed's carpentry has already helped make this house livable."

Ellen began dishing up the soup. "Let's pray, so these hungry men can eat."

Johnie looked to Warren and Corrine to begin the prayer. Then in unison Matthew and Ellen began, "Come, Lord Jesus...."

The prayer ended. Johnie noticed how good the soup tasted—vegetables and chicken and dumplings. No one cooked better than his mother.

Ellen repeated her question. "What happened out there?"

Matthew answered. "I'm not sure. Jake's been sassy. He must have said something to Ed. Ed flew off the handle and ended up beating him. He was out of control."

Johnie couldn't help adding, "Jake never cries, but he was crying. Uncle Ed beat him with that stick. It was terrible."

"I'm afraid he might have killed Jake if you hadn't stopped him," said Warren.

Matthew interrupted, "No, that wouldn't have happened. Ed gets angry easily, but then he's sorry for his actions. He's probably feeling sorry for what he did. And apologizing to Jake right now."

James looked across to Johnie and his father. "I'm glad you're our dad and not Uncle Ed. Jake bullies the way he does because his father treats him that way. Uncle Ed is always criticizing Jake and putting him down."

Johnie agreed. "I feel sorry for Jake. He's become a jerk and a bully because he's treated badly."

"We have to do something about this," announced Ellen. "I have a large beef roast that's thawing out. It's time to ask Ed and the kids over for Sunday dinner. We've got to try to make things better."

Johnie wondered how this would help.

"We have to try," his father added.

The group ate in silence for a few moments, but began to chat with animation as second and third bowls of soup were dished up.

As they finished the soup, Ellen brought out big pieces of chocolate cake with thick frosting.

Johnie and James gobbled down their pieces. The others were more restrained in their enthusiasm.

Later after the dishes were washed and put away and the Andersons got up to leave, Warren's tough-looking features were soft as he spoke haltingly. "I don't know if we could have made it through the winter without your help. You've been kind. We're beholden to you."

Corrine's eyes filled with tears. "You brought food and you brought warmth. The house is comfortable, now. Thank you."

"Ed was part of this too," reminded Matthew.

"I know," said Warren. "Watching his anger today has taught me a lesson. I've been angry, especially with P.J. and Larry. But I can't hold on to that anger. I have to let it go."

Johnie saw his parents exchange glances. Then his father spoke. "Forgiveness is the only way and it can only be done with God's help."

Johnie felt proud of his father. He wanted to become that kind of man—a man with strong convictions.

Warren hesitated. "I have a long way to go, but I'm learning. Thank you."

As Johnie drove the car home he said, "I wish we could do something about Jake."

"All we can do is try," said his mother. "People don't change all at once. Some people never change. But with God's help, we'll do the best we know how to help him."

Chapter 16

That Friday afternoon in December, Matthew enjoyed the delicious aroma of Christmas cookies the women were baking. "Ma, there's something we need to talk about."

"No time like the present." Ma handed the pan to Ellen. "These can go in the oven."

"I think you'll like what Matthew has to tell you," said Ellen. "We've waited because P.J.'s death was still too fresh in our minds."

Ma sat down at the kitchen table. She took off her apron.

"I have a letter from P.J. He has directed Rita to sign the farm back to you and me though he keeps the lake property and signs eighty acres over to Larry."

Ma looked down. "So he did regret his deeds at the end. I hope he really meant it."

Matthew remembered only too vividly what Dr. Baker had said. Somehow the picture of his tormented brother would never fade. He hoped that in some way P.J. became a believer during his last moments.

"I've felt way down in the dumps lately." Ma folded her worn and wrinkled hands. "I've wondered how I could go on living."

"We're here," said Matthew. "And we go on because of the kids."

Ma looked up at Matthew. "I don't know what I would have done if it hadn't been for you and Ellen and the children. I think I would just have lain down and died."

"We're family." Ellen opened the oven door to check the cookies.

"We felt you should know what we're doing. We're going over to see Rita and Larry." Matthew hesitated. "We wondered if you would stay with Michael and see that he's OK until the kids come home from school."

Ma laughed. "I'll watch. But I can't possibly keep up with that boy."

A half-hour later Matthew and Ellen knocked at the door of P.J.'s mansion. Someone seemed to be rushing around inside. Finally the door opened.

Rita greeted them. "Won't you come in? I'm surprised to see you."

Matthew sensed a kinder attitude in his sister-in-law than he had ever felt before. "We have something we want to talk over with you."

"Why don't you come into the living room and have some coffee. I was just having some myself."

What a surprise! Except for that one Christmas celebration, Matthew could not remember a time when Rita had warmly welcomed them.

Ellen responded to the invitation.

"It seems awfully quiet around here." Matthew looked around into the hallway and saw no activity. "You usually have so many people around."

"The guests and business people have gone." Rita sighed. "I don't know when I've felt so alone."

Matthew and Ellen both expressed their sympathies. Ellen added, "But to use the old cliché, life must go on."

"I'm trying."

Matthew sipped his coffee and waited for the right moment to bring up the subject.

Finally, Ellen brought out the letter that P.J. had written before his death. "We have this letter. That's what we wanted to talk with you about."

Rita read the letter, showing little or no reaction.

Matthew waited for her to speak. "We feel this should be taken care of soon. It's what P.J. wanted."

Rita looked over to the mantle above the fireplace to the portrait of her and P.J. She wiped away a tear. "I don't know what to say."

Chapter Sixteen

"What P.J. said is quite clear." Ellen put down her cup. "The farm should be back with the family."

Rita remained silent.

Matthew thought of more arguments. "Larry can stay here with you. He should not be living in Ma's house. That is clearly hers."

Rita looked away. "I have no control over Larry. He's supposed to be farming, but he's deep in business deals. I don't even know what those deals are."

"Now that your business associates aren't here, Larry can move in," argued Ellen. "You have plenty of room for him even if the business people come."

Rita ignored Ellen's comment. "Yes, but I can't figure out Larry. For some reason he wants to be in that little house." She hesitated. "Sometimes he scares me. He's angry and determined."

Matthew couldn't understand Rita's changed attitude.

"We're sorry to bring up this business, but we felt it was time." Ellen stood up. "Is there anything we can do for you? I know this is a difficult time."

All at once Matthew felt sorry for his sister-in-law. "Come visit us."

"Why don't you come for Sunday dinner? We're going to ask Ed and the kids to come too."

Rita hesitated. "That would be a good break. I'll see."

The threesome talked about earlier times before life had become so complicated. Matthew yearned for those simpler times.

After a while, they returned to the subject of Larry. Almost abruptly Rita blurted out, "If you want to carry out Paul John's wishes, you'll have to talk to Larry."

Matthew and Ellen stood at the door to the little house that Ma and Pa had lived in so many years. They knocked. No one answered.

"Matthew. Ellen. I'll be there in just a minute. I'm finishing some work in the barn," called the voice. "Walk in. Larry should be there."

Matthew turned to see Joan hurrying toward the house.

Ellen called to Joan. "Should you be doing all that work now that you're pregnant?"

Matthew and Ellen waited as Joan came up to them.

"I'm a healthy farm girl. I like being outdoors working. And besides Larry has all kinds of business to take care of."

As Joan came near, Matthew noticed a bruised lip. "What happened?"

Joan covered her lip. "Oh, I guess I'm just accident prone. One of those cows bumped me. Pay no attention."

Matthew knew something was wrong. These were not just accidents. Something else was going on.

Joan led Matthew and Ellen into the kitchen. She called to Larry.

Larry's voice came from upstairs. "Don't interrupt me. I'm busy. You're getting to be more trouble than you're worth."

Joan avoided the gazes of Matthew and Ellen. "Larry, we have company."

Larry came down the stairs. "I didn't realize you were here. I'm busy. I'm taking care of Dad's business. There's a lot more than you realize."

Matthew hesitated, feeling some of the same anger he had felt for P.J. It was as if P.J.'s shadow fell across his life even now.

Ellen replied quickly. "We do have business, Larry, your father's business. Matthew, show him the letter."

Matthew handed him the letter.

Larry glanced at the letter, hardly taking time to read all of the details. "I don't know that this letter means much. Dad's mind wasn't clear at the end. He was having weird hallucinations."

"The letter states your father's wishes. It is up to you and your mother to see that they are carried out."

"Nothing is up to me. The legal inheritance will take care of itself. When and if I'm ready, I'll move on."

Matthew stiffened in anger. He said nothing.

Ellen's commanding tone caught the attention of Larry. "You forget something else, Larry. Your grandmother has lifetime rights to this house. You have no business being here."

Larry stumbled over the next words. "I don't think Grandma would kick me out of this house into the cold."

Ellen cleared her throat. "Your mother has room for you."

"But," Larry interrupted, "that's so far from the barn and other outbuildings and the cattle. That would be inconvenient."

Matthew finally found words. "If Corrine and Warren had been here, we wouldn't have these problems."

Chapter Sixteen

"Uncle Matthew, you can't blame me for their problems."

Matthew realized silence was the best response. Even though he had been learning to be more forceful, he knew that the soft answer or no answer could turn away wrath.

All this time, Joan stood by, looking fearfully at her husband.

Larry turned to Joan. "And besides, you don't want my wife to go to all the work of moving again."

Matthew looked at Joan's bruised lip. "Larry, you shouldn't have your wife doing all those chores. It's not good for a woman in her condition."

Joan didn't hesitate. "Remember, I'm a farm girl. I like the outdoor work. Milking cows and feeding chickens are second nature to me."

"It's Joan's choice." Larry went on with his argument. "This farm was legally my father's farm. Now, it comes to me. The law will back me up."

An awkward silence followed.

"It's time to go," said Ellen. "I think it's about time we have a lawyer look into this situation. I think we might be able to prove the deception and lies."

Larry looked visibly shaken by Ellen's words.

Matthew gazed directly at his nephew. "Larry, you need to take care of your wife. She can't afford to have any more of those 'accidents'."

"We'll work things out." Larry shifted uncomfortably. "Besides, we'll see that Grandma can move back into her house in the spring."

Matthew again looked at Joan and then at Larry. "You need to take care of your wife. Get her to a doctor. It's your responsibility!"

Larry did a mock salute. "Aye, aye, Sir."

Ellen moved toward the door with Matthew following. "Larry, you plan to take care of things, or we will."

"Yes ma'am."

Joan's eyes were filled with tears as she spoke. "I don't want trouble. You're my family too. I love you."

Ellen turned back and gave Joan a hug. "I know, dear, this is not an easy time for you. We'll be praying for you."

Matthew and Ellen left the little house. Matthew drove down the driveway. As he turned on to the township road, he looked back to the spot where the big house had once stood. "It seems unreal. Larry is exactly like his father, only P.J. had a conscience. It seems that Larry doesn't."

"Larry's headed for trouble. Serious trouble."

Beyond the Storm

Sunday morning, the strains of a familiar hymn came from the Reed organ. Matthew often used these moments to think through problems. Solutions often seemed clear after such a time of meditation. Today, though, no solutions came. The problems of the world seemed impossible.

Matthew began to pray about each of the problems. Mary in the TB sanitarium. Ed and the children's difficulties. Ed's violent temper. Jake and his bullying. Corrine and Warren in a run-down house. Larry and his questionable dealings. Control of the home farm. Ma's health. He silently named Ellen and each of the children.

Matthew turned around and looked two pews back to where Ed and his three children were seated. Ed nodded. Jake sat sullenly next to him, probably objecting to church attendance.

As the organist modulated into another hymn, Matthew continued to pray. "Thank You, Lord, for Ellen and my children. I know my kids aren't perfect, but they're on the right track. I don't know how it's ever going to happen, but guide all of these people into a relationship with You. Please guide Larry so that He doesn't follow in his father's footsteps. I'm afraid his end could be even worse."

The prelude ended and Pastor Strand announced the opening hymn. Matthew felt himself being led into the presence of the Lord as he sang, "Rejoice, rejoice believers. And let your lights appear." Anticipation and hope filled his whole being.

The family dinner turned into a large family gathering. Ellen managed to stretch the beef roast dinner with all the good trimmings for the unexpectedly large number. Rita accepted the invitation. Martha and Victoria came after a last-minute invitation. Ed and his children came as well as Corrine and Warren and their three girls. This gathering was about as complete as an Anderson gathering could be.

Matthew liked the time after dinner when the men relaxed in the living room. Ed and Warren and he sat back as the women chattered in the kitchen and washed dishes and did the other clean up. It didn't seem fair that the men had it so easy at this point, but then this was a brief break from man's hard work outdoors. And the children, eleven of them now

Chapter Sixteen

with Corrine and Warren's three girls, were outside skating and playing other winter games. Even little Michael was outside.

Matthew was about to doze off. He found there were times he needed some extra rest. But both Warren and Ed kept on talking. After talking about the threat of war and the changing world situation, Warren spoke some encouraging words.

"For the first time, I think I can make it through the winter. The house is warm and livable, and I got the first decent paycheck from the creamery."

"Do you have enough feed for the winter?" questioned Ed.

"My mother-in-law came through. She bought a load of oats from Glenn Robertson. That's paying off. You have to feed the cattle to get the milk production."

Matthew yawned. "That's what family's for."

"But," Warren responded, "I think a man needs to make it on his own. It's up to me to provide for Corrine and the girls. If I don't work and take care of my own family, I'm worse than a pagan."

Ed clenched his fist. "That's not true. You're working. You're doing your best. But when there are rough times, neighbors and family have to look out for one another. The time will come when you can help out someone else."

"I'm indebted to both of you."

Ed's fist unclenched, and gentleness replaced his harshness. "Your father, John Anderson, helped Mary and me just after we married. I couldn't have gotten ahead without that help."

"Pa was the salt of the earth. I'd give anything to become the man my father was. I miss him," said Matthew.

Ed continued to talk. "I know I've made some mistakes. I'm learning I can't make it on my own. I need the family. I need the cooperation of my kids. And...," his voice cracked, "...I need God's help."

Matthew sat up and leaned toward Ed. "I'm finding that out again and again. I wouldn't be alive if the Lord hadn't spared me."

Sounds of children returning from outside interrupted the conversation. Apparently Jake's bullying had not been a problem today.

Ed grew restless. "It's time to get home for chores."

Farm folk move through their days like clockwork with definite schedules. In a farm gathering, visits are cut short and people quickly leave when it's time to get home for chores. Ed and his children left, followed by Corrine and Warren and the girls. Martha and Victoria drove back to town. Ma returned to her room to take a nap. Only Rita remained. Today she was not acting the part of a fashionable socialite. She had said little, but it seemed she wanted to talk.

Matthew signaled for the boys to go outside and start the chores.

"Why don't you stay for supper?" invited Ellen. "The boys will do chores, and we'll eat afterwards."

"You've been so very kind," began Rita. "I know I have often been unfriendly. Paul John and I were always so busy."

"We understand you've had a hard time since P.J. died."

Matthew sat back and waited for Rita to go on.

"I need to say some things." Rita hesitated and went on. "I'd like to carry out Paul John's last request. I'm afraid Larry's gotten things messed up. He has control."

Ellen stiffened. "But you have control. You have the say."

"I'm afraid not. After my husband died, Larry came with some papers. I signed them without thinking. And there are some other factors."

"But," Ellen interrupted, "you can't let him get away with this. And besides the property must be probated to you before that can happen.'"

Rita's hands shook as she spoke. "I'm afraid of Larry. He becomes angry and violent. I know my husband wasn't completely honest. He had dealings with crooks. Those crooks were always kind and polite and pleasant to me."

Matthew spoke in disbelief. "I can't believe Larry would harm you in any way."

"He probably wouldn't. He's under pressure from those men who seem to have control. He becomes violent with words. And I'm afraid what he'd do or say when he doesn't get his way."

"You can't let this go on." Matthew stood up. "I think I should go help the boys with chores."

Rita stood. No longer did she appear the lady who was always in control. "I must be on my way. Yes, I have to do something. I can't go on this way."

"We're still your family." Ellen placed her hand on Rita's shoulder.

"But I have to face my own problems."

"Come again, soon. We can always set one more place for Sunday dinner."

"Thank you."

Rita hurried away.

Chapter 17

Christmas was fast approaching. Ellen sat down in her rocking chair to mend socks and listen to her radio programs. For those moments it seemed that Ma Perkins became her mother. And then the Youngs of "Pepper Young's Family" became her family. Her mother-in-law listened quietly and knitted.

Elizabeth Anderson had seemed more quiet than usual. No doubt she was still mourning the death of her son.

"I think I need to do some cleaning upstairs in the kids' rooms," Ellen announced. "They're so busy with school and others things, and they're not doing a good job."

Her mother-in-law set down her knitting. "I only dusted my room. I guess my 'get up and go' has gone."

"That's OK. You've earned some time off."

Ellen oiled the old dust mop and gathered the dust rags and went on upstairs to the boys' room.

As she dusted the floor of the room, she thought of her two boys and how different they were. Johnie, the younger, strong and athletic, the dependable mechanic and farm helper. And James, the artist and writer and dreamer.

In some ways Ellen felt James had a whole world within that she did not understand. He read books that she knew nothing about. He had a fascination for geography and faraway places.

Beyond the Storm

A sheaf of typewritten papers caught her eye. She always respected her children's privacy, but this seemed to invite her to read. Once she started to read, she couldn't stop.

"I have dreams. I look at the beauty of this place: the trees, the rolling hills, the fields, the lakes, the pasturelands. This area is almost the Garden of Eden in its beauty.

"Then, I look at the people around. Most do not see and appreciate this beauty. They work hard. They are good people. But they do not look to the hills and beyond. Some seem to see only the satisfaction of hard work. And that is good. I can work hard and feel satisfaction too. But I want something more. I look for something beyond these hills.

"There are good, honest people. I appreciate their struggles. I see the families around. I see my own family. There are stories to tell, and I would like to tell them. And there is music, and I'd love to play that music.

"I guess I'm different. Some people think I'm strange, and that hurts. Perhaps I shouldn't pay that much attention to Jake and those other hoodlums. But ridicule hurts. Being called a sissy or a girl is humiliating. I think it takes real strength to stand up and go against the crowd and be different.

"Most people here are not like Jake. I've met some of the kindest people I could ever imagine. Grandpa was big and strong, but I've seen how gentle he was with the horses. Yet, he could be firm at the times when firmness was needed. I would like to be that kind of man.

"And Grandpa loved people. I don't think he had any enemies. People looked on him as a giant among men. On the day he died, I saw the love he had for me and his family. He was like the Old Testament patriarch blessing his children and grandchildren.

"I think of Thomas Wolfe and *You Can't Go Home Again*. I hope he's wrong about not being able to go home after you leave. I have this incessant need to read and to learn and to make music and I don't think I can learn them here on the farm. There's an urge within me that I do not quite understand.

"I look at my family. I could not ask for a better mother and father. I don't think Dad understands me, but he has Johnie. I'm glad Johnie loves to drive the tractor because I'm no good with machines. At least Dad has one son who will stay and run the farm. Mother understands me better. I think I'm more like her. She understands my desire to learn.

"Now, back to my dreams. Going beyond the hills is something symbolic. In my mind I have already gone beyond this place. I want to

Chapter Seventeen

write the great American novel. My teacher says I have to write about what I know. I must write about life in these hills.

"When I look at other parents, I think I am the most fortunate of sons. I see fathers who try to force their sons and daughters into their molds. An oldest son must take over the family farm. A daughter is supposed to marry the neighbor boy. It becomes a rigid pattern."

At this point Ellen stopped reading. Should she go on? James was saying something very personal, and that might hurt. But something within her compelled her to continue reading.

"Matthew Anderson is probably one of the most kind and sensitive men around. He somehow feels he doesn't measure up because he has less education than the rest of the family. He's had some failures that have hurt. Perhaps those experiences have helped to build in him a kindness that most men do not possess.

"Dad loves the land. And he loved the old home place. When P.J. said he had ownership of it, that practically destroyed Dad. How could a brother do such a thing? Though Uncle P.J. did some kind things, I sometimes felt he was dark and evil—at least he had a dark side that wanted to manipulate and control people.

"There's a lesson Dad knows well. You can't control people. You have to let a person become who he really is.

"And Mother. How precious she is! Ellen Anderson is one of those exceptional ladies. As a teacher, she is probably better educated than others in the community. Everyone respects her. The kids call many women by their first names, but they always call Mother, Mrs. Anderson. I think she deserves that respect.

"Mom knows I have dreams to go beyond this place. She inspired me to be who I am. She taught me to play the piano even though most farm boys wouldn't think of doing such a thing. I guess she's responsible for encouraging me to be different. Mother has taught me to be tough and even stern and determined. She has the ways of a teacher that command respect. I'm not like Johnie so that I can win a fist fight, but I can win a verbal battle. And I aim to be good at that. After all, "the pen is mightier than the sword." Mother is my inspiration. She's the one who has taught me to go on resolutely, to study, to learn, to go beyond these ordinary expectations.

"Mom and Dad have brought five children into the world, all with distinctly different personalities. Look at me: I'm the bookworm and probably the future teacher. Then, there's Johnie, the athlete, the fighter, the mechanic, the future farmer. And Margaret probably will be a farmer's wife and teacher like her mother. She cares for people and for children. And who knows what Carol will become or do. I'm afraid she's headed for trouble. And, then, little Michael. He looks like Johnie. And I think in ways he is like Johnie.

"Well, that's the family.

"My brain is teeming with stories. I've met people who have dark secrets. Mother has told me some confidential stories that she knows. There are many more. People hide things; there are truths beneath the outward respectability. But there is the good and simple life. I want to capture this. There is excitement and joy in little things of life. How can I make these people and stories come alive?

"I remember that trip to Minneapolis with Cousin Pete. He's like an uncle. When I saw the city last summer, I was fascinated. I must go there as a student. But now I appreciate even more the life that I have here.

"Yes, I must tell of the rest of the stories of life. The humor, the tragedy, all that is a part of life.

"I must go beyond these hills I have seen almost every day of life. I must travel to New York. I want to see London and Paris and the highlands of Scotland and the beautiful Lake Country of England. Yes, I must live life to the fullest.

"Will I find someone to share the dream? I sometimes doubt it. My likes and interests are so different from those of anyone I know. But I will travel on until I find my dream. Dreams are the stuff life is made of."

Ellen put down the writing. "I didn't realize how determined James is. Now I understand." She felt guilty for uncovering her son's innermost thoughts. She shouldn't have snooped.

Her thoughts were interrupted by the opening of the outside door. She heard a voice calling, "Mrs. Anderson."

She hurried downstairs to the kitchen. There stood Carol, sullen and obviously unhappy. Beside her was her teacher, Miss. Wilson.

Before Carol could say a word, Miss Wilson spoke. "I'm sorry to barge in this way, but I felt we needed to talk."

Ellen surveyed the situation. "Should we send Carol to her room?"

"I think Carol needs to hear what I have to say."

"Why don't you take off your coat and sit down?" Ellen turned to Carol. "Take Miss Wilson's coat. You can lay it on my bed."

Carol obeyed without a word.

Chapter Seventeen

"I don't know exactly how to say this." Miss Wilson hesitated and then continued. "Ever since Margaret was promoted out of eighth grade into ninth at town school, Carol has been sullen and uncooperative. She's done sloppy work. And her grades show that carelessness."

Ellen turned to her daughter. "What does this mean?"

Carol looked down. "Miss Wilson thinks I should be as good a student as Margaret. But I don't have her brains. I'm not that good."

"Carol," interrupted Miss Wilson, "you know that's not true. Margaret studied hard and passed all the State Board Examinations so that she could go directly into high school. I'm afraid that if you keep going the way you are, you might fail the geography examination and the seventh grade."

"It's not fair," whimpered Carol.

"And, today, you were just plain nasty to me and your fellow students. You should be having fun when we practice the Christmas program."

"The program's stupid." Carol looked toward the door.

"That's no way to speak to your teacher. You owe Miss Wilson an apology."

Miss Wilson placed her hand on Carol's hand. "Most of the children are younger, Carol. It's written for them. But your part is different. You're reading Scripture, and your part is an adult part."

Ellen repeated, "You owe Miss Wilson an apology."

"I'm sorry for being rude," Carol began. "I guess I'm just an obnoxious kid."

Miss Wilson smiled. "Well, you have a good vocabulary. Where did you learn that word?"

"James used it on me. He said I was obnoxious." Carol's demeanor changed. "But Margaret's always getting breaks. I look just as old as Margaret."

Ellen used her teacher tone. "If you keep on this way, you won't be ready for high school a year from now. Your attitude needs to change."

Both mother and teacher looked at Carol.

"I guess you're right," said Carol reluctantly. "OK, I'll learn my part."

Ellen's eyes told Carol she needed to say more.

"I'm sorry. I'll work harder and be nice to others. But," she added, "I don't want anything to do with Freddie Smith."

Miss Wilson laughed. "Just ignore him."

Beyond the Storm

"How about some coffee and Christmas cookies?" invited Ellen. "Coffee is always a good ending to any discussion."

Matthew wanted to savor each moment of the Christmas season. He had to do the chores by himself because the boys and Margaret were staying after school to practice and get ready for the evening Christmas concert. Matthew was proud of the fact that these country kids had gone to town school and were doing well.

Christmas season always brought memories of the past to Matthew. He thought of all the years at the home farm when he and his father had done chores together. But that was in the past. This was a better farm, but even so he missed the home place.

He moved as quickly as he could to milk the fourteen cows and feed the calves and then the cattle. He was thankful the boys were around to help most of the time. Life would be more complicated if Johnie left.

Matthew finished the chores, quickly washed up, changed clothes, and joined Ellen and Ma and Carol and little Michael for supper. He learned of Carol's misbehavior. For punishment she would have to stay home from the high school concert with Michael. Her task was to study and be ready for her Christmas program the next day.

Matthew often wondered about Carol. The other three seemed to be on the right track, but Carol's behavior left something to be desired.

As they entered the gymnasium/auditorium, Ellen led the way. Matthew and Ma followed. The place was filling up quickly. Many proud parents and friends were gathered to hear the choir and band concert. The Christmas tree lights on the stage brought out that Christmas spirit within Matthew and signaled memories of Christmases past.

The program began with a flurry of activity. The Lake View High School band played a medley of Christmas carols. James had a trumpet solo with one of the Christmas carols. Johnie reluctantly played the trombone, and Margaret played her clarinet. Three of their children exhibited musical talent beyond his expectation.

As the audience applauded, many of the band members got up to take their positions with the choir. James moved to the piano, where he would accompany the group. Matthew saw James as the little boy who

Chapter Seventeen

loved to run off to the woods and dream. And now here he was performing in front of several hundred people.

Johnie, always the reluctant one in these matters, stood out as bigger and huskier than most of his classmates. He must have inherited Pa's height and strength. It's a good thing he was named John Anderson.

And Margaret. How quickly she had learned to play the clarinet. There was little question about her academic and musical abilities.

As the program neared its end, another accompanist came to the piano. James joined the other choir members for several numbers. Then, he stepped forward to sing "O Holy Night!"

What a voice James had! When he finished, the audience applauded enthusiastically. Matthew reached over and clasped his wife's hand.

As the applause died down, some choir members returned to the band section. The grand finale ended with "Joy to the World." The audience rose to sing along with the choir as the band played the triumphant strains of the hymn. These songs ushered in Christmas.

As Matthew, with Ellen and his mother, began walking out of the auditorium, he was surprised at the way people greeted them. "Mr. Anderson, your son has real talent. He should be a music teacher. Or even a minister." Another said, "Matthew and Ellen, I can't believe all the talent you have in your family."

An hour later at home, Ellen heated milk for hot chocolate. The Andersons sat around the kitchen table, enjoying the satisfaction of jobs well done. Matthew noticed Carol. She looked sullen as usual, probably feeling left out. But Ma showed more life than she had in a long time.

Friday night, the family readied themselves for another event, this time the Christmas program of District 185. This was Carol's night to shine, so to speak.

James, Johnie, and Margaret decided not to go to the Lake View High School basketball game. That meant the whole family, including little Michael, would attend this rural school program.

Matthew had read about a push for consolidation of rural schools. The absence of these small country schools would be a big loss. Large towns and large schools could become big and cold and impersonal.

These rural schools almost burst at the seams for the Christmas programs. The whole family came, as well as aunts and uncles who lived nearby. This was truly the extended school family—a community gathering.

Though the program was predictable, Matthew never tired of the sameness. He loved the Christmas carols and the readings and small plays. In a fast-changing world, he appreciated that which remained the same.

Matthew held Michael and Ma sat between him and Ellen. Margaret had found one of her friends, and James and Johnie found their friends as well.

All at once, Matthew's attention turned to Carol. Miss Wilson had handed her a piece to read. Carol began confidently, but then she stumbled over several words. Matthew knew she wasn't the student that either Margaret or James had been. As she finished reading, Matthew thought he saw tears in her eyes.

Matthew's mind went back to the times when he had not done well in school. He had not finished eighth grade. It had been handy for Pa to have him at home doing farm work. Somehow he felt inferior to his brother and sisters who had gone on to school. He sensed that Carol too felt she didn't measure up to her sister and brothers.

Carol made up for the poor reading as the final play was presented. She played the part of Mother Christmas, and she said the words with gusto. She knew exactly how to bring out the drama of the play.

The play ended with loud applause. Food and community fellowship followed.

Snow fell gently as they returned home. God was good. Life was good.

Chapter 18

"Just coffee, today," said Ellen as she poured a cup for Matthew. "We want to be hungry for Christmas Eve lutefisk and Swedish meatballs."

Matthew's mouth watered. "Another Christmas," mused Matthew. "I wonder what life will be a year from now."

"Would you mind making a quick trip into town?" Ellen held up the butter dish. "I baked all those cookies, so I'd like you to stop at the creamery and pick up several pounds of butter. We need a good supply for the lutefisk. And I think you should stop at the locker plant and see if you can buy some ground pork that isn't frozen. We're going to be a full house for our Christmas Eve meal. I'm afraid I may run out of meatballs."

Matthew was only too happy to drive into town. "Be sure the boys have the cattle fed and ready to milk in time."

"Here's the locker key. No. 143. Pick up some frozen meat for later in the week."

Matthew got into his '35 Chevy and drove to Lake View. It took only minutes to pick up the butter and the ground meat. Stores were closing early for Christmas Eve. Most people were at home getting ready for the real celebration.

The Christmas lights of Lake View showed off even more with the light snow coming down. The clouds made the late afternoon seem like night.

Beyond the Storm

As Matthew drove away from Lake View, he glimpsed a figure walking on the highway. Who would be walking on this snowy Christmas Eve?

Matthew stopped the car and backed up. "Can I give you a lift?"

A young man, out of breath, opened the car door. "Thank you, sir. I'm hoping to get to a friend's house."

"It's not a nice time to be out on the road. Most people are at home for Christmas. Where are you headed?"

The young man got in the car, threw a knapsack into the back seat, and closed the door. "I'm not sure exactly where he lives. I know it's supposed to be on the township road a mile or two south and west."

Matthew looked over at the young man, noting his light jacket and no gloves. "You're not dressed for this kind of weather."

"I'm not from around here."

Matthew drove on. "Where are you from? What's your name?"

"I'm from down South—Tennessee." Matthew noticed the southern accent. "My name's Greg."

Matthew introduced himself. "And whose place are you headed for? I think I'm driving near the place."

Greg reached into his pockets and brought out a piece of paper. He leaned forward, trying to read. "It's the township road going south one mile. Then turn west for less than a mile. It says there's a house that's been burned down and a smaller house nearby."

The words startled Matthew. He knew this had to be the home place. "What's the name of the person you're going to see?"

"I think it's Lawrence—or Larry."

Something didn't seem quite right about this situation. "Don't you know this person?" Matthew wondered why a stranger would be going to Larry's house on Christmas Eve.

"It's a long story. Let's say he's a friend of a friend. I'm deliv…." Suddenly he stopped himself.

Matthew's mind filled with questions. "So you're in business, are you?"

"I guess that's what you'd say."

The passenger rode on in silence. He fidgeted, obviously uncomfortable.

Matthew hesitated, though he had many more questions. There was something about this young man that seemed strange or odd.

"I know exactly where you're going," said Matthew. "Larry is my nephew."

Chapter Eighteen

"Oh."

"What kind of business is this?" Matthew couldn't help thinking of P.J. and the questionable associations.

"Well," Greg hesitated "Larry will have to tell you about it."

"Where did you say you were from?"

"I didn't say. I'm from lots of places."

Matthew began asking more questions. "Where are your parents? Or your wife? Shouldn't you be home for Christmas?"

Greg groped for words and then he spoke quickly. "My Dad's…. My parents are dead."

"I'm sorry. You must miss them—especially at Christmas."

"I do."

By this time, Matthew was driving toward the little house. Lights gleamed from the windows and reflected in the snow.

Matthew decided to get out of the car at the same time Greg did. In the darkness, he saw a bulge in Greg's light jacket, a bulge that appeared to be a revolver. For a moment he froze in fear.

Larry's voice broke into his awareness. "Uncle Matthew, what are you doing here? I thought you'd be busy with chores."

"I picked up your friend along the way."

Larry looked surprised. Apparently, he didn't know this young man.

Greg spoke up. "I have something for you."

Larry backed away. "Come inside."

Matthew sensed he was not wanted. "Merry Christmas to you and Joan. And your mother."

"Thank you," Larry replied. "I'm sure you need to be on your way."

Larry hurried ahead with Greg following.

Matthew heard the words as he got in the car. "It's a delivery from Thornton. You're to take care of it until…."

The remaining words faded as he closed the door.

Thornton? That name was familiar. Were P.J.'s business associates now Larry's? What would this lead to?

Matthew sensed danger. "Lord," he prayed, "keep this family safe from harm."

The young man frightened Matthew, but there was nothing he could do. He'd keep this to himself for now. After all, he didn't want to spoil the joy of Christmas Eve for the rest of the family.

175

Beyond the Storm

The friendly lights from the kitchen and dining room windows spilled out onto the snow. Ellen and Ma were busy in the kitchen. He saw Victoria's car, so he knew Martha and Victoria were also helping. In a short time the Andersons would once more celebrate the birth of the Christ Child.

Johnie sat on top of the feed bin, watching the cattle eagerly eating the ground feed. He and James had followed Dad's directions to give an extra portion to each of the animals. Johnie was proud of his father. Matthew Anderson had that gentle and kind way both with animals and people.

The barn door opened. Dad and James entered.

"Let's get going early." Johnie took down his pail and handed one to his dad. "James, why don't you get the separator ready?"

"You gave the cattle the extra feed I suppose." Dad took his pail and moved toward the cow farthest down.

"We can never forget that. It's a tradition."

Johnie noticed something in Matthew's mannerisms and voice. Something was wrong. He was getting good at understanding people, especially in knowing when something bothered his dad.

As Matthew and the boys milked the cows and did the other work, they said little. The smells of cattle and a few horses made Johnie think of the way it must have been in the Bethlehem inn. The smells of a stable or barn must have been the same whether in Bethlehem or in rural Minnesota.

When they finished the milking and the other chores, James left. Johnie lifted the cream cans into the water tank. He walked back to the barn, wanting to talk with Dad.

"Dad, is something wrong?"

Matthew started to say no, but then he began to tell of the stranger, Greg. "I can't believe Larry would carry on the same sneaky business P.J. did."

Johnie felt anger within. "We read *Julius Caesar*, and there was a saying about how men's evil lives long after them. That's the way it is with P.J."

His father looked surprised. "Son, I guess you're school-smart after all. Sometimes, the wrong that people do affects the next generation."

Chapter Eighteen

"But look at how good Grandpa was. And yet Uncle P.J. went the wrong way."

"I hate to admit it, but every family has its black sheep. I denied it for a long time, but P.J. was our black sheep."

Johnie began to think aloud. "Dad, some people say I look like P.J. because I'm tall. I don't like that comparison. I'd be afraid to go his way."

"You're tall like P.J. But you're not at all like him."

"When people do wrong, I just want to punch them out. And I've punched Jake and a few others."

Matthew said nothing for a moment. "You'll find better ways to take care of problems. These things take time."

"I want things to happen fast."

"Patience, son." Matthew reached down for his pocket watch. "I think we better get in, or your mother will wonder what happened."

Father and son left the warmth of the barn. Johnie looked back and thought of the gentle peacefulness of the animals. All seemed right in that world except for Larry.

Johnie, usually the talkative one, was quiet this Christmas Eve. The dining room was filled with many family members as Mother and Aunt Victoria and Aunt Martha brought out the lutefisk and Swedish meatballs and potatoes and all the other good food.

When Mother got everyone seated at the tables, she asked Victoria to say a prayer. Victoria looked around and spoke. "Thank you, Ellen, but I think someone else would do a far better job. I know Matthew is shy, but he's the kindest most thoughtful brother I could ever want. Maybe he doesn't like to speak in front of a group, but he has a kindness and way that we can all learn from."

The words surprised Johnie. He always thought of Aunt Victoria as a good teacher, but a little strict and harsh with people. This kinder, gentler side surprised him.

The eyes of the group turned toward Matthew.

"Thank you, Victoria." Matthew hesitated. "It's good for us to think and be thankful. Last year, Pa was with us. P.J. was also here. From year to year, we never know what changes will come. We must appreciate each other."

Matthew paused and began his prayer. "Dear Lord. We praise You now for the wonderful God that You are. You have created this world and given us many blessings. Thank You for this family. We remember Mary tonight, and we pray that You will give her health. We love her and miss her. Guide us during the days ahead. And now, thank You for this food, this feast. May we remember You as we feast together. In Jesus' name, amen."

Victoria's eyes and nod told everyone she appreciated the prayer.

In minutes they passed the food and people ate hungrily.

Johnie looked across the table at Cousin Jake. He didn't like the guy, but he felt sorry for him. Uncle Ed, who sat nearby, no doubt missed Aunt Mary. And there sat Grandma, who looked so very much alone without Grandpa. Aunt Martha and Mother seemed to sense her alone-ness.

Johnie observed the other children, some of whom weren't really children. Beth wasn't bad for a cousin. She sat next to him. They got along well. James also was strangely quiet. His sisters sat at another small table with Irene and cousin Corrine's three girls. The younger girls were noisy in their fun.

Corrine and Warren were here for the first time at Christmas. They had become such a part of the family this past year.

Missing were Aunt Rita plus Larry and his wife. And Cousin Noreen was nowhere around. And Martha's other daughters were far away.

The traditions continued. Everyone seemed to enjoy the meal. After the meal the women washed dishes. The men sat in the living room, talking farm problems. And age separated the kids into two groups. Johnie found himself with James and his cousins Jake and Beth. Beth, something of a tomboy, always fit in with the boys. He used to be a good buddy with Jake, but the last year he and Beth got along famously. This foursome quickly organized a game of Pit, a lively game of trading.

Margaret and Carol played more quietly in the girls' room with Irene and the three younger girls. And little Michael wandered around, finding the people who gave him the most attention.

The volume of the Pit game became louder and louder until Uncle Ed appeared at the door. "This noise is ridiculous. Stop right now." He stooped down and picked up Beth's cards.

The game came to an abrupt end.

James quickly apologized. "We didn't realize how loud we were."

"This is no way to celebrate Christmas." Ed threw the cards on the dresser and left.

Johnie decided this was enough game playing. "Let's go downstairs. It's about time to open presents."

Christmas tree lights had been plugged in. The bulbs of various colors reflected a soft gentleness on the windows. The men's conversation had ended, and the women had finished washing dishes.

Chapter Eighteen

Aunt Victoria entered and announced, "We have another tradition. It's time for Ellen to read the Christmas story. And then let's sing 'Silent Night'."

The younger children came downstairs. The adults sat on the chairs and davenport while the children stood or sat on the floor. His mother sat by the lamp and began to read the story that never grew old.

Johnie's mind moved to the animals in the barn. Maybe there was some truth in the old Scandinavian legend that those animals came alive on Christmas Eve and worshiped the Christ Child. Mother's reading of the story and the warmth of family made this teenage boy become warm and sentimental.

He moved over and sat in front of Grandma. "I miss Grandpa. I wish he were here."

Tears came to Grandma's eyes. "I miss him all the time. But he lives on in this family. He lives on in you."

"I've got his name. I'm proud of that."

The children received some of the usual gifts such as sweaters and mittens and books. Johnie paid little attention to those because the roller skates captured his full attention. That gift was more than he expected. These were hard times, but the tag showed him that Aunt Victoria had helped out. Without her help, Mother and Dad and Uncle Ed couldn't have afforded such gifts for their children.

In minutes, the room was a mess of noise and wrappings from the gifts.

Ringing from the telephone brought noise and conversation to an end. The telephone did not usually ring at this time on Christmas Eve.

His mother quickly moved to the kitchen to answer. "Mary, it's good to hear from you. Merry Christmas. We miss you. We wish you were here."

The word "Mary" brought Ed and the three children to the kitchen. Soon the girls were talking with their mother.

Uncle Ed's gruff manner became gentler. Johnie had never heard him use such a quiet tone. He noticed Jake was strangely quiet, trying to hide his feelings.

After Ed and the children had spoken with their mother, Ed motioned for Grandma to come to the phone. Grandma spoke words that encouraged. "We love you. We want you back home with us. We all miss you so terribly much."

From the conversation on this side, it was evident that Aunt Mary was crying. Johnie couldn't help wondering why God permitted someone as good as Aunt Mary to have TB. Why couldn't He just heal her?

As Grandma hung up the phone, she turned to her family. "Mary says she'll be home for Christmas next year. I believe she will. The Lord will bring her home."

For a few moments the quietness was like the quietness of a prayer service. In a sense Grandma's words were a prayer to which the family agreed.

A loud crash followed by a scream interrupted the quiet moments. Johnie knew instantly what had happened. Michael had been grabbing at the Christmas tree lights. The tree had fallen against the piano with branches scratching him.

Johnie hurried to the rescue, straightened the tree, and picked up little Michael. His brother seemed more frightened than hurt. "You're OK little brother."

"It's bedtime, Michael," announced his mother.

"And," added Uncle Ed, "it's bedtime for us. If we're going to Julatta, we need to do chores early. I'm not sure this early morning Swedish service is such a good idea."

As soon as the company left, Mother made an announcement. "Come to the living room. There's something more—something special."

Johnie looked at both Dad and Mother. His parents must have something up their sleeves.

Grandma and four sleepy children quietly sat down in the living room. Mother took out two envelopes.

"Dear Matthew and Ellen, Aunt Elizabeth and children. I hope you have had a blessed Christmas. Alice and I wanted to let you know that we're accepting your invitation at New Year's. We would like to do something special. We know that only rarely do you go out to eat. I know there's that fancy place in River Falls. We would like to take you there for Sunday dinner. And let's spare no expense. We look forward to seeing you. Merry Christmas. And may God bless you all. Love, Peter and Alice."

The letter roused the interest of the children.

"We've never been out to eat at a fancy place," announced Carol.

Others chorused agreement.

"Going out like that is a waste of money," announced Grandma. "It's expensive, and that money could better be spent on other things."

Chapter Eighteen

"But, Ma," said Dad, "we've helped Cousin Pete. Now, he wants to show appreciation."

"It's Peter's gift," said Mother. "We must graciously accept it."

"I guess so." Grandma got up to leave. "It still seems a lot of money to spend."

"There's one more thing." Mother took out the second letter. She began to read.

"Dear Mom and Dad Anderson, Grandma, James, Johnie, Margaret, Carol, and Michael. I'm not much good at writing letters, but here goes."

Johnie knew who this was from. He couldn't help noticing Margaret's broad smile.

"I wish I were with you. I'd take a cold Minnesota winter any day to the heat of these islands. Nothing much is happening. We keep hearing rumors that there could be trouble at any time. I miss you all. Thanks, Margaret, for your letters. Keep on writing. I'm sorry I'm not good at answering. You see, I don't have much time, and I'm a terrible writer. I wish I could give gifts to each of you, but that's not possible. I'm sending a $20 money order. I hope you can buy a little something for everyone. I miss my grandma and grandpa so very much. I don't think my own parents miss me. You're my family, and I love you. Love, Joe."

"Poor boy," said Grandma. "I'd like to have a word with his parents. They never knew how to be parents."

"Think of how blest we are to have Joe as part of our family." Ellen put down the letters. "Now, it's time for bed. Chores and Julatta come awfully early."

In their bedroom later that night, Johnie felt like talking. "This was the best Christmas Eve ever."

James answered, "Yes, but do you remember last year? Many things were different."

"And I remember three years ago. We were in our old home then. That was our last Christmas there."

"I think about the future." James sat up. "Two years from now I'll be out of high school. I want to go off to college. I love this farm, but I can't stay here."

"I don't ever want to leave. But I'm afraid I'll have to go fight in a war. We'll be fighting those Nazis in Germany or some place else. It's our duty to go."

"Somehow, I can't see myself ever killing anyone. It's seems too awful to think about. But I know if the government says I have to go, I'll go."

Johnie remembered something Pastor Strand had said. "The pastor says it's the government's duty to protect us. Citizens must fight for our freedom. That's our duty to our country."

The boys continued talking late into the night. When a voice called them in the morning, Johnie realized Dad and Mother had done all the chores. That was just another way of Dad being kind to his children.

This year Julatta was later in the morning than usual. The church in town had the earlier service. This service, part of an old early-morning Swedish tradition, celebrated the birth of the Christ Child. The family, minus Carol and Grandma and little Michael, walked into the country church.

Johnie loved the smell of candles in the church. For this service, electricity was not turned on. The candles provided a gentle light, like the gentle light emanating from God.

A peace and calm filled the sanctuary—a peace that would be shattered in the times ahead.

Chapter 19

January 1941

"I'm worried about you," said Ellen. "Or perhaps I should say I'm concerned."

Matthew set down his coffee. "You know Christmas was such a warm and pleasant time. And now it's a year since…" He left the sentence unfinished.

Ellen reached across the kitchen table and grasped Matthew's hand. "Yes, I know. Your father was a wonderful man, truly the 'salt of the earth'."

Matthew felt a strength and reassurance from his wife. They sat for a moment in silence.

"I don't think I realized how important Pa was in my life until these last years."

"It's a cliché, but life goes on. We have your mother here, and the children."

Matthew kept remembering other things. "I can't help thinking of P.J. He's dead, but his shadow keeps coming across our lives. I'm finding it hard to think of the good he did; instead I think of the awful things he did. And Larry keeps right on going down the same path."

"Aren't you glad we're away from the home place? Wouldn't it be terrible to live close to that whole situation?"

Matthew's mind took him back more than three years. "You know, Dear, it was hard to leave the home place, but now I can see the Lord was in all of this. We're better off now."

"You've come a long way, dear Matthew. You're more like your father all the time."

"That's the highest compliment you could pay."

"Let's think of some of the other good things that have happened. Cousin Pete and Alice are back together. Peter knows he has a drinking problem and he's dealing with it. It was good to have the old Peter back with us at New Year's."

"Maybe there's still hope for Larry."

"And Rita," added Ellen.

Life often involves strange coincidences. At that moment a knock interrupted their talk.

Ellen opened the door. "Come in, Rita."

"I'm sorry if I interrupted something," Rita apologized.

"We're finishing our afternoon coffee," invited Ellen. "Why don't you sit down and have a cup?"

"I guess that would be nice. I've been rushing around, packing. I haven't thought about coffee or eating or anything."

Rita slipped off her coat. Ellen took it and laid it over a chair.

"Packing?" Ellen questioned as she brought out a cup and poured the coffee.

"I've made some decisions. That's what I've come to talk about."

Matthew observed his brother's widow. There was something different about her. That was probably because she didn't have makeup on, her hair was not neatly in place, and she was not wearing a carefully tailored outfit.

Ellen offered her some of the freshly-baked cookies. Rita accepted the offer.

"What's wrong?" Ellen sat down and faced Rita. "Can we be of some help?"

"That's kind of you." Rita had never been at a loss for words, but this now seemed to be the case. "I've been doing a lot of thinking."

"We know it's been hard for you since P.J. died. You've had to make many adjustments."

"I've realized some things," began Rita. "I've not treated you right. I guess I never tried to look at things from your point of view. I listened only to Paul John. With Larry taking over, I've begun to see things differently."

Chapter Nineteen

Matthew looked from Rita to Ellen. His wife's eyes registered surprise.

"There's so much I want to say. I don't know where to start."

"You said you were packing. What does that mean?"

"I've decided to go back to Illinois. I have relatives there."

Matthew managed to speak. "We'll miss you. What about the business? What about Larry?"

"Larry's been taking over the business. One of Paul John's partners and his wife will be living in our—my—house. He's going to work with Larry in the business."

Matthew hardly dared ask the next question. "Well, are you going to sign the farm back to the rest of the family? Then, Corrine and Warren could live there."

Rita looked down, avoiding the gaze of Matthew. "Shortly after my husband's death, I had Larry take over everything. I don't know what's happened."

"But the property has to be probated." Matthew felt that old anger returning. He thought those hurts were far behind him, but scars remained.

"I've washed my hands of that whole situation."

Matthew felt his hands tighten into fists. "But P.J. wrote the letter. He asked you to make things right."

"I'm sorry. I gave all the business over to Larry several months ago. Some of the business partners seem to have some claim on the land. I'll talk to Larry."

"Larry doesn't want to farm, does he?" questioned Ellen. "Why would he want to stay?"

"With the draft re-instated, he could be drafted. And if war comes, it's even more possible. That's what Paul John was thinking."

"But," interrupted Ellen, "with a baby on the way, his chances might be less likely."

Matthew saw the usually composed and in-control Rita, suddenly break into tears. He began to feel sorry for this woman.

"I didn't mean to upset you." Ellen got up from her chair and went over to stand by Rita. "We know you've been through terrible times."

"I'm afraid." Rita began to tremble visibly. "I don't know what to do. That's why I have to get out of here."

Matthew and Ellen were speechless.

"I don't know what Larry's into. I always knew Paul John's business associates. They weren't honest, but they had their limits."

"Yes, we learned about his questionable connections."

"I'm afraid about Larry. Some of those people look dangerous to me. Larry could get hurt."

Matthew and Ellen listened to Rita's concerns. At least there was some evidence that this woman was trying to make a change.

"Why don't you stay for supper?" invited Ellen.

"Thank you. That is very kind of you, but I need to finish packing tonight. I'm leaving early in the morning. But there's something I'd like to ask you to do."

Matthew couldn't help thinking about P.J. Whenever something difficult came along, P.J. had come to Matthew for help.

Rita went on. "I know Larry hasn't been the nicest nephew, but I'm afraid he needs help with farming. He knows so little. I was hoping you would check on him every once in awhile.

Ellen looked at Matthew.

For a moment Matthew pictured Larry as a child. "I guess I could do that."

"And I'm arranging for something else. When spring comes, Larry will move to my house. I might be back, I don't know. That will leave the little house empty so Grandma can return."

Matthew breathed a sigh of relief. "That's good. Ma wants to move back. But I don't know if she'll be ready."

Rita rose to leave. Ellen picked up her coat.

"Thank you. You've been kind to me even though I've not always been hospitable to you. I wish I could change what is now past."

"We'll miss you," said Ellen. "All we can do is to go on with life."

Rita extended her hand to Matthew. He shook it awkwardly. Then, she awkwardly embraced Ellen. Without looking back, she made her exit.

That evening after supper and chores, the family gathered in the dining room. James and Margaret were doing their homework, writing answers on worksheets. Even Johnie was trying to read a book. Carol was playing with Michael. Ma knitted as usual. Ellen darned socks. Matthew read the paper.

Chapter Nineteen

"It's time for Dr. Christian," said Margaret.

Johnie turned on the radio, and the familiar strains of organ music and the voice of the announcer came on. "Dr. Christian. Stories right from the heart of America. The only show in radio where the audience writes the script."

"A car just stopped outside." Johnie walked toward the kitchen door as a car door slammed. Before the person could knock, Johnie opened the kitchen door. There stood Sheriff Walker.

"I'd like to talk with your dad."

"Come in," invited Ellen.

"No, this is business. I'm wondering if I can see you and Matthew alone. Perhaps you could come out to the car."

Matthew and Ellen got their coats and went outside.

Sheriff Walker started the car, and the warmth felt good. "Some strange activities have been going on."

Ellen quickly responded. "I suspect it centers on the usual place."

"I'm sorry to say you're right. Matthew, I understand you gave a ride to a stranger on Christmas Eve."

"Yes."

"Could you describe him?"

Matthew tried to think about the rider. "Well, he said his name was Greg. It was dark so I didn't see much. He had a slight beard. He wasn't very large, probably average height with a slight build."

"Do you remember anything else about him?"

Matthew scratched his head. "He bothered me. He seemed frightened."

"Now, I understand you let him off at the home place, where P.J.'s son now lives."

Matthew began to remember more. "Yes. And Larry didn't seem very happy to see him at first. He had a package that he was supposed to deliver."

"Did you see what was in that package?"

"No. It seemed important."

"There've been some break-ins over in the next county. And some of the activity around that time seems to come right back to this area and P.J.'s place."

Have you talked to Larry?"

"Yes. But we can't get any satisfaction. We have no concrete evidence. And he's pretty smart."

Beyond the Storm

Ellen commented, "It's almost as if P.J. is still around; only it's Larry."

"Well, thanks. If you become aware of anything, please let me know. I know he's your nephew, but you don't want him to break the law."

Matthew and Ellen got out of the car. Sheriff Walker shook hands with each. "I appreciate the way you cooperate."

"We'll help any way we can," said Matthew "even if he's my nephew."

That night, Matthew and Ellen talked late into the night. Sleep evaded them.

The next afternoon Ellen sensed something was wrong. Could it be crying she heard in her mother-in-law's room? She tiptoed to the room and gently opened the door.

"Grandma," she said. "Are you ill?"

"No. I'm OK. I know it's not right to worry, but I do."

"It's not easy when you truly care for someone. Would you like to talk?"

"Sharing a burden can make it easier."

"Come out of this dark room. Why don't you come to the kitchen? I'll start another batch of cookies."

Soon Elizabeth Anderson was seated at the kitchen table as her daughter-in-law stirred the dough for some Old Fashioned White Cookies. She began to talk.

"It's almost exactly a year since Pa died, and I still can't get used to his death. I miss him terribly."

Ellen went on working, waiting for her to go on.

"You know, Ellen, I loved my son. But P.J. did some terrible things. I know that what he did upset John so very much. In some ways I feel P.J. brought on my husband's heart attack. And now I feel terrible that I would even think such a thing."

Ellen wanted to say the right thing. "I miss Grandpa, but he lived a full life. I believe it was his time. I believe it was God's timing to call him home."

"I think you're right. But I still want him back, and I can't seem to help myself, thinking about P.J."

"Our family has suffered big losses."

"And those last hours with P.J. He was in torment. I'm afraid P.J. was lost eternally."

Chapter Nineteen

"Isn't it good, Grandma, that we don't have to make those decisions? His destiny is in God's hands."

"You know, Ellen, sometimes I think it's my fault. I didn't experience this real closeness with the Lord until the three older ones were almost grown. Martha and Victoria were fine, but P.J. never really accepted our ways. He pretended to for a long time. And, then, when Lucille died, I almost felt it was a punishment for the kind of person I was in my earlier years."

Ellen knew she had to object. "No, Grandma, God isn't that way. He's not out to punish you. You've come before Him, sorry for your sins. He's forgiven you. Isaiah says that though our sins be scarlet, they are as white as snow."

Elizabeth Anderson wiped a tear away. "Thanks for reminding me."

For a few moments the women remained silent. Elizabeth added, "I miss Mary."

The two women went on talking as Ellen rolled out the cookie dough and cut the forms and placed a pan in the oven. The aroma of fresh cookies would greet Matthew when he came in from doing chores.

As Elizabeth got up and moved to the door, she made an announcement. "Next spring, I'm going back to my own home. I have things to straighten out before I leave this world."

Ellen was not surprised by her mother-in-law's announcement. "We'll see if you're ready then."

CHAPTER 20

March 1941

The kitchen clock inched toward 10 p.m. Something strange was in the air. Matthew thought he heard a crash of thunder, hardly what he expected on March 15.

The day had been one of those spring days with mild temperatures. It seemed too early for spring in Minnesota. Winter had a way of returning suddenly and without warning. Matthew thought of his children.

Ellen also looked at the clock. "It's strange Carol isn't home. Glenn should have had her here at least half an hour ago."

"I started to think the same. Something's not right."

Ellen went to the telephone and called central, giving the Robertson's number. Matthew could gather little from the conversation that followed.

As she hung up, Ellen announced, "Carol's gone to the Smiths. She's been talking about these new kids and wanting to stay there."

"I think I'd better check on her. Since the boys have the Chevy, I'll have to take the Model A."

"Perhaps I should go with you." Ellen moved toward the bedroom to get her coat. "I didn't say anything, but I had a talk with Miss Wilson. Carol's been uncooperative again. Ever since Margaret skipped a grade and went on to high school, Carol's been unhappy."

Beyond the Storm

"Don't you think you should stay here? The weather out there seems strange. Thunder and lightning aren't normal for this time of year."

The sound of someone coming down the steps interrupted Matthew.

"I feel it in my bones," said Ma. "Something's happening. We're going to have a storm. It feels like a different kind of storm."

As he looked through the kitchen window, Matthew noticed lightning, orchestrated by thunder. The sound of raindrops hitting the windows and roof announced the truth of Ma's statement.

"I hope the boys and Margaret make it home safely from River Falls. The tournament basketball game won't be over for another forty-five minutes."

Matthew made a quick decision. "Ellen, you stay here. I'll drive to the Smiths."

Darkness and black seemed to cover everything. As Matthew got out of the car, he realized that the wind contained dirt as well as rain. And the temperature was dropping. A flash of lightning revealed the Smith house as one of those smaller two-story houses badly in need of paint. The porch sagged, indicating much more was wrong with the house.

He knocked on the door. He heard activity within.

A five-year-old answered the door. "What do you want?" she whined.

"I've come for Carol. She belongs in her own home tonight." He looked around the empty room. "Where are your parents?"

"Mom and Dad went to town."

Matthew wondered how parents could leave small children like this alone on a dark and stormy night. "I've come for Carol," he repeated.

Carol and another one of the Smith girls appeared. Carol looked sheepish.

"Mother said I could stay with the Smiths some time this week. We decided on tonight."

Matthew looked directly at his daughter, who avoided his gaze. "You did not tell your mother—or me."

Carol began her tearful routine. "You let Margaret do whatever she wants. She gets to go to town school and have lots of fun. You never let me do anything."

Matthew tried to hide his annoyance. He quietly said, "You belong at home on a stormy night. And you should have been in bed long ago."

Chapter Twenty

The Smith girl hung back and Carol added, "We were going to have some fun for a change. Can't I stay? Mother said I could."

Matthew knew Ellen had not given permission. "We'll talk to your mother right now. I'll call her."

The Smith girl hesitated and then spoke. "Mr. Anderson, we don't have a phone. Ma and Pa don't have enough money."

Matthew looked around the kitchen and into the dining room. Everything about the place spoke of poverty. He wondered if this family had enough food to eat. Even so, the parents were in town on a blustery Saturday night. He was at a loss for words.

"When are your parents coming home?" Matthew felt a growing concern that these children should not be left alone. He began to realize the temperature in this house was far below a comfortable level.

The five-year-old began to cry.

The older girl spoke up. "I'll take care of you. Don't be afraid. And Grandpa and Grandma are just down the road."

Matthew made another decision. "Carol, you are coming home with me. And I'm taking you kids down the road to your grandparents."

The girls looked relieved. Carol reluctantly found her coat and put it on.

Matthew loaded the children into his car and drove down the driveway. Strong winds and dirt and rain limited the visibility. He was relieved when he found the grandparents home and ready to take in their grandchildren.

Carol had been silent all the way. Matthew tried to start a conversation but failed. Anyhow, he had to concentrate on driving and not landing in the ditch. He felt ill at ease with a twelve-year-old who remained in an angry frame of mind.

Finally, they arrived at the crossroads just below the hill that often gave drivers trouble. A coating of ice had formed on the road. Matthew hoped he could somehow drive the last quarter-mile without going off the road.

The car began sliding toward the ditch. Matthew hit the brakes and the car spun around. He had an empty feeling in his stomach. The rain was changing to snow, and the snow blinded him.

Matthew stepped on the clutch and shifted into low gear. Slowly he maneuvered the Model A to the top of the hill. These old Fords were pretty good when it came to winter driving. The blowing snow and dirt again blinded Matthew.

Beyond the Storm

"I'm scared," whined Carol.

"We're almost home."

Matthew drove slowly, finally reaching the driveway. He breathed a sigh of relief as he drove into the garage.

Carol started to run ahead toward the house. Except for the snow coming down, darkness dominated everything. And some of those flakes had dirt mixed in. Apparently the yard light was not working. That meant no light guided them.

For a moment Carol disappeared into the darkness. Then she cried out, "I'm lost. I can't see where I am."

"Come here," Matthew called. "This is a bad storm. And you know you can get lost in minutes."

Carol returned, running to her father. Even though she was twelve, she was perfectly happy to have her father guide her to the house. She relaxed in his arms and all her anger seemed to disappear. The dim kitchen light had never been more welcome.

Both Ma and Ellen were sitting at the kitchen table, waiting.

"What happened?" asked Ellen

Carol gave her mother a hug and hurried upstairs to her room.

Ellen called after her. "We'll talk in the morning."

Matthew took off his coat, handing it to Ellen. "She wasn't a very happy girl. She thought she was going to stay with the Smith girls."

"Carol's been a problem most of this year. She's jealous of Margaret."

Ma, looking tired, took off her glasses. "At least she's home safe in bed."

Three long sharp rings of the telephone abruptly interrupted their talk.

Ellen quickly took down the receiver. Matthew sensed tension as Ellen said few words with most of the talk at the other end.

Ellen hung up the receiver. "It was Mr. Allen. The bus left the tournament game early. The roads are treacherous. He didn't know if our kids would be able to make it home if they waited until the game ended. The kids may have to stay in town."

Matthew walked over to the window and looked out at the snow blowing violently. The house cracked as a wind gust blew against it. "If the kids don't stay in town, I hope they have sense enough to find shelter before they stall some place."

Chapter Twenty

Ma sighed. "I can't help thinking of the Armistice Day blizzard. And, of course, I remember that blizzard of 1888."

Ellen walked over to the ice box and took out a jar of milk. "I'm afraid we won't sleep well tonight, but some hot milk might help."

Matthew thought of the treacherous trip he had made. "It's dangerous out there. I wish they had the Model A. It would get them through more snow than the newer car will."

James had to admit his brother was the better driver. "OK, Johnie, you drive. See if you can get us through."

During the last fifteen minutes, snow had begun to fall ferociously. The road was icy part of the way, and then drifts would almost stop the car. The time was fast approaching midnight.

James got out of the '35 Chevy and Johnie moved over to the driver's side. Margaret stared out at the blinding snow. James wiped snow off the windshield and got into the car.

"Do you think we should go on?" questioned Margaret. "Dad always said we should find a warm place in a farmhouse or even a barn."

"We'll make it." Johnie shifted into low and managed to get through the next drifts. "I can get us through almost anything. A few big drifts won't hurt."

"There are more than a few," James cautioned. "And there's ice underneath."

Johnie drove the next quarter-mile without any delays or difficulties. James felt a certain literary fascination with blizzards. He had just finished reading a novel about the famous blizzard of 1888. And he couldn't help thinking of that Armistice Day storm of the previous November. He had sent a story to *The Young People* and hoped the editor might want to publish it.

More than that, he wanted to write the great American novel. Or maybe he could write a story of a family struggling just the way his family struggled against the elements. Perhaps he could write a modern story like *Giants In The Earth*. Someone needed to tell the story of the generations beyond the pioneers.

James managed to dream of exciting happenings that always took place at times like this. He would work these events into the writing he would do.

"We should have stopped at that last farm," said Margaret. "It's not safe to go on."

Johnie ignored his brother and sister. James heard her words, but continued in his world of imagination, not even considering the possibility of danger.

"I'm scared," called out Margaret. "People can freeze to death. Remember what almost happened to Carol."

"We're only about two miles from home. We can make it!" shouted Johnie, very much annoyed.

No sooner were those words out of his mouth than he abruptly hit the brakes. In front of him and barely visible was a man trying to get his car untangled from the snow. James's head hit the windshield, and Margaret flew forward. The car slid into the ditch. Fortunately a ditch that was shallow.

James heard his brother mutter under his breath something about stupid drivers.

Johnie opened his door and got out.

"Sorry about my car," said the man. "I don't think anyone will get any further. The drifts are even higher around this next corner. I walked on to see. I was trying to turn my car around."

Johnie surveyed the situation. "I guess we're stuck. We'd better go to the Hanson place."

By this time, James had helped Margaret out of the back seat. The gust of wind and heavier snow brought visibility down to a few feet, and it was evident the temperature was dropping rapidly.

"This storm is dangerous," said the stranger.

"Take those blankets with you," ordered Johnie. "We need anything that can keep us warm. This is another killer blizzard. Let's get inside to safety."

James didn't like taking orders from his younger brother, but he knew Johnie was right.

The stranger moved ahead and seemed to know exactly where to go. Johnie, with James and Margaret behind, followed. In no time, they knocked on the door. It was strange that lights would be on this late in the evening.

Chapter Twenty

Mrs. Hanson opened the door. "Come in out of this terrible cold. You're the Anderson children, aren't you?"

James recognized this friendly, jolly, slightly over-weight woman, obviously a good cook who enjoyed the fruits of her work. He never had appreciated the warmth of a house as much as he did at that moment. Mrs. Hanson motioned where they could lay their coats.

Johnie began to explain what had happened. The stranger injected comments as well.

"That's fine. You stay here. We'll make room, and you stay the night." She walked over to the new refrigerator. "I have a feeling you children are hungry. How about some sandwiches? And then we'll see about blankets and a place for you to sleep."

James and the others murmured acceptance of the offer. The stranger remained quiet. No one knew his name.

"We need to call Mom and Dad," said Margaret.

Mrs. Hanson pointed to the telephone. "There it is. Go ahead and call."

After calling central, Margaret announced. "Our lines are down. I can't get through."

"I think Mom and Dad know that we'll look for shelter," said Johnie.

Mrs. Hanson walked over to the window and glanced out at the blowing snow. "I'm afraid we have a problem. I have to ask you for help."

"We can help," agreed Johnie.

"The weather's been so nice that we neglected to carry in wood from the woodpile. And now Mr. Hanson has been ill. I'm not able to get out and do that work. Do you suppose you could get some wood? We don't have enough inside to last the night."

James and Johnie put on their coats and went out to the woodpile. Soon an ample pile of wood stood next to the kitchen stove, and another pile stood next to the Coleman heater in the living room.

The three Andersons talked excitedly as Mrs. Hanson fed them sandwiches. The stranger remained silent. James wished their parents knew they were safe. They would be worried.

It was well after midnight when Mrs. Hanson showed her guests to the spare bedrooms upstairs. James shivered as he and Johnie pulled the warm blankets over themselves. "I think a glass of water would freeze up here!"

Beyond the Storm

Before sleep took over, James thought over the events of the evening. The excitement and cheering of the basketball game still rang in his ears. Blizzards always posed a problem, but then difficulties and challenges bring out the best in people. The blizzards brought them to the Hansons, who desperately needed help. If Johnie and he hadn't carried in the wood, their fires would have gone out.

The next morning, James heard activity downstairs. This was Sunday morning, normally the time they would be getting ready for church. A gentle knock on the bedroom door awakened him.

Mrs. Hanson opened the door. "I'm sorry to waken you, but I have to ask a big favor. Mr. Hanson is still under the weather. Could you boys do the milking? I'm afraid I'm not feeling so well myself. Otherwise, I'd do the chores."

James saw his brother was waking up. "Sure, we'll take care of it."

Within minutes the boys were dressed. Mrs. Hanson provided them with jackets that had been worn in the barn. The stranger, still saying very little, followed them. Outside everything was blank and dirty white, a strange and different world. In some places the ground was almost bare while nearby there were drifts several feet high.

Johnie quickly figured out where the pails and other things were. In a few minutes the two brothers were milking the eight cows. The stranger stood by awkwardly, not quite knowing what to do. As they were finishing milking, Johnie showed the stranger where the feed was so that he could take care of that task.

When they entered the house, the aroma of eggs and bacon greeted them. Mr. Hanson sat by the kitchen table.

"You kids are a godsend. I don't know what we'd have done without you. We'd have frozen if you hadn't carried in wood. And now you've done the milking as well. That was great. As I said, God sent you."

"We're used to milking cows and hauling wood." Johnie yawned as he took off his coat. "The breakfast smells great."

"You sit right down. Margaret's been kind enough to help get breakfast ready."

The rest of the day was filled with winter chores and tasks. The stranger, who had seemed to guide the Anderson children, decided to try driving back to town. James and Johnie helped him get his car started. Then the boys took care of cleaning the barn as well as gathering eggs and other chores.

Chapter Twenty

Margaret cooked the noon meal, and the afternoon work proceeded with small breaks. The storm had left enough drifts so that the outside work took more time.

That evening, the boys did the milking once more. Margaret prepared the evening meal.

As they sat down to eat, Mrs. Hanson entered. "This day of rest has made me into a different person."

Margaret brought out the platters of food, and Mrs. Hanson sat down. They prayed and enjoyed more good food.

As they finished eating, Mr. Hanson pushed his plate aside. "That was quite a meal, young lady. I don't know what we would have done if this blizzard hadn't happened. You boys took care of the things I couldn't do."

"And, Margaret," added his wife, "I can't believe how you cooked such a delicious meal. I feel ever so much better."

"I love to cook. And besides you gave us shelter. We owe you something for that."

"We have much to be thankful for." Mr. Hanson turned to his wife. "We need to thank our good Lord for sending help."

Mrs. Hanson's gentle and kind face reminded James of Grandma and other kind older women he had known. Somehow, he wanted to paint a picture in words of strangers coming together to help one another in time of trouble. These people would find their way into his stories.

Mrs. Hanson bowed her head as did each person in the room. "My dear and loving heavenly Father. Thank you for warmth and safety during this dreadful blizzard. You have sent us James and Johnie and Margaret to help us in our time of need. Thank You for these wonderful children. Be with them throughout their lives as they face many problems in a changing world. Keep them safe from harm. I know that You will be in their lives, and may they let You guide them in all Your Ways.

"And thank you for the stranger who quietly pointed out some of our needs. Thank You for pointing to our need for more wood on this cold night. Lord, You provide and guide us in such unusual ways.

"We praise You now for Your wonderful world. We see the danger in this storm, but we also realize the beauty that is all around us.

"Thank You for fellowship with You. And thank You for this wonderful warmth and fellowship with one another. In Jesus' name, amen."

James was tired but did not want to sleep. His mind kept working the way farmers work at harvest time. He re-lived the events of the day and thought of ways to put them into a story. Rest would not come until he completed the story even if only in his mind.

He wondered about the stranger who had not given his name.

Matthew and Ellen slept little that night. Were the three children safe? Matthew thought of the lives lost in the Armistice Day blizzard. He hoped the kids would have sense enough to find shelter at such a time. He had taught them this kind of caution. Yet, youth often felt invulnerable in the most dangerous of situations.

"Matthew, I know they're safe." Ellen's words didn't help.

She got up from bed and knelt. Matthew slowly rose and knelt by her side.

Ellen began to pray. "Dear Lord, You are the shepherd. You are our shepherd and the shepherd of our children. We come to You, imploring You to keep them safe on this stormy night. We love You, and we love them. Please, Lord, please…"

Her voice trailed off. Matthew kept repeating the same pleas within. A sense of quiet reverence filled the room, making it as sacred as any chapel or church.

That morning, Matthew struggled through the chores. He had to shovel snow so he could open the doors to the barn. The cattle were restless as they reacted to the sudden changes in weather. Ellen soon made her appearance, and Matthew milked the cows as Ellen took care of the cream separator and other chores. Michael would be safe in the house with Carol and Ma near by.

At breakfast the two said little. Ellen tried calling the operator, but the ringing seemed to fall on deaf ears. Telephones in the country were not dependable in times of a storm.

Matthew went about doing the usual morning chores, but his mind was elsewhere. In reality, there was nothing to do. The roads were blocked, and it was no use trying to open them until the winds subsided.

Though it was Sunday, there would be no worship service. This Sunday would become a workday because of the storm. Ten o'clock coffee time arrived. Matthew felt heaviness within as he opened the kitchen door. Michael rushed to meet him. This two-year-old had learned the art of walking and seemed to be everywhere.

Chapter Twenty

As Matthew picked up Michael and held him in his arms, his cares disappeared.

Ellen poured his coffee. Carol seemed strangely silent.

"The radio had so much noise, but I heard this storm was as bad or worse than the Armistice Day storm. Only this time, people were more careful."

"Where can those kids be?" Matthew looked out the window, hoping he would see something.

"I'm positive they're safe. They know the dangers of being out in a blizzard."

Carol suddenly broke into tears.

"What's wrong, honey?" asked her mother.

"I'm so afraid something's happened to Margaret and to Johnie and James." Carol walked over to the window. "And I haven't been very nice to Margaret."

Matthew knew Margaret was used to the antics of Carol.

There was no news from the three older children that day. Ellen and Carol tried to help with the extra work outside because of the storm. Ma looked after Michael. The hard work helped them forget about their concerns for the three who were missing.

Nothing happened until mid-afternoon the following day during three o'clock coffee. Matthew and Ellen, along with Ma and Carol and Michael, were seated at the kitchen table.

"Look!" exclaimed Carol. "There's a horse and sleigh coming. I think I see Johnie with the man in front."

Matthew grabbed his jacket and went out the door, closely followed by Ellen and Carol. "It's Hanson!"

In the next minutes, Johnie as well as James and Margaret stumbled out of the sleigh into the snow.

"We're home!"

"I brought your kids back to you," said Hanson. "We couldn't have made it the last two nights without them. You have some great kids."

"Thanks. Thanks for bringing them home." Then Matthew added, "Come in and warm up."

"Sorry, no," Hanson called out. "This is tough weather for the horses. I need to get back home."

James, Johnie, and Margaret were soon inside, relating the events of the past days. Matthew felt at peace with the world.

James disappeared to his room. Matthew knew he was busy writing.

The March blizzard would soon give way to spring.

Chapter 21

April 1941

"It's time for me to go back to my own place," announced Ma that April morning. "I'm perfectly capable of taking care of myself."

Matthew set down his cup of coffee. He said nothing.

"Are you ready to be alone?" Ellen questioned. "You haven't been back to your house for months."

"I'm not so young, but I think I'm pretty healthy. I've faced tough times before. Besides, you're busy with your children, and I'm afraid I'll get in the way."

"Oh, no, Ma, you could never be in the way. You've helped us take care of Michael. And you've helped cook at other times." Matthew felt hurt that his mother could think such a thing. After all, it was the obligation of children to take care of older parents.

"I'd really like to go over to my little house. After all, that was home to your father and me for almost fifteen years."

Matthew thought a moment. "Well, Ma, I'll finish the chores and take you over."

Ma sighed. "I wish I could drive, but a lady of my generation just wasn't supposed to."

"Remember, Larry and his wife have been living there," Ellen reminded.

"But he's moving to the big house down by the lake. That was understood."

Matthew began to wonder what actually would happen. "We'll drive over. Then, we'll check things out."

An hour later, Matthew and his mother approached the home place. The charred remains of the big house served as a grim reminder of that autumn fire. He thought of his growing up years in that house as well as the happy years Ellen and he had spent there.

Ma remained silent. Matthew knew she was thinking of the wrongs done and of the frightening fire. He wished he could somehow erase the terrible Armistice Day storm and death of P.J. In this life his brother would never again speak to him, except in his memories and imagination. Yet, P.J. Anderson would be a part of his life through all his days.

Ma slowly got out of the car. She looked at the remains of the big house and then at the little house where she had lived. Matthew could see the last months had changed her to an old woman.

"It's like a nightmare. I can't believe your father's gone. And then P.J.'s death seems even more impossible. Children aren't supposed to die before their parents. And Mary now so ill."

Matthew's eyes turned to the barn that needed paint. He half dreaded going up to the door of the little house. He glanced at the fences that were badly in need of repair. Larry was definitely not a farmer.

Ma walked ahead of him slowly, looking down. He took her arm and guided her up the steps.

Ma knocked gently. There was no response.

Matthew gave several hard knocks. "They certainly can't be sleeping. It's almost ten o'clock. Half the day's gone."

Matthew heard movement. He tried the door. It was locked. Strange, he thought, most people around here never locked their doors. They waited. Finally, the door opened.

The heavy smell of cigarette smoke greeted Matthew. "Good morning. I brought Ma over to check on her house. She's moving back!"

Larry, hesitantly motioned for them to come in. "I was up late last night; I'm afraid Joan hasn't been feeling well."

Matthew saw his mother's eyes move about the living room and kitchen, observing the unwashed dishes and pans on the table. She cleared her throat and looked down.

"Hello, Grandma." Larry stooped down and kissed her on the cheek. "It's been awhile."

Chapter Twenty-one

An awkward silence followed.

"Why don't you sit down? I'll make some coffee." Larry looked over at the empty water pail. "I guess I'll have to go out to the pump."

Matthew realized the coolness of the room even on the spring morning. "I think you might have to get the fire in the stove going."

"We don't need any coffee," said Ma. "I thought you were moving to your father's—no your mother's—house."

"We haven't gotten around to it. Besides, Joan's not been feeling well with the baby coming and all."

Matthew was getting used to the heavy smell of cigarettes, but he thought he caught a whiff of something else—liquor. He hated that smell for it was part of what brought P.J.'s early death.

Matthew cleared his throat. He knew he had to be firm. "Larry, this is your grandmother's house. It's time for you to get out. We are giving you notice."

Larry didn't have a ready answer. He might be charming and good looking, but he didn't have the quick wit of his father.

Though Ma had tears in her eyes, she spoke with determination. "I am moving back here. This is my home. Most of my things are here."

Larry avoided the gaze of his uncle and grandmother. "Dad always said that this farm was his. He had the title."

Matthew found anger welling up within him. "Your grandmother has life-time rights to live in the house. And on his deathbed, your father said this land should go to your grandmother and the family. It is all written in the letter."

"Oh, Matthew," pleaded his mother, "we'll give Larry a few days."

Matthew breathed a silent prayer. If he ever needed help in knowing what to say, this was the time. Larry started to mumble something, but stopped.

Matthew, usually slow to speak, found the words coming quickly and easily. "Larry, for one thing, you're no farmer. The barn looks terrible, the fence is run down, and those cattle have not been taken care of. Farming's no good for you. Find another job."

"I need to stay on the farm now. Joan's baby will soon come. And if I leave the farm, I'll be drafted."

Matthew wanted to speak his mind, but he held back his words. A weak voice interrupted Matthew's thoughts.

"You're not going to kick us out, are you?" Joan, still in her nightgown, stood at the doorway. "I can't stand the thought of moving now."

"You need to take care of yourself," said Ma. "We'll all help you move. Besides your father's house has many conveniences. You don't even have running water here."

Joan looked so weak and frail that Matthew wanted to take her in his arms and comfort her. Her blonde hair and blue eyes reminded him of his own daughters. The contrasting features of Joan and Larry made them into a handsome couple.

"Grandma," Joan said, "Larry's mother doesn't want me there."

Once more Matthew knew he needed to speak. "That's too bad. It's time for you to move out. We're giving you no more than a week. By the way. is your mother back now?"

"Yes, but she's here for only a few days."

Larry and Joan both tried to apologize for their lack of hospitality. Larry started the fire in the kitchen stove and prepared to go out and pump a pail of water for the household use.

Matthew and his mother left and drove to P.J.'s lake home.

Rita, dressed in a stylish tweed suit, met them at the door. "I'm sorry, but I need to be on my way. I'm already late." She set down a heavy suitcase on the front porch.

"This business is important." Matthew had learned to be firm with his sister-in-law. She was usually in a hurry. Her earlier pleasantness had been replaced by annoyance.

Rita greeted her mother-in-law. "Hello, Mother Anderson. I'm sorry I'm in such a hurry. I'm catching a train for the city."

Ma returned the greeting. "I thought you just came home."

"Rita," said Matthew firmly, "Ma is planning to move back to her house. Whether you like it or not, it is her house."

"Well, you'll have to get Larry to move out."

Matthew found his stomach churning. "That isn't our job. It's *his* and *yours*. Whether you like it or not, they must get out."

Rita could see Matthew was not about to give up. "He's planning to move in here—not that I'm happy about that."

"And there's something more. You said you would check on the matter of P.J.'s dying wishes. You need to take care of that."

Rita's face reddened. "The lawyer will take care of that, I suppose."

"You need to do your part."

By this time it seemed Rita had regained her composure. "P.J. had the rights to the land. Now, I depend on Larry to settle those matters."

Matthew interrupted. "It is still your duty."

Chapter Twenty-one

"I am Paul John's wife. I inherit whatever is his. It's my land, or if I choose, it's Larry's. I'm leaving everything up to Larry."

Ma turned and walked down the steps and away from Rita and Matthew.

Matthew turned to Rita as he followed Ma. "Look what you've done to P.J.'s mother. How can you be so selfish? How can you treat us this way? I thought you'd changed, but you haven't."

Ma's muffled sobs stopped Matthew from saying more. "Don't make trouble," she said. "Rita is family, and Larry will move out."

Once more, it seemed Rita had the upper hand. "Matthew, don't forgot that I lost a husband. I have my life to think about."

"I'm sorry," said Matthew, "but Ma has her rights as well. And so do the rest of the family."

Ma covered her eyes. "I didn't think someone from my own family would put me out of my house."

"We'll make sure you get moved in," reassured Matthew. "Don't worry."

Rita picked up her suitcase, pushed her way past Matthew and his mother. "I have no more time for this. I need to be on my way."

Rita unlocked the trunk, quickly adding the suitcase to what was already there. Then she moved to open the driver's door.

"Stop!" Matthew commanded. "If you're leaving this family and everything here, then it's time you returned the land to the rightful owner." Matthew stood, blocking her from entering the car.

"Let me go! If you don't, I'll scream and then I'll call the sheriff."

"The sheriff might be interested in checking this place," said Matthew. "Larry must be out of the little house within one week."

"Don't try to stop her, Matthew," pleaded his mother. "It won't do any good."

Matthew stepped aside and walked over to comfort his mother. Rita slipped into the car and sped down the driveway.

"Oh, Matthew, that woman is not good—she is evil. She was never good for P.J.; she was part of the reason he went the way he did."

Matthew led his mother to his car. "Ma, don't worry. You'll always have a place with us. And I can assure you this little house will be yours."

"My little house is home to me."

Matthew couldn't help repeating a line he remembered, "The evil that men do lives long after them."

Beyond the Storm

A week later, Elizabeth Anderson moved back to her little house. She made sure all the windows were open. The stale cigarette smoke was gradually disappearing, though not completely. Today, she would hang all the bedding on the clothes line. Spring cleaning would bring a new freshness to everything inside and out.

Elizabeth poured her cup of coffee for "ten lunch" as her husband used to call this break. "I'm not giving up!" At this moment she missed John more than ever. "I'm not giving up," she repeated.

She took her coffee cup and walked into the bedroom. Her face reflected in the mirror on the dresser. At times it didn't seem possible she was an old woman. "I have more wrinkles," she said. "But I don't feel that I'm 73."

Elizabeth picked up her Bible and returned to the kitchen table. She began her daily Bible reading and meditation. The words didn't seem to say anything special to her. She felt empty and lonely.

She closed the Bible and then opened it and began turning the pages. An underlined verse caught her eye. "They that wait upon the Lord shall renew their strength. They shall rise up like eagles...."

"Lord, I've been feeling sorry for myself," she prayed. "I'm tired of having people look after me. I want to help others, but I don't know where to start. Lord, show me what I can do to be a real help to people in this life. I don't know where to start."

The Anderson family moved through her mind. Children. Grandchildren. Great-grandchildren. Her brothers and sisters. Some of the nieces and nephews. She prayed for each person by name.

Deep in thought and prayer, she didn't hear the gentle knock followed by the opening of the door.

"Hello, Grandma."

"Why, Joan, I didn't hear you. Come, sit down. Have some coffee." Joan had come to feel more like a grandchild than an in-law.

Joan sat down. "Coffee isn't agreeing with me these days. I'll have a glass of water."

During the next hour, the two women talked about children, about having babies, and the whole business of farm life.

"You're still milking cows and doing other chores, aren't you?" Elizabeth asked.

"Yes," Joan replied hesitantly.

Chapter Twenty-one

"Are you sure you should do all that lifting? Those chores are too much for you."

"I've worked hard all my life. I don't know what I'd do with myself if I didn't work hard. Larry's gone again today."

Elizabeth held back a comment. After all, Larry was supposed to be farming. "You need to take care of yourself."

"The baby's not due until late June."

Elizabeth eyed her granddaughter-in-law. "You keep on working the way your do, and the baby could be early. I was lifting and washing clothes and my oldest came almost two months early."

Joan shuddered. "I'm not ready for that."

"When that baby comes, you'll be ready." Elizabeth couldn't help thinking of her prayer earlier that morning. "Joan, you're an answer to prayer. I've been realizing I don't want people looking after me. I want to help others. I need to help you get ready for your baby."

"I've been so busy, I haven't done much."

The old woman smiled. "I've been knitting and sewing. I know just what I'll do. The baby will need a quilt. And that's what I do well. I've made quilts for each of the grandchildren. And now I can make a quilt for the first great-grandchild with the Anderson name."

Joan responded by reaching over to Elizabeth's hand. "That would be wonderful. Mother's so far away, and she has my younger brothers and sisters."

Joan stood to leave, and the two women hugged warmly.

"Why don't you stay for dinner," invited Elizabeth. "Larry's gone, and I have plenty of meatballs. I'll just throw in some extra potatoes and cream a few extra peas."

During the next hour, Elizabeth felt new purpose and a hope for the future.

Several hours later, Elizabeth turned off "Pepper Young's Family." She always enjoyed immersing herself in the problems of the Youngs.

A familiar voice greeted her. "Mother."

"Come in Martha."

"I just came from the City Café. I have some news."

Elizabeth's ears perked up. Automatically, she moved the coffee pot to a warmer spot on the stove.

Martha began to relate the news. "I've gone to work at City Café. Corrine and Warren have agreed to buy 120 acres of Robertson's land next to ours. I'm earning money to help."

"What are you doing at the Cafe?"

"I'm baking pies and rolls and other goodies. And I'm waiting tables. And one gentleman from Minneapolis even gave me a dollar tip. That's pretty good."

"Isn't that work hard on you. Your legs aren't too good."

"I've done fine these last few days."

Elizabeth knew there was something more. She poured two cups of coffee and put out some crackers and cookies.

"I'm going to talk to Victoria and Matthew. Larry isn't doing any decent farm work in the fields. There's still time for Warren to get the fields seeded."

"Larry's no farmer." Elizabeth didn't want trouble in the family, but she knew something had to be done. "Larry has little idea of what to do. Matthew's trying to help."

"Mother, I know you don't want trouble, but we have to do something. P.J. wasn't taking care of this place, and Larry is doing even worse."

Elizabeth had a trembling feeling within. "Yes, I know."

Mother and daughter continued their visit.

As Martha prepared to leave, Elizabeth remembered something. "I forgot to get the mail this morning. I might just hear from my sister or have some other good mail."

"Let me get it for you." Without another word Martha hurried to the mailbox. She came back with the daily paper plus two letters. She handed the letters to her mother.

Elizabeth's eyes brightened. "Two letters. And one from Mary."

"I'm curious, I must admit."

Elizabeth glanced over the letter and then began reading a part. "Mary says I have good news. The doctor says if I keep improving, I should be home in a few months. And that's for good."

"Thank God!" shouted Martha.

"Amen," Elizabeth added. She thought of that precious family. They would soon be back together, and the old way of life would continue.

"You have another letter. Who's that from?"

Chapter Twenty-one

Elizabeth cut the letter open. She recognized the handwriting. "It's from Pete and Alice." She scanned the letter. "I guess Ellen wrote and told them that I was back here. Well, Pete says he'd like to spend his August vacation with me if that's OK."

"That'll be good. I think it helps for you to have people around. By the way, Mother, I'm thinking about this weekend. After I finish work on Friday, I'd like to come out. I haven't rambled over the hills for awhile, and I'd like to do that."

Elizabeth knew what Martha was trying to do. "You certainly don't have to. I'm getting used to being by myself. I can handle it."

"Mother, perhaps I need to get away from my sister once in awhile. Victoria has her ways. And I don't like being alone; I want to be around people."

She laughed at her daughter's honesty. "In that case, by all means come. You can help me with the quilt for the baby."

Somehow Elizabeth felt less lonely after Martha's visit. Yes, she lived alone, but she had family nearby. Her family didn't need her in the same way as before, but they still looked to her as their mother and grandmother and aunt. They needed her in a different way.

She found the writing tablet. She had two letters to write. One to Mary: a letter of encouragement and optimism. A second letter to Peter: welcoming him to stay for his August vacation.

Life was good. She looked outside to her garden spot. In a few months flowers and vegetables would fill the empty space.

God had answered her prayers.

Chapter 22

Matthew had probably drunk too much coffee when Glenn stopped over. They had talked about farm problems as well as fears of a Japanese expansion. And the thought of Germans bombing London and killing innocent people was reprehensible.

That night he had one of those nightmares. The nightmare took its usual form. P.J., tall and dark and menacing, stood above him. Matthew again became a child. P.J. held the baseball just beyond Matthew's reach. Then he pushed Matthew into the milk shed and locked the door on the outside. Matthew kept screaming, but no one heard. Ma and Pa and the rest of the family had gone to town.

The nightmare then took a different form. P.J. lay on the hospital bed, writhing in pain and calling for help. "I'm burning up. This heat is insufferable. I can't stand it. I can't get out. Save me, Matthew. Help me!"

In the nightmare, Matthew reached out to him. The hospital bed disappeared. Instead there was what seemed to be an abyss, a dark hole. He wanted to save P.J. The more Matthew reached out, the farther P.J. slipped from him. The dark abyss enveloped P.J. He disappeared, but his agonized cries became louder and kept echoing in Matthew's mind.

Matthew felt Ellen's hand on his shoulder. "Matthew, you're having a nightmare!"

Matthew sat up, relieved that it was morning and Ellen was beside him.

Beyond the Storm

"Happy birthday, Dear. This is your day."

Matthew had a feeling that this day would be eventful. Being forty-one was hardly an event, but other things were happening.

After chores that morning, Matthew took a walk into the pasture and woods. Once more he looked to the hills. "I will lift up mine eyes unto the hills, from whence cometh my help. My help cometh from the Lord, which made heaven and earth."

Last night's nightmare had faded. The spring planting was done, except for corn. He welcomed this short break from hard work. Often, this break came at the time of his birthday. Tonight, the family would celebrate. Ellen had baked a cake, and the family would be there.

There are times when events and revelations all come together at once. Matthew's birthday was such a day.

Ellen and the girls were washing and wiping dishes, and Matthew and Johnie were changing from their "barn clothes" into something dressier when Victoria drove up the driveway. Matthew always knew which sister was driving. Law-abiding as she was, Victoria drove a little too fast.

Victoria stopped the car. James had come with his aunt because he'd worked after school on the newspaper. Martha and Ma were in the back seat. James helped his grandmother out of the car. Martha held her birthday card for her brother. They hurried into the house and the kitchen.

In the midst of noise and activity, Matthew received birthday greetings. A few minutes later, Ed and the kids drove up. And within a short time, Corrine and Warren and the three girls arrived. Matthew's birthday gathering was in full swing.

Matthew always enjoyed people—especially his family, but it seemed too many people descended on him all at once. After the children went outside, Victoria pulled Matthew aside. "We have to talk—later."

In typical fashion, the children remained outside with their activities. The women stayed in the kitchen, and the men moved into the living room.

Matthew sensed that that both Warren and Ed had something on their minds. They had talked about hog prices and milk prices, but they had more urgent concerns.

Chapter Twenty-two

In the midst of talk about the likelihood of war, Warren spoke up. "You know something: I need more land. If I could only plant another eighty acres, I think I could manage to come out ahead this year."

Matthew couldn't help thinking of a possibility. "I'm looking at the way nothing is being done with the fields on the home place. Perhaps we could work something out."

"Do you think Larry would let that happen?" questioned Ed. "If you ask me, Larry's a lazy, good-for-nothing jerk. I hope he gets drafted and the army disciplines him."

Matthew thought of the circumstances. "It's almost May, but there's still enough time for wheat or oats to mature."

Warren shifted in his chair. "I think things are different now. I don't know what Larry's into, but he's doing very little work on the farm. Joan milks the cows, but how long can she do that?"

Ed grunted. "It's lucky Larry married a farm girl. I don't know what he does all day."

"The family needs to step in," said Matthew. "P.J. said the land should go back to Ma. And she can make use of any rental income from that land. We need to act."

"We all seem to have our problems." Ed clenched his fist.

"We need to act," Matthew repeated. "Warren, I have some extra seed grain. You go ahead and plant those fields on the home farm."

Warren quickly consented and began speaking aloud his plans.

Ed seemed to have a need to talk. "This world is filled with problems. For one thing, I have Mary to think about. I don't know when she'll be home. And then there's Jake." His voice trailed off.

Matthew waited for him to go on.

"I guess I've been too tough on him. I tried to treat him the way my father treated me. If I got out of line, he gave me a good whipping. And that's what helped make me the man I am today. But I'm afraid whipping a kid doesn't work anymore."

Matthew thought of his brother-in-law's ferocious temper. He said nothing.

"Jake's been skipping school. His grades have been terrible. He talks about quitting."

Both Matthew and Warren spoke at once. "He needs to get an education. These days you need more than an eighth-grade education."

"I know that," said Ed. "Some people make fun of a high school education. And that gives Jake big ideas."

Their discussion ended as Victoria entered, followed by the other women. "We have family business. We need to talk."

Ed frowned since his talk had been interrupted. "What's up? What can be this important?"

Victoria's teacher authority came through, and even Ed submitted to her direction. "I think this involves all of us here. And if we're united, I think we can take care of the situation."

Matthew wondered what this could be.

"Mother received a notice about the delay of insurance money for the house. There was a clause in the policy stating that the house must be re-built on the same area. That makes a big difference."

Matthew wondered where this was leading.

"Mother and Father have always paid the insurance. That means, without question, this money belongs to Mother."

Matthew began to realize the impact. "I see what you mean."

Victoria talked faster and faster. "First, Larry's staying at Rita's house. And I think we can convince him to give up on milking cows."

She paused briefly and went on. "We'll have the new house built with the insurance money. "And," she looked at each person, "we can have Corrine and Warren move in. From there on, I have a lawyer who thinks we have a good chance of enforcing P.J.'s last wishes in that letter. We're going to get the farm back in the right hands. And we can go further and prove that the original signing away of the farm was done fraudulently."

Warren was speechless.

Corrine moved over, looking into Warren's eyes. "That's almost too good to be true. I always loved the home farm."

The conversation became animated. For the first time in more than three years, Matthew saw a real answer to the P.J. problem. He didn't want to move back to the home farm, but if somehow it went to Corrine and Warren, that would be the solution.

Once more, Victoria took charge. "We need to confront Rita and Larry. Tell them that we've got a case and that we mean to take action. We'll let Larry use the pasture for beef cattle, but Warren will take over."

Ma had been quiet all along. "This is an answer to prayer."

"Ma, I know you don't want trouble." Victoria cleared her throat. "However, my lawyer friend said we have a case against P.J.'s estate. We can prove P.J. defrauded his own father."

Matthew could see his mother trembling.

Chapter Twenty-two

"Let's pray it doesn't go that far," she said. "After all, Larry is family, even if he doesn't act like family."

This time, Martha interrupted as Ellen returned to the kitchen. "Matthew, it's time to celebrate your birthday. Let's call the kids. Ellen made a cake and so did Mother. We'll have cake and coffee and other goodies. Happy birthday, my brother."

Martha gave Matthew a hug. God's love was evident in the way the family could come together. And this rich land and home was more than he had ever dreamed of. God was good.

In minutes the happy group boisterously sang "Happy birthday." Matthew liked the second verse. "Happy birthday, God bless you, another year through."

To Matthew, the cake and coffee and Jell-O and other goodies never tasted so good. Underneath the celebration, he felt hope that the wrongs of P.J. would come to an end.

An hour later, the visitors left. No one seemed ready to go to bed. Even Michael remained quietly content with his older brothers and sisters. Matthew felt a kind of peace that seemed rare these days. All seemed right with the world.

"It's bedtime," announced Ellen. "Morning comes fast."

Matthew yawned. "I think I'll take a look at the paper. We've been so busy I haven't read the news."

Johnie picked up the paper and handed it to him. "It's a day old."

Matthew took the paper and opened it. A letter fell out. He looked at the address. "James, this letter is for you."

James's eyes lit up as he saw the return address. He trembled as he opened the letter. He had the attention of the rest of his family.

"Wow! I can't believe it."

Matthew knew this was something out of the ordinary.

"I've sold my story to *The Young People*. And I've received my first check as a writer."

Ellen and the others crowded around James. Matthew always knew this would happen.

James began reading. "We are happy to accept your story, "One Stormy Night." You've done a fine job. Your story, however, will not be published until next winter. I'd like to encourage you to do more stories and send them to this periodical."

"How much is the check?" asked Carol.

"Nine dollars and thirty-five cents. I get paid half a cent for each word I write."

"You'll have to write lots of words," said Johnie.

"I'm proud of you," said Ellen. "You'll go far." She turned to the others. "And the rest of you will go far in whatever you do. We have much to be thankful for."

Matthew experienced pride and happiness, but he also felt sadness. James would soon leave home and go away to school or the army—far beyond those hills. He loved having all the children near by, but this changing world would take them far away.

"Why don't we end the day by singing our family song?" Ellen went to the piano and played the introductory notes. Matthew and the children began to sing:

Children of the Heavenly Father,
Safely in His Bosom gather.
Nestling bird nor star in heaven,
Such a refuge
Ne'er was given.

Chapter 23

May 1941

Elizabeth Anderson looked again at the psalm she had been reading. "Thy word is a lamp unto my feet." Many times she had been guided by those comforting words. God was in control, and He would be with her in these times of being alone.

She had been in the habit of praying aloud. "Thank You, Lord. You have answered my prayers about loneliness. I'm busy now. Thank you that I have tasks to do. I'm happy to be useful."

Even as she prayed, she heard the carpenters get out of their cars. Men in the family and community had cleaned up the remains of the burned-down house. Today carpenters would be working on the foundation for the new house. She found comfort in their voices and the pounding and other noises and activity. She would be doing the cooking, but she wondered if she could handle all those tasks.

One thing about Victoria: when she moved into action, she moved fast. Mr. Edwards, who had built the first house thirty years ago, was building this house. It would be much like the house she had enjoyed and loved.

Even so, Elizabeth missed the house that had burned. It contained a host of memories from that earlier time. Most of all she thought of John and how hard they had worked that summer when the first house was built. Each of the children had been a part of that exciting venture. That summer perhaps had been the happiest of her life. They were all together, working and playing and laughing. But now those were only golden memories of an old woman.

A light knock on the door interrupted her reverie. "Mother, I'm here."

Martha stood by the door with her suitcase. "I'm staying here as long as those carpenters are working, and I'll do the cooking. I quit my job at the café. They didn't really need me. I'll take the upstairs bedroom."

Elizabeth breathed a sigh of relief. "I guess I'm old and don't get around as fast. I could use the help."

"When you're over seventy, you shouldn't be doing all that hard work. I'll run out to the car. I prepared something. The chicken's all ready to go."

"I planned to have ham for dinner."

"We'll save that for tomorrow."

Elizabeth wasn't quite ready to sit down. "I have some sponge cake, and I discovered a jar of raspberry sauce. We can have raspberry shortcake."

"The men will love that."

Martha hurried out to her car and returned with the groceries.

Elizabeth set out the jar of raspberry sauce. She was beginning to feel her seventy-three years. Martha scurried about the kitchen, getting everything in order for the noon dinner.

Elizabeth began to feel she was in the way and sat down. It felt good to have someone else taking the responsibility and doing some of the work. Martha found the potatoes and began to peel them.

"Mother, there's something I need to tell you."

Elizabeth knew this was something serious. "What is it, dear?"

Martha began slowly and deliberately. "I know you've agreed that we should carry out P.J.'s wishes in that letter."

Elizabeth nodded her reply.

"And that Larry should live down at the lake home with Rita as he is now. And we agree that Corrine and Warren and the girls should live here in the new house."

Elizabeth hardly needed to think about this. "That would be wonderful. Since Matthew isn't living there, I'd like nothing better than to have my granddaughter next door."

Chapter Twenty-three

"That's what we hope to accomplish. Victoria is coming over early this evening, and so is Matthew. We're going to talk to Rita and Larry. We have to work with them."

Tears clouded Elizabeth's eyes. "Please, I hope there won't be any trouble. I know Larry's done wrong things and so has Rita. But I don't want trouble."

"We'll take care of everything. You can come along if you want to."

She thought a moment. "No. I think I'd rather not. I'll pray instead."

"I feel confident. This will all work out."

Elizabeth wasn't so sure. Next to P.J., her daughter Victoria could be about as stubborn and bullheaded as anyone. Victoria was not afraid of trouble. But trouble and conflict Elizabeth did not want.

Matthew hated conflict of any kind, but there were times a person needed to stand up for what was right. He drove down the road to P.J.'s lake home with Victoria in the front seat and Martha seated in back. The two sisters were silent.

The fragrance of spring was everywhere. Apple and plum trees were blooming along with the first violets and other flowers of spring. Matthew loved this season. In another week the lilacs would blossom. New life brought joy, but he felt apprehensive about the meeting.

Matthew and his sisters walked to the front door. Much to his surprise, Rita opened the door before they could ring the door bell. "Good evening. Won't you come in?"

The three greeted their sister-in-law. Rita greeted them in a pleasant and cordial manner.

"I made some coffee. Let's sit in the living room." Rita motioned for them to go to the living room, and she went to the kitchen for the coffee and cups.

Matthew saw the knowing glances that passed between his sisters. Rita was trying her pleasant approach.

Matthew and his sisters sat together on the davenport. Rita returned with the cups of coffee already poured. She then hurried back to the kitchen and returned with a plateful of cookies.

Beyond the Storm

"Larry's cleaning up after milking. He'll be here in a few minutes."

Some awkward small talk followed. Matthew had never felt comfortable around Rita. She had ways he did not understand. Her attitude could change like the shifting winds.

Larry entered, mumbling a greeting. Matthew stood and shook hands with his nephew.

Victoria began to take charge. "We need to talk." She looked over at her nephew. "What's wrong? You look terrible."

Larry avoided his aunt's steady gaze. "I had some bad luck today. The creamery returned yesterday's milk. They said the milk was infected and couldn't be used. They put something in it, so I couldn't even feed it to the pigs."

Matthew knew what had happened. "Larry, you said you had a sick cow. Well, the milk from that cow is infected. Whenever that happens, that milk can't be used. If you keep that cow's milk away, the rest of the milk should be OK."

"Thanks Uncle Matthew."

Victoria cleared her throat and then continued, using her voice of commanding authority. "We came here tonight because something has to be done. We have the letter with P.J.'s wishes. We aim to see that these are carried out."

Rita looked to Larry for a response, but he said nothing. She re-positioned herself on her chair. "If you check in the court house, the land is in now deeded to P.J. The probating will take place."

Matthew felt that churning in his stomach once more. How could Rita ignore the family who rightfully should have this land?

Victoria stood up, her tall dark features commanding respect outside the classroom. "I think we have some news for you."

Matthew waited for the next words. He felt his muscles tighten as if he were about to fight. He was not a fighter, but he remembered those few times as a boy when he had fought an obnoxious schoolmate.

"I don't think there's much you can do." Larry's dark features seemed a duplicate of his father's. The nephew he had known was now a stranger. "The insurance was in Mother's and Dad's names. The insurance money comes to Mother. She and Dad would have life-time rights to the homestead."

Larry stood up and began to pace. "Grandma's an old lady. She might not be around that much longer."

Chapter Twenty-three

This time the gentler Martha responded. "I'm embarrassed that I have to call you nephew. Shame on you."

"Well, I spoke the truth."

Victoria folded her arms in her determined manner. "There's more."

The eyes of everyone focused on Victoria.

"I've done some investigating. And I've had others do a more thorough investigation. And I don't think you'll like what I'm finding."

Both Rita and Larry looked visibly shaken.

"First, we've retained a lawyer. He's checked all the documents. We don't want to take this to court, but we will if we have to. My lawyer says that P.J. committed fraud back when he had Dad sign over the farm. And there are some other legal technicalities. If we take this to court, we will win. I'm confident of that."

"You wouldn't do such a thing, would you?" questioned Rita. "We're family. We shouldn't get involved in litigation."

Victoria looked directly at Rita and then Larry. "We'd rather not, but the rest of the Andersons have been defrauded, and we're going to make things right."

"But you can't do this," stuttered Larry.

"Oh, yes we can. And there's more. Much more."

Larry groaned. Rita looked perplexed.

"I hired an investigator, and I've talked with Sheriff Walker." She walked over to Larry, standing close to him. "And there are some dealings you've had with Chicago people. Those dealings are highly questionable. When we do more investigating, we are likely to find illegal transactions."

"You couldn't do this to your own nephew." Rita began wringing her hands.

"Oh, yes we could—and will!"

Larry walked toward the front hallway as if he wanted to escape.

Rita followed him and then spoke. "We'll do something. I don't know if we can meet all your demands."

"For starters," began Victoria, "when the house is built, Corrine and Warren will live there. And for now, Warren will farm the land. We'll settle details of ownership later."

Rita started to say something but stopped.

"In addition, Warren will use the barn for his cattle. You, Larry, will move any cattle you have to the old barn. That is good enough for your cattle."

Matthew had wanted to say something, and finally the words came. "Larry, you're not taking decent care of your milk cows. That's why you're having problems. Work with your beef cattle. There's plenty of pasture for the beef."

Larry's face showed a look of defeat. Then his eyes began to spark anger. "I hate this place. I should never have come here."

"Don't say that, son. I need you here. And you do have your father's business to take care of."

By this time Matthew spoke the words that Victoria very well could have said. "Young man, the best thing that could happen to you would be the army. Some good discipline would straighten you out."

Rita's manner had changed by this time. "Listen here, Matthew, you have no right to say that. I won't stand for it."

Victoria interrupted. "Matthew speaks the truth, and you know it. Now, let's get back to business. You will take care of the necessary signing of the legal documents. The farm should belong to Mother and all her children."

"You're not going to order me about, Victoria. You know that P.J. had the title to the land, and there is nothing you can do. The land is now mine and Larry's."

Victoria stood tall to her full height, making Rita look small by comparison. "If you don't do what I say, you'll have to accept what the court is going to say. And, Rita Anderson, you know that we have a solid case. Right always wins."

Rita turned aside from her formidable opponent.

Larry moved over to his mother. "They can't do anything, can they? The land is ours, isn't it?"

"Don't worry, Larry." Rita's words did not carry much conviction.

"There's something else I haven't told you." Victoria stopped abruptly. Matthew could see Rita's puzzled reaction. "We have a witness to that agreement years ago. P.J. should have been legally bound to sign back the land. This testimony will stand up in court. There was fraud, no question about it."

Rita cleared her throat.

Martha broke the silence. "We just want you to do the decent thing without having to go to court. But we do mean business."

Chapter Twenty-three

Tears came to Rita's eyes. "So this is the way you treat Paul John's widow. It's as if I was never part of the family. How can you be so cold and callous?"

Victoria did not hesitate. "We are not the ones who are cold and callous. You, and I'm sorry to say, my brother P.J. were callous and hard and manipulative."

Rita dried her tears. "OK," she said, "for now you will have the house. And Larry will use the old barn. But I'll see my Chicago attorney. Then, we'll see what happens."

Victoria stood up and walked toward the hallway. "I hoped we wouldn't have to take legal action, but we will. Good night!"

Matthew and Martha followed Victoria and silently went to the car.

Rita and Larry said nothing.

Elizabeth knew her children weren't telling her everything. It didn't seem possible that Rita would just deed the land back to her and the family.

Martha reached over and touched her mother's hand. "In just a few months you'll have neighbors in the new house. Corrine and Warren will be there, and they'll look in on you."

Elizabeth turned to Matthew and Victoria. "I can't believe it's all that simple."

"Mother, things will work out." Victoria kissed her mother on the cheek. "I've got to be going."

Matthew stooped down and gave his mother a hug. "I've got to get home. Early morning chores come much too soon."

Elizabeth understood farm life all too well. The early hours could be used as an excuse for almost anything.

After Victoria and Matthew left, she turned to Martha. "I know there's more. Please tell me. Don't keep an old lady in the dark."

Martha hesitated. "Victoria can be forceful, and she was."

"I know that all too well."

"Victoria retained a lawyer. She has a strong case. Mrs. Robertson was witness when you signed the land to P.J. with a clear stipulation that he would return the ownership to you. We could go to court if necessary."

Elizabeth gave a deep sigh. "I guess we can't avoid trouble."

"We're only following P.J.'s wishes as presented in that final letter. It's what he wanted."

"I'm tired." Elizabeth felt aches everywhere in her bones. "I'm going to bed. Only a miracle will solve this problem."

Elizabeth lay awake for hours. In the middle of the night she stood by her window, looking out at the spot where the new house would stand. She couldn't help wondering what the future would hold.

"Dear Lord," she prayed. "Bless each and every member of my family. Take care of Larry and let him seek Your guidance. And bless Joan and take care of the precious new baby that will soon come. I don't know what to do. Please, Lord, show me the way. I commit all these problems to You."

Finally, sleep settled over her as the first light of morning began to appear.

Chapter 24

June 1941

Three sharp rings wakened Matthew. This had to be an emergency. Ellen, already awake, hurried to the kitchen to answer the phone.

Matthew wiped the sleep from his eyes. The alarm clock on the dresser read 3:30.

Ellen returned to the bedroom and began to dress. "It's Joan. She's having sharp pains. She needs help."

Matthew moved slowly, beginning to dress. He wasn't quite awake. "Where's Larry anyway?"

"Obviously, not there. He's never around when he's needed or when there's work to be done."

"But there's Rita." Then he remembered Rita had left to visit her sister. And Martha should have been at Ma's, but she was called away to her daughter Rachel's. That meant none of the closest people were around.

"We'd better let the boys know about doing chores." Ellen put on her plain blue dress. "I think I better go with you in case the baby comes early. I've been through a home delivery before."

Matthew and Ellen moved into action. Within twenty minutes they were driving by the home place. He hoped Ma wouldn't awaken. She'd been having trouble sleeping lately. He glanced at the partially-built new house.

"The carpenters are moving fast, aren't they?" Matthew said.

"Your mother should do just fine when Corrine and Warren move in. That's a perfect solution."

Matthew looked at the barn and thought of the milk cows that Larry didn't seem to care for. "That is if Larry doesn't somehow stop Corrine and Warren."

"With Victoria fighting and hiring a lawyer, I don't think he's likely to."

"I know I let go and forgave P.J. long ago, but he's hurt and cheated the rest of the family."

"Scars remain," replied Ellen. "And the effects of his actions will live on indefinitely. Look at the way Larry is following in his father's footsteps."

By this time, Matthew stopped the car in front of P.J.'s house.

They hurried up the steps and went inside, not bothering to knock. The kitchen light was on. Painful moans came from somewhere nearby.

"Joan. Joan, where are you?" Ellen called out.

They hurried into the kitchen where they found her seated at the kitchen table. She kept calling. "Why did you leave me here alone? Why, Larry? Why?"

"We're here," reassured Ellen. "We'll get you to the hospital. Did you call Dr. Baker to let him know that you're in labor?"

"No, I didn't think. I just knew I had to get help."

Ellen hurried to the phone and called central. "Central. Emergency. It's Ellen Anderson. Could you just notify Dr. Baker that Joan Anderson is in labor? Matthew and I are taking her to the hospital."

Ellen hurried ahead to open doors. Matthew carried Joan to the car and placed her in the back seat. He kept praying that nothing would go wrong.

Matthew shifted the car into gear and began racing down the township road onto the state highway, ignoring stop signs and driving faster than he ever had. "I'm glad this is June and not February when Michael was born."

By the time they reached River Falls, Joan's cries had subsided and she had calmed down. Matthew carried her into the hospital and felt a sense of relief when he saw Dr. Baker waiting.

Chapter Twenty-four

"She's better," said Ellen. "I think she was afraid of being alone with the baby coming."

Dr. Baker took one look. "I don't think she'll have long to wait."

Several hours later, Matthew wakened from a nap when Ellen poked him. "The baby's here. We can see Joan."

He looked up at the clock that told him 8:30. It seemed as if he had slept for hours. He straightened himself slowly. "Is the baby a girl or a boy?"

Ellen reached for his hand. "A boy." He stood up and followed her to Joan's room. Silently they entered her room. A sleepy young mother greeted them. The same protective feeling welled up within him that he had experienced as each of his own children was born. Birth was a miracle, revealing God at work.

"Thank you, Uncle Matthew and Aunt Ellen. I don't know what I would have done if you hadn't come."

"We're glad you came through so well." Ellen placed her hand on Joan's forehead. "We'll just stay a few minutes. You need your rest."

Joan strained to talk. "I'm afraid. I don't know what to do. Larry's gone all the time. He won't say what he's doing."

Matthew thought of his own journey as a father. "He's going to have to change. Change happens when a man becomes a father."

"I hope so. I can't be outside and take care of the baby at the same time."

"Have you thought of a name?" asked Ellen.

"Yes, I've decided. One of my favorite authors is James Russell Lowell. I want to name my boy Lowell."

Ellen stooped down to kiss Joan on the forehead. "What a beautiful name!"

"I want him to grow up to love poetry and everything beautiful around him. I don't want him to be thinking only about working and making money."

The nurse quietly entered. "I knew you'd want to hold your baby." She placed the child in Joan's arms.

Joan's voice filled with emotion. "What a responsibility I have. This beautiful child came from me. I must teach him to do what is right."

Matthew looked at the sleeping baby. In that moment he saw the dark features of P.J. as well as those of Larry. Whose footsteps would he follow? Could this child somehow break away from the hold of his father? He breathed a silent prayer for the young child.

Later that morning when they drove into Ma's yard, Matthew heard the cows bellowing. The cows' loud protests almost drowned out the hammering of the carpenters who were now working on the roof of the new house.

Ma stood on the back porch and called out. "I don't know what to do about those cows. What's happened anyway?"

"Well, Ma, Joan's in River Falls, and you have a new great-grandson."

"I thought I heard cars early this morning. But I guess I slept through everything."

Ellen explained the early-morning phone call and what had happened.

"Where can Larry be? He should be with his wife. And he's not done the morning milking."

At that moment a car drove in and stopped behind Matthew's car. Larry, looking tired and bedraggled, got out.

Matthew, feeling intense anger, walked over to his nephew. "Larry Anderson, where have you been? Your wife desperately needed you at three o'clock this morning."

"I had business to take care of. Important business."

Ellen walked over to stand beside her husband. "What could be more important than taking your wife to the hospital and being with her when she gives birth to your son? That's more important than any business you might ever have."

Larry objected. "But the baby wasn't due for a few weeks. I have to earn a living."

Matthew eyed the cows that were impatient to be milked. "Yes, and you're supposed to be a farmer taking care of your cattle. You'll have no milk to sell if you don't take better care of your cows."

"I can make more money elsewhere."

Chapter Twenty-four

"Yes, and if you don't do your farming, you might just find yourself working for Uncle Sam."

Larry's tone changed to one of quiet persuasion. "Uncle Matthew, I should go and see my wife in the hospital. Do you suppose you could milk the cows?"

Matthew started to say something, but his anger choked back the words. Then the words came forcefully. "Young man, you take care of your business. I will not do the work that you're too lazy to do." He pointed to the barn. "You get going right now. Let those cattle into the barn. They need to be milked immediately. And as soon as you finish, you get to River Falls and see your wife."

Larry, usually glib and ready with a quick answer, turned back to his car and grabbed a pair of overalls. Without another word, he walked to the barn.

Matthew surprised himself that he had been able to speak so honestly and forcefully to his nephew.

Ma smiled as she also noticed Larry's humble response. "Come in. I have almost everything ready for dinner. Why don't you stay? There are only three carpenters today, and I have plenty of food."

"Isn't all this cooking a little much for you?" asked Ellen. "Now that Martha's gone, you have all the work."

Ma quickly responded. "Oh, I've managed quite well. And in a few days Victoria is coming to help."

They entered the kitchen. Ellen surveyed the situation. "Why don't you let me set the table and get the potatoes ready?"

Ma agreed. She sat down and then yawned. "I guess I'm tired. I'm not as young as I used to be. But what about dinner for *your* children?"

Ellen laughed. "Margaret's in charge of the kitchen when I'm gone. She does quite a good job. She's turning into an excellent homemaker. In fact, she does much of the cooking and baking even when I'm there."

Matthew moved over and sat down near his mother. "Is there anything we can do to help? This time of year isn't quite so busy with farm work."

"Well," Ma began, "I'm afraid I'm running short of flour and a few things. When Martha left so suddenly, I wasn't quite ready. Matthew, do you suppose you could pick up some groceries in town."

Matthew and Ellen both nodded agreement.

Within the hour, Ma and Ellen had the noon dinner on the table. The three men, along with Matthew, Ellen, and Ma, ate heartily of roast beef, mashed potatoes, and creamed corn, topped off with rhubarb pie. Once again, Matthew thought, life is good.

After dinner, Matthew left Ellen and Ma as they washed the dinner dishes and did other cleaning. He took Ma's list and drove into town, going straight to the grocery store. After that, there was enough time to have coffee. Since Glenn Robertson happened to be in town, the two friends headed to the restaurant for coffee. Glenn always had the most up-to-date news.

The café was empty after the dinner crowd left so that meant the two friends had the place to themselves. Matthew knew that Glenn had something he couldn't wait to tell. This story must be a good one.

Glenn set down his coffee cup and leaned toward Matthew. "Some strange things have been happening around here. Have you heard?"

"No." Glenn obviously knew his answer.

"This morning, First National Bank in River Falls discovered they'd been robbed. The safe had been jimmied open. It seems it was an inside job."

"I didn't think anything like that happened around here."

Glenn continued with his news. "The sheriff and the police are puzzled by the whole thing. There have been some similar robberies a distance away. Nothing has happened nearby, so that makes it scary."

"It's been safe around here. Most people are honest." Matthew could sense that his friend had more to tell.

"Also, I heard that Ed had a big fight with Jake. And now Jake's taken off to who knows where."

Matthew thought of Mary in the TB sanitarium. "Things have gone from bad to worse with Mary away at the sanitarium. We don't see Ed and the kids the way we used to."

"Ed's been pretty tough on Jake. And Jake's turned into a bully. He's been running around with a wild crowd."

Matthew remembered the way Jake had made fun of James. "It seems worse when the kid's part of your own family."

The men's discussion changed to talk of war and "rumors of war" and the recent happenings. The sinking of the Bismark. The Germans invading Russia. Just a few days ago, President Roosevelt had announced

Chapter Twenty-four

a national emergency. It seemed inevitable that the United States would soon send men into battle.

Glenn concluded his comments, "The world's pretty messed up."

"I don't know where this will lead."

Before their discussion could go further, Sheriff Walker entered the café and headed to their booth.

"Hello Sheriff," greeted Glenn. "Have you solved the bank robbery case? I hear it might be an inside job."

Glenn moved over and Walker sat next to him.

"I've been investigating. And there's another case. I've been following some car tracks and skid marks. The robbers seem to have had another target after the bank."

The waitress brought the sheriff his coffee and re-filled the other cups.

"I don't suppose you've ever heard of old man Jenkins. No one knows much about him. He moved to a remote farm house five or six years ago, lives alone, has little to do with anyone. And rumors say he has a large amount of money hidden in his house. Well, his place was broken into."

Matthew remembered hearing about the man. "It seems to me that P.J. knew this man. I'm trying to remember more."

The Sheriff eyed him with interest. "If you can remember something, that might help."

"If P.J. had dealings with him," said Glenn, "it can't be good. I know I shouldn't speak ill of the dead."

Matthew knew Glenn was right and he began to remember. "I recall something my brother said. As you recall, P.J. seemed well-off at times, and then other times money was very tight. It seems he borrowed money from Jenkins. And I recall he had to pay him back."

"That bit of information may help." Sheriff Walker went on with his report. "It seems the car that went into Jenkins' place took many back roads and came here to Lake View. And with tarred roads, I can't see where the car went. I'd investigate south and east of town, but I'm afraid the rain shower wiped out the tracks."

The men continued to visit and drink coffee. The local situation looked as bad as the international problems.

An hour later as Matthew drove down the driveway to Ma's little house, he recalled the events of the night. Where had Larry been all night?

He knew P.J. and Larry had not been honest. But could Larry have been party to a bank robbery? Would he harm a helpless old man?

The disturbing thoughts remained with him the rest of the day.

CHAPTER 25

July 1941

Matthew sensed a fight was about to take place. Victoria's guarded words on the phone had told him Larry was making trouble for Warren. A month ago, Warren had moved his cattle to the barn on the home place. That was the beginning of the solution to the ownership question. But now it seemed Larry was once more interfering.

Matthew stopped the car, and he and his sons got out. He saw Victoria marching toward the barn where Larry faced Warren. For a moment he hesitated, wondering what he should do.

"Looks like trouble," said Johnie.

Matthew and his sons walked toward the barn as Victoria raised her voice.

"Larry, it's time you find your place. You don't belong on a farm, milking cows. You're not taking care of the cattle you have. This place is Warren's."

Larry began to yell like a man out of control. "What do you think you're doing with your cattle in my barn? You may think you've won this battle, but I have some plans."

Warren spoke quietly. "This is the family farm. I have been given the right to be here. And I will stay here. My cows will stay just where they are. Your cattle, that you never seem to take care of, will go to the old barn."

Larry shook his fist at Warren. "We'll see about that."

Matthew and his boys stood spellbound by the display of anger.

"Yes, we will see about that." Victoria stood between the two men. She stood tall with her dark blue eyes flashing sparks of anger.

Matthew stepped forward. "Larry, this farm will be back in the family legally where it belongs. If you and your mother do not cooperate, there will be more trouble than you have ever dreamed of."

Larry backed away from Matthew and Victoria. He mumbled something under his breath.

Victoria signaled the boys to come closer. "You might as well hear everything close up."

Matthew found the old anger returning. "We are claiming the land that belongs to the family. I should have been the rightful owner if P.J. hadn't manipulated and contrived to get the ownership."

"But Dad was the oldest son."

Victoria spoke up and seemed to say what Matthew was thinking. "Your dad had little interest in the farm until he needed a place to build a house and hide out. I'm embarrassed to admit that your father was my brother. At least at the end, he wanted to do the right thing. And it would be wise that you would agree to those wishes."

Larry turned toward the barn and pointed beyond. "You people talk of tradition. It's tradition that the farm goes to the oldest son. That goes far back in history."

Victoria started to say something, but Matthew interrupted. Ma remained on the porch steps.

Raising his voice only slightly, Matthew went on. "You, Larry, have ignored all the rest of tradition. There's something about morality and helping the rest of the family."

Victoria began speaking in her most commanding tone. "I've been with my lawyer, and I've talked to my friend, the judge. Your father fraudulently became owner of this property. That will stand up in court. Now, you can avoid all of this if you and your mother follow the last wishes of your father."

Larry's face reddened. "You accuse my father of bullying and manipulating." He turned to Matthew and Victoria. "You're the biggest bullies I've ever met."

Chapter Twenty-five

Matthew couldn't help smiling, though he tried to hide that smile. Victoria was the strongest woman he had met, but underneath she had a heart of gold. However, gentle Matthew had never been accused of being a bully.

Victoria moved close to Larry. "If I'm strong, I get that strength from being right and from getting what is rightfully Mother's and the whole family's. Getting what is a legacy of faith and determination and hard work of John and Elizabeth Anderson. You have absolutely no right to what you are claiming. I only regret that I didn't do this for Matthew four years ago."

Larry mumbled something under his breath. It sounded like a curse.

"Young man, watch your language. I am a lady, and I do not tolerate any profanity whether mumbled or spoken."

Larry began to back away. "You can't tell me what to do," he yelled. "And you get young kids to be your back up. These boys have no business here. They're too young to know what's going on."

Matthew followed Larry as he backed away. "This home place should have been mine. And these boys would be rightful heirs. There's no question about that."

Warren had been silent all this time, but he now began to speak. "This farm belongs to a family that cares about what happens to the land. I will preserve this place so that it can be passed on. You would exploit and destroy it. That's all you do."

"You're not family," sneered Larry. "You married Corrine. You've been a failure. You lost your farm back in Wisconsin."

Warren looked down, his face showing the hurt he must have felt. "Yes, and you've ruined your milk cows. You've had to sell all except three or four."

"Larry," said Matthew calmly, "you'll be getting what you deserve."

"If I were a man," shouted Victoria, "I'd give you a punch in the nose. But that's not the way to settle matters. You will get a punch in the nose through the legal system."

"We'll see." Larry turned and faced all of them. "It looks as if you need five people to face one of me. I've got friends too." He began walking away.

Victoria raised her voice. "Your friends won't even dare show up in respectable society. They sneak around in the dark when respectable people are sleeping."

Larry got into his car and drove away.

For a few moments the group remained silent and then walked toward Ma's little house.

Ma stood on the porch, looking sad and concerned. "Come in, all of you."

Victoria was the first to speak. "I think we have the situation under control. Larry knows he has the law to reckon with."

"I'm not so sure about that," said Warren. "I begin to wonder if we should move in when the new house is ready. I'm not so sure I want to deal with Larry."

Victoria led the way into the house. "You will not have to deal with Larry at all. I shall deal with him. I'm staying here to help Mother with the cooking for the carpenters. I'll be watching that rascal closely."

Matthew knew his sister meant business, and she was not a person to tangle with.

Johnie chuckled. "Aunt Victoria, I don't think I'd want to get on your wrong side. And I'd say Larry better watch out. But I don't trust him."

"Neither do I," Victoria added.

Warren repeated his concern. "I'm not sure I can stand living in a war zone with Larry."

Matthew calmly reassured Warren. "Your family is behind you. We're going to make sure you have a place to stay. And this new house that Ma's insurance money paid for is the right place for you."

Warren sat down next to Matthew. "What's right doesn't always win. That's a lesson I've learned."

Victoria firmly asserted, "Right will absolutely win in this case."

Matthew and Warren and the boys eagerly ate Ma's sandwiches. Then James and Johnie devoured several pieces of their grandmother's chocolate cake.

Just as Matthew approached his car to leave, he saw two cars driving down the lane to P.J.'s lake home. One glance told him it was Sheriff Walker's car. Was the law catching up with Larry Anderson? He could only hope.

Chapter Twenty-five

"Boys," Matthew announced after supper that evening, "would you come with me to check the wheat field out east? And we should also check the fences. One of the cows was out yesterday."

The boys seemed happy to go with their father.

At that moment a car drove up and Sheriff Walker got out.

James and Johnie eagerly followed their dad as he went out to greet the visitor.

Sheriff Walker hesitated when he saw the boys. "Matthew, I'm not sure what to think. I've got a problem, and I'd like to talk with you."

Matthew nodded. "Glad to be of help if I can."

"Maybe I shouldn't involve the boys."

Johnie didn't hesitate to respond. "Oh, Sheriff, we know more than you think. We'd make good detectives."

Walker smiled. "You think so."

"I don't know that you need to shield the boys from knowing what's going on. In fact, they're becoming suspicious as it is."

"Actually, I'm asking for your help. We had a search warrant because the car from some break-ins and the bank robbery appeared to go to P.J.'s house. Well, we searched the house and the grounds and found nothing. I don't know what to think."

Matthew began to realize the truth about his nephew. "I'm afraid Larry's a lot smarter than I thought. He's not too good with cattle and farm work, but I guess he inherited some of his father's brains and smooth talk."

Walker leaned against his car. "The old man east of River Falls had another break-in. It looked like the same person or persons. This time, Jenkins landed in the hospital. He's in serious condition. He may not make it."

Matthew thought of his nephew and the way he had been as a little boy. "I can believe Larry would cheat and lie, but I can't believe he'd beat up on an old man."

"He appears to have accomplices. Are you aware of other people coming and going?"

This time James interrupted. "Aunt Victoria said there had been traffic late at night. And sometimes Grandma has a hard time sleeping because of the cars."

"I hate to upset Mrs. Anderson," Walker included James and Johnie in his invitation, "but if you think of anything or hear anything, I'd like to know. And I'll talk with Mrs. Anderson."

Walker opened his car door, preparing to leave.

"We'll help you any way we can."

The trip out to the east fields to check fences and look at the grain was an excuse for Matthew to talk with the boys. James and Johnie had questions.

"How can a brother or cousin do these terrible things to other family members?" questioned James. "How could Uncle P.J. come from such a good home and do so much wrong?"

Both boys looked to Matthew for an answer. Matthew motioned for Johnie to start the John Deere. Johnie started the tractor. Matthew and James got on the platform.

"We'll talk about it, but I don't know if I have an answer."

The noise of the John Deere drowned out the conversation. The breeze and speed of the tractor made Matthew feel good inside. Here he was with two people who meant more to him than anyone else, other than Ellen and the girls. A male bonding, something beyond the ties of family, was taking place.

Johnie stopped the tractor. The three got off. Matthew pulled off a few heads of wheat. He rubbed the heads together and shelled out the grain. "It looks ready to cut."

James began again, "I can't understand how people can do such terrible things."

"There are rotten people around," stated Johnie. "And Larry is a rotten person."

Matthew walked along the barbed-wire fence, the boys following. "Sometimes people are hard to explain."

"Larry's just taking after his father." Johnie, quick to answer, didn't hesitate.

James, a little more thoughtful, added, "Uncle P.J. had his good side. He could be generous when he had money."

"Son, you're right. Your uncle did have a good side."

Chapter Twenty-five

Matthew saw the spot where the fence needed mending. The three worked, tightening the barbed wire and nailing the wire securely.

Matthew very much wanted to make sense of his brother's actions, and he did know some of the history. "Your uncle was always ambitious. He didn't like the hard work of the farm even though he was big and strong and could do good work. He wanted to get away."

Johnie poked his brother. "James wants to get away too."

James objected to the comparison. "I only want to learn about the world out there. I want to write and somehow make this world a better place."

"Sorry, brother."

"There are dangers out there," began Matthew. "P.J. stayed with a cousin in Prairie Center. They had values that were different from the values of our family. Liquor was a regular thing in their household. P.J. started down the wrong road."

"Is liquor really that bad?" questioned Johnie.

"Some people can't handle it. P.J. could handle quite a few drinks, it seemed. I never could. A few drinks changed me completely."

James looked surprised. "I can't see you drinking."

"Well, I did. But I soon realized it wasn't right."

James walked ahead as the three checked the fence. "Tell us more about P.J. and what happened."

Matthew stopped and went on with his story. "P.J. went away and seemed to be making good money. He was tall and dark and good looking. He was a born salesman. People were impressed with him."

"Good-looking people have an advantage," said James. "Some people look honest, and they can fool others."

"That was P.J. When P.J. came back with fancy cars and nice clothes, people were impressed. And then he married Rita and she was a beautiful southern belle. But as she visited, we found that she didn't fit in with ordinary people like us."

"What happened to make people dislike P.J. and become suspicious?" asked Johnie.

"I don't know exactly when it happened. He would show off his fancy cars and clothes. I think some people were jealous. People here work hard and don't have a lot of money. They began to think he was doing something illegal. That happened when some of his friends and business associates started showing up."

"Was he doing something illegal?" asked Johnie.

"He was involved with illegal bootlegging during Prohibition. Afterwards he was involved in questionable business operations."

Johnie pulled up a large weed and threw it into the woods. "If he knew these things were wrong, why did he keep doing them?"

Matthew thought a moment. "When a person doesn't listen to his conscience, he can do wrong without feeling any pangs of regret."

James responded. "Uncle P.J. had all the things a person could ever want. Yet, he wanted more. I don't understand. Enough is enough, isn't it?"

Matthew's sons never ceased to surprise him with their insights. He had to credit Ellen with teaching them great spiritual truths of life. "There's something terrible about greed. Greed never satisfies. A person always wants more."

James stopped to pound another nail. "Was Uncle P.J. ever happy?"

Johnie came back with another question. "Can someone be happy if he's such a jerk? I don't think so."

Matthew wanted to be fair but honest. "I don't know that he was ever really happy. Your uncle seemed to be two people. He could be kind and helpful. But he could be vicious and controlling. I couldn't begin to understand my brother."

"He was like Dr. Jekyl and Mr. Hyde," said James. "Two people. A split personality."

Matthew and his boys came to the property line and turned back.

James fell behind and then ran to catch up with his father and brother. "Look at what he did with Cousin Pete. He knew Pete had a drinking problem and wanted to stop. Yet, he got him to take another drink."

Matthew remembered only too well the way P.J. had taunted Pete, calling him weak. "When someone does something wrong, he likes to have company. P.J. wanted others to look up to him and do the same things he did."

Almost in unison James and Johnie mimicked, "Watch who your friends are. A person is known by the friends he keeps."

Matthew laughed. He realized the boys had listened.

As they approached the tractor, Matthew began to tell of his last visit with P.J. "Your uncle was in torment when I saw him last. He was remembering things he had done, but it was too late for him to make change. That last visit still haunts me."

"What did he say?"

Chapter Twenty-five

"It wasn't exactly what he said, but it was the fear and hopelessness that I saw in his eyes."

The three stood on that spot, talking quietly about life and matters of right and wrong. This was one of those times Matthew would long remember.

When Matthew and the boys returned to the house, the light and voices from the kitchen invited them to hurry and join the company. Ma and Victoria and Ed had joined Ellen and the girls in drinking coffee. Ed looked troubled.

Ellen poured the cups of coffee and nodded to Ed. "Ed came to tell us something he wants us to know."

"Is something wrong with Mary?" Matthew blurted out.

"No. Mary's actually doing quite well." Ed looked down. "It's Jake. He's taken off. I think he's gone to Dakota, looking for work."

Victoria didn't hesitate to comment. "Ed, that might be a good thing for him. He can learn what the world is like out there. He'll find things are better at home."

"I hope you're right. But, Victoria, some rough characters work in those threshing crews."

Johnie interrupted. "I know Jake can take care of himself. He's a good fighter."

Ed smiled and looked away. "Yes, Jake likes to think he's tough, but some of those characters are into gambling and drinking and more. They'd enjoy teaching a kid the wilder side of life. Jake doesn't need that."

Everyone seemed to have an idea about Jake and how he would meet the situations. Others tried to soothe Ed's concerns.

When a pause in the conversation came, Ma trembled even as she spoke. "We're facing so many big problems. We need to pray. We need to pray for Jake."

Ed looked uncomfortable. "You do that, Elizabeth."

Ma reached her hand out to her son-in-law. "We all need to."

The phone rang several rings, interrupting the quiet. Ellen hurried to answer. Matthew listened but could tell very little from the one side of the conversation.

Ellen returned to the table. "Matthew, it was Larry. He'd like to see you. I said you'd stop tomorrow morning."

Victoria set down her cup decisively. "I think I should have more words with him. He had better listen."

Ma replied gently, "But, dear Victoria, you might need to listen to him."

Victoria, looking surprised, said nothing.

Matthew said what he hoped would be true. "It's all going to turn out right." But underneath he wasn't so sure.

Chapter 26

August 1941

A week later, Matthew sat spellbound, looking at the dark clouds and sharp streaks of lightning. He looked to the west, where black rolling clouds covered the late afternoon sun. Something within him said this storm was serious.

Ellen and the girls were finishing supper dishes. James was in his room as usual, probably writing another story. Johnie sat silently, enjoying the strange kind of beauty of a summer storm that was about to happen.

Matthew thought back to that last conversation with Larry. He saw a side of Larry so different from the side he usually saw.

Larry's words still repeated themselves in his mind. "Please, Uncle Matthew, I'm afraid. Don't let Victoria go to court or to the police. We'll work out something. But I need to be on the farm. I don't know where else I could go. I feel safer here than anywhere else. I want to start doing things right if you will only give me a chance."

Larry had gone on about living in his mother's house and renting out tourist cabins. To Matthew it seemed he was finally looking after Joan and his young son.

Larry's last words Matthew would not forget. "If I have to give up all of the farm, I don't know what I'll do. There are people out there who were out to get my father. Now, I'm afraid they may be out to get me. I'm safer here than anywhere else. I love Joan and I love my son. I have to stay and try to do what's right."

At times Matthew doubted his nephew's words. Like P.J., Larry seemed to have the knack of saying the right thing if it was convenient.

Ellen's voice jolted Matthew back to the storm. "The storm is getting worse. Should we go to the basement?"

The wind velocity had increased. Box elder trees bent low to the ground. Loud cracking of breaking branches followed. The wind propelled those branches into the air as if they were small match sticks.

"Yes! To the basement, everyone!" shouted Matthew. "Leave everything. I mean business! This storm is dangerous."

Johnie loitered behind. Ellen called to James. Little Michael, frightened of the loud noise and wind, clung to Matthew.

In moments the Andersons stood close together near the bottom of the basement stairway. Sudden darkness followed a loud clap of thunder. Lightning must have struck nearby.

"Go to the northeast corner. This is a tornado. If the house goes, we'll be safer there."

Michael held Matthew tightly. Ellen moved to the northeast corner. The girls followed close to Ellen. Johnie and James stayed close to Matthew.

Carol whimpered, "I'm scared."

"You're safe here with us," reassured Matthew.

"I think we need to ask God for protection," said Ellen. "We haven't had a storm like this in years."

Matthew agreed. "You pray, Ellen."

"Dear Lord," began Ellen. "Help us. We ask for Your protection in this time of storm. Make us safe in Your care. Shelter us from the dangers of this storm. And we ask for Your safe keeping of all those nearby. For our family. For our neighbors. You are our shelter in the time of storm. In the name of Jesus, amen."

The house creaked. For a moment, Matthew thought the storm would take it. He had heard about storms like this, but had never experienced one.

The next minutes seemed like hours. Finally, the winds quieted, and the basement room was flooded with light. The electricity had come back on.

Chapter Twenty-six

Matthew peered through the basement window. "It's safe," he announced. "Let's see how much damage has been done."

The family hurried upstairs and looked outside. Much to Matthew's relief only a few branches lay scattered around the yard. One giant elm tree had blown down. He and the boys would take care of that.

"Come on, boys, we'll check the cattle," Matthew shouted to the boys.

Matthew and the boys hurried to the barnyard. He wanted to shout for joy when he saw the cattle huddled close together near a clump of trees. Johnie quickly counted them. They were all safe.

The clouds opened, and the sun broke through. In a short while the sun would set. Once more, the family gathered on the front porch to watch the clouds and the sunset.

Ellen moved forward, opened the screen door, and went outside. "Look! There's a rainbow. Its colors are beautiful."

The rest of the family followed and stood quietly in the front yard, amazed at the colors of the rainbow.

"It's a sign of hope after the rain—after the storm," Ellen added.

A troubling thought came to Matthew. "I wonder if everything's OK with Ma and Victoria. I think we better check."

As he and Johnie approached the home place, Matthew saw a stack of wheat tipped over and tree branches scattered on the driveway. He felt panic. Johnie stopped the car halfway to the little house. "We're going to have to move some branches."

"First, let's make sure Grandma and Victoria are OK."

They hurried out of the car. Johnie ran ahead to the little house. Matthew couldn't quite keep up with his agile and athletic son. In the darkness Matthew stopped himself from stumbling over a branch. Dim lamplight showed through the kitchen window, indicating that the storm had cut off electricity.

Victoria appeared on the porch steps with a lamp. "We're all right. But it looks as if we lost some trees and branches."

Matthew looked to the almost-completed new house. From what he could see, the new house had survived in good shape. They exchanged news of the storm and its development. Apparently, the storm was much worse over here on the home farm.

Matthew began to take charge. "Let's get the driveway cleared so we can drive in and out."

Ma went inside, obviously to make a pot of coffee. Victoria didn't hesitate to help her brother and nephew clear away branches. A half-hour of moving branches cleared the road and other paths.

Johnie drove the car to the house, and Ma announced, "There's coffee on. You've worked hard."

Lunch always followed hard work. In minutes Ma and Victoria with Matthew and Johnie sat down to lunch, which included Ma's egg salad sandwiches.

Ma began to reflect. "This storm was bad, but I think the grasshoppers of the nineties were worse. And those dry years of the thirties. They were unbearable."

Matthew looked out at the darkness. "Back in the thirties during those dry times, I said many times that I would never complain about too much rain."

Victoria smiled. "Yes, and we certainly got it tonight—along with a real storm. I think we'd call it a cyclone or tornado. The last serious cyclone came in 1919."

"I've never been through one of these before," said Johnie. "I suppose James is in his room, writing a story about it."

At that moment lights from a car reflected through the window.

"It's Corrine and Warren and the children," said Victoria. "Glenn's driving." Victoria, followed by the rest, hurried outside.

Glenn Robertson stepped out of the car. "Their house is in pretty bad shape," he announced.

"It was so terrible," cried Corrine. "I thought for sure we'd all be killed."

Ma hurried down the steps and threw her arms around her granddaughter. "Come in, my dear, you need to dry off."

The three little girls clung to their mother.

Victoria, as usual, began to take charge. "We need to get you some dry clothes. Come inside now."

While the women went inside, Warren stood back. He was still trembling from the frightening event. "I can't take any more of this. The house is in bad shape. It's off the foundation. And I don't know what's left of our possessions."

Chapter Twenty-six

Glenn began to reassure. "We'll see in the morning. It's not raining now. And you'll find there's more left than you think. My uncle was in the cyclone of 1919, and they recovered many of their personal goods."

Victoria and Ma took the children inside the house. Matthew heard Ma's voice giving comfort to the children. And Victoria was close by, directing and telling the children what to do.

"How about the barn?" questioned Matthew.

"That's completely gone," said Glenn.

"I'm glad we moved the cattle over here." Warren wiped his face with an old bandanna.

"I wonder if they're all right," he added.

"The cattle seem to be near the barn now," said Matthew. "You went to the cellar, didn't you?"

"The storm happened so suddenly we barely made it. There was this sudden roar, the loudest roar I've ever heard. Then in that small cellar we heard all that cracking and crashing."

"That's the way these storms go," said Glenn. "I drove over here because I figured something might be wrong."

"I don't know what I'd have done if Glenn hadn't come. The car's blocked in by fallen trees."

Glenn put his hand on Warren's shoulder. "That house wasn't fit to live in. I let you live there because it seemed you didn't have anywhere else."

"We didn't." Warren rubbed his eyes. "And I wonder what happens now."

Matthew felt confident now that things would work out. "You and Corrine will live in the new house. In fact, the downstairs is ready so you can move in. There's no question about it: you'll be living in the house next to Ma."

"This is more than I hoped for. The timing is good."

Glenn said, "And the neighbors will see to it that you have beds and chairs and tables. We take care of people when they've had tough times."

Matthew remembered the storage shed. "We have an extra bed and some other furniture."

"It's hard to accept all this kindness."

"I remember years ago," began Glenn, "when I was just a kid. Dad became seriously ill during spring planting. Well, the whole neighborhood came and did the planting. They gave of their own seed and didn't expect anything in return. That's the way neighbors are."

Matthew added, "When I had my illness, neighbors were nearby. We were lucky enough to get Joe as hired man. When it was moving time for me, the whole neighborhood turned out, and we had everything moved in one day."

"I guess there's still hope." Warren shivered as a cool breeze blew.

Matthew walked up the porch steps and motioned to Warren. "You come on in and get out of those wet clothes. We don't want you getting sick after all you've been through."

As they entered the house, Victoria held up night clothes. "Warren, you go upstairs and get out of those wet clothes. We found Dad's old pajamas. They'll fit you for one night."

Warren accepted the pajamas and trudged wearily up the stairway.

"I've heated some milk. The kids had some hot milk and they're sleeping. Now it's time for the rest of us to have some."

A few minutes later, Warren and Corrine sat at the kitchen table, sipping hot milk. To Matthew they seemed like children who had gone through more than anyone should have to go through.

"We may have lost almost everything," said Corrine, "but we have each other and the children."

"And we have our friends and family," added Warren.

Johnie had been a silent observer and finally spoke. "Isn't there something about loving your neighbor as yourself?"

Ma quoted, "Thou shalt love the Lord thy God with all thy heart and soul and mind and thy neighbor as thyself."

Matthew felt a warmth and togetherness far beyond human understanding.

Chapter 27

September 1941

"It feels good to be alone," Elizabeth Anderson said aloud to herself. Cooking for the carpenters had been a big task for a seventy-three-year-old woman. Even though Victoria had taken over the work much of the time, Elizabeth felt responsible. And now Victoria had returned to town to prepare for another school year.

Elizabeth walked to her garden and looked at the colorful zinnias and a few gladiolas and her vegetable garden. The garden was late this year; after all she had not moved back into her little house until late spring.

She looked across at the big new house where Corrine and Warren now lived. Matthew and his boys along with Ed and Glenn Robertson were doing the final touches of painting the outside of the house. Ellen and the girls were inside her house, getting noon dinner ready. She would join them in a few minutes. Ellen was a wonderful daughter-in-law and had told her, "Go outside and enjoy the beauty of autumn. You're tired from all the hard work of summer. Just take it easy. We'll do the work."

Even after almost two years, she missed John as much as ever. She felt she was not a complete person; there was a void. But she was not about to give up. With help from her family, she would go on living here and being a part of life. After all, she would have Corrine and Warren nearby, and three little girls would visit her and play in her house.

She loved this land just as her husband had. It was Anderson land. If she felt strong enough, she would walk down the lane into the east pasture and enjoy the beauty of the hills. She often looked to those hills as she thought of the Scripture, "I will lift my eyes unto the hills from whence cometh my help. My help cometh from the Lord, who made heaven and earth."

An unusually bright red gladiola caught her attention. "Lord, You reveal Yourself in the beauty of these flowers. Thank You. Creator God, give me the strength to grow and be strong and go on."

"Grandma," a voice nearby called.

She turned. It was Margaret.

"Is it time for dinner?"

"Not quite. Grandma, I have something to show you."

Elizabeth looked closely at her granddaughter. She had grown into a beautiful young woman. Petite like her mother Ellen, her blonde hair and blue eyes reflected the joy of an autumn day.

"I have a letter from Joe."

Elizabeth thought of the way Joe had helped as hired boy when Matthew and Ellen desperately needed him.

"Did you want to read me the letter?"

Proudly, Margaret held up the letter and began to read. "'Dear Margaret. Thanks for your letter. I can't begin to tell you how much it means to me.'"

Elizabeth smiled. "That last line doesn't really sound like Joe."

"I think he had help. He has help from a buddy who's been to college."

"Go on with the letter."

Margaret spread out the letter. "'I can't say too much because these letters are censored. All I can say is this army business is tough. I hate this dreadfully hot weather and the dampness and rain. I guess we're in the jungle part of the time. The training is tough, but I've got some good buddies. Especially Tim. He's educated and he corrects my spelling and helps me say things a little bit better. Sometimes I wonder where they're sending us. I think we may be going to Hawaii. I hear that place is beautiful. I can't wait to go there. Though I'm afraid Uncle Sam might change his mind.'"

Margaret stopped reading, her face reddened.

Elizabeth waited, saying nothing.

Chapter Twenty-seven

"'Margaret, your letter transported me back to your farm. You are my special girl. I'm lonesome. I miss all of you so terribly much. I'd give anything to have you right here. I wish I could have your mother's chicken dumpling soup. And I still remember your chocolate cookies and the chocolate cake. I don't know what I'd do if I didn't have the Anderson family back in Minnesota. I'm afraid I'm really homesick now. Love and kisses to my favorite girl.' He signs it Joe."

Elizabeth couldn't help remembering her awakening awareness of John as she was becoming a young woman. "What a perfectly lovely letter." Then she noticed tears in Margaret's eyes. "Come now, dear, what's wrong?"

"I'm so afraid that something's going to happen to Joe. He's such a good person. Someone said that the good die young. And he's one of the kindest boys I've ever met."

"That's not true—about the good dying young. God often rewards people by giving them long life."

"Like you and Grandpa?"

"Yes like your grandpa." She looked into Margaret's eyes. "You care deeply for Joe, don't you?"

"I think I love him." She blushed. "But don't tell Johnie or the others. They already tease me about Joe. They think it's a joke, and it isn't."

Elizabeth reached out and clasped her granddaughter's hand. "This will be our secret. I know lots of things, and I'm good at keeping secrets."

Carol suddenly appeared. "What's this about secrets? I'm not good at keeping secrets."

"I know that all too well," responded Margaret.

"It's dinner," said Carol. "And we're having a big community house-warming tomorrow afternoon for Corrine and Warren. It's supposed to be a surprise, but I don't think it will be."

The two granddaughters ran ahead, and Elizabeth walked up the hill to the big house. She felt a new confidence and security now that Corrine and Warren would be nearby.

Beyond the Storm

This September Sunday reminded Matthew of a similar day almost four years ago when Ma and Pa celebrated their golden wedding anniversary. But there had been radical changes since that day.

Today some of the same people were gathering to help and encourage a young couple with three young girls. Corrine and Warren had had more bad luck than anyone should have. And now a community was showing its love and concern in a tangible way.

Matthew and Johnie stood in the driveway, directing people to park in what had been a wheat field a few weeks ago. He was surprised at the number of people who had showed up so far. Each family brought household goods such as sheets or blankets or towels or kitchen goods. The new house would be well supplied.

Matthew glanced at the new house that was very much like the house he and Ellen had lived in. He caught a glimpse of Larry. He hoped Larry would not cause trouble for Corrine and Warren. That would be a repeat of what P.J. did to him.

"Brother, a penny for your thoughts." Martha walked toward him. "I haven't had a chance to see you since I got back last night."

Matthew opened his arms to embrace his sister. "I'm so glad you're home where you belong."

"I belong where people need me. I needed to be with my two girls."

Matthew looked down at his sister who seemed to look more and more like his mother. As daughters grew older, they often resembled their mothers.

Martha seemed to understand her brother's thinking. "Matthew, is something wrong?"

Matthew wanted to find the words to express his mixed feelings. "Just a moment ago, I saw Larry. He looks exactly like our brother. That brought back memories."

"Oh, it's just four years ago, isn't it?"

"Yes. It was Ma and Pa's golden wedding anniversary. And P.J. almost destroyed my life."

"I never did understand him."

While Johnie directed the visitors, Matthew and Martha visited. They talked of the growing and changing family.

Matthew and Martha returned to the crowd that had gathered outside the new house.

Someone gave a loud whistle.

Chapter Twenty-seven

Victoria stood on the front porch with Pastor Strand close behind. "I want to welcome all of you and thank you for coming. Corrine and Warren and the girls have had some hard times. On behalf of my family, I thank you for coming and bringing furniture and all the items that are needed in a home. We are now happy that my niece and her family can settle in this community."

She paused and went on. "This time, we don't have a piano. But even so, let's sing a few songs as we celebrate. As we think of our nation and world, why don't we join in singing 'God Bless America'?"

Ellen found a good pitch, and people joined in, lustily singing this favorite song. Afterwards, they sang several other songs.

Matthew observed his own children. Johnie, almost sixteen and becoming a handsome blond athlete, had several girls near him. James, a senior in high school, seemed satisfied to remain on the sidelines, observing life around him.

Margaret had been given the job of keeping track of Michael, who was intent on moving everywhere he could. Margaret would be a wonderful teacher and wife. He couldn't imagine anyone who would be quite good enough for this daughter. Carol remained in the midst of a group of girls. Carol's actions would always be unpredictable.

It was always customary for the pastor to say a few words and ask a blessing on the home and family. Pastor Strand had become such a part of the fabric of life at the Oak Ridge community and church that it was hard to imagine life without him.

After the singing of several songs, Pastor Strand stepped forward. "I remember standing in this same place just a few years ago. Some things have changed. There's a new house on this spot. There's a different family living in it. And one member has gone on to be with the Lord. We miss John Anderson for the strong and loving man that he was. This family has also lost a son and brother.

"I'm reminded of the scripture I used at John and Elizabeth Anderson's golden wedding celebration. 'Jesus Christ the same yesterday, today, and forever.'"

Matthew's mind left the words of his pastor and traveled to the day four years ago. He thought of the family gathering at that time. The brothers and sisters had been all together. Today, Pa was gone. Even after more than a year, it seemed somehow as if Pa should walk out of the little house.

Beyond the Storm

As he heard the last words of Pastor Strand's talk, Matthew looked at the hills. In one sense he would never go beyond the hills. But he looked to them. His strength and his help came from those hills.

Pastor Strand began to pray. "Lord, we thank You for this magnificent day. The colors of gold and red have appeared. Those colors reflect Your beauty. We thank You for the reflection of Your love in the love that people have showed in helping our friends here. We dedicate this home to You. May this family enjoy love and prosperity and all good things as they go on living. And now, Lord, bless this food which we are about to receive. We thank You for these and all our bountiful blessings. Guide and bless our fellowship together. In Jesus' name, amen."

Immediately, Warren stood up beside Pastor Strand. "I'd like to say a few words."

Warren's forwardness surprised Matthew.

"First, I want to thank you for all you have done. I'm not good with words, but I want to say something about what's on my mind."

Warren paused a moment, obviously overcome with emotion. "I'm not good at saying thank you and showing people that I care. I guess it's hard for a man, especially a stoic Scandinavian."

By this time, he had everyone's attention. Matthew realized these words had more serious implications than he had thought.

"I'm afraid I came here a bitter and angry man. My farm had been taken from me in Wisconsin. Then, when I came, I got help from so many of you, but there were other problems. And you are all aware of those. But what you didn't know about was my anger at several people. Worst of all, I was angry at God. I felt He had let me down."

Warren's composure had evaporated by this time. He was holding back tears. Matthew wanted to run up and tell him, "That's OK, I've gone through the same thing."

Warren wiped away his tears. "I'm sorry about this. I wanted to say that you people, my family and friends, have taught me a powerful lesson. Your love and concern in words as well as in what you have done have proved to me that God's love is out there. You showed me what love is all about. More importantly, you showed me that God is love."

First, there was complete silence. Then several people called out "Amen!" Then, the crowd broke into a spontaneous applause.

As the applause died down, Pastor Strand stepped forward. "That's the best sermon I've heard in a long time."

"And it was short," someone called out.

Chapter Twenty-seven

Laughter and further applause followed.

"What better response can we have than if we sing the Doxology." The crowd lustily sang the words:

Praise God from whom all blessings flow.
Praise Him all creatures here below.
Praise Him above ye heavenly host.
Praise Father, Son, and Holy Ghost.

The amen swelled. Matthew had never experienced such a visible evidence of a loving God.

Two days later Matthew stopped to visit his mother. As Matthew stood at the door on his way out, his mother startled him.

"Warren's upset about something. Really upset. I don't understand why."

Matthew quickly changed his plans. "I see he's out by the barn working. I'll stop to see him."

"You can talk man to man. He didn't want to talk to me about it. And I didn't want to pry."

Matthew hurried out to the barn where Warren was cleaning the last of the manure left by the cows that morning. Matthew greeted him.

Warren began to tell his story. "I thought everything was working out just fine. That was until Larry talked to me last night."

"What's Larry doing now?"

"He came to me as I was finishing work last night. I don't exactly know how he said it, but it was something like this: 'You think you've won the battle for this house and farm. You may find that I'll win the war.' I asked him what he meant."

"What did he say?"

"He sneered and said, 'Just you wait. You'll see.'"

Matthew tried to reassure Warren, but Warren remained troubled.

As Matthew left he called to Warren. "Don't worry. Things will work out." However, Matthew wasn't sure he believed his own words.

Chapter 28

October 1941

If there was one season Ellen disliked, it was the October hunting season. All the routines were ignored and organized life became a mess. She had coffee and cake ready for the hunters. Matthew and Johnie and Cousin Peter would be in shortly. She was also getting hints of a problem.

Sometimes she wished she drove a car the way Victoria and Martha did. But in her growing up years, women did not drive. The man of the house would always take care of driving. Of course, Victoria was hardly a traditional lady. And Martha, out of necessity, had learned to drive.

She called to James, who was in his room. "Do you suppose you could take me over to your grandmother's? I think there are some things I need to talk over with her."

James did not answer. Ellen suspected he was deep in some writing project. She hesitated as she knocked on his door.

"I'm sorry to interrupt."

"Come in."

She went on to repeat her request.

"Sure, Mom, it's a nice day for a drive. I need to get inspired and a drive might help."

It was at this moment that Ellen heard heavy steps on the front porch. The hunters had returned. She hurried downstairs to pour the cups of coffee. For awhile the talk seemed to exclude her. The conversation was the male hunters' domain.

During a break in the conversation, Pete spoke to Ellen. "Last night, a number of late night calls came on the party line. They were either for Rita or Larry. Aunt Elizabeth seemed to be upset."

Matthew's attention shifted to his wife. "I'm wondering if Rita and Larry are getting back into the business. Whatever it was, it's not good."

"Maybe it's a good time for me to go and talk with Mother Anderson. I haven't visited with her for awhile. I've asked James to drive me over."

Margaret and Carol appeared. Margaret announced, "I'll take care of dinner. I'm a good cook."

Not wanting to be outdone, Carol added, "I can cook too."

It was time for Michael to make his presence known. "I'm going hunting with Johnie. I'm big enough to hunt."

Ellen smiled as she realized once more that at two-and-a-half-year-old Michael was a duplicate of Johnie: always active, always wanting to go places and do things. She said nothing.

Obviously Johnie didn't want a little brother tagging along. "You're not old enough yet, Squirt. You have to keep up with the big guys."

"I can run fast," said Michael as he pushed himself over to Johnie.

"Guns are dangerous to little kids," added Johnie.

Michael moved away from Johnie over to his father. Ellen knew that Matthew had a hard time saying no.

Ellen saw that look in Matthew's eyes, a look that said, "Go ask your mother."

Michael ran over to Ellen. "Please, Mom, please."

"It's up to Johnie and your father." She reached for her coat. "James and I are going out for a little while."

Ellen stooped down and gave Michael a kiss. He seemed to accept the refusal.

At times Ellen felt Elizabeth Anderson was more like a mother rather than a mother-in-law. She entered the little house and found Elizabeth

Chapter Twenty-eight

at the kitchen table with her Bible open. James left for one of his walks to the hills.

"I'm glad you're here. I've been troubled."

Ellen took off her coat, laying it on the chair. "Peter said you heard some late phone calls."

Elizabeth pointed to the coffee pot. Ellen found a cup and poured coffee into her cup and added fresh coffee to Elizabeth's.

"I'm sorry, I'm not being a good hostess, but my joints and muscles are aching today. I didn't sleep well last night. That phone kept ringing."

"Maybe you need an afternoon nap."

Elizabeth took soda crackers out of the package. "These crackers always taste good with a little coffee. I guess the Bible and a bit of coffee help a person to think better."

Ellen's thoughts traveled back a few years. "I can't help thinking of life here five years ago. Matthew and I were right next door."

"I miss you and Matthew ever so much. Even though Corrine and Warren are wonderful. I'm afraid I'm a little older, and those three darling girls are a little much to handle."

"Life keeps changing. It keeps moving on," Ellen reflected.

"Something else happened also," began Elizabeth. "This morning Peter went out hunting, and there must have been ten or twelve city fellows there. I suppose that's Larry's or Rita's doing. And it's not right."

"We need to have words with Rita and Larry. I'll talk to Matthew."

Elizabeth looked away. "I hate these constant problems."

As Elizabeth said those words, a loud knock sounded on the door. She jumped and so did Ellen.

Ellen, seeing the pain her mother-in-law was experiencing, stood up and went to the door. Sheriff Walker stood there.

"Good morning, Mrs. Anderson. Do you suppose I could come in?"

Elizabeth called out, "By all means, Sheriff. I hope this isn't anything serious."

In traditional Scandinavian hospitality, Ellen went to the cupboard and brought out another cup. She motioned for Sheriff Walker to sit down. "Everything goes a little better with a cup of coffee."

"Yes," agreed Elizabeth, "and I baked some good old-fashioned white cookies yesterday." She reached over to the cookie jar and put some cookies on a plate.

Sheriff Walker sat down and reached for a cookie. "You remind me of my grandmother."

The two women waited in silence. Ellen wondered what the problem was, though in the past she had known the sheriff to stop just to see if everything was all right.

"I don't know how to say what I have to say, but I thought I should stop. I have some questions, and I may need to caution you."

Elizabeth's facial muscles tightened and she wrinkled her brow. "You might as well get it out. I'm an old lady, but I prefer knowing the truth."

"I hate to put you on the spot." He reached out for Elizabeth's hand. "But you are truly the salt of the earth—just like your husband. But I'm afraid some things are happening around here."

Ellen spoke up. "We knew P.J. wasn't honest. It's almost as if his business is going on with Larry—same as before."

Elizabeth held back a yawn and then apologized. "I'm afraid I'm terribly tired. I had very little sleep last night. There were cars coming and going all night. And the phone ringing."

Walker finished his cup of coffee. "Just as I thought. We don't know who these people are. There have been some break-ins. Everything leads this direction. We've questioned Larry, but we can never prove anything. So far, there haven't been any big thefts after the last bank robbery."

"You haven't caught the bank robber?" questioned Ellen. "I have a hard time believing that Larry would do something like that. He's sneaky. He'd cheat in other ways."

"That may be true. But everything leads in this direction. We did manage to get a search warrant. We searched P.J.'s house and the premises as well, but nothing turned up."

Elizabeth Anderson gasped. "You mean you searched my son's—no my daughter-in-law's house. They could be arrested as criminals?"

"Sorry, Mrs. Anderson."

"I never thought anyone in my family would come to this."

Ellen saw tears in the old woman's eyes. She wanted to comfort her, but she knew words wouldn't help.

Sheriff Walker reached over and grasped the old woman's hand. "My dear Mrs. Anderson, your son would have become a saint if he had followed in your footsteps or Mr. Anderson's. It's hard to explain, but most families have a black sheep."

"And my grandson is following in his father's footsteps."

Chapter Twenty-eight

The sheriff rose to leave. "Thanks for the coffee. I wish I could help. Be watchful and careful. And tell Corrine and Warren to be very careful. Some of those guys could be dangerous if they think you know too much."

"Mother Anderson, maybe you should come stay with us," invited Ellen.

Elizabeth did not hesitate. "No, this is my home and I intend to stay here, hopefully until the day I die. If good people leave, that leaves only the bad guys to take over."

"You're a gutsy lady." Sheriff Walker stooped down and kissed her on the forehead. "Even the worst criminal couldn't hurt a grand lady like you."

Elizabeth laughed. "You are a charmer." She stood up. "And if I have to, I can play the part of a helpless old lady who doesn't know anything."

"Corrine and Warren will always watch."

Elizabeth walked into the bedroom and came out, holding a bat. "I have this right by my bed. If I have to, I could use it."

"I bet you could." The sheriff stooped down, this time to give her a hug. "But please, I think you might get further by being that helpless old lady."

"I pray a lot. Sometimes, that's all I can do."

Walker opened the door to leave. "I didn't used to feel that way, but I'm learning that prayer is more powerful than the gun."

After the sheriff had gone, Ellen spoke softly. "Walker's more like a friend than a sheriff."

"I think of him almost as a son. He's the kind of man that P.J. could have become. I just wish Larry were on the right side of the law."

At that moment the door abruptly opened. Victoria greeted her mother and sister-in-law. "Was that the sheriff I met? He wasn't in a sheriff's car. What's been happening?"

"We just had some coffee," said Ellen. "He came to ask questions, but I think he was concerned about Mother Anderson."

"I heard about all the noise last night. I drove over and saw Matthew. He said you were here. It's time we had words with Rita and Larry."

"I guess there's no avoiding trouble," said Elizabeth.

"Mother, we are beyond trouble. This is a war. And if Larry and Rita think they are winning, they will treat us worse than ever. I'm becoming a high school football fan, and in football we say the best defense is a strong offense. I intend to fight."

Ellen had no doubt that Victoria would fight, and this woman was indeed a formidable fighter.

Victoria turned to Ellen. "I'd like you to come with me. I'm going over to see Rita. It's just about noon. Larry and the hunters will be coming in for dinner—or lunch as they call it."

"Maybe Matthew should be here. After all, I'm an in-law."

"You're family. That's it!" Victoria turned to leave.

Elizabeth's hands trembled as she spoke. "I'll pray."

"This situation means action. Prayer may help, but we need action."

With those words Victoria left, and Ellen followed.

Five minutes later, Victoria rang the doorbell at Rita's home. When she came to the door, Rita looked dismayed.

"This is not a good time."

Victoria swept past her sister-in-law and Ellen followed. "We have important matters to discuss."

"Can't those matters wait?"

Victoria cleared her throat and began, "Your company or business associates have driven by Mother's house at outlandish hours. They are loud and disruptive."

"Oh, come now. Just because she goes to bed early doesn't mean the rest of the world does."

Victoria straightened herself. "You and your son will have your day in court. So far we have been following the unofficial wishes of P.J. However, if you persist in your present actions, we will lay claim to all that land that should rightfully belong to Mother. That includes your house and all the land."

Rita looked startled. "You can't do this. Paul John and I built this house as well as the tourist cabins. These are ours."

"If you don't listen to what I am saying and accept the proposed agreement, you may be in much deeper trouble. After all, we can prove fraud."

Ellen couldn't help adding, "And we have ethics and morality on our side."

Rita moved toward Victoria. "So this is the way you treat me. I was married to your brother for more than twenty years. I don't deserve this."

Chapter Twenty-eight

Victoria quickly responded. "We didn't deserve your unwelcome treatment when we came. You come to the Anderson family when it's convenient and when you want something."

The outside door opened. The hunters entered. Suddenly there was the noise of men talking and milling about.

Rita motioned for Ellen and Victoria to go into the office.

"Hello Aunt Victoria," said Larry. "These are my friends and business associates."

Victoria and Ellen nodded and walked down the hall.

Rita announced, "Lunch is ready in the kitchen. The hired girl has soup ready." Then she added, "Larry, you better come to the office."

With the door closed, Victoria stood tall and stately and spoke sternly to Larry. "Your so-called business associates made life miserable for your grandmother. What do you have to say?"

Larry tried looking penitent. "I'm sorry."

"What is happening here must stop. I don't know what business is going on, but it's no good."

Larry's apologetic approach ended. "My business is none of your business. And don't try getting me in trouble with the sheriff. That hasn't worked."

Victoria shook her fist. "Perhaps a legal battle will make a difference. We Andersons were willing to give over this lake property and some acreage to you. But if you proceed this way, we're going to court to get *all* the property. Your father was fraudulent in his dealings, and we can prove it."

Larry's confidence was obviously shaken. "You can't do that."

"Oh yes we can."

The raucous noise of the men in the kitchen stopped the next words from being spoken.

"I expect things to change. I'm staying with Mother tonight, and there better not be any traffic or loud noises after nine o'clock. Or late telephone calls."

Larry edged toward the door. "I'm sorry. I'll see what I can do."

Victoria's voice carried that commanding authority. "Don't *see* what you can do, *do!*"

"Yes ma'am."

Ellen felt keenly the awkwardness of the next moment. Troubled and strange thoughts lurked in the back of her mind.

Beyond the Storm

Ellen was not prone to dream and have nightmares. At least she usually didn't remember anything she dreamed. That night was an exception.

In her nightmare, Victoria kept pointing at Larry. Suddenly Larry's figure merged with P.J.'s. And she saw P.J. as he called out during those last tormented moments when he struggled to breathe and screamed about the intense heat.

Then Matthew and she were in P.J.'s office. She took down a picture that hid a handle. She grasped the handle and a door opened to a short passage. She opened another door that opened into a hidden room. Suddenly the door closed. The light went out. Darkness enveloped her.

An evil presence dominated the room. P.J. appeared. His face was the face of evil incarnate—the face of the devil himself. And then a dreadful laughter followed.

"I've got you now! I've got you now!"

All at once she was awake. She reached over and touched Matthew. She felt safe, but she was troubled.

For days to come she remembered the dream, and she remembered the time she and Matthew had gone into the hidden room that might well contain evidence against Larry and his associates.

Ellen was surprised she had not thought of this sooner.

Chapter 29

November 1941

"Everything's changing. Nothing stays the same." Matthew looked out the kitchen window as Carol walked down the driveway on her way to school. Ellen handed him a cup of coffee.

"Yes," replied Ellen, "I'm afraid Carol thinks she's much older than she is."

Matthew thought of his contact with the world away from these hills. "The kids are growing up way too fast. I dread the thought of James going off to college. It's a tough world out there."

"College is the only place for James. His brilliant mind will take him many places."

Yesterday's newspaper caught Matthew's eye. "This world is becoming a scary place. Just a few weeks ago, two Navy ships were torpedoed and one sank. The world is not safe from the Germans. And I wonder about those peace talks with the Japanese."

"There shall be wars and rumors of wars," quoted Ellen.

"And I think of Joe somewhere in the Pacific."

"Life has never been easy. The Lord will see us through."

Matthew sighed. "I'm afraid I keep doubting. So many things are different. With Mary in the sanitarium, life has been tough for Ed and the kids. We haven't seen much of them—not the way we used to."

"Let's hope Mary can soon be back home."

"There've been so many setbacks. Sometimes I think she'll never come back."

"That reminds me," said Ellen, "I need to talk with Victoria about our family Thanksgiving. I think the family will come here. Corrine isn't quite up to having the whole family. We need to do some planning."

Matthew always looked forward to these family gatherings. At the same time he was reminded of the absence of Pa and P.J. And the rift in the family still bothered him.

Ellen yawned. "I had trouble sleeping last night."

"You were thrashing about for hours. What was wrong?"

"I've been having these dreams—no they're nightmares. I'm always in that secret room in P.J.'s house. Do you remember the time we had to go in and get the money and documents for P.J.?"

Matthew remembered P.J.'s strange request several years ago. Matthew had felt he had to help his brother out of a desperate situation. He and Ellen had done what P.J. had requested.

"Well," Ellen continued, "I'm locked in that room. It's dark, and I can't get out. Then, I'm suffocating. And then P.J. appears, and he seems to have the face of the devil. I want to run and get out, but I can't. Then I wake up, sweating."

"I thought we were done with P.J. and his business dealings. But it seems it's started all over again with Larry."

Ellen paused a moment. "Yes, Larry could have an even more dreadful ending. Joan has been hurt, and she and the baby are back with her parents. He may find he's permanently separated from his own son."

"There's only so much we can do."

Ellen excused herself. "I need to get some potatoes from the basement."

As Matthew was getting on his jacket for more outdoor work, the telephone jangled. "Matthew, you answer," called Ellen from the basement.

"Matthew," Victoria's business-like voice came through, "there's some family business. Could you and Ellen come over tomorrow morning? I think it might be better to talk without the kids around."

Matthew agreed. He wondered what new developments had taken place.

Chapter Twenty-nine

The next morning Victoria greeted Matthew and Ellen. "I have an apple pie ready for you, Matthew, along with egg coffee."

She ushered Matthew and Ellen into her kitchen.

"Since when did you have time with all your school duties to bake pie?" asked Ellen.

"The bakery does homemade pies," laughed Victoria. "I knew we needed to talk and I didn't want to meet at Mother's because this talk upsets her."

"Is it about Larry?" asked Matthew.

"Yes. Larry still won't give up his claim to the farm. We have to try again before we take drastic action."

"There's something else," began Ellen. Then she stopped.

Victoria took their coats and then motioned for them to sit down at the kitchen table.

Ellen continued hesitantly. "I don't know where to begin, but something's come to mind, and it's been bothering me. Matthew and I have been talking. If you remember, Sheriff Walker suspects that the bank theft is somehow connected to Larry or some of his business partners. The trail seems to lead to P.J.'s house."

Victoria nodded. "I had hoped that Larry hadn't sunk quite that low."

"Several years ago when P.J. was in trouble, he asked Matthew to go over to his house to get some documents and money. There is a hidden room behind the office-library. Well, I've been having nightmares as I keep remembering that place."

"What are you saying?" interrupted Victoria. "Are you thinking that the evidence or the loot is to be found in that room?"

"That's right. That room may contain incriminating evidence."

"We can't be sure, though," added Matthew. "Larry is pretty sneaky. He's smarter than I thought. Actually, smarter than P.J."

"Let's eat this pie and drink some coffee." Victoria filled the cups. "We'll plan a little strategy and then talk to Larry. And Rita, if she's there."

The three ate pie and planned their strategy.

Beyond the Storm

Victoria led the way to the front door of P.J.'s mansion. The trees were now bare of leaves, and snow covered the ground.

Matthew remembered other times they had come here. For some reason his mind went back to the first Christmas in this new house. P.J. had been at his best. The electricity had just been turned on and they celebrated Christmas in P.J.'s grand style. P.J. had been especially kind and generous that Christmas.

Victoria rang the doorbell. Rita opened the door. "Good morning, I'm surprised to see you."

"We have business. We wish to see Larry also."

"You're in luck. He's here."

Rita led the way to the kitchen.

"Everything seems quiet here," said Victoria. "A few weeks ago your house was full of activity."

"It's just Larry and me."

Larry greeted them. Everything in his manner said he didn't want to see them.

Rita offered coffee, but all three declined the offer. "Why don't you sit down?"

"I prefer to stand," said Victoria. "We'll be brief. We want to settle this ownership of the land business. We're giving you one last chance to claim this lake property and surrounding acreage. Otherwise we're going to take further action and claim all the property."

Both Rita and Larry showed surprise.

Rita took out a cigarette and prepared to light it. "I don't think you're being fair with me, the widow of your brother."

Victoria did not hesitate. "We're being more than fair. We need to have an answer right now."

Larry avoided his aunt's steady gaze. "We'll think about it."

Victoria straightened herself. "I suggest you give an answer immediately. We have uncovered some new information. We'll be using it if you don't act."

"What information?" asked Rita.

Victoria cleared her throat. "We will not get into that. We're just warning you: we'll use this negative information only if you don't agree to something that is fair. Otherwise, you may lose the rights to this house."

Chapter Twenty-nine

Rita's demeanor showed she didn't quite believe her sister-in-law. "You wouldn't do that, would you?"

"Just try me. Or try us."

Larry looked visibly shaken. "Give us a day to talk this over. We'll think about it."

"All right. We'll expect to hear from you by one o'clock tomorrow."

Victoria turned and walked toward the door, followed by Ellen and Matthew.

As they drove away, Victoria spoke forcefully. "Ellen, you must go to Sheriff Walker. You must tell him what you know."

"Yes," Ellen agreed. "Justice will be done one way or another."

Chapter 30

The hall clock struck eleven. Ellen poured herself a cup of hot milk. That was always her solution to a sleepless night.

This night before Thanksgiving had followed tradition. Victoria had come from town early in the evening and had helped get everything ready for the big feast. Victoria and Ellen had sisterly talks while doing the work. This year was different. Mother Anderson and Martha remained at the little house and prepared their pies.

Ellen rarely had sleepless nights, though sleep came slowly if she started thinking about problems. And tonight she couldn't stop thinking of her trip to see Sheriff Walker the other day. What if a search warrant brought up nothing in that hidden room? Then, Larry and Rita would know that she or Matthew had talked. After all that P.J. and Larry had done, her act was hardly one of betrayal.

Ellen couldn't help remembering Larry as a little nine-year-old. His sparkling dark eyes and handsome features endeared him to her and others. This oldest Anderson grandson had shown much promise.

When did he begin to go wrong? Or were his actions and ways simply an extension of his father? It seemed the ways of the father were being visited upon the son. Where would all this lead?

She took a sip of milk. Her mind took off in many directions.

She thought about Ed and his problems. Would Mary ever come home and be her old self? It seemed so unfair to deprive a family of the mother.

"Mother, what's wrong?" James stood in the doorway. His intense blue eyes told Ellen that her son sensed she was troubled.

Ellen tried to avoid the truth. "O, Victoria and I talked about so many things. My mind just keeps going on. I can't seem to turn off my thinking."

"That's me, too," agreed James. "I think I could use some hot milk and crackers."

Ellen went to the new refrigerator and took out the jar of milk and poured it into a pan. "I think something's bothering you."

"I'll tell you if you tell me."

Ellen laughed. James had figured right. "I don't know that I should say anything because I don't know if anything is wrong."

"You suspect something, I bet."

Ellen had to agree that her son was right. She hesitated and then began to tell of Larry and the suspicion about Larry's activities and about the hidden room.

"That's no surprise," said James. "After all, P.J. did lots of illegal things. He just never got caught."

Ellen sighed. "His conscience tormented him at the end."

Mother and son drank their milk in silence.

Ellen finally spoke up. "Now, it's your turn to tell what's bothering you."

James looked away. "I've been reading the papers and listening to the news. I'm afraid we're going to war. I know what my duty is, but I don't know if I could kill another man even in war."

Ellen shuddered. "Let's hope you don't have to."

"I have nightmares about facing enemy soldiers in battle. I read *Red Badge of Courage*, and I identified with the soldier who ran. I don't want to be a deserter. That would be a disgrace."

"Courage comes when courage is needed."

"I hope I have the courage."

Mother and son continued to talk. The hall clock struck twelve.

"I think it's time for bed," said Ellen. "Morning will come soon."

Chapter Thirty

Morning came quickly for Matthew. When the alarm rang, he realized that Ellen was sound asleep. He wouldn't waken her. He'd get Johnie to help, and the rest of the family could sleep.

Chores went like clockwork. Johnie and Matthew said little during the work time, but as they finished feeding the cattle, Johnie began to talk.

"Jake's back home. He was hanging around school."

Matthew wasn't sure whether this was good news or bad. "I hope he's learned a few lessons. At least he doesn't need to bully James."

"I don't think he'll be back in school. Jake's bought an old Chevy, and he wants to look like a tough guy. He was smoking cigarettes and I think he had some booze."

Matthew thought of his sister Mary. "I'm afraid Mary's time in the TB sanitarium has been hard on the kids, especially Jake."

"I wish things could be the way they used to be. We cousins used to have fun together. We played games and did some crazy things."

Matthew thought of the way he had grown away from some of his cousins and friends. "Life goes on. We drift away from some relatives. We have new interests. We may have little in common."

"I thought cousins would always be close, but I guess it's not that way."

"We haven't been together with Ed the way we used to be. He's been different, too."

Johnie picked up a sack of oats, emptying it into the bin. He turned to Matthew. "I'm glad you're my dad. Uncle Ed can be nice, but he's been really tough on his kids, Jake, especially. He spanks Jake even now."

Matthew thought aloud, "Even if he deserves a spanking, he's too old to spank."

"Dad, you've never whipped us the way some parents have. I can't imagine what that would be like."

"Son, you have a remarkable mother. Neither your mother nor I have felt that was the way to bring up children. We could discipline you in other ways."

Johnie smiled. "Mom's words can be as tough as any spanking. She knows how to let me know when I've done wrong."

"Your mother is a good woman."

"You're a good man. And Grandpa was a good man—no a great man. I hope I can be that kind of man."

Matthew opened the barn door. "It's time for breakfast. And son, you're growing up too fast."

The delicious aroma of ham and eggs welcomed Matthew and Johnie as they entered the kitchen.

Victoria greeted them. "Breakfast's ready for our hard workers. The lazy ones aren't even up."

The Thanksgiving morning proceeded like the one last year. After breakfast, Matthew and his sons went out to do the rest of the morning chores. They let out the cows, cleaned the barn, and fed the cattle. Margaret gathered the eggs. The indoor preparations for the Thanksgiving feast moved along.

Thanksgiving church service followed the pattern of so many others. Matthew wondered if that was why the attendance was down. He was more aware of the people who weren't there than the people who were. His friend Glenn's mother wasn't in her usual seat. Mrs. Robertson had been ailing.

And then there were Ed and Beth and Jake and Irene. That family was not present. They were supposed to come to Thanksgiving dinner. Perhaps part of Ed's problem was that he was forgetting what was most important.

Matthew was delighted that Martha was back home. He had missed the way Martha always mothered him. She sat in the pew with Ma. Corrine and Warren and their three daughters were next to them. Matthew was thankful for Warren as both a family member and friend.

Matthew sang the familiar words. He loved the lines:

All is safely gathered in,
Ere the winter storms begin.

He felt a satisfaction that the harvest was complete, and everything was ready for winter. The last verse caused him to think about the whole of life:

Even so, Lord, quickly come
To Thy final harvest-home;
Gather Thou Thy people in,
Free from sorrow, free from sin;
There forever purified,
In Thy presence to abide:

Chapter Thirty

Come with all Thine angels come,
Raise the glorious harvest-home!

Matthew's rich tenor voice swelled with that final verse. Even with clouds on the horizon—clouds of war, clouds of problems with Larry and Rita—life was good. And ultimately God was in control.

Pastor Strand's sermon was the type of sermon Matthew expected. He knew he should focus on God and how much there was to be thankful for, but his mind traveled elsewhere. He wondered why Ed hadn't come. And Mary, would she ever be able to come home and assume her role as mother and wife?

Life seemed to be moving forward fast, much like the news reels at the movie theater. He felt sometimes that he couldn't keep up with all these changes.

Pastor Strand spoke in a quiet but earnest manner. "The Lord has blest our nation most generously and abundantly. But are we seeking Him first? Now that the Depression is over, are we not looking to material wealth for our security? Are we not making a god of material wealth and property?"

Matthew realized the truth of what his pastor was saying. Then, Pastor Strand began to speak of Israel and the times that nation went astray. Forgetting God and going astray had serious consequences.

It was easy for Matthew to look at Larry and Rita and the way they lived. Money and power did terrible things to people. Maybe he was better off being a poor farmer. But God had made him richer than ever before.

"Good sermon," Matthew said to the pastor on the way out of the church.

A few hours later, the house was filled with delicious aromas of food of the Thanksgiving season. The special turkey had been butchered and now was filled with dressing. Several dishes of fresh cranberry jelly added color to the table setting. The enlarged oak dining room table plus the added outdoor picnic table meant there was room for everyone.

Ellen, along with Martha and Victoria and Corrine, worked in the kitchen. Ma had been told to take it easy, and the girls had their girl talk or games upstairs. Margaret and Carol seemed to like the idea of entertaining their three younger cousins. The boys were outside.

Matthew and Warren talked about the problems of being ready for the winter. Matthew wondered why Ed and the kids hadn't come yet.

The women began to put the food on the table. "Matthew," said Ellen, "why don't you go upstairs and get the kids to come down. They're probably in the middle of Sorry or Uno or some other game. And get the boys, wherever they are."

"Where are Ed and the kids?" Matthew asked.

"Beth called just as I came into the house. They'll be a little late. She said to go ahead and start eating."

"That's strange,"

In minutes the members of the family were all seated, except for Ed and his children. Ellen turned to Matthew, "Why don't you lead us in the table prayer?"

"Don't make it too long," said Johnie.

Someone else piped up, "We're hungry."

Matthew felt he never measured up as a speaker. He began slowly. "Dear heavenly Father, we come to You thankful for Your bounty. Thank You for bringing our family together. We pray for those who are not here—especially Mary. Make her well and bring her back to us. And now, thank You for this meal. Bless the food. Bless us all. In Jesus' name, amen."

At that moment the door opened. "We're here!" called out Ed. Matthew hadn't heard that kind of happiness in his voice for years.

Jake and Beth and Irene crowded forward.

"We have a surprise!" The words came almost in chorus from Ed and the three children. Even Jake was there, minus his sullen look.

Mary stepped forward. "I'm home." She gave her coat to Ed, and tears of joy filled her eyes. "I'm home at last."

The next moments were utter confusion. Thoughts of eating had been forgotten.

Matthew could see that Mary looked thinner and older. Her dark hair now had strands of gray. Her face had lines that had not been there before. The past year had been a hard one.

As the commotion quieted, Ed called out. "We're here to feast. Mary's home for good, so she'll be here for all our family gatherings."

Chapter Thirty

Mary spoke through her tears. "I can't tell you how much I missed all of you. And I just have to say I love you all more than I can say. God has been good to me."

"We love you, too," was the response from many.

Ellen motioned for people to sit. "We have much to be thankful for. Let's sing the Doxology." She set the pitch, and the family joined her:

Praise God from whom all blessings flow.
Praise Him all creatures here below.
Praise Him above ye heavenly host.
Praise Father, Son, and Holy Ghost.

Matthew scarcely noticed whether the food was hot or cold, and that was true of the rest of the family as well. The feast of Thanksgiving became a family reunion that Matthew and others would long remember.

That afternoon, Matthew felt he had returned to the happier times of the past. Dinner ended. Matthew, Ed, and Warren went into the living room. Ed joked about his cooking and was his old self once more. Warren expressed his happiness about the bumper crop. Matthew felt a good tiredness come over him.

He listened to the women in the kitchen. Victoria and the others were trying to get Mary to lie down and rest, but she refused. Otherwise, it was the women's talk that Matthew had heard every year since his earliest remembrance.

The children went outside. However, James and Johnie were hardly children. Johnie was two inches taller than Matthew and James was almost the height of his father. Margaret and Carol had changed from girls into young women. His niece Beth in some ways reminded him of Ma. After all Beth was short for Elizabeth. And Jake, tough-looking like a wrestler, seemed happy to be home. Then there was Irene, who could have passed as a sister to Carol and Margaret. Finally, Corrine's three girls joined the older cousins.

Problems seemed to disappear. The children were simply having fun. Matthew relaxed completely. "This is a good life. We couldn't ask for more." In moments, the hard-working men were dozing off.

All good times come to an end. That evening, Ma and Martha stayed after the others had left.

"Matthew," Martha said, "I have something I'd like to talk with you about."

That was a sign to Ellen and Ma and the kids that brother and sister had something private to discuss.

"You can go up to the guest room," said Ellen. "I think you've made the kids curious."

"It's not that private, really, but I think I'd like to go outside."

Matthew agreed, and soon brother and sister were walking outside beneath the yard light. Matthew loved the peacefulness of an early winter night.

Martha walked slowly. "I find it hard to believe there's all this bloodshed in the world when I look at the peace we have right here."

"There's nothing like a quiet winter night."

"Winter slows people down. Farm life is cut down to the essentials of life."

Matthew stopped. "That's not what you wanted to talk about, is it?"

"I'm troubled, and I don't quite know how to say this."

Matthew felt a fear grip him within. "What's wrong?"

"I saw and heard something strange this morning at Mother's. I wakened early, probably about four o'clock. Everything was very quiet. I decided to make a trip to the outhouse. In a way, it was a good excuse to get outside."

"That's the advantage of not having indoor plumbing."

"I heard something when I was in the outhouse. I looked outside. A car drove up the driveway, slowly, with no lights on."

"I begin to see what you're telling me."

"There's more." Martha stiffened. "For some reason the two men really scared me. One got out of the car. He's one of the biggest men I've ever seen. Then, Larry drove up, no lights on his car either."

"Did you hear anything?"

"I sneaked up behind a clump of trees so that I could hear what they were saying. The big man handed Larry a box. He said, 'I think we made it OK. I don't think anyone suspects. But you keep the loot for another week. Then, we'll be back.'"

"Where did the loot come from? Did you hear?"

"No, but Larry said, 'I want my cut.' What's Larry into anyway?"

Chapter Thirty

"We don't know, but I think we had better let Sheriff Walker know."

"I heard more. The man said there was another rich old man who didn't trust banks and had lots of money hidden in his house. They were going to 'relieve the man of his heavy burden of money'."

"These robberies are part of a pattern. The sheriff just can't seem to prove anything."

Martha shivered. "I'm afraid for Larry."

In that moment Matthew knew that Larry's downfall had to come soon.

Chapter 31

December 1941

Snow whirled around Matthew as he walked from the barn to the house. On stormy days like this, the chores and cleaning the barn took longer. Ever since Martha told him of the clandestine meeting of the two thugs and Larry, he had felt uneasy.

As he entered the house, the radio was tuned to the "News at Noon." The words of the announcer caught his attention. "We have just received word from the State Police of a bank robbery in Prairie Center. The robbery probably happened last Thursday, as several employees were ill on Friday so the bank was closed. The robbery was not discovered until this morning. The thief or thieves got away with about $1,000. The banker was relieved that the thieves did not discover the bigger packet of money. This robbery is similar to the River Falls robbery that took place a few months ago. It appears that the same robbers are at work. The robbery has been cleverly planned, said the police. No other details are available."

Matthew gasped. He remembered what Martha had told him about the strange meeting early that Thanksgiving morning. Could Larry be connected with this criminal act?

Ellen looked at him, knowingly. "I dare to bet that money is in P.J.'s hidden room."

"We should have done something sooner, but we didn't know enough."

"Matthew, you know what we have to do. We've got to call Walker before the money disappears."

Ellen went to the telephone and stopped. "We can't do this by telephone. If we do, the whole community will know. We have to see Sheriff Walker in person."

Matthew and Ellen moved into action. On the way to town, they stopped at Ma's so that Michael could stay with his grandmother.

"I have an idea," said Ellen as they neared Lake View. "Let's go to the telephone office and call Walker. That way what we say won't be public knowledge. Only Phoebe will know."

"Yes, but I bet she will spread the news."

"I think we can prevail upon her to say nothing—at least until Sheriff Walker makes his moves."

In minutes Matthew and Ellen explained the situation to Sheriff Walker.

Matthew listened carefully to the sheriff's words. "We must move carefully. I'll need to get a search warrant. We don't want to clue them in so that they get away one more time."

"We'll do whatever we can."

Matthew could almost hear the wheels turning inside Walker's mind.

"It's going to take an hour or so before we can get out there. I'll be bringing deputies and some federal officers as well. I'd like to have you go to your mother's and caution her. Also you'd better caution Warren and Corrine. We don't want a lot of activity. After you've talked to them, meet me a half mile down the road. I want you to point out some of the back ways to P.J.'s house."

Matthew agreed to the sheriff's plan. Deep down, he felt guilty. Larry was, after all, a member of the Anderson family.

When Matthew and Ellen entered his mother's home, Ellen spoke immediately. "Something's going to be happening that we need to warn you about." She turned to Matthew, "Maybe you should go over and get Corrine and Warren."

Chapter Thirty-one

Matthew hurried up the hill to the big house. In minutes he returned with Corrine and Warren. "You explain," he said to Ellen.

She told them what had happened and what was about to happen.

When the explanation was finished, Warren spoke vehemently. "I hope the jerk gets what he deserves!"

Corrine cautioned her husband. "Larry is my cousin. He is family."

Warren clenched his fists. "He doesn't act like any member of the Anderson family."

Ma had said very little. "Yes, he's family. He bears the Anderson name. We must be concerned about his destiny. Not just his destiny on earth, but his eternal destiny."

"I keep remembering," said Matthew, "how we played together. He was my young friend. He followed me everywhere."

Matthew heard a car drive up followed by a car door slamming. An abrupt knock came next.

Sheriff Walker spoke quickly. "We've got our plan worked out. We think there may be others at Larry's place." He turned to Ma. "I think you should get out of here."

Ma stood up, folded her arms, and spoke with authority. "I will stay right here. I don't think Larry or any of those business associates will harm an old lady."

"But you could get caught in the crossfire."

Matthew interrupted. "Ma, you are not going to stay here. This is not something you have to see or put up with."

Ma protested. "I am staying."

Warren turned to Corrine. "We need to make sure the girls are safe. You come with me. We can't have them coming home from school in the middle of this situation."

The two stood at the door, ready to leave.

"That's a wise course of action. We may wait awhile before we do the search and hopefully make the arrests. However it could happen immediately."

"I should do chores," said Warren. "The cows won't wait for anything."

Sheriff Walker scratched his brow. "You know it may be best if things look normal—at least that you're doing the usual chores."

"I want my wife and girls safe."

"They can come to our place," suggested Ellen.

"Matthew," said Walker, "I need to see some of those other ways of getting down to the lake house. We'll check the whole area carefully."

Warren motioned to his wife. "Corrine, you take Ellen and Michael and pick up the girls at school and go to Matthew's place. Then, Matthew can show the sheriff some of the best ways to go. And I'll go ahead and do chores. But I'll have my gun handy."

"You shouldn't have any need of it," said Walker. "Anyway, be careful."

Once more, Matthew tried to get Ma to leave, but again she adamantly refused.

Warren left the house, followed by Corrine and Ellen and Michael. Ellen returned in a moment and went over to Matthew. "Darling, don't you dare take any chances."

"I'll send him home as soon as he's shown me my way around," Walker reassured.

Matthew stooped down and gave Ellen a kiss. Then she left.

"Sheriff," Ma responded, "I will lock the doors. You go and do what you have to do. If Larry is responsible, he must be brought to justice."

Sheriff Walker looked down at this small woman. "Mrs. Anderson, you're one of the finest ladies I've ever met. You're also one of the gutsiest."

Ma walked over to the sheriff. "Mr. Walker, I'm praying for you."

Matthew saw Sheriff Walker choke with emotion. Walker stooped down and kissed Elizabeth Anderson on the cheek. "Matthew, come with me."

Ma went into the bedroom and found the rusty key and proceeded to lock the back door.

Matthew followed Sheriff Walker. "Ma, you be careful." He heard the key turn as his mother locked the door.

At this time of day the shadows lengthened. Darkness claimed a major part of the day in early December.

Both men drove their cars out to the township road. Matthew showed how the men could follow a line fence and conveniently find the house and cabins. Then, he showed some other pathways so that the sheriff and deputies could quickly surround the area.

As Matthew finished giving directions, he became aware of a number of cars coming down the road. Lights were switched off as they approached the area.

Chapter Thirty-one

Matthew felt a deep fear. The tentacles of greed of P.J. and now of Larry had reached into the lives of innocent people. He breathed a prayer for his safety as well as for the safety of the family.

Elizabeth Anderson had the habit of talking to herself. "Did I do something wrong when I raised P.J.? The others are fine upstanding citizens. And now, Larry. What can I do?"

Elizabeth sought refuge in her favorite chair. As she took out her Bible and opened the pages, her mind moved elsewhere. She thought of her husband. If he had lived, none of this would have happened. Or would it?

Darkness enveloped the world outside. There was no moon. The blackness seemed to say that evil was encroaching on the light. She found some comfort in the lights in the barn, where Warren was doing the milking.

Elizabeth's mind drifted to that earlier time when her family was safe within her home. The best time of her life was when she knew all her children were safe in their beds. She sat for what seemed like hours. Finally, sleep brought an escape from the harsh realities of the day.

A loud knock sounded. "Mother, are you OK? Is something wrong?"

She awakened abruptly, remembering she had locked the door for the sake of safety. She recognized the familiar voice of Mary.

She fumbled in her pocket for the key and opened the door. Mary and Ed greeted her.

"Mother, why on earth are you locking the door?"

Ed made a crack about someone robbing her.

She invited her daughter and son-in-law to come in. She left the door unlocked.

"There's more truth to what you say than you think." Elizabeth went on to explain how the sheriff and deputies were on their way to Larry's. "I decided I wasn't about to let anyone scare me out of my house."

"Good heavens, Mother, we should get you out of here."

Ed came with a quick reply. "No, we shouldn't leave right now. We'll stay. I don't think even the worst criminal would do anything to a kind old lady."

Elizabeth began to collect her thoughts. "Mary, I don't think I told you how happy I am that you're home. It's almost like old times."

"You can't be any happier than I am," said Ed.

"You know what happened just now. I was exhausted and dozed off. I haven't had supper and I'm really hungry. I think I need a sandwich."

"Mother, let me take care of that." Mary knew where everything was. She found the roast in the ice box and the freshly-baked loaf of bread on the cupboard ledge.

"I think I'd like a sandwich, too," Ed added.

Soon the three were sitting at the table, eating sandwiches. Elizabeth's concern and loneliness disappeared.

"I've missed home more than I could ever imagine," said Mary. "Beth and Irene seem the same, but Jake is like a different person. I don't know him any more."

Elizabeth could see her daughter's concern. "A boy growing into manhood needs his mother as well as his father."

Ed looked away. "I guess Mary's time away was harder on us guys. I don't know what's gotten into Jake along the way."

"He'll turn out all right," said Elizabeth.

"I hope you're right, Mother."

In the distance, shots rang out. Elizabeth felt herself gripped with fear. She, as well as Ed and Mary, looked in the direction of the lake home. Then two more shots rang out.

"Oh, no!" groaned Elizabeth. "Oh, Lord, I hope no one's been hurt."

Ed raised his voice in quick reaction. "You'd better lock the door. They could be coming this way."

Elizabeth picked up the key. Ed grabbed it from her and locked the door.

"Turn out the lights," said Mary. "Then, they won't see us or the house." She moved over and switched off the lights.

Ed looked toward the big house. "That's what Warren has done. His lights are off."

The three stood in the dark, peering out the window. They were greeted only by the silence of a December night. They whispered back and forth as they stared out the window. The waiting seemed to take hours.

"Mother, I don't think you should be here alone. You come with us," said Mary.

Chapter Thirty-one

"They're not going to harm a helpless old lady."

At that moment several cars drove through the yard and on out to the township road. The three tensely watched. Then, another car drove up and Sheriff Walker got out.

Ed turned on the lights. "It must be all over. It has to be." He unlocked and opened the door.

Sheriff Walker greeted them and announced. "It's all over."

"Those shots? Was anyone hurt?" asked Elizabeth.

"Those were warning shots. Several big city crooks were there. We got them all. Some tried to make a break, but we stopped them."

Elizabeth breathed a sigh of relief. "Thank God. My prayers are answered."

"I thought I should tell you in person. Larry was arrested. He is clearly connected to the robbers. He was definitely an accomplice. I think he'll be in jail for awhile."

"What about Rita?" Elizabeth couldn't quite feature her elegantly-dressed daughter-in-law in jail.

"We've taken her in for questioning. She's one smart woman. We'll probably let her go though she probably knows more than she lets on."

Elizabeth interrupted. "What about that hidden room that Matthew and Ellen knew about?"

"Mrs. Anderson, that was the key to catching the criminals. We found much of the money as well as other solid evidence. There's no question about their guilt. We have proof beyond a shadow of a doubt."

"I'm just sorry my grandson and daughter-in-law are involved."

Sheriff Walker leaned over and gave Elizabeth a hug. "It's not your fault. Every family has a black sheep or two."

Elizabeth looked away. "That's no consolation."

When the sheriff and Ed and Mary left, Elizabeth felt very much alone.

"Lord, help me. Comfort me. I miss John ever so much. I'm not afraid, but I'm terribly lonely."

Elizabeth saw the school pictures she had recently been given. There were Corrine's three girls along with Matthew's children, James, Johnie, Margaret, Carol, and a baby photo of Michael. She felt as if these children were actually present.

Then she saw a plaque on the wall. "I will never leave you nor forsake you." She knew she was not alone.

Beyond the Storm

A day later, Matthew walked toward the house for his afternoon coffee. A car drove up. He recognized the Cadillac as Rita's. Her manner of driving told Matthew she was upset.

There was no preamble. She spoke without any greeting.

"You betrayed your brother. You ought to be ashamed of yourself. How could you do such a thing?"

"What do you mean?"

"You told the cops about the hidden room. You're the reason that Larry's in prison. You could have prevented this."

Ellen must have heard the car. She stood on the porch steps and answered her sister-in-law. "Larry is in prison because of what he did. That is the only reason."

Rita began to scream out her words. "I thought you Andersons looked after one another. Isn't that what families are supposed to do?"

"Come, Rita," invited Ellen. "Come in and calm down. Maybe Larry didn't rob a bank, but he aided and abetted those who did. And they broke other laws. This is the result."

Rita reluctantly followed Ellen into the kitchen. Matthew wondered what would come next. At Matthew and Ellen's the coffee was always on the stove. Ellen poured Rita a cup.

Rita began to talk. "I knew they were not completely honest, but I didn't think it was that bad." The first sips of coffee seemed to have a calming effect.

Ellen had a way of getting Rita to talk about other things. Soon Rita was able to laugh. This was the side of Rita that Matthew could appreciate.

Later, as Rita got up to leave, she made an announcement. "I don't know if I can stay around here. I think I'll be going back to the city. That big house is far too lonely."

Matthew wanted to ask questions but didn't.

"Who's going to take care of the house?" asked Ellen.

"One of Paul John's business associates will probably live there. He and his wife have been interested."

Matthew wanted to groan as he wondered about the activities of the new tenants.

After a few pleasantries Rita made her exit.

Chapter Thirty-one

"I hope this takes care of the problems," said Ellen. "Larry will be away for a long time."

"Yes, justice will be done." Even so, Matthew felt a growing uneasiness that December afternoon.

Chapter 32

Sunday, December 7, 1941, dawned like any other day.

Matthew had much on his mind. He hated conflict of any kind. Victoria had called and announced another family session with Rita. Now that Larry was out of the picture it was time to force her to make a decision before she left for the city. That meeting would take place in the afternoon.

An image of Larry, sitting in a jail cell, haunted Matthew. He remembered how he had played with this innocent and lovable young nephew. How could that innocent child change into someone so corrupt? Matthew knew he should visit this nephew in jail. But would Larry even want to see him? Would Larry understand there was a principle involved? He couldn't let a crime go unsolved when the puzzle could be solved by investigating that secret room.

Life used to be much simpler.

The world news bothered him. Japanese troops in China meant trouble, even full-scale war. And submarines destroying British ships meant another kind of trouble. The happenings in Germany and Italy were disturbing too.

Could these wars and rumors of wars be a sign? Were these signs that Christ would soon return? Could someone like Hitler or Hirohito be the anti-Christ? Matthew didn't quite understand the mysteries of prophecy.

Today, church services would be held in the early afternoon. As usual, Ellen was in charge of Sunday school, and they were practicing the children's Christmas program. James and Johnie were in a teenagers' class, and Matthew had become a part of an adult Bible study group.

As Matthew and Ellen were dressing for church, Ellen interrupted his thoughts. "Matthew, I can tell something's wrong. What's bothering you?"

Matthew often hesitated to express these deeper thoughts. "The world's sure a mess these days. And look at Larry and the mess he's in. I don't know where this will end."

"The world's been in a mess before."

"I can't help wondering if we're living in the last days. Hitler overrunning Europe and those death camps we hear about. Evil is everywhere."

"You may be right. You read and listen to the news much more carefully than I do."

Matthew tied his tie and put on his suit coat. He always believed in dressing his best for church. Ellen checked his tie and coat.

In a matter of minutes the family was in church. Family members scattered to their Sunday school classes to practice parts for the Christmas program. Life went on very much as it had done for years—even decades.

After the Sunday school hour Matthew sat with Ellen and Michael in their usual spot at the church service. The girls sat on the other side of Ellen, and the boys went to sit with some of their friends nearer the back of the church.

Matthew recognized some of the Advent music the organist played. He looked forward to Christmas decorations and celebrations. Today there seemed to be much talk during the quiet time before the service. Matthew had always felt this was not a time to visit, but a time to prepare for worship.

It was easy to go through the motions in church. Sometimes, Matthew feared this was happening to him. During the opening part of the service, Pastor Strand spoke with great intensity. The familiar scripture reached deep within Matthew. "If we confess our sins, he is faithful and just to forgive us our sins, and to cleanse us from all unrighteousness."

The words reminded Matthew of his own need. And the world was more needy than ever.

Chapter Thirty-two

As the time came for the sermon to begin, Pastor Strand stood at the pulpit. He bowed his head, saying nothing. Then he looked out at the congregation. Something must be seriously wrong.

Pastor Strand held up some notes and put them down. "My sermon for this Sunday in Advent is ready, but I'm not preaching the sermon I had prepared. Instead I need to talk with you about something of grave importance."

Matthew turned to Ellen. She had that puzzled look. Others looked around. His sister Mary, sitting a row back, nodded to her brother. Glenn Robertson and his wife sat across the aisle.

"This morning, the Japanese bombed Pearl Harbor. All the damages have not yet been assessed, but many ships were destroyed. Hundreds, perhaps thousands, of men have been killed. There is no doubt we will be at war with Japan."

For a few moments members of the congregation made comments, whispering to one another, looking around in concern. Then, silence returned.

"At a time like this I scarcely know what to say. But I believe God is speaking to us loud and clear. He has a message for us on this fateful day of Sunday, December 7, 1941. It is a day we will always remember.

"We have read the Advent scriptures that point to the coming of the Messiah. In a sense we wait with eagerness for the joys of Christmas. We, too, are looking for the Messiah. And we wait also for His second coming. That coming could be today, or it could be in a thousand years."

Pastor Strand had expressed the very thoughts on Matthew's mind.

"What is God's message today? Christ first came to a world that was in turmoil. The chosen people were waiting and wondering. There had been false messiahs. Israel was under the domination of the Roman Empire. It was a time of corruption and high taxes. Radical groups had risen, ready to fight the Romans.

"Isn't this a time to journey to Bethlehem as children would? We come believing that the babe in Bethlehem is still the hope of the world."

In those next moments as the pastor preached, Matthew experienced a strange anticipation. He felt that Christ was outside, waiting and wanting to come in. Christ stood above the devastation saying, "May I come in?" At the same time, Matthew struggled with questions. Why would God permit such a terrible thing to happen? As the sermon ended, he felt an assurance that God was sovereign and ultimately in control.

The service ended, it seemed almost too soon. Matthew wasn't ready to go out into the world.

Glenn Robertson approached Matthew as they walked toward their cars. "I was afraid this would happen. Our boys are just the right age. Unless the war ends quickly."

"This could be a bloody one. We both missed the Great War, but I'm afraid our boys won't miss this one."

The next moments the two men stood close to their cars. There was no need for words. Matthew felt comfort by being in the presence of his friend who was in many ways closer than a brother.

He felt Margaret come to stand next to him and put her hand in his.

"Dad, I'm afraid for Joe. I think he might be at Pearl Harbor."

The approaching war had come close to home. Just a year ago, Joe had helped with the harvest and had been like one of his own boys.

The war seemed to have tentacles of evil, reaching this peaceful community.

The Sunday family gathering took place at the home place, now the home of Corrine and Warren. Ed and Mary arrived with their three children. Matthew and Ellen brought their five. Ma came up from the little house. Martha was present, for she had remained for some time after Thanksgiving, and Victoria drove out from town.

For awhile the sounds of children filled the new house. Then, the children decided to go outside to play. Matthew felt relieved when all the children left. The original seven children of a few years ago had now increased to eleven with little Michael as well as Corrine's three daughters. The ice on the lake would provide a skating and play activity for all eleven.

The gravity of Pearl Harbor made a big difference that day. The mood was somber. Yet Matthew and the others realized that life goes on. With war coming, farmers would need more than ever to feed a hungry world.

Later in the afternoon, Victoria announced to Matthew. "It's time to visit Rita before she leaves. Matthew, I think it should just be you and me."

Chapter Thirty-two

Matthew dreaded the confrontation. He would let Victoria do the talking.

Ellen agreed. "Yes, if more of us go, she might get the feeling we're ganging up on her. Matthew was most involved in this land. He should go."

Martha quietly added, "Don't forget Corrine and Warren. They have the most to lose."

Warren didn't hesitate. "I'm afraid of what I might say to that woman if I went. It's better that I don't go."

Ma placed her hands over her heart. "I loved P.J. And Larry is my oldest grandson, but they've done some terrible wrongs. I hate to see this rift in the family. But you have to go and make things right."

Matthew and Victoria left the family group. Matthew drove down the road that had previously been a trail to the far pasture. As he looked beyond P.J.'s mansion, the place didn't look like the lake and beach where he had played as a child.

When Victoria rang the door bell, Rita appeared immediately. "Come in," she said.

Matthew wasn't sure what to expect.

Rita invited them into the living room. Her neatly tailored dark suit and her words and manner gave the impression of a woman who was very much in control.

Victoria hesitated and then spoke. "We need to settle this matter of land ownership."

Rita appeared to choose her words carefully. "We can't rush into this. There are some legal ramifications."

Victoria glared at her sister-in-law. "Yes, there are. And we will proceed with court action if you don't cooperate."

Rita continued, "Yes, we'll do something. We need acreage to go with our lake property."

Victoria didn't hesitate. "We need to keep the pasture land."

"I'll have to check with Larry."

Victoria gave a groan of agitation. "Larry has given up his rights. He has no right whatsoever. He is in jail, and he'll stay there for a long time."

"Where's your family loyalty? You can't give up on a young man who's made a mistake."

Matthew couldn't hold back. "He's not just made a mistake. He's been an accomplice in a bank robbery. That's a crime. And there's more."

Rita looked surprised. "You're too harsh on Larry. And, Matthew, Larry used to look up to you. He idolized you when he was a child."

"I remember that. I love my nephew, but I can't approve of the things he's done."

Victoria stood up. "This is your final notice. If you're not ready to act, we'll be in court after January 1."

"Let's compromise," pleaded Rita.

Victoria clenched her fist and the paper she carried. "You can avoid this by coming to our lawyer's office tomorrow."

"I'm sorry I can't. I'm leaving early tomorrow morning."

"Then," said Victoria, "we have no choice."

Rita followed Victoria as she walked toward the front door. "I'll be back right after Christmas. Then we'll work things out."

Matthew felt he was in a war already.

Victoria, with her hand on the door knob, announced, "We'll see what the Andersons will do."

Without another word Victoria opened the door and walked out, followed by Matthew.

Rita tried to re-open the conversation, but Victoria ignored her.

On the way back to the house, Matthew spoke with conviction, "We must stand strong against Rita."

A day later, Matthew decided it was time for him to visit Larry in jail. He and Ellen left Michael with his grandmother and drove on to River Falls.

Matthew had moments when he wondered if he should make this visit.

"This is something you have to do," Ellen told him. "You won't rest well until you do."

Matthew knew his wife was right. Ellen remained in the waiting room.

When he was ushered into the jail cell, Matthew experienced a terrible shame and feeling of being closed in. For anyone who loved the freedom of open spaces, confinement to a jail cell must be stifling.

Chapter Thirty-two

For a moment Matthew felt he was seeing an innocent young child. He groped for words. "I'm sorry" was all he could say. For a moment it seemed Larry was a child and Matthew a young uncle.

Larry turned toward Matthew and stood up. The spell was broken.

Matthew repeated the words. "I'm sorry."

A flood of words came from Larry. "You should be sorry. You betrayed your own family. It's your fault that I'm here."

Matthew said nothing. He wanted to comfort Larry as he would comfort a child.

A torrent of more angry words came from Larry. Matthew backed away.

Finally, Larry's anger subsided.

Matthew prayed for wisdom, and the words flowed easily. "Larry, my nephew, I love you and care about you. But you are responsible for being here. You were an accomplice in a bank robbery. You have done much that is illegal. You can't do such things without getting caught. The Anderson family is honest and law-abiding. You have left the good and honest life."

For the first time, Matthew felt his words had gotten through to Larry.

"You can't go on this way." He groped for the next words. "You weren't around when your father died. He died in torment. He saw clearly the wrong that he had done. He wanted to do something about it, but it was too late. You have time to change."

Larry's face softened.

"Please think about it. You can't go on this way. You have disobeyed man's laws. And you have disobeyed God's laws. There is a price to pay."

Larry cleared his throat. "I'll have plenty of time to think. I'll be here for a while."

"Remember when you were a child. You weren't like this. You enjoyed the beauty of the land around you. You loved the animals. You loved being on the tractor."

"That was a long time ago."

Matthew somehow wanted to help his nephew, despite all that Larry had done. "When you get out of jail, we'll do all we can to help. You'll have to make changes."

"I'm not sure I can."

"Think of your own son." Matthew thought of his own responsibility for his three sons. "You will play a big part in his life."

"I'm not sure about that. Joan's with her parents. I don't think she ever wants to see me again."

"Larry, there's no question about Joan. She loves you deeply, but you have treated her badly."

"I know that now. I was intent on getting money."

"Joan will be coming to see you. I know that. And you can count on me and the rest of the family."

Larry turned away. "I'm not sure about anything any more. But, thank you."

Matthew knew it was time to leave. Maybe there was hope after all.

Chapter 33

The aroma of Christmas cookies greeted Matthew as he entered the kitchen for afternoon coffee.

Ellen set out a cup of coffee. "I'll give you some of these broken sunbackle cookies. I'm bringing cookies for the lunch and coffee after the choir concert tonight."

Matthew took off his jacket and sat down. He had been looking forward to the concert. He felt nervous though because James was playing the piano for several pieces. James would always do a good job, but even so Matthew felt his son's nervousness.

Ellen went on to add, "I thought we should take in some Christmas goodies to Larry. After all, he'll be alone at Christmas. Rita's nowhere around, and she would never think of anything like that."

Just as Matthew took a sip a coffee and tasted a cookie, someone knocked on the door. He wasn't expecting company at this time of the afternoon.

When Ellen opened the door, Glenn Robertson entered. "Just thought I'd stop by. There's something I heard that I wanted to tell you."

Ellen reached for the pot of coffee and immediately poured another cup. Glenn joined his friends at the table.

"What's the news?" Matthew appreciated his friend's honesty and wondered what piece of information he was now bringing.

"I was in River Falls this morning," began Glenn. "I talked with my brother, and he had heard about the case against Larry."

"There are lots of rumors out there," said Ellen.

"This is more than rumor. I believe the story will be in the paper tomorrow. Your nephew, it seems, is connected with a large number of small crimes and robberies. His place was the hideout for the goods and money."

Once more Matthew thought of Larry as a young child. "I'm afraid we suspected as much."

"Anyhow, the word has leaked out that Larry will face a number of criminal charges. He'll be put away for years."

Ellen sighed. "I feel sorry for Joan. She's such a sweet girl. And then Larry's son will have to live with the knowledge that his father was a criminal."

"There's something else." Glenn hesitated. "The neighbors have been talking. They don't want that criminal element living down at P.J.'s lake home. We know that P.J. gave some of our people good jobs for awhile, but we still want those people out of here. They'll contaminate a good community."

Matthew needed no time to think. "I agree. One hundred per cent."

"My friend, you have to move ahead with your case against Rita so that you own the land. You can't let Rita have any control."

Ellen offered more cookies. "We're working on that."

"If I could help, I would," offered Glenn. "My mother can testify to the agreement your parents made when they signed the property over to P.J. Ma was present, and I believe that agreement had a time limit."

"That testimony would help a great deal if we go to court."

"We'll be seeing Rita right after Christmas." Matthew paused as he sipped his coffee. "If she doesn't agree, we're going to court. We have a good case."

Ellen added, "We don't want these criminals around here any more than you do. But there's only so much we can do."

If it hadn't been for the return of Carol from school, Matthew and Ellen and Glenn would have continued the talk. Glenn soon went on his way.

It took only a moment for Matthew to realize how unhappy Carol was.

Chapter Thirty-three

"It's not fair," she sobbed, "that I have to stay in this hick country school. You let Margaret skip a grade and go to town school. I hate being in this stupid Christmas program."

Matthew saw Ellen's wisdom in allowing Carol to let off steam.

Ellen finally spoke. "Remember, dear, that Margaret passed all the state boards ahead of time. And she had almost perfect papers. Your school work has been nowhere near that level."

"You can't expect me to be as good as Margaret. No one can be that good."

Ellen hung up Carol's jacket, which had been thrown over the chair. "We've been through this before. I'm not expecting you to be a repeat of Margaret. However, I do expect you to do the very best job you can. And your work has been extremely careless."

Once more, Carol objected and continued to repeat the same reasons.

Matthew could see Ellen had listened long enough. "Carol, go to your room. You are enrolled where you are, and you will do the best job you can in the Christmas program."

Carol left the kitchen, mumbling something about Margaret always being the favorite.

Matthew began to put on his jacket. It was time for late afternoon chores. At the same time he heard the Model A come up the driveway. James, Johnie, and Margaret were now home from high school.

"We've got to be early for the concert tonight," announced James.

"And guess what," added Johnie, "I have a solo this year. I didn't think I was good enough."

Matthew felt pride in all his children, but he felt a special pride in this husky son.

"I'm on my way to start the chores," said Matthew. "We'll all leave early tonight. The lights on the Model A haven't been working. We'll have to go in the Chevy."

Finally, Margaret was able to ask her question. "Was there any mail for me? Did we hear from Joe?"

Ellen gave her daughter a motherly hug. "No, my dear, we haven't heard anything. But he's not on any of the lists of dead or missing."

Matthew hurried out to begin the evening chores. It was Johnie's turn to help tonight, so everything would move fast. Matthew couldn't help wondering if Joe was dead or alive.

Beyond the Storm

Ellen's mind was on other things as she and several other women worked in the home economics room. There were ample Christmas cookies and bars for a large number of people from the concert. If she knew the propensity of her two boys, those cookies would quickly disappear.

Once the coffee pots were filled and ready, Ellen left for the gymnasium. She didn't want to miss any of the performance.

She entered the gymnasium just as the lights were turned off, except for the lights in front. The band began playing the strains of "Joy to the World."

Ellen couldn't help thinking of all the opportunities these children had. She thought of leaving a country school for town school in the eighth grade. And then she saw herself as a frightened girl of fifteen as she left home for Normal School to train to be a teacher. Life could be scary with strange places and new people.

Her eyes strained to see her own children. James had musical talent. A year from now, would he be in college fulfilling his dream? Or would he be drafted into the army to fight this war? She heard the part of the song where the trombones stood out.

And there was Johnie, hardly as industrious with music and school work. It would just seem natural that Johnie would take over the farm. Or would this war interfere with his plans as well?

"Joy to the World" ended, and the band began playing a medley of other Christmas carols. The band director motioned for Margaret to move to the front of the reed section. Margaret had caught on to the clarinet quickly and had surpassed the older students.

Margaret had seemed distracted lately, and Ellen knew why. It had to do with Joe. This almost-fifteen-year-old girl had a crush on this older boy. Joe could very well be in danger or even worse. She thought of her own brother killed in the last war. She would never get over that dreadful experience.

Carol moved over and pushed herself between her parents. This young daughter wanted to act so mature; yet she was the little girl needing the assurance of her mother. And little Michael, who was large for his age, wanted to be in her lap rather than his father's. Michael seemed to be growing into a duplicate of Johnie.

The band ended its part of the program, and the students rearranged themselves. Choir members walked to the risers. James went to the piano.

Chapter Thirty-three

He played the introductory strains, and the choir soon sang out the joyful songs of Christmas.

One song ended, and Johnie moved forward. In a clear baritone voice he sang:

O Holy Night, the stars are brightly shining,
It is the night of the dear Savior's birth.
Long lay the world in sin and error pining,
Til he appeared and the soul felt its worth.
A thrill of hope, the weary world rejoices,
For yonder gleams a new and glorious morn.
Fall on your knees...

Ellen felt herself transported to a quiet town of Bethlehem, a peaceful place, far away from these rumors of war. But for now, these children were safe within hers and Matthew's care. She must enjoy the beauty of these moments.

As the choir members left the risers, Ellen found herself looking across the aisle and ahead a few rows to Mary. She was thankful to have her sister-in-law back home, but Mary looked so thin and tired. Would Mary be able to face all the rigors of farm life this winter?

Ellen thought back to the many times she had been in charge of rural grade school programs. Children always exhibited so much enthusiasm and excitement. But also these programs brought a community together. There was something indescribably beautiful about such a gathering. This high school concert meant a blending of town folk and country folk, all coming to celebrate Christmas and being together as a family.

As the program neared its end, Ellen hurried out. The coffee and nectar and cookies were all ready for the students and the families and community members. Ellen and several other ladies poured coffee.

The program ended with delightful confusion as people hurried down the hall to the home economics room for the coffee and goodies. Ellen thought there was something about a meal or coffee and cookies that encouraged friendship. Conversation could lag or a gathering could become dull until the coffee was brought out. Then, new life came to people.

Within minutes, the generous plates of cookies and bars were depleted. Just a few cookies remained. Ellen and the other women relaxed with their cups of coffee.

As she relaxed, a stately woman with clothing obviously of expensive quality addressed her. The woman reminded her of Rita with her city-bought, tailored clothes.

"Mrs. Anderson," she spoke and extended her hand. "I'm Mrs. Jeffrey Donovan Grant. I'd like a few words with you."

Ellen responded with a greeting. She couldn't help thinking how cold and formal this woman was. What could the banker's wife possibly want?

"It has come to my attention that your family farm has been the scene of criminal activity. We do not appreciate that sort of thing going on in our law-abiding town."

Ellen wasn't sure how to respond. "That farm is not Matthew's. We lived there until three years ago."

"I want to give you notice that we in Lake View do not tolerate that kind of thing. You are a part of that family. Such criminal activity does not reflect well on you."

Ellen found anger arising within. She hesitated, saying nothing.

"It is up to you and Mr. Anderson to see that something is done."

Ellen cleared her throat. "At present, we have no ownership of that land. Rita Anderson, widow of P.J. Anderson, is the owner. You need to talk with her."

"I expect you to take care of that."

Ellen, petite as she was, stood tall to face her adversary. "The law is taking care of all that has been done illegally. I am not the sheriff. Sheriff Walker has done a fine job of getting to the bottom of this."

"But we don't want any of these crooks around here."

Ellen quickly responded, "There's something in the law about being innocent until proven guilty."

"I believe it's up to the rest of the family to do something."

Ellen tried to stay calm. "I can bring up my own children in the fear and admonition of the Lord. However, there's nothing I can do about my brother-in-law's widow or her son."

The crowd was thinning out. The other ladies were cleaning up after the celebration. And Ellen could see Matthew in the back of the room, waiting for her.

Mrs. Grant obviously had something more on her mind. "You know, there's something I'd like to say. My son, Jeffrey Donovan the third, should have had the solo that your son had. He could have done a far better job."

Chapter Thirty-three

"The choir director made that choice. I had nothing to do with it."

Mrs. Grant seemed to be in the mood for a fight. "I guess some people are a little pushy for their children."

If there was anything Ellen knew she wasn't, it was pushy. She was a strong believer in children's responsibility and making their own choices. She said nothing.

Mrs. Grant apparently expected a response. She repeated herself. "Some parents are pushy."

Ellen smiled. "It's time for me to go. Matthew is waiting."

Mrs. Grant's face reddened and she walked away.

Ellen and Matthew left the school along with the five children. The Christmas lights on Main Street served as a reminder of the warmth and beauty of the season.

The next evening, Matthew entered the white frame country school for the Christmas program. He thought of past Christmas programs when the children were smaller. And he couldn't help thinking of the people moving away from farms to work in the city. Time moved on, and with it came change.

Tonight Matthew's own family seemed smaller. James, Johnie and Margaret had gone into town with one of the neighbors to a basketball game. It seemed that the family members now tended to go in many directions.

Only a few years ago, all four children were in the Christmas program. At that program it seemed James and Johnie had stolen the show in the Christmas play. But that program was in his home school. He still missed some of the old neighbors and the home farm. But in many ways he was better off.

The program began with the small group of seven or eight children singing the old carols. Matthew never tired of Christmas music, but he had to admit this singing lacked energy and liveliness. At this point, he wondered if they shouldn't decide to send Carol to town school to finish the eighth grade.

There seemed to be an endless number of recitations by the little children. Then came the traditional play. Carol had the lead part of an old grandmother. She was obviously having fun as she put everything into the character.

The program ended. Matthew reached down and took out his watch. That was a short program, but with so few students it could hardly be longer.

A flurry of activity followed. The older children distributed gifts. Several women went to the back of the room to get the lunch ready. The room had become warm. Matthew felt he wanted to get outside. Several other men had the same idea.

A few of the men smoked. Matthew detested the habit, so he moved away from the smokers.

"Matthew," a voice called to him. "Could I talk with you?"

"Certainly," Matthew replied to the man he didn't know very well. It was Lee Smith, a neighbor a few miles down the road.

"I guess we haven't seen much of each other." Smith seemed at a loss for words. "You had an older brother, P.J. And I believe Larry Anderson is your nephew."

Matthew began to wonder where the conversation was going. He nodded.

"Well, my wife's been nagging me about this. And she's been talking a lot. She blames Larry for getting her brother into trouble."

"Why would Larry be responsible?"

"Larry was older. Her brother idolized him."

Matthew repeated the wisdom he had heard as a child. "Each person is responsible for his own actions. And, besides, Larry's in prison. He can't be a bad influence any more."

Lee abruptly changed the subject. "We're wondering about the crooks who stay in your brother's old house."

"Well, Lee, I believe there's an older couple staying there. I'm positive they're not crooks. And besides the sheriff will keep close watch."

Lee started to walk away. "We want you to know the neighbors have been upset."

Matthew thought back to the building of the house and the other times P.J. offered jobs. "We know that. It seems you weren't upset enough to turn down the work and pay when P.J. built his house. If you really didn't want those people here, you should have refused the jobs."

Lee walked away, saying nothing.

Chapter Thirty-three

That night, long after the children were home and in bed, Matthew reviewed the conversation in his mind. He felt like a child blamed for something he didn't do.

"Matthew, what's wrong?"

Matthew told of Lee Smith's talk.

Ellen added to Matthew's story. "His wife said just about the same thing, and before that Mrs. Jeffrey Donovan Grant."

"We need to fight to get that land back. We're not giving up."

"Somehow right will prevail," Ellen reassured.

Matthew drifted off to sleep, dreaming dreams filled with hope.

Chapter 34

Elizabeth Anderson awakened Christmas Eve morning. Something wasn't right. She usually got up in the dark. But today light shown through the window. She sat up in bed. Suddenly everything was whirling around. "What's happening to me?"

She had heard of people having strokes and experiencing exactly what she felt now. The whirling seemed to accelerate. She placed her hands firmly on the bed. It would not be wise to stand up.

Elizabeth thought of the many Christmases she had celebrated. More than fifty had been celebrated with John as part of her life. And, now, she was alone.

Should she bother Corrine and Warren? The girls had been ill with the flu, and Corrine was busy.

The dizziness subsided. She stood up, still feeling weak.

She moved carefully, dressing herself. "Lord, what should I do? Do I call Matthew? But I hate to bother him."

She filled the coffee pot with water. Maybe she'd feel better after a cup of coffee and some oatmeal. The weakness persisted.

It seemed to take forever to complete the smallest tasks.

Finally, she finished eating. A light knock at the door interrupted her thoughts.

Matthew's familiar voice called out. "Ma, I'm here to take you to our place for Christmas."

"Hello, son," she managed to say.

"Is something wrong?" That question and others followed before she could answer.

"Matthew, I'm not sure. I got up and felt terribly dizzy. And now I just feel weak. I don't know what's wrong."

"Ma, you're staying at our place tonight—and for a few days. And if this keeps on, we'll head for the doctor's office."

"I don't want to be a bother."

"Ma, you're no bother. Remember you took care of me. And now it's my turn to take care of you."

"The dizziness is gone now. I'm feeling better." With only a few words Elizabeth went into the bedroom and placed some clothes in her small suitcase. She would feel safe and secure with her son.

For Matthew, Christmas Eve was always a time for reflection, a time for remembering. At the same time Matthew thought about an uncertain future. Where would this war take the country and the people he loved?

Johnie interrupted his thoughts. "Dad, we're giving the cows extra ground feed. You always said to do that on Christmas Eve."

Matthew smiled a smile of satisfaction. "You're catching on."

"You used to tell us that story."

Matthew remembered what he used to say. "It's not really a story. Each Christmas, the legend says, the animals remember the Christ child. And for one evening they are given the power to speak. They kneel in their stalls and speak their praise and worship to the Christ child."

"That's quite a story."

Father and son herded the cattle into the barn. The cattle took their places, eager to eat their portions of feed.

"Where's James? Isn't he going to help so we can get ready early?"

"He's been acting strange. All quiet. Moody," said Johnie. "He seems to be in another world."

"Writers are that way, I guess."

"He's not been writing much. He's been quiet and glum."

Matthew knew why. "I think it's the war. We can manage without him."

Chapter Thirty-four

The barn door opened and James entered. "I'm here, Dad. I want to remember and savor all the traditions of Christmas."

"At least you're talking," said Johnie.

James ignored the remark.

"I can't help thinking," said Matthew, "what next Christmas will be like. We're missing Pa and P.J. And Mary's been at the sanitarium most of this year. I wonder if we'll all be together another year."

Johnie flexed his muscles and then picked up the milk pail. "I might be out in the jungles, fighting those dirty Japs."

Matthew was quick to respond. "No, Johnie, you will finish high school no matter what. Then, if you have to go, you can go."

"Aw Dad," Johnie answered, "I think school's a waste of time. And we Americans have to stand up for ourselves."

James began milking a cow down at the far end, ignoring the conversation. Johnie and Matthew proceeded to milk their cows, saying little.

Johnie hurried as he always did. James took his time, seemingly in deep thought.

When the cows were milked and the cream separated and the pigs fed, Johnie hurried to the house. James rinsed off the milk pails carefully.

"Son, is something bothering you?" asked Matthew.

"I've been reading *The Red Badge of Courage* again. War is something awful. I know I need to help protect my country, but I'm afraid I might run just the way Henry Fleming did. I don't know if I could kill someone."

Matthew remembered his own thoughts as he registered for the draft back in 1918. "I had some of those thoughts."

"This world is a scary place. I want to see the city and the rest of the world. I want to see what life is all about. And maybe I have to fight in a war to see what that part of life is."

Matthew wished he could shelter his son from the harshness of the world. "I hope you don't have to fight. I wish this world were a safer place."

James looked away from Matthew and walked over to a young calf. "Everything seems safe and secure here. These animals have it pretty good."

"We have it pretty good, too."

It seemed James needed to talk. "I know I'm looking beyond those hills to the south and east, but there is so much right here. Perhaps there's no better life than the life right here in the hills."

Beyond the Storm

"I used to think," began Matthew, "that I'd like to travel to far away places. Now I realize I know all the good people I need to know. These lakes and hills and fields are in some ways like the Garden of Eden. When I'm plowing the fields, I like to look at all the beauty that is practically at my fingertips."

"I want to tell our stories," James said. "I want the rest of the world to know what we have right here."

At that moment Matthew felt he saw into the future. "Son, that's what you are meant to do. Your grandfather and I knew almost from the beginning that you were not meant to farm."

"I have these dreams. I want to write. This is something I have to do."

In those moments, Matthew had one of those rare glimpses into his son's world. Father and son stood for several moments in silence.

"I'm hungry." James's words broke the spell.

An hour later as the family ate their Christmas Eve meal, time seemed to be suspended. That family included Ed and Mary and the children, Ma, Victoria, Corrine and Warren, and the three girls as well as Matthew and Ellen and the five children. Matthew and the others had enjoyed the lutefisk and Swedish meatballs and other Christmas goodies. He savored a cup of coffee as the family finished eating the rice pudding with raspberry sauce and rich farm cream added.

The table leaves had been added almost beyond limit along with several card tables and the kitchen table moved into the dining room. That way, the whole family could be together at the same time.

Ma seemed to have recovered after her dizzy spell. She remained quiet though as if to take in all the little conversations around. The children had become quiet following the dessert. They seemed to realize something beyond gifts and excitement. The adults' talk had also tapered off.

Mary was the one to break into the reflective silence that followed a good meal. She stood up. "There are some things I'd like to say before we wash dishes and open presents."

Matthew couldn't help noticing the lines in his younger sister's face as well as the gray hairs that now dominated the previously black head of hair. She was no longer that youthful little sister.

Chapter Thirty-four

"My year away from home made me realize some things about life. Life is more than working and earning a living. Life has to do with people living together. I never realized how much my family meant to me until the time away. Life means that we take time to listen to and know each other."

Mary began to choke up. Matthew noticed tears coming to his mother's eyes.

"People are more important than farms or money or power. Life is short, and we are together on this earth only these few years. We must show our love to one another. Saying I love you is hard to do. But I want to say that to each of you right now. I love you all. I want you to know that. Let's all just enjoy our love for one another because we never know when we'll be separated from each other."

Matthew looked at the other family members. No one said anything for the next moments. Even the youngest of Corrine's girls seemed to share the mood.

Ed cleared his throat. This man, usually so lacking in showing love, began to speak. "I learned something too. I don't know if I could have gone on much longer without Mary. We need each other. All of us need each other."

Matthew looked to Ellen. She usually knew the right thing to say. Or there was Victoria, who was rarely at a loss for words.

Ma slowly stood up. "Somehow, I feel that my husband, your father, and grandfather, and great-grandfather, is present. Right now, I feel close to him. And Mary, my youngest, I want to say how much your words meant to me. The good Lord has said that we should love one another as He has loved us. Love isn't something you can touch. It's not something we can see. But it's that something that we know is there. It's something we live and practice and show. I have felt your love this evening. And that love has had a healing effect." She paused a moment. "I must thank you. And I must thank God."

A few moments of silence followed.

Victoria broke the silence. "I think it's time to clear the table. Why don't you children sing? James, you play the piano."

"Yes," Ellen agreed. "Why don't Victoria and Corrine and I do the dishes? Mary, you need to take it easy. And, Grandma, you've had so many years of work, you deserve the time off."

"No," said Mary, "I'm helping. I'm tired of being an invalid. I'm much stronger."

Ma also objected. "I have no intention of sitting in some corner. I'm helping, too."

In minutes, the children gathered around the piano. Matthew, along with Ed and Warren, remained at the dining room table. And the women with their ready skills in the kitchen picked up the dishes and were soon washing and wiping and visiting at the same time.

Matthew noticed the words to the songs—words he had never noticed before:

No more let sin nor sorrow grow,
Nor thorns infest the ground.
He comes to make His blessings flow,
And wonders of His love.

Those were words he didn't quite understand. The words told him the millennium would come some time in the future. The thorns and thistles that Matthew struggled with would be gone.

As the men sat in the living room, the children sang. Johnie's voice had become a deep bass, and James had a rich tenor voice very much like Matthew's. Ed and Warren said little. He heard the women's voices in the kitchen. Ma and Mary kept insisting that they would be part of the clean-up crew.

The carols, mixed with talk and laughter, were the sounds of Christmas.

A short time later, with dishes washed and put away, the family members crowded together in the living room. The lights of the tree added a glow and warmth.

"Mother, it's time for you to read the Christmas story," James called out.

Some other voices added, "Let's get going so we can open presents."

Ellen sat down in the chair nearest the tree, a chair that was left for her. "I thought we'd be in such a hurry for gifts that we'd skip this tradition. Anyway, it may be the time for someone else to take over."

Several objected to any change in the tradition.

As Ellen opened her Bible to read, James spoke quietly. "This is something I'll remember the rest of my life."

Matthew wanted to reach out and touch his sons. He thanked God that they were safe in the warmth of this home and family.

Chapter Thirty-four

"'In those days there went out a decree from Caesar August that all the world should be taxed.'" She went on reading the other familiar words. "'And there were in the same land shepherds abiding, keeping watch over their flocks by night. And the angel of the Lord...'" Michael snuggled close to his mother.

Matthew found himself thinking of other Christmases. He saw Michael close to Ellen. Just three years ago when Ellen read the story, she was "great with child." Each of the children was special, but Michael was special in a different way. He came into the world after many problems had been resolved. He was God's gift after some hard struggles. Ellen finished reading. There was a reverent silence.

Ma broke the silence. "I think we should pray a prayer of thanks."

"You pray," were the words from several.

Ma objected. "I'm not good with words. Victoria, I wish you would."

Victoria nodded agreement and stood. "Let us pray. Dear heavenly Father, I thank You for my family here and for this beautiful room and gathering. I thank You for each family member, from Mother to the youngest. We thank You for memories. We thank You for the memory of my father and for others who have gone from our midst."

Victoria's voice, filled with emotion, remained silent a few moments.

"Thank You for Mary's return to health. We feel our circle is complete now that she is here. We pray for Martha and for her children and grandchildren who are far away. We thank You that Corrine and Warren and their girls are now with us.

"We look to the future. We think of the war that has just begun. We pray for our safety and the safety of our soldiers. We pray for Joe, who has seemed like one of the family. We pray for his safe return, and we pray that we will hear from him soon."

Matthew uttered a silent prayer for Joe. Losing Joe would be almost like losing a son.

"We face so many uncertainties. We pray for peace in our family. We pray that Larry will realize the error of his ways. And we pray for Joan and little Lowell that they may find warmth and love with her parents.

"Most of all, we thank You, God, for sending Your Son to save us from the bonds of sin. And may we honor You by enjoying fellowship with one another. Amen."

There was only a moment of silence. Then Michael walked over to the tree and reached for a package. "I want my presents."

And in times to come Matthew would not remember anything about the gifts given. He would remember those who gave.

Christmas Day arrived. The family arose shortly after four a.m. By five, they were seated in church for the Julotta service. Matthew loved many traditions, but he sometimes wondered about getting everyone out of bed this early in the morning. Perhaps there might be a better tradition. The service seemed to attract fewer people each year. Only the most hardy and loyal showed up. After chores and breakfast and more chores, the family rested. After the noon dinner, they drove over to the home place, where Corrine and Warren had invited them for the afternoon. The children would walk down to the lake and go skating and do some tobogganing or even some skiing. These familiar places evoked many memories for Matthew.

While the rest of the family celebrated Christmas Day, Matthew drove to River Falls. Ma felt she wanted to visit Larry and take him some Christmas cookies. Matthew knew he must talk with his nephew.

As they walked toward the jail cell, Matthew saw how frail his mother looked. He held her arm and felt her tremble. "I don't know what to say," she said. "I hope he realizes the terrible wrongs he has done."

"I hope so too."

The guard unlocked the cell, and Matthew and Ma went in. Larry sat in the corner, face buried in his hands. He looked up.

"Merry Christmas." Ma handed him the plate of Christmas cookies. "I knew you'd like these."

"Thank you, Grandma. This hasn't been much of a Christmas."

Matthew searched for words. "We wanted to come. You are family no matter where you are."

Matthew and Ma sat down on the cot. Larry accepted the plate of cookies and eagerly tasted one.

"These cookies were my favorite when I was a kid. Thank you, Grandma."

"I'm concerned about you, Larry." Ma reached out and took her grandson's hand. "I hate the thought of you in this jail."

Chapter Thirty-four

"I've been doing a lot of thinking. I was angry at Uncle Matthew for leading the authorities to me. But I have begun to realize the terrible mistakes I've made."

Matthew breathed a sigh of relief.

"I guess I'll be in jail for awhile."

Ma grasped Larry's hand more tightly. "But you're young. When you get out, you can change and make a better life for yourself."

"I know I have to make changes. It won't be easy. My own mother hasn't even been to see me. And Joan has been here only once. I haven't seen my son for months."

Matthew knew that Larry's treatment of Joan had led to this separation. "Joan loved you very much. When she sees you change, she'll come back to you."

"I hope so. She's planning to come tomorrow."

Matthew saw the deep sadness in Larry's eyes. At the same time he saw the little boy he had known not so many years ago.

Ma tried to keep the conversation going. They were soon laughing over Christmas memories from the past.

The guard appeared. "I'll have to ask you to leave. Anderson, you have another visitor."

Ma stood up and gave her grandson a hug. "God bless you. You can and will make these changes in your life."

Larry, obviously overcome with emotion, tried to speak. "It'll be years before I get out. But I'll try. I'll do the best I can."

"You must turn to the Lord." Ma spoke with stern conviction. "That's the only way."

Matthew and Larry shook hands, saying nothing. The handshake told Matthew there was hope.

The guard unlocked and then locked the cell. Matthew felt a relief and freedom as they made their exit.

"Merry Christmas." Rita greeted them as they reached the main room. "I want to talk with you." She turned to the guard. "I'd like to talk with these people before I go in."

Matthew felt a moment of uneasiness. He wondered if Rita was going to cause more trouble. The guard returned to his desk.

"I've made a decision." Rita looked directly at Matthew and then at her mother-in-law. "I'll agree to sign the farm back to you."

Matthew gulped. He said nothing.

"There's one stipulation. The lake home and cabins will remain in my name."

Matthew couldn't help wondering what this would mean. "Are you going to live there? What are your plans?"

Ma reached out to touch Rita's arm. "My dear, you are still family. I consider you my daughter-in-law even though P.J. is gone."

"I'll be going back to Chicago for now. But I'll visit. I'm not sure what I'm going to do."

Matthew remembered the neighbors' concerns. "Keep in mind, Rita, we don't want these Chicago characters hanging around."

"I don't think they'll want to come back. The law seems to watch even when people are honest. The caretakers are going to rent out cabins in the summer."

Matthew knew in advance what Victoria would say. He tried to speak carefully. "We don't want anyone driving through the main yard by Ma's and Corrine's and Warren's. You will need to build a different road to go into your home."

Rita's tone became sharp and business-like. "Then, if I am to sign this agreement, I'll demand a right of way to build a road to my home."

"We'll talk that over with Victoria. And it will be up to Ma."

Rita began to walk away. "No, it's up to me at this point. Remember the land comes to me as Paul John's widow. I'm in charge."

Matthew couldn't stop his next words. "If this goes to court, we'll win."

Rita raised her voice. "I'll see you at the court house Wednesday morning. You can take this offer or leave it."

Rita turned away, and the guard led her toward Larry's cell.

"There's hope, at least," said Ma.

Matthew and Ma returned to the warmth and love of the family celebration.

Chapter 35

Wednesday, December 31, 1941.

New Year's Eve Day arrived. It was a typical winter morning. Snow lay on the ground, covering the dirt and dreariness of late autumn. Frozen lakes and ponds and white snow gave the world a freshness that Matthew enjoyed.

Matthew and Ellen, along with Ma and Victoria, waited in the large entry room of the courthouse. Mary had decided to stay home because she didn't feel well. Rita was late as usual.

As they waited, Victoria fidgeted. "I probably should have brought our lawyer, but I hoped we could settle this peacefully."

Matthew longed for the way good farmers did their business. A handshake and the right words would seal the bargain. Why did life have to be so complicated?

They waited what seemed like hours, but finally Rita appeared. "I have the papers here. We can take care of this in the county auditor's office."

Rita handed the papers to Victoria.

Victoria glanced at the papers and pointed to one part. "Yes, but you will have access along the line fence, not through the yard between the big house and Ma's house."

Rita hesitated. "I guess so."

Matthew was quick to respond. "We used to drive there. There's still a track. And Warren will put up a new fence so there won't be any gates to open and close."

Rita tightened her grip on her purse. "You realize I'm giving away a great deal. I don't have to do this."

Victoria straightened herself and moved toward Rita. "Listen here, Rita Anderson. If we go to court, fraud will be proven and Mother will get everything. You have had no right to this land in the first place."

Rita turned and walked toward the office. "Let's go in, and get it over with. I'll sign. Then the rest of the legal work can proceed."

"Good!" exclaimed Victoria.

Matthew breathed a sigh of relief. A major battle had been won.

An hour later Matthew stopped the car outside Victoria's home. She invited them in for coffee. They could relax. The farm would be in the hands of the rightful owner.

As Matthew and Ellen and Ma were about to sit down at the kitchen table, Ellen turned to Victoria, "Victoria, you're not spending New Year's Eve alone. You come out to our place. We're going to the New Year's Eve Watch Night Service at church."

Victoria hesitated. "I don't mind being alone." She began getting the coffee ready as well as some noon lunch.

"Well, Victoria," said Ma, "they've convinced me to stay a few days. Why don't you come and stay over tonight. We're having our usual New Year's Eve meal—much the same as the Christmas Eve meal."

"Sometimes," began Victoria, "I regret that I didn't marry when I had my chance. There are moments I feel very much alone."

Matthew could remember only a few times when his sister had showed that personal side. She might appear to be business-like and hard, but underneath she had a heart filled with love.

"You'll stay, then?" asked Ellen.

Victoria smiled. "Why don't I take care of a few things this afternoon? Then, I'll drive out."

Ma began to reminisce. "I'm thankful for all the family gatherings that John and I had when we were younger. Now it's much more difficult to get the family together."

Chapter Thirty-five

These words seemed to invite the others to think of years gone by. The next hour passed quickly as they ate lunch and told family stories.

Just as Matthew and Ellen and Ma were about to leave, the doorbell rang. Victoria hurried to answer.

Victoria gasped with surprise. "Rita, I didn't expect to see you."

"I'm sorry to intrude," she apologized. "Something has come up and I need to ask a favor of Matthew."

After the family differences that might have involved a court case, Matthew hardly expected Rita to ask for help.

Victoria softened in her attitude. "We've just had a noon lunch. Could I invite you in?"

"Thank you, Victoria, that is kind of you. I'm returning to Chicago immediately. Noreen needs me. And our friends who were to take care of our house have left. They backed out."

Matthew grasped what had happened. Some of Rita's friends weren't all that loyal. Then, she always came back to the family.

"Matthew, we have to close up the house for the winter. Could you drain the water or have someone do it? It looks as if no one will be there until spring or summer. We don't seem to have other friends around."

Ellen gave Matthew a knowing look.

"I guess I can take care of that."

"Here's the key to the front door." She handed him the keys and turned to the others. "I hope my signing the land over to you will make you feel better about everything. Paul John thought the world of all of you."

"We knew that," said Ma. "At times his actions showed how deeply he cared."

Rita moved toward the door and then turned. "I wish things could be different. I'm truly sorry for any misunderstandings."

She closed the door slowly.

Victoria was the first to speak. "I can't believe what just happened."

"Come, Matthew, it's time to get on home. We'll have plenty of time later to spread the good news."

Matthew thought to himself. There's one less problem for 1942. The farm is back in the rightful hands of the Andersons.

Beyond the Storm

Matthew closed his eyes, ready to take his afternoon nap. He heard a light tap on the bedroom door. "Come in," he called.

"Dad, I've written something, and I'd like you to hear it."

Matthew sat up. He was surprised at this request for James was not inclined to share writings or inner thoughts with anyone. If he did share, he shared with Ellen.

"I'll listen."

James sat down on the chair near the bed. "I've been thinking about graduation. I decided to write a commencement prayer as a poem."

Matthew looked at his son: blond hair, piercing blue eyes, small-boned, now very much a young man. In a few months, this boy would be eighteen, and he would be registering for the draft.

"Mother thought I should read this to you." He cleared his throat and read:

Dear Father in heaven, I pray this night,
I ask Thee to be my Guiding Light.
My life is not certain, my way is not clear,
So wilt Thou not help me my Father, most dear.
I ask Thee to guide the decisions I make.
What is right? What is wrong? What path shall I take
Where shall I go? What shall I do?
Dear Lord, may I always call upon You.

Tears came to Matthew's eyes. He had to respect his son for his learning. "I'm proud of you, son. I wish I had gone further with my education."

James read more of his poem. It seemed he wanted to talk. "Dad, I love this farm and the old home farm as well. But I want to do something special with my life. I want to write and maybe teach. I want to make a difference in the world."

Matthew couldn't help thinking of the dreams he used to have, dreams of going far beyond those hills. But that changed and his dreams centered right here now.

Matthew spoke slowly. "I used to wish I could do something big and special. But I'm caught up in the day-to-day work of running a farm."

James must have realized his words could hurt. "Dad, you've made such a difference in my life. And you are helping to feed a hungry world. It's homes like this that produce people who can go out. I'd like to do some big things, but you may have done more than I'll ever do."

Chapter Thirty-five

"No, Son, you have been born with talent. God meant for you to go into the world and get an education and do things that will make a difference to many people."

Matthew would long remember these moments.

"If I ever make anything of myself, I owe it to you and Mom. I could never have done it otherwise."

In the next moment, Matthew opened his arms, embracing his oldest son. They stood that way, oblivious of time. Words were not necessary. The silence was beautiful. Father and son made the connection that would bind them for life.

Ellen's call from the kitchen interrupted the silence and their closeness. "Coffee and afternoon lunch are on. This is special. We've got some news."

The call had reached everyone. Ma walked into the kitchen at the same time Matthew and James did. Johnie came bounding in from outside, and Carol skipped down the stairs. Margaret sat at the table. The news was apparently hers.

Ellen poured the coffee and set out the cookies. This timing of coffee and cookies surprised Matthew. Usually, they had no lunch in order to have big appetites for the traditional New Year's Eve supper.

"What's this all about?"

"Margaret has something to read to us," announced Ellen.

Margaret began to read. "I'm thinking of you, sitting around the table at dinner or supper or lunch. Perhaps Grandma Anderson is there with you. You are probably enjoying some of Ellen's good cookies. Or maybe you girls have tried your hands at baking.

"You are the reason I'm here fighting in this war. I think of those harvest days when we were all together, working. I treasure those memories. They will be with me forever. And the warmth and love of your family is helping me go on."

"I know who this letter's from," interrupted Carol.

"I can't tell you much about where I am or what I am doing. The government does censor all the mail. They cut out anything I would say about fighting and such details.

"What I want you to know is that I am well. I am safe at present. I was not one of the victims of that terrible bombing. I intend to come back home and buy a farm in the Oak Ridge area. I want you to know that all of you are worth any sacrifice I might have to make."

Margaret stopped reading.

"I think Joe's been getting help from that buddy of his," said Johnie. "He can't write any better than I. That letter is something James would write."

Margaret explained, "He said in the earlier part of the letter that he had someone help write the letter. In fact, the letter isn't in his handwriting."

"There's more," Ellen said.

Margaret blushed. "He just says how much my letters mean to him."

Matthew glanced at Ellen. His little girl had the feelings of a young woman.

"Thank God, he's safe." Ma turned to Ellen. "Let me help you peel potatoes."

Ellen served New Year's Eve supper later than the usual time for supper. That was also a tradition. In this community, families most often shared supper with immediate family only and then went out—usually to the watch night service at church. Families also tended to include special people who would otherwise be alone. Ma and Victoria were included.

Tonight, Matthew noticed how quiet and reflective the family was. Conversation had been slow. Everyone at the table, from oldest to youngest, seemed satisfied to eat quietly and enjoy being with others.

Matthew ate the last spoonful of rice pudding with raspberries and whipped cream. He reached for his cup of coffee.

Carol broke the silence. "Dad, why can't you let me go to school in town? You let Margaret go a year early."

"We've been through this before," reminded Ellen.

"But I'm tired of being the only one in my class. Ever since Bruce moved, I've been all alone."

"Carol," reminded her mother, "Margaret's situation was different. We're not going into that again."

"Oh, Mother," Carol pouted. "Margaret always gets all the breaks."

It was Johnie, who spoke with his usual honesty. "Margaret always studies. You don't."

"I can't help that Margaret's smarter than I."

Chapter Thirty-five

Matthew could see Ellen had heard enough. "Carol, you will finish eighth grade right where you are. And, furthermore, each of you children has different talents. God made you each as individuals. And all we expect of you is that you work hard to the best of your ability."

Victoria had been unusually quiet. "Carol, you'll be much better off where you are. Then, next fall, you can come in when all the other country students come to town for high school. If you come now, you'll be the only new kid in class."

Carol gave a little sniff. She mumbled something under her breath.

Victoria turned to her brother and then to Ellen. "You have five remarkable children. You remind me of what I've missed out on. It's such a comfort to have children."

James spoke up. "But Aunt Victoria, you have hundreds of kids at Lake View High School. You wouldn't have time for a family of your own."

Ma reached over to touch her daughter's hand. "Victoria, not all women were meant to be wives and mothers. You've had a remarkable career as teacher and principal. I'm proud of you."

"We're all proud of you," said Matthew.

Victoria smiled, deeply touched by the affirmations of her family. "I don't know what I'd do without my family."

"You've enriched our family," said Ellen. "You have become like a sister to me and a special aunt and teacher to the children."

Victoria reached for her coffee, took a sip, and set the cup down. "I think it's time to look forward to 1942. What will our lives be like in another year?"

Matthew felt a fear creep in—fear for his two boys.

"I've led a full life," said Ma. "I have children and grandchildren and great-grandchildren. I've lived more than my allotted time of seventy years. But I feel in good health. I'd like to go back to my home and live. I want to knit and sew and help my family."

"You can continue to stay here," said Ellen.

"Or Mother," added Victoria, "you can come to town and live with me."

"I don't want to be a bother. It's best if I can stay on my own."

They talked some more about Ma's living arrangements until she interrupted. "Please, let's talk about something else."

"All right! Let's talk of the future." Victoria assumed a leadership role. "I hope Mother will be in her own home. And I suspect that I shall continue as teacher and principal for several years to come. I'll be in Lake View."

Matthew thought back to his brush with death almost four years ago. "I hope to be here, but we never know. At these times I wonder how many of us will be together a year from now. Life can change suddenly."

Ellen didn't waste time. "I know this is true. But I expect we'll be here, Lord willing. And I hope we can all gather together here for many years to come."

Victoria raised her cup. "Let's drink to that."

Each person raised his or her coffee cup and took a sip, if there was any left.

"I guess it's my turn." James looked around at each family member. "I hope I'm home from college. I've dreamed for years of going away to college. That's what I want to do. I don't want to be fighting in some war, but I'll go if I have to."

This was pretty much what Matthew expected.

It was Johnie's turn. "I might just go off and enlist in the army. We've got to win the war against the Japs and Germans. And if I've got to fight, I'll go. I think it sounds exciting."

Ellen was first to object though others added their objections.

"And now let's hear from Margaret," said Victoria.

"I'll be a junior next year. I want to be ready for normal teacher training. I want to be a teacher just like Mother. And right now, there's a shortage, so I want to teach."

"Maybe you should go on and get your degree," suggested Victoria.

Margaret's answer was quick and decisive. "I want to keep going to school to learn, but I want to teach in a country school."

Johnie joked, "Now you've heard from the good students. We'll hear from one that's not quite so good."

Carol gave her brother a dirty look. "I'll show you. When I get to town school, I'll really work. I'll be a freshman next year. And when I finish high school, I want to take off for the big city and work and wear fancy clothes."

Ellen's concern showed in her voice. "There's more to life than parties and nice dresses."

"Oh, I'll be a good girl," said Carol.

Chapter Thirty-five

Ellen began to gather the plates near her. "It's time for dishes. We need to get ready for church. Most people come early before this late nine o'clock program."

"Don't forget me," whined Michael.

"It's a long time for you," said Ellen. "But what about your future?"

"I'll grow up and be big like Johnie, and then I'll go off and fight."

Ellen quickly interrupted her son. "The war will be over by that time."

Ma gathered the plates near her, ignoring or not hearing her youngest grandson's words. "We have much to be thankful for. Mary is back home with the family. And Corrine and Warren are settled on the home farm. Those problems have been worked out."

Noise and activity followed. Victoria and Ellen insisted on doing dishes with Carol and Margaret wiping. Ma reluctantly sat down in the living room. Matthew could see she was tired.

Somehow this New Year's Eve watch night service was different. There were fewer people. Ed and Mary came, but Jake and Beth and other young people had stayed away. And others who were usually present did not attend this year.

People gathered before nine o'clock and visited. At nine, the young people put on a short program of songs and readings. Pastor Strand seemed preoccupied as if something was wrong. He gave his meditation that seemed something like a farewell speech. After the program, there was the lunch. The adults sat and drank coffee, visiting. The youth and children played games. The level of noise sometimes rose quite high. The church basement was filled with fun and fellowship.

Then at 11:30 the bell tolled, announcing the watch night service. Matthew listened to the scripture that Pastor Strand read. Then he introduced a hymn and prayer. "On this eve of 1942, we will pray for peace. Yes, above all, we want this war to end and peace to come. But more important is the peace within our soul."

The pastor continued and told how the hymn writer had lost all four daughters when two ships crashed together at sea. The words took on a new meaning:

Beyond the Storm

When peace like a river attendeth my way,
When sorrows like sea billows roll;
Whatever my lot,
Thou hast taught me to say,
It is well, it is well with my soul.

Matthew thought of the storms, both physical and spiritual, that had passed through his life. He thought of the future with its war and uncertainty. He felt a peace settle over him as the congregation sang the remaining verses and the final words, "It is well with my soul."

The pastor's voice seemed more fervent than ever before. He prayed for the servicemen and for the country and for peace in the world. He ended his prayer with an invitation for everyone to pray silently.

Silence filled the congregation. Matthew thought of Joe and then his own boys. He wanted to keep all of his family safe from harm. Darkness and evil seemed to reach out its tentacles to suffocate and destroy.

The tolling of the bell interrupted the silence. The prayers of individuals continued. What would this new year bring? Matthew felt both hope and uncertainty about what lay ahead.

The bell stopped tolling. Pastor Strand began a closing prayer. "And now we move forward into a new year with strengthened confidence that You, Lord, will guide us in all our ways." He then pronounced the benediction.

As Matthew walked outside, light snow flakes greeted him. A new year meant new hope.

Epilogue

January 1942

An hour after the watch night service ended, Matthew and Ellen and the four older children sat at the kitchen table, drinking their hot cocoa. Michael was asleep in his bed. Victoria and Ma had gone to bed.

Matthew didn't feel tired, and neither did the others. They had talked of many things, including their expectations and hopes for 1942.

After a lapse in the conversation, James spoke. "I don't understand all this evil in the world. I learned the word *unleashed* the other day. It seems evil has been unleashed over half the world."

"Don't use all those big words," interrupted Johnie, "you're not in college yet."

Johnie's interruption didn't stop the flow of conversation.

"I don't understand Uncle P.J. Why did he do those terrible things? And Larry, why would he lie and steal?" questioned Margaret.

"How can people be so nasty?" Carol yawned.

Johnie cleared his throat. "Well, what about you?"

Ellen gave a sharp look. "Johnie, that's not fair. You've acted less than perfect at times. 'He that is without sin among you, let him first cast a stone at her'."

James must have ignored the intervening comments. "I don't understand how people can do good things and then do such awful things."

Matthew had often been puzzled by the same question. P.J. had almost destroyed Matthew's life. At the same time this wayward brother had been generous and kind.

"Some matters we will not understand in this life," began Ellen. "P.J. started out in the same family that your father and Victoria and the others did. But P.J. made some choices along the way. And some of those choices were bad choices."

"But," questioned James, "how could P.J. be so dishonest? And how could Larry do those terrible things?"

Ellen continued. "We can't completely understand, but Larry made choices. And his choices led him to be a part of businesses making fast money. He was overcome by greed." Matthew began to remember happenings out of the past. "P.J. always seemed to want more than we had. He would always get away from hard work. He managed to get jobs where he did just a little work and was paid well. Then, he didn't care how he made money, just so he made it."

Matthew listened intently as Ellen and each child talked about greed and what it could do to people.

After a break in the conversation, James came through with a question. "Isn't greed causing war? Countries and people want more than is rightfully theirs."

"I think you know the answer," said Ellen. "People throughout time have dealt with greed. And there have been other dark and difficult times."

"This somehow seems worse today." James put down his cup.

"Difficult times always seem darker when you're going through them." Ellen left the kitchen and returned in a minute. "I have a clipping that might be good to look at as we start a new year. I cut this out of the paper about two years ago. This is what King George VI said in his Christmas address in 1939. He quoted Minnie Louise Haskins. At that time, London was being bombed, and the people's very lives were threatened."

Matthew couldn't help noticing how intently the children were listening.

Ellen read:

I said to the man who stood at the gate of the Year,
"Give me a light that I may tread safely into the unknown."

Epilogue

*And he replied, "Go out into the darkness
and put your hand into the hand of God.
That shall be to you better than light and safer than a known way."*

"Read that again, please," asked James.

Matthew heard the words again.

Ellen yawned. "It's late. It's long past bedtime."

James said goodnight and kissed his mother on the cheek. "I have some ideas." He hurried upstairs, taking three steps at a time.

Matthew knew James would be in his room writing.

"It's been a wonderful New Year's Eve." Margaret kissed both her parents. "And Joe is safe." She left quietly.

Carol simply kissed her mother and ran into Matthew's arms, giving him a big hug and kiss. She followed her sister.

"Chore time comes soon, Dad, doesn't it?" Johnie awkwardly gave his mother a kiss on the cheek.

"Son, I'll do the chores myself. You need to sleep."

"No, Dad, I'll help. You're not so young any more."

Matthew smiled and thanked his son. Johnie hurried upstairs, taking four steps at a time.

Matthew took Ellen's hand. "I'm proud of our children. They're turning out well."

"We've come through a lot, haven't we? But we've done it together and with God's help." She looked up into Matthew's eyes. "I couldn't have done it without you."

Matthew felt an overwhelming love for this woman. "I love you, my dear. You know, Ellen, let's step out in the darkness. That clipping you read has some deep meanings."

Without saying a word, Ellen found her jacket, Matthew put on his jacket, and they silently walked out into the night. Clouds had rolled in. They looked out on the darkness.

As they walked away from the house, Matthew found words of the old hymn coming to mind. He began to say them:

*Jesus, Lover of my soul,
Let me to Thy bosom fly,
While the nearer waters roll,
While the tempest still is high!
Hide me, O my Saviour, hide,
Till the storm of life is past;*

Safe into the haven guide:
O receive my soul at last!

"Matthew, you have such a good memory."

"There's another verse that I'm not so sure about. But I think of the storms of the past year. The Lord didn't spare us from the storms. He guided us through them. And I know He will guide us the rest of our days."

Ellen moved closer to him. "Your faith strengthens mine."

Matthew began to remember the other verse:

Other refuge have I none;
Hangs my helpless soul on Thee,
Leave, ah, leave me not alone,
Still support and comfort me.

Matthew and Ellen stood in silence, looking into the night. Matthew held out his hand in a symbolic gesture. Ellen, knowing what he was thinking, did the same. In the darkness, they had placed their hands in the hand of God.

To order additional copies of this title call:
1-877-421-READ (7323)
or please visit our web site at
www.pleasantwordbooks.com

If you enjoyed this quality custom published book,
drop by our web site for more books and information.

www.winepressgroup.com

"Your partner in custom publishing."

NORMANDALE COMMUNITY COLLEGE
LIBRARY
9700 FRANCE AVENUE SOUTH
BLOOMINGTON, MN 55431-4399